NO WAY IN HADES WAS HE GETTING NAKED . . .

As an Argonaut, Zander had never been one to just "go with the flow." It went against his nature. If someone said sit, he stood. If he was told to go one way, he went the other. So listening to Callia boss him around right now was seriously pissing him off.

However, he knew there were times when it was better to bite his tongue rather than let the rage rumble through. And right now—though he hated it with a passion—was one of those times. Still, no way in Hades was he getting naked for this physical.

Take me, Zander. Fast. Before someone gives me a reason to say no.

Thirteen simple words from eleven years ago. She'd known exactly what to say to turn his entire world upside down in the span of a heartbeat.

Perspiration dotted Zander's forehead as he remembered the feel of her silky smooth skin, the taste of her wet heat, the way she'd come apart around him right in this very spot.

And—dammit—the rod of steel now nestled between his legs was an in-your-face reminder that Callia, and not the woman he was about to marry, was his soul mate.

Other *Love Spell* books by Elisabeth Naughton:

Eternal Guardians Series
MARKED

Stolen Series
STOLEN FURY
STOLEN HEAT
STOLEN SEDUCTION

ENTWINED

ELISABETH NAUGHTON

LOVE SPELL NEW YORK CITY

LOVE SPELL®

August 2010

Published by

Dorchester Publishing Co., Inc.
200 Madison Avenue
New York, NY 10016

ISBN 10: 0-505-52823-1
ISBN 13: 978-0-505-52823-0
E-ISBN: 978-1-4285-0915-3

For Lisa,
My archaeology expert, Greek myth–loving, smart-ass, snarky and too-damn-cute-for-words BFF.
This ride wouldn't be half as sweet if I couldn't share it with you.
(BTW, I'm still waiting for that e-slap.)

ENTWINED

Sing, Goddess, of the rage of Peleus's son Achilles. The accursed rage, which brought pain to thousands . . .
—THE ILIAD

CHAPTER ONE

If he could die, this would be the perfect place to take the plunge.

Zander stood on the edge of the cliff, transfixed by the massive canyon below. A thin layer of day-old snow crunched beneath his boots as he shifted his weight on the rocks and wondered . . . *What if?*

The temperature was in the teens, the wind howling past his face, numbing what little he could feel of his skin. As an Argonaut, born of the guardian class descended from the greatest heroes in all of ancient Greece, he was stronger than mere humans. Stronger still than the Argoleans and the newly discovered half-breed race he now protected. Stronger, even, than his warrior kin.

No, hypothermia wouldn't kill him, dammit. Frostbite was nothing but a minor annoyance. And shit, since he was *him*, he could take a bullet to the chest and still his frickin' heart would go on beating. But this—he stared down into the abyss some six hundred yards below, which opened and darkened until all he saw was a river of deep green shrouded in a layer of thin mist—this might just do the job. A little voice in the back of his head whispered, *Just do it.*

He wasn't stupid. He spent more time with humans than any of the other guardians from his world and knew taking this leap would be nothing more than a major-ass Nike commercial gone wrong. But still . . . it was damn tempting. There was always the possibility he could hit that one vulnerable spot on the way down that would kill him instantly and end his immortality once and for all.

His brother in battle, Titus, stepped up next to him before

he could make up his mind and peered down into the canyon below. "Fucking nasty way to go. But you're right. It wouldn't kill you. And I'm not in the mood to pick up your broken-ass pieces and nurse you back to health today."

Zander glared at the younger Argonaut—the *way*-younger one, who, wouldn't you just know it, could take that fall and die . . . the lucky bastard. "Stop reading my mind. You know it drives me bat-shit crazy."

Titus smirked. Reached up to rub his hand over his mouth. In the waning light of early evening, the markings on his forearms and hands that all the Argonauts shared stood out against his light skin. It wasn't a full-out grin, but then Titus never truly smiled. "You're already bat-shit crazy, old man. And do you think I like knowing what goes on in that twisted brain of yours? 'Cause let me tell you. It's definitely not high on my thrill-ride list." He waved his big hands. "You're projecting your crap all over the place. Trust me. I'm trying not to listen."

Zander's scowl deepened, and he stepped back from the ledge, frustrated he hadn't taken the plunge before Titus started bitching, even more irritated because he knew that little free fall wouldn't snuff him out like he wanted. He was in a foul mood and it was only getting worse the longer they went without running into any daemons.

It didn't help that he and Titus had been patrolling this particular mountain range for the last frickin' week looking for stragglers and that they'd come up empty so far. He didn't want to go back to Argolea; he didn't want to head to the colony or look for any more half-breeds hiding out in the woods. He was itching for a fight in a dark and dangerous way, which was only making him moodier than Hades. And if he didn't get one soon, bad things were going to happen. For everyone.

"Let's go," Titus said, stepping back and rubbing his hands together to ease the chill. "There's no one hanging out here, and if there was a settlement down below, we'd have spotted it. We'll head north, cut toward Mount Hood and see what we can find."

Though he didn't want to, Zander nodded. The closest half-breed colony was hidden deep in the Willamette National Forest to the south, unknown to the humans who lived around it. Consensus among the Argonauts was that there were other half-breeds, or Misos, those with both human and Argolean parentage, in hiding from the daemons who hunted them. Thanks to the colony's leader, Nick, a man who was both a half-breed himself and something else that none of the Argonauts could quite pin down, they now knew of three other colonies spread out over the globe. One was in Africa, one in the frozen wasteland of northern Russia, and another in the jungles of South America.

"Hey," Titus said with that smirk again as they started walking toward a trail that led back into the trees. "It could be worse. You could have drawn shit patrol in Siberia like Cerek and Phineus."

The mention of his two guardian brothers didn't lighten Zander's mood. "At least then I would have been away from you and your constant mind-probing."

Titus chuckled. "You need to change your outlook, Z. Immortality? It's a gift. Shit, I'd give my left arm to have that power instead of reading mi—"

Zander turned on his guardian kin so fast, Titus sucked in a breath. "It's not a gift. It's a fucking curse."

Titus glanced down at Zander's meaty hand pressed tight against his jacket. A dark warning flashed over Titus's features. He didn't like to be touched. Not anywhere. Not even by a brother. "You need to step back. Right now."

Zander's eyes met Titus's. The guardians were roughly the same size, both six and a half feet, two hundred and fifty pounds of pure muscle, but that's where the similarities ended. Titus's wavy dark hair was tied with a leather strap at the base of his neck. Ice crystals clung to his thin mustache and dark soul patch. Sure, he looked human to the average passerby, but he wasn't. And his hazel eyes sparked of knowledge and danger. The kind that were a fiery combination for anyone who crossed him.

Zander slowly dropped his hand. But he didn't back away. In a fight, he'd win, even against a hothead like Titus. He could take a beating like no other and still go on ticking. But he could be hurt. And it'd take a while to heal. As much as he wanted a good knock-down, drag-out bloodletting today, he didn't want it with Titus.

He did, however, want the brother to get it. Especially if he had to keep prowling this fucking earth for shit only knew how long with the mortal bastard. He clenched his jaw. "Watching everyone you care about die is not a blessing, Titus. I served with your father. I served with all the Argonauts' fathers. I was around when Eurandros was king and Leonidas wasn't even an itch in his pants. And now King Leonidas is dying of old age, but not me. I'm still just as strong and healthy as ever."

The rage Zander kept buried deep inside built by the second. "You might not want to die now, Guardian, but one day you will. One day you'll be ready to go to the Elysian Fields or wherever the fuck it is the rest of you get to go when your days are done. But not me. No, I'll still be here. Doing the same damn thing I've done for the last eight hundred twenty-nine years. Watching you all die and wishing like Hades I could go with you."

He stalked off into the trees before he did something he knew he'd regret, knowing, okay, he sounded like a major pussy having one gigantic pity party. But he was sick of it. Sick of holding up his head and acting like he was all rosy and chipper at the way fate had bashed in his brain. There'd been a time—a long time—when he'd thought like Titus. When he'd actually believed the fact he hadn't yet found his vulnerability, or Achilles' heel, like his father and grandfather and every other male from his line had, was a gift. But that was before. Before he'd realized he was going to be stuck here for all eternity while everything that truly mattered was taken away from him. Before ten years ago. Before he'd figured out Hera's curse was real.

"Zander. Wait up."

He ignored Titus and kept going. Head down to block the wind. Temper and self-loathing warming his blood. Yeah, he was in the mood for a major-ass pounding. And if he didn't get away from Titus quick, he wasn't gonna care that the Argonaut was friend, not foe.

He made it thirty yards into the trees before the miserably cold temperature went bone-jarring frigid.

He came to a standstill. His head darted up. Ahead and to the right, six daemons stalked through the trees, obviously on patrol themselves. Searching for half-breeds to decimate.

A slow smile spread across his face—the first he'd felt in days. All were easily seven feet tall, with horns and fangs, catlike faces, dog-shaped ears and the bodies of men. Really big-ass, don't-mess-with-me ugly men you might meet in a dark alley on the wrong side of town after hours, looking for nothing but trouble. His smile only widened.

"Just who I was looking for. You freaks want to come out and play or stand there and look stupid like your bitch of a leader, Atalanta? 'Cause you know, you do it so well. In fact, I see the family resemblance. You there, in front." He pointed toward the ugliest one, with something vile dripping from its fangs. "You're like, what? Her brother? No, I know." He snapped his fingers. "Her son."

The one in front, the one clearly in charge, looked at Zander and growled, "Argonaut," then sniffed the air and added, "Two." The other five daemons spread out in a U formation, surrounding Zander, then crouched, ready to strike.

And yep, that was indeed steam coming out of the leader's ears. Hot damn. This was gonna be a good one. Six against one. Maybe he could get his ass kicked once and for all. And maybe he could take a few daemons out with him in the process.

Titus jogged up behind him just as Zander reached for his

parazonium—the ancient Greek dagger all Argonauts carried—from the scabbard hidden at his back. "Aw, hell. You just had to go and antagonize them, didn't you?"

"Sure as shit, I did."

Titus reached for his own dagger. "Okay, smart guy. Which ones do you want?"

"All of them."

"Zander—"

"Just stay back until I need you," he growled. "I can't die, remember? You can."

He took a step into the melee and ignored Titus's protest, but knew the Argonaut would listen and let him have the first go. If only for a few moments. Hopefully, that's all it would take to end this for good.

"Come on, motherfuckers. Show me what you've got."

With a roar, the daemons bared their fangs and charged.

This was one family squabble Callia definitely didn't want to be a part of.

"This is ridiculous. Isadora, tell him no!" Casey Simopolous turned in exasperation toward her half-sister, the future queen of Argolea.

From the far side of the extravagant bedroom suite, Callia chanced a sideways glance toward Isadora. The princess stood with her blonde head down, studying something between her pale pink slippers. Her hands were clenched behind her back, the gossamer pink dress all but swallowing her fragile frame. The perfect picture of submission. Not once had she flinched since her father, the dying King Leonidas, had issued his dire announcement.

This was their soon-to-be queen. This waiflike *gynaíka* who would rule over their land, command the Argonauts and lead them in this dangerous time of war. Atalanta was roaming the human realm, looking for a way to destroy the half-breeds and cross into Argolea to exact her ultimate revenge for being cast out of the Argonauts. Now more than ever it was imperative they have a leader with resolve.

But that clearly wasn't Isadora. Callia had suspected that for a while. And she couldn't help wondering if maybe Leonidas's decree was best for everyone after all.

"Isadora, you cannot let him do this to you," Casey said louder, stepping toward her sister. "This is archaic!"

"Enough!" the king rasped, attempting to sit up higher in the pillows of his gigantic four-poster bed.

Ignoring the buzzing in her head that had been going on for the last ten minutes, Callia set down her instruments and eased over to help him shift up in the bed.

The king frowned, irritated he needed any kind of help, but he didn't fight Callia. Today his mind was clear and he was making use of it while he could. "Isadora will marry by the next full moon. And that is final."

Casey's jaw twitched. "It's not right and you know it."

The king's head swiveled toward his dark-haired daughter—the one who would never be queen, simply because her mother had been human, even though Casey was the stronger and wiser choice and they all knew it—and he squinted to see clearer. Callia knew he saw nothing more than dark fuzzy shapes. "Isadora's binding to a guardian of *my* choosing will ensure the Council cannot overrule her authority. You already commandeered my first choice, Acacia. You do not have a say in whom I choose to replace him."

A heavy silence settled over the room. One Callia felt all the way to her bones. She knew all too well about domineering, controlling *patéres*. And she knew when they laid down the law, there was very little for a *gynaíka* to do but obey. Silently, she cursed their patriarchal society that gave females the opportunity to be anything they wanted so long as the male in guardianship over them approved.

Isadora still did not lift her head or look to either her father or sister. And though Callia and Isadora had never been close, a part of Callia went out to the princess. A part she didn't want to acknowledge or dredge up.

Ready to be done with the family drama, Callia gathered

the rest of her things and snapped her bag closed. As personal healer to the king, she'd spent a fair share of her time here lately, making him comfortable, seeing to his maladies during his last few months, but she didn't relish it a bit. Especially not when she had a headache like this one. And every time she came to the castle there was the chance she'd run into an Argonaut. Which was a rendezvous she avoided at all costs. "I'll be back to check on you tomorrow morning."

His gnarled hand snaked out and snagged her arm before she got a step away. Even at 684 years and with his body finally giving out from old age, he was still strong. Stronger than most. "I'll need you to stay."

Anxiety pricked Callia's skin. "That's not necessary, Your Highness. And I have work at the clinic I really have to get back to."

"The new moon is but a week away. After I make the announcement to the Argonauts, I'll need you to verify my choice is in peak physical shape. I need to know he can sire an heir immediately. You'll use my office for the exam."

Callia darted a look at Isadora, who, if possible, hung her head even lower. How great it must feel to be seen as nothing but a breeding machine.

But, oh, good gods. Callia had worse things to worry about right now. The king wanted her to perform a physical exam. On the Argonaut of his choosing. Today. She could think of a thousand other tortures she'd prefer to this one. "Um. I'm sure another time would be—"

"It is not a request." He released her hand and barked, "Althea!"

His maidservant scurried into the room with a bow. "Yes, Your Majesty."

"Get me Demetrius. He's with the Executive Guard at the portal, training the newest recruits. I want him and the rest of the Argonauts assembled here within the hour."

Althea's eyes widened with the same anxiety suddenly spiking Callia's chest. "All of them, Your Majesty?"

He waved off her question with a weak flick of his wrist. "Go. Now."

"Um, Your Highness," Callia started as Althea rushed from the room. "I really think—"

"Isadora," he said, ignoring Callia's urgent protest. "Show Callia to my study and see she has everything she needs for her examination. I want you both back here when the Argonauts arrive."

Isadora didn't bother to argue. She turned silently for the door, her slippers making not even a whisper of sound across the stone floor. Callia sighed in defeat as she watched the princess leave. She had no choice but to follow.

"Acacia." The king's attention swung to his other daughter. "Find that husband of yours. Have him call back his guardians from whatever patrols they're on. I don't want to hear excuses. I want them here. All of them. Is that clear?"

Arms crossed over her chest, Casey frowned and stepped close to his bed. Dressed in a sleeveless white blouse and crisp black slacks, she didn't cower in front of the king like Isadora. And she had no qualms about putting him in his place. "Oh, I'll find Theron and tell him exactly what you're up to, don't you worry about that." She tipped her head when she reached his bedside. "This is going to backfire on you. You know that, don't you?"

The king only harrumphed and looked ahead.

"It will," Casey reiterated as she leaned down and kissed his wrinkled cheek. "Mark my words, Dad. Isadora is not going to sit back and let you run her life for her."

"Yes, she will," he mumbled. "Because she's not you."

Casey straightened, and though it was clear she was fired up over what was being done to her sister, Callia could see the compassion the half-breed had for her long-lost father. A compassion Callia wished she felt for her own father.

"You're right," Casey said. "She's not. She's stronger than I am. Stronger than all of us. And one day soon, you're going to realize that for yourself. Everyone will."

The king didn't answer. Not when Casey turned and

disappeared through the door. Not when Callia grabbed her bag and followed. But as she reached the threshold, Callia was almost sure she heard the old *ándras* mumble, "I hope you're right. And for all our sakes, I hope this motivates her to finally prove me wrong."

CHAPTER TWO

Zander was bloody and bruised. He took a punch to the kidneys that nearly sent him to his knees, but he didn't fall. If anything, it steeled his resolve. He whipped toward the daemon at his back and plunged his parazonium deep into the unholy's chest. "Eat that, you piece of shit."

A roar erupted from the beast. It fell back, a loud sucking sound echoing as the blade exited its body. But before Zander could swing the blade out and to the side to decapitate the monster and send its soul to Hades for good, another jumped on his back and sank its fangs deep into his shoulder.

He hollered as blinding pain shot to his skull. Somehow he managed to twist and throw the beast off. He saw only red as he kicked, punched, swung his dagger right and left. Blood spurted, hit him in the eyes to run down his face. His back ached, his lungs burned. His shoulder was on fire where the beast had ripped through his jacket, tore open flesh and shredded muscle. But he didn't stop, didn't call out for help. This was exactly what he wanted. Adrenaline zipped through his veins, blending with years of pent-up rage as his arm arced out again and he took down another daemon. "Come on!" he yelled. "Is that all you've got!"

The two he'd sent to the ground seconds before charged again from different angles. His blade was a blur as he fought them back. From the corner of his eye he saw the others were gearing up for the next round. He was holding his own, but he wasn't going to win this. Not six against one.

"Zander! We have to leave. Now!" Titus jumped into the fracas then, his sword whipping through air and flesh, decimating right and left. Zander heard shouts and screams, grunts and the crack of fist against bone. Dammit, he had mere seconds before Titus changed the tide. And he hadn't taken enough damage yet.

The rage built deep in his chest—as it always did. And that's when it hit him. Just as he sent two of the uglies to the ground. The solution. Smack in the center of the forehead.

Stop fighting.

Titus could hold his own. They weren't protecting any half-breeds on this mountain. There was no one to get to safety. If things got hot, Titus could open the portal and flash back to Argolea and save his own ass. So why was Zander fighting this when he could possibly finish it once and for all?

Before he could change his mind, he dropped his weapon. Stood up straight. And stared at the three daemons around him. They looked as dazed and bloody from the fight as he felt, but they weren't nearly done. They each had the strength of ten men pumping through their veins. And from the menace rolling off them in waves, were getting ready for the final kill.

Yes. That's what he wanted.

Zander held his hands out to the side and closed his eyes. Sweat ran down his forehead to mix with the blood and other things on his face he didn't want to think about. He cleared his mind and thought about . . . nothing. Just sweet, empty nothingness. Which was all he really wanted anymore.

"You goddamned prick!"

A body hit him hard. Took him to the ground. His head cracked against rock. But when he peeled his eyelids open and looked up, he realized it wasn't a daemon on top of him. It was Titus.

Fire flashed in the other Argonaut's eyes. The daemons growled behind him.

"You asshole. Get off me!" Zander struggled beneath him as a familiar, uncontrollable urge rolled and boiled inside him. *What the . . . ?*

"Saving you, you son of a bitch!"

Before Zander could comprehend that Titus had just read his mind again, the Argonaut brought his arms together between them. Titus's elbows dug into Zander's ribs, but who the hell cared? The only thing that mattered was the fact Titus was going to fuck this up.

"No!"

Titus's hands came together, and the markings that ran from his forearms down around his fingers glowed from the inside out. A flash erupted as the portal opened. And then all Zander felt was air as they both spiraled through space.

He landed on his back against cold, unforgiving stone. Knew without even opening his eyes that he was at the Gatehouse, the portal into Argolea. But it was the bone-jarring right hook to his jaw that had stars firing off behind his eyes.

"You motherfucking son of a bitch!" Titus hit him again. This time hard enough to rattle brain against skull.

"Titus! Enough!"

Titus was yanked off Zander's bruised and beaten body with a grunt. Dimly, Zander heard voices. Theron. Demetrius. A lot more swearing—mostly from Titus. Feet shuffling. Heavy breathing. And Gryphon chuckling in his ear. "Way to go, Z. What'd you do to light him up, anyway?"

Ah, hell. Just his friggin' luck, all the Argonauts were in the Gatehouse.

Strong arms wrapped around his biceps. Pain shot through his left arm as Gryphon eased him to sitting, but he shook it off. When he opened his eyes and looked across the massive room with its soaring ceiling, he saw Demetrius holding Titus back in a death grip and Theron up in the Argonaut's face trying to talk him back from a blowup.

The portal glowed and popped behind them. Titus glared around Theron's massive shoulders toward Zander. Jerked against Demetrius's hold.

Zander shook off Gryphon's help and pushed to his feet. Rage boiled just beneath the surface of his control. Fuck it.

Fuck Titus. Fuck this damned war and his never-ending life. Fuck all the Argonauts, for that matter, and their constant interference.

"You nearly got me eaten because of your goddamned death wish!" Titus roared.

"Stop being such a pussy," Zander tossed back. He felt like his shoulder might be broken. A rib or two. He'd lost quite a bit of blood, but he could already feel his body trying to heal, dammit. "You can save your own sorry ass anytime you want with that light show you just pulled."

"That's it." Fury flashed in Titus's eyes just before he yanked free of Demetrius's hold. "Your ass is mine, you sick fuck."

Zander's adrenaline pulsed with the prospect of another fight. And that rage he worked so hard to keep a lid on boiled up to the top. He threw his arms out wide. "Bring it on, asshole."

Titus moved like a flash of lightning, and he was nearly on top of Zander before Theron got hold of him from behind. "I said *enough!*"

The leader of the Argonauts threw Titus across the room as if he weighed nothing. Titus's body hit a column on the far side, cracking stone and plaster with a deafening thwack. Titus slid down the column to land in a heap on the ground.

"Pussy," Zander mumbled. "Is that the best you can do?"

"You." Theron turned on Zander. "I should let him pound you into the ground after the stunt you pulled."

Oh, yeah. Big-mouthed Titus had already spilled the beans. Zander narrowed his eyes. "So let him."

Theron got right up in Zander's face, nice and personal. And though Zander didn't mind unleashing his fury on Titus, his rage had dimmed enough in the last few seconds to remind him egging Theron on right now was a bad idea. A descendent of Heracles, the greatest hero ever, Theron was strong enough to rip Zander from limb to limb and make him feel pain like he'd never experienced. Except once.

"You'd better pull it together right now." Theron's voice was so low, his face so close, Zander barely heard him. And Zander knew that was the point. "Find something to live for or leave the Argonauts for good. Because I won't have you risking one of my guardians again. Are we clear?"

Zander's chest went cold. Leave the Argonauts? That was not an option. "Yeah, we're clear."

Theron's eyes narrowed. Behind him, the portal popped and sizzled again. Cerek and Phineus came through, snow-flakes still stuck to their shoulders and hair, and glanced around with what-the-hell-happened-here? looks on their faces.

"We'd better be," Theron said. "I'm not kidding this time, Zander. Loyalties only run so deep. I will remove you if I have to."

Removal from the Argonauts was not a simple process. It involved the king and the Council and an assload of red tape Zander didn't even want to think about. And doing so was the equivalent of slicing a guardian's throat, taking away not only his job, but his identity.

But that wasn't the worst of it. Reality hit Zander as he stood there staring at their leader. If he was kicked out of the Argonauts, he'd be banned from crossing the portal and going into the human world. And if that happened, he'd lose the one thing that gave him any pleasure in his godforsaken life.

"You won't have to."

Theron sent him one more steely look before turning toward the rest of his Argonauts. "The king has called a meeting." He looked toward Titus, now standing and dusting rubble from his body. "You have fifteen minutes to get cleaned up and over to the castle." He glared at Zander. "And that time line is nonnegotiable." Then he stormed out of the Gatehouse, all 280 pounds of pissed-off Argonaut.

Tense silence filled the air. Finally Demetrius, never one to care about any of the others, stalked out, followed by

Cerek, Gryphon and Phineus, until Zander was once again alone with Titus.

And shit. Now that his rage had ebbed and his adrenaline was flagging, Zander knew he needed to break the ice, but he wasn't sure what to say. Apologizing had never been his strong suit. Even when he'd been a total ass.

Titus crossed the floor, his heavy boots clomping on the stones beneath his feet as he headed for the door without a word.

"Wait up, T."

"Save it, Zander. I'm not in the mood for your shit right now. I've got my own hell to deal with. We all do. But then you never think about that, do you? You only think about yourself."

Alone, Zander blew out a long breath. The Executive Guards, protectors of the portal, had turned their backs and were doing their best to ignore him. No surprise there. Word would undoubtedly spread to the Council about this little brouhaha, but he didn't really give a rat's ass. When it came down to it, the king had the final say in what happened to the Argonauts, not the Council. It had always been that way. Would always be that way.

Still not ready to join the others, Zander stalled in the Gatehouse, a massive marble structure patterned after the Temple of Hermes in Arcadia, Greece, with soaring columns flanking every side. The stagnant portal sat in the center of the room, a looming doorway from one world to the next, edged all in solid stone. His eyes drifted to the words inscribed into the rock, to the ones he'd read a thousand times but had never really seen.

Herein lies the boundary of worlds. Protected on this side, bound only by sacred land on the other. Those who cross do so at their own risk. But be forewarned: passage herein invites the bringer of nightmares, the watcher of madness, the light and dark in constant flux. And always, waiting . . . the thief at the gate taking stock for the deathless gods.

It always came back to that, didn't it? To the fucking gods and their immortality. To what Zander had and didn't want. He never worried about crossing the portal because he knew he'd always come back. But others didn't. Others like Titus. Every time his kinsmen crossed, they put their lives on the line. And they did so for their race without question.

A heavy weight pressed on his chest. Okay, maybe Theron had a point. Maybe he needed to get a grip and stop being such a downer. So he was old. Who the hell cared? So his life was shit. Nothing new there, right? It didn't look like death was an option, and bailing from the Argonauts was the last thing he wanted, which meant he needed to find something to live for fast—before Theron made good on his threat and threw him out on his ass, once and for all.

Problem was, he couldn't see a damn thing worth living for at this point.

Callia glanced around the king's royal study. Bookshelves lined every wall. The gilded ceiling was at least three stories high. Behind the antique desk, which was empty but for a lamp on the front right corner, a bay of windows looked down to rolling green hills and a lake shimmering far off in the distance.

The room smelled of tobacco and leather, was cozy and warm with a great stone fireplace and a trio of couches ripe for sinking into. Callia knew, because she'd once sunk into one after hours when the castle was asleep. And she hadn't done it alone. If that little memory wasn't enough to drop her mood a notch, nothing was.

"Is there anything else you need?" Isadora's soft voice made Callia turn. The princess stood in the doorway with a strange look on her face, almost as if afraid to cross the floor inlaid with the royal seal.

It's just routine. You've done this a thousand times. Doesn't matter that this time it's with an Argonaut. "No, this should be fine."

"Very well, then. We should get back." But Isadora didn't

make a move to leave, and there was a flat, almost emotion-less look in her eyes that said going back was the last thing she wanted to do too.

Torn between what was none of her business and the re-gret she knew she'd experience later if she kept quiet, Callia heard herself say, "Tell him no, Isadora."

Isadora's brown eyes slowly lifted, and Callia sucked in a breath at what she saw. No, they weren't flat. They looked dead. As if she'd given up all hope.

"It won't do any good."

"It will," Callia protested, unsure why she felt the need to help the princess so strongly. "Stand up for yourself. Prove him wrong. Prove them all wrong."

Isadora's eyes didn't even flicker. And Callia had a sicken-ing sensation in the pit of her stomach. What had happened to the princess? This was more than simply being beaten down by her father.

"Stay out of things that do not concern you."

She turned before Callia could even respond, and Callia sighed as she watched the princess go. Maybe Isadora was right. This wasn't her concern. Sure, she felt bad for the *gyn-aíka*, but really . . . it was foolish to worry about someone else when Callia had bigger problems.

Resigned, she left her bag in the study and followed Isa-dora back to the king's chambers, thankful, at least for now, that the buzzing in her brain was gone. They made it as far as the grand staircase before voices drifting up from below stopped Callia's feet.

Male voices. Mixed with heavy footsteps that sounded like a herd of elephants had stormed the castle.

The Argonauts. All of them, just as the king had ordered. Callia's stomach jumped into her throat and perspiration popped out all over her skin even though she'd mentally prepared for this moment from the second she'd heard the king's command.

Theron led the group and bowed his head quickly when he saw the two of them standing at the top of the fourth floor. "Isadora. Callia." His dark eyes homed in on Callia. "How is the king today?"

"Holding steady." She tried to focus on his features, but the Argonaut was huge—six feet five inches of solid muscle, broad shoulders and legs like tree trunks. Alone he was intimidating, but followed by five more Argonauts, each equally big and imposing as he was? He was like the beginning of a tidal wave about to sweep her under.

"That's good," Theron said. "I take it he's ready for us, then?"

She would have answered, she really would have. But her eyes were searching of their own accord, skipping right over Demetrius and the other Argonauts until they finally landed on Zander. Alone at the end of the group, turning at the base of the stairs and heading her way.

Okay, mentally preparing herself and actually being in the same room with him again were two very different things. She sucked in a shocked breath, even though—dammit—she tried not to. But it wasn't just *him* that elicited the reaction—at least she told herself that much—it was what had been done to him.

His face was black and blue from temple to jaw on one whole side. A myriad of cuts and scrapes marred his tanned skin. While his short blond hair was wet and slicked back as if he'd just splashed water on his face, and the white shirt he wore was clean and crisp, neither hid the pain etched into his features or the way his left arm hung at an odd angle.

He'd obviously been in the human world, fighting daemons, which was what he'd been bred to do. But a small part of her quickened with fear just as it did every time she thought of something bad happening to him.

Which was . . . bone-brain idiotic. Because he couldn't care less about what happened to her.

"Callia?"

Theron's voice finally registered, and her gaze jerked back to the leader of the Argonauts, studying her with curious eyes. In a rush she realized several other guardians

were also looking at her funny, and even Isadora was wring-
ing her hands, watching her with a perplexed look.

"Y-yes?"

"The king?" Theron asked with raised eyebrows.

"Oh. Right. Yeah." She shook off the flood of emotions
seeing Zander always conjured, pushed them down deep,
as she'd gotten good at doing over the years, and turned for
the king's chamber. "He's ready and waiting."

Her anxiety lessened when they stepped into the room.
But that damn buzz picked up all over again.

Althea, who had been helping the king get situated with
his mountain of pillows, went scurrying out as soon as she
saw the Argonauts. Casey turned from the window as they
filed inside. Wishing she had some lavender for her suddenly throbbing head, Callia took up a space in the far corner of the room, near the king in case he needed her, but
well out of the way. She didn't miss the warm smile spreading across Casey's face when she spotted her new husband,
or the way Theron's eyes lit in response.

"*Meli.*" Theron went to the king's half-breed daughter.
Kissed her cheek and temple. They exchanged quiet words
as the room filled with more people than it could contain.
And though he probably didn't realize it, Theron trans-
formed from badass-biker-dude intimidating to downright
handsome as he smiled at Casey and took her into his arms.

A hollow ache hit Callia midchest as she watched. There'd
been a time, not all that long ago, when she'd felt the same
consuming, electrifying emotions. Her eyes skipped back
over the group to where Isadora was leaning against the far
wall, also well away from the others, a far cry from the
happily-ever-after her sister had found. Then to Zander, standing only inches inside the doorway, ready to bolt at the first
possible opportunity.

Yeah, she knew that feeling all too well. It was the same
one she got whenever she saw him. Anger welled up in her
chest as his gaze bounced anywhere but at her. He'd shaved

off the little bit of facial hair he had the last time she'd seen him, but even bruised and beaten he looked more like Adonis than his ancestor Achilles. Bronze and blond, buff and beautiful. He was the oldest of the Argonauts. The only one rumored to be immortal. The one she'd once foolishly thought she'd spend her life with.

"I'll get right to the point," the king said, cutting through Callia's dark thoughts, bringing her attention back where it needed to be. His voice wavered from his illness, but didn't break. "The situation with the Council is getting out of hand. They've made no overt threat, but rumblings are filtering through and it's clear they're preparing to strike as soon as I pass. While Theron and I have had our disagreements of late"—the king inclined his head toward where he'd last heard Theron's voice—"we both believe that the future of the Argonauts cannot fall into the Council's control. Lucian has made no qualms about the fact he wants the Argonauts replaced by the Executive Guard. I don't have to tell you that doing so would be our greatest downfall."

He paused to take a breath, and this time Theron dropped his head and focused on Casey's hand, which he held in his own, as if he knew what was coming but didn't want to hear it.

"While I am pleased that Theron chose to marry *one* of my daughters, now that their binding is complete, it has left the monarchy once again vulnerable to the secret plottings of the Council. I see no other choice but for the same solution as before. Theron and I are both in agreement that Isadora must marry—"

"You knew?" Casey's head jerked up, and she pinned her new husband with an outraged look.

"Shh, *meli*." Theron patted her hand.

"—and that her husband must be from the Argonauts." The king's words didn't seem to appease Casey. She glared from her husband to her father. But lucky for the king, he couldn't see her reaction. Just as he couldn't see the sudden tightening of the shoulders of every Argonaut in the room. "We have disagreed on just who that should be. But as king, the decision falls to me."

He pulled in a breath and seemed to grow a foot, looking very much the regal king he'd once been, commanding an impressive amount of authority from his deathbed. "Because Jason's line is the second strongest of the Argonauts, that responsibility falls to you, Demetrius."

Silence filled the chamber. All eyes shifted to Demetrius, in the back of the group, leaning one shoulder against the wall, only half paying attention to what was happening around him.

And then, when he noticed everyone looking his way, it was as if the king's words finally hit. Shock ran over Demetrius's face just before he dropped his crossed arms and pushed away from the wall. He was the biggest of the guardians, at nearly six feet eight. And the shadowed eyes Callia had often thought were soulless narrowed and darkened to ebony as he homed in on the king. "No. Fucking. Way."

"Demetrius . . ." Theron warned in a low voice, letting go of Casey's hand and rising to his full height.

"I won't do it," Demetrius said, shaking his head. "And you cannot make me. No one can make me."

Theron crossed quickly to stand in front of the giant Argonaut, who was now shaking with a mixture of contempt and resentment that seemed to roll off him in waves. Callia swallowed and wondered if the other females were thinking the same thing she was—namely, that a brawl was about to break out if someone didn't do something fast.

"Demetrius, stand down."

"I will not bind myself to *that*," Demetrius ground out, his face twisting in fury as he glared over Theron at the king and lifted a hand to point at Isadora. "And you cannot make me."

Theron said something Callia couldn't hear, but she didn't miss Demetrius's response. No one did. Especially not Isadora, who, standing in the other corner of the room, seemed to shrink into herself even more.

"Kick me out of the Argonauts if you want. Banish me to the human world. I don't care. But hear me now, Theron. I will never marry *that*. I'll choose death first."

Theron slapped a hand on the bigger Argonaut's chest and pushed hard.

Oh, jeez. This was not good. Not good at all.

Voices broke out in unison: Casey's as she rushed to console an obviously shaken Isadora; Theron's from the doorway, where he was talking Demetrius down from inflicting bodily harm; the other Argonauts as they whispered about what had just happened.

The king, surprisingly, was silent, until a voice from the back of the room called out, "I'll do it."

A voice Callia knew all too well.

"Who said that?" The king's ears perked, and he leaned to the side to peer around the massive guardians toward the speaker, though it did no good.

Conversation quieted. Heads turned toward the doorway. Even Theron and Demetrius stopped arguing long enough to glance sideways.

And Callia's stomach twisted into a knot as the sea of bodies parted to reveal Zander standing there, staring at the king with nothing but resignation across his bruised and handsomely familiar face.

No, no, no. He can't possible mean—

"I'll do it," Zander said again in the quiet. "I'll marry Isadora."

CHAPTER THREE

Okaaay. Not the reaction Zander had been hoping for.

No one in the room said a single word. And oh, yeah. He *totally* should have thrown himself off that cliff. At least then he wouldn't have to endure this soul-rattling silence or see the what-the-fuck? looks on his kinsmen's faces.

He shifted his feet, rested his hands on his hips and waited. As the seconds passed and no one said a word, his unease peaked. Finally, he broke the stare-down and said, "Look, don't everyone thank me all at once."

Theron glanced over his shoulder at the king. "We need a minute."

Before Zander could respond, Theron pushed him back into the hallway with a force that nearly knocked Zander off his feet. The leader of the Argonauts didn't speak until they were well out of earshot of the king's chamber, and then he let loose.

"What the *fuck* do you think you're doing?"

Resentment brewed as Zander's back hit the stone wall. It wasn't like he expected Theron to be all rosy cheeked and gracious that he'd finally manned-up. Theron had every reason to be suspicious. But a little thanks wasn't too fucking much to ask, especially now.

"Helping."

"This isn't a joke, Zander."

"I don't see anyone laughing."

"Why in Hades would you make light of this situation?"

"I'm not—"

"*Skata.*" Theron raked his hand through his shoulder-length hair. "I'm already so pissed at Demetrius I can barely see straight. I hate that Isadora is forced to marry anyone, but there's no way around it. Not if we're to keep the Council out of Argonaut affairs and Atalanta out of Argolea for good. And I don't need you adding fuel to the fire and fucking it all up when I—"

"I'm not adding fuel, Theron. I'm serious. I'll marry her."

"Serious? You?" Disbelief raced across Theron's chiseled features. "I doubt that. This isn't something you can casually volunteer for just to make up for what happened earlier. Or to get you back in the king's good graces. Marriage to Isadora isn't until you get bored of her and decide to go back to your human women. This is permanent. The binding ceremony joins two together for—"

"A lifetime. Yeah. I get that. But let's be honest here. We're only talking about her lifetime. Not mine."

Theron's mouth snapped shut, and Zander took a deep breath, because okay, yeah, there was no turning back from this. Not now that it was out there. And part of him . . . part of him didn't want to turn back. "Isadora's got what, five hundred years until she passes, if that? That's a long time, but in the grand scheme of my life? Probably nothing, and you know it."

"Zander, you're not really—"

"Immortal? Yeah, don't go there. We both know you'd be wrong anyway." He wasn't about to let Theron change his mind. "Demetrius obviously doesn't want this, and you can't force him to marry her when he's so adamantly against it. Not to mention, he's volatile. He scares the crap out of her on a good day. What do you think he'll do to her if they're alone? Do you want her to be miserable for the rest of her life, or worse, be thinking about what he could be doing to her whenever the doors are closed?"

"No." Theron winced. Looked down at his boots. Seemed as sickened by the idea as Zander was. "Of course I don't want that. Demetrius is the last guardian I'd choose for her, but the king won't listen."

"None of the others want to marry her either," Zander

said quietly. "You could see it in their eyes. Let me do this. I want to. I'm the only one who doesn't have anything to lose."

"Zander," Theron said cautiously, bringing his dark eyes back level with Zander's, "if you marry Isadora, you sacrifice potentially finding your—"

"My what? My soul mate?" Zander scoffed. "I already found her, Theron. Years ago. Only she didn't want me. Not enough." At Theron's pitying expression, Zander nearly laughed at the irony, even as he felt the ache he'd gotten good at ignoring bubble deep in his chest. "Yeah, Hera's curse about an Argonaut finding his soul mate and losing her, then being nothing but a shell? It's true. I know from experience. Before her? I didn't know what I was missing. Since? It's like one long-ass day that keeps repeating itself over and over, only there's no way I can get past it. And you know what? I'm tired of it."

"Zander . . ."

The sympathy he heard in his kinsman's voice was too much, and he ran a hand over his brow. If he didn't get this conversation back on track he was going to spill the beans to Theron about all the really ugly shit that had gone down, and he didn't want that. He needed to keep it locked inside. Where it was his and no one else's.

"Look. You told me to find something worth living for. That's what I'm trying to do." He dropped his hand. "The only thing that means anything to me these days is the fighting, which, if I keep going down the path I've been on, I won't even have anymore. No one else wants to do this and I can. So"—he blew out a long breath—"say yes. Save the other guys from having to make a sacrifice you know they can't handle and tell the king you support my binding with Isadora. And let's be done with this."

Theron studied him so long, Zander wasn't sure the Argonaut had heard him. His heart thumped hard in his chest as he waited. If Theron said no . . . he wasn't sure what he'd do. He felt like he'd just been thrown a lifeline, something real to grasp onto. Something that would give him a reason to live instead of just going through the motions. And now Theron alone had the power to crush the one spark of hope he'd had in years.

Finally, Theron said, "The king wants heirs. It's the entire reason he's forcing this marriage on Isadora."

"I know."

"And you're okay with that?"

Was he? It meant sex. With an Argolean. *Not* a human woman. "I have to be, right?"

"He won't let you fight. He'll take you out of the rotation and keep you in Argolea until she's with child or an heir is born."

Zander hadn't thought of that. "Okaaaay. Yeah. I guess . . . that makes sense."

"And there's always the question of your . . . virility. You've taken more than your fair share of beatings over the years."

That was Theron's polite way of saying Zander may have been kicked in the balls one too many times to sire a child. On this, at least, Zander knew he was certain. A sound that was half chuckle, half harrumph came out of him. "I'm fertile. Don't worry about that."

"How do you know—?"

"Because I've worked that particular magic before."

Theron's brows drew together. "You have a child?"

Had was more accurate. Or, *almost had.* The ache intensified in his chest. "Not anymore."

"*Skata.* Zander . . ."

Okay, now things were getting *way* too real for Zander. He rubbed a hand across his lower lip. "Look, they're waiting for us. Just say yes, Theron."

Theron sighed. The battle raging inside him was palpable. He, of any of the Argonauts, would know the sacrifice Zander was making. Because he was the only one who'd found his soul mate. And obviously, just the thought of losing Casey was enough to tear him apart. "You can't change your mind. Once the ceremony is final, that's it. No one else but her."

"I know."

"You're willing to make that commitment to Isadora? Even knowing she's . . . still out there?"

Zander thought about the "she" Theron was referring to. Wondered what the Argonaut would say if he knew that *she* was right in the next room. Then thought about all the years he'd wished things could be different, that she'd made a different choice, that she'd picked him over her domineering father. Or that he could just get beyond her betrayal and forgive her. But he couldn't. Every time he looked at Callia, he didn't see the beauty that she was or the power that she held, he saw what she'd done. And even now, as he remembered, it pierced his chest as fresh and sharp as it had that day.

"I am," he said with more conviction than Theron needed. But then, that conviction wasn't for Theron, was it? It was for him. And what he was about to do.

"Isadora will never be your soul mate, Zander," Theron said quietly.

"That's why I want to bind myself to her."

Theron turned and glanced toward the king's door, rubbed a hand over his face as if he was exhausted. Blew out a long, long breath. "Okay," he finally said. "Okay, you have my endorsement. It's up to the king, but . . ." He looked back at Zander with a mixture of pity and respect that was oddly reassuring, then placed his large hand on Zander's shoulder. The Argonaut markings, the ancient Greek text, ran down his forearms to entwine his fingers, just like they did on Zander's arms, just like they did on the arms of all the Argonauts. "You have my respect. And my gratitude. What you do here, you do for all of us. I won't forget this. None of us will."

The emotion swirling in Zander's chest was unfamiliar. Not excitement, or even happiness really, because he was neither excited nor happy. No, this was different. It was warm and encapsulating, and it radiated from the center of his being.

It was . . . pride, he finally realized. For the first time in longer than he could remember, he was proud of what he was doing. For someone else. For his people. For their protection and way of life. And it felt good. Damn good, because . . . it meant he wasn't numb anymore.

He was too pansy-assed choked up to say anything, so he only nodded and followed Theron back into the king's chambers.

The room quieted once more as they entered, and he met the expectant looks of each of his guardian kin with a reassuring nod. But he didn't look at Callia, standing near the king's bed. Couldn't. And he told himself that was a good thing. Because his past with her ended here. His future— for the next five hundred years, at least—was with the *gynaíka* on the other side of the room. The one he intended to marry, bed and impregnate all in the next week.

His stomach tightened at that little reality, but he lifted his head, held still and let Theron take the lead.

"Your Highness," Theron said, his deep voice like a boom to seal Zander's fate. "I recommend you reconsider your choice. Zander has my full support as the guardian best fit to marry Isadora."

No one said a word. Behind him, Zander could hear Demetrius suck in a breath and hold it. Across the room, Isadora and Callia stared at him. The king frowned, obviously contemplating his options. And he didn't look altogether ecstatic at what he was thinking.

Just say yes. Beads of sweat broke out on Zander's forehead as he waited. His conversation with the king weeks ago—when Theron had nearly walked away from the Argonauts—flashed in his brain. The king hadn't been happy when he'd sided with Theron. Looked less than thrilled now. If the king held that against him . . .

Just say yes . . .

Finally, the king said, "So be it."

A breath Zander hadn't realized he'd been holding rushed out. At his back, he heard the same from Demetrius.

"The binding ceremony between Zander and the princess Isadora will take place in seven days' time," the king announced. "On the eve of the full moon. You are dismissed."

Collectively, the Argonauts turned to leave. Muttered voices echoed around Zander, but the only one he fully caught was Demetrius's grateful one as the guardian said, "I owe you, Z."

That pride hit Zander again in the chest full on, even though . . . the thought of what lay ahead solidified that ice around his heart.

This was the right thing to do. The only thing he could do. He was saving the others from something they didn't want. Hopefully saving a small part of himself too.

He turned to leave with the other guardians, but the king's sharp voice stopped him. "Zander." He looked back. "Do not disappoint me. The repercussions will be fierce."

Yeah, that wasn't glowing thanks either. Zander bowed once, indicating he'd heard the king, but his pride wavered.

"Before you return to duty," the king went on, "you'll report to my private study for a complete evaluation by my personal healer. If you pass the exam, the binding ceremony will go on as scheduled. If not, I'll choose another Argonaut. You are excused."

Zander's gaze hopped right to Callia. Who was staring at the floor as if it might just jump up and bite her.

For shit's sake. This was supposed to put his feelings for her behind him. Not give her an opportunity to grope his naked body. And holy Hades, his blood did *not* just warm at the thought. Or at the possibility of being alone with her one last time.

Callia waited as long as she could. The Argonauts filed out of the room. Casey and Isadora left. She took her time helping the king get situated so she didn't have to make the trek downstairs with Zander.

When he finally turned to leave she swallowed hard. Oh, gods. He was binding himself to Isadora. Never in her wildest dreams had she ever expected . . . *that.*

"If you find anything even remotely questionable in your exam, Callia," the king said, "I want to know about it. Do you understand?"

She nodded, though inside she felt like screaming. Zander was binding himself to someone else. And now she had to go into that room with him. See him naked. Touch his body. Remember everything they'd done with each other. What had happened after . . .

She was so lost in her thoughts, she didn't feel the king's hand wrap around her wrist, only registered the tug when she tried to leave and couldn't. She turned to look back at him and found his violet eyes focused in on her. Violet eyes that couldn't possibly see her, but were focused just the same.

He didn't speak. Only stared at her as if searching for . . . something. Finally, he said, "Your mother was a great healer, Callia. Fervent in mind and body. She served as Royal Healer for a long time, and she did it well, much to the chagrin of your father. I see a lot of her in you, and it pleases me to know that you carry on her work, when your father would have chosen something else for you. But your powers are stronger than your mother's ever were. Your future brighter." When Callia opened her mouth to protest, he cut her off. "No, it's true. And you know it to be so, deep in your heart."

She closed her mouth. Stared at him. Unsure what to say or do.

"Callia, dear, I for one know what it is to want something you cannot have, but I also know the only thing that matters in this world is that which we leave behind. Your mother knew that too. Do not forsake what might have been for what can never be. A true leader sets aside his personal wants for the good of the whole. And he makes sacrifices. Ones that, in the end, justify all that came before."

Her pulse thumped hard in her veins. A strange tingling lit off at the base of her hairline. She searched his face for a clue as to how he knew what she was feeling. Only she came up empty. Did he know about her past with Zander? Had someone told him what had happened between them? Or was he talking about Loukas, Lucian's son, the *ándras* who would one day lead the Council of Twelve so at odds with the monarchy, and the male she'd been betrothed to from the time she was just a child?

"I . . . I am not a leader, Your Majesty."

His eyes softened, just a touch. Just enough to tell her he knew more than she'd ever expected. "Not yet. But maybe one day."

He let go of her as quickly as he'd grabbed her, then leaned back in the pillows, closing his eyes as if the last hour had drained him of his energy. Gone was the gentleness and wisdom in his voice when he said, "Report back to me after you see to Zander. I want to know that he can produce heirs. If this binding is to be sanctioned, I need confirmation of his virility. Once the ceremony is complete, I cannot choose another. And tell that useless maidservant Althea on your way out that I do not want to be disturbed."

Callia's stomach clenched into a knot as she stared at the old *ándras* and he drifted off to sleep as if he had not a care in the world. The king expected her to . . .

Skata.

She lifted a shaky hand to her forehead, swiped at the sweat beading there and turned for the door. This exam had suddenly taken on a whole new form of personal torture.

She left the room as anxiety and anger boiled in her gut. After relaying the king's message to Althea in the antechamber, she reluctantly headed down the great marble staircase toward the king's study on the second level.

Damn the king. Her temper soared as she reached the bottom step and turned the corner toward the study. Damn the politics of this war. Damn the Argonauts and Zander especially for making her feel, when she'd been doing a helluva job just getting by these last ten years. She didn't want to sacrifice. She didn't want to think about marriage and bindings and doing what was right. And she especially didn't want to be alone with the one Argonaut who had ruined her entire life.

She pushed the study door open to see Zander turn from the bay of windows, late-afternoon sun highlighting the gold in his short blond hair, backlighting the muscles and planes of a well-defined body she'd known more intimately than any other. But he didn't greet her, not that he ever did. And there was absolutely no reaction whatsoever on his face at seeing her. Not that there ever was.

He turned his gaze out the window again without a word.

She let the heavy door snap closed at her back and walked toward the desk, her shoes clicking across the king's seal as she crossed the marble floor. Calm. Clear. Completely professional. That's how she'd play it with him, no matter how much she wanted to throw something. If he was going to act like they were complete strangers, two could play that game.

"Strip," she said as she cleared the ancient mahogany desk of its lone lamp so she could use it as her exam table. "Everything off."

Stormy blue-gray eyes shifted her way. And oh, yeah, that was definitely not happiness reflected there at the prospect of being alone with her. Like she cared.

"I'm not getting naked for you."

She ignored the little thump in her heart at the sound of his deep voice and narrowed her eyes. "Then you're going to have a hard time binding yourself to the princess." She glanced at his hips. Smirked. Wanted to gouge out a wound in his chest big enough to dump a truckload of salt into. "Or soft, as the case may be. Rumor has it you can only perform with human women. Whether you like it or not, the king wants to make sure you're . . . up to par, you might say, before he lets you marry his daughter."

She knew she was antagonizing him, but just couldn't stop herself. It had been building for a long time. Since the moment he'd turned his back on her all those years before. She wanted to make him hurt the way he'd hurt her. To feel . . . something . . . instead of being the stone-cold bastard he really was. And since this was the first time they'd spoken in ten years, was it really a shocker their conversation was about to be a doozy?

She focused on his darkening eyes, saw the temper flare there and felt marginally better over the fact he was finally exhibiting some kind of emotion, even if it was contempt. "Of course," she went on, "you can save yourself the burden of this little exam by simply admitting you're impotent."

"You'd like that, wouldn't you?"

"No." What little humor she had faded. "What I'd like is to get this over with so I can be on my way. Contrary to what you might believe, Zander, my world stopped revolving around you a long time ago. Now either strip, or I'll tell the king to choose someone else."

CHAPTER FOUR

There were times when the bitter cold was something you reveled in. When the shiver running down your back was a stark and blessed reminder that you were alive. For Max, this was not one of those times.

He stared up at the seething seven-foot monster in front of him. Blood and sweat and other disgusting things he didn't want to think about dripped down its ugly face. The shiver that ran through Max was a mixture of the near-zero temperatures this far north in mid-October, and the fear that lanced through every cell in his small body.

"You. Will. Pay!" The daemon lunged, his sword slicing through air, coming dangerously close, but one thing Mr. Ugly didn't count on was how quick someone only four and a half feet tall could be.

As if fueled by some outside source, Max darted between the daemon's legs, whipped back and sliced out with his own blade, cutting deep into the daemon's thigh. The monster howled, dropped his sword and went down to one knee. Blood spurted from what could only be his femoral artery, spraying over Max and the ground. Bile welled in Max's throat, but he lifted his sword again, ready to strike. To finish this. The need to annihilate stronger than anything he'd felt before.

"Good. Good, Maximus." Atalanta's voice echoed in his ear. "Let your hatred guide you. Finish him. Plunge your blade deep into his chest. Then send his soul to Hades for all eternity by decapitating the beast."

He wanted to. His muscles ached to kill. But the pride he heard in Atalanta's voice stopped his forward momentum.

The monster lifted its face, his glowing green eyes now level with Max. There was fear there, true fear at what would happen to him. And in that instant Max saw himself reflected back in those eyes. He saw the weeks of training, the years of hopelessness and his own fight just to stay alive. And he saw that Atalanta was winning.

He dropped his blade, stumbled backward. Couldn't seem to tear his eyes from the daemon in front of him. A kind of respect passed between them. And on the daemon's part, a thanks, if you could call it that. But it was probably more relief. Tomorrow he'd be healed of this wound and be ready to take Max on again. This time to the death.

"Spineless." Atalanta swept by Max, picked up his blade and thrust it into the daemon's chest. The monster's eyes went wide. He reached for the blade, but she yanked it from his body, swung out and decapitated the beast without so much as a grunt. His grotesque head hit the ground just before his body fell.

Max's eyes grew wide, but he didn't run or even gasp. He'd seen her kill before. Knew he would see it again.

She rounded on him, leaned down and narrowed her black-as-night eyes. "I grow tired of your humanity, Maximus. Kill or be killed. That is the world in which we live. The sooner you accept that, the sooner you will take your place at my side."

She was tall, close to six and a half feet, he guessed, and with her jet-black hair, which fell straight to her waist, her snow-white skin, her coal eyes and those high, sharp cheekbones, probably pretty to some, but not to him. This close she smelled sweet, of honey and spun sugar. But he knew how deadly she was. The beauty was a mask. Inside she was as sick and twisted as the daemons who served in her army. And when she struck, her sting was worse than any scorpion's.

"Yes, Maximus," she whispered, a wry smile sliding across her perfect face as she leaned in closer. "I feel your hatred for me right now. You want to lash out. To hurt me. But you can't. Because I am your *matéras*. Feed the feeling, *yios*. Channel it. Direct it back to the ones who created me. To those who are responsible for your misery now. You know the root of all evil lies with the Argonauts."

She let the last word linger near his ear, her hot breath running down his neck, under the collar of his thin shirt. The sickness he'd been fighting condensed in his stomach and rose to his throat, and it was all he could do to swallow it back.

Her eyes were filled with victory as she eased away, but there was also something else there. Disgust at how he had failed her yet again.

He stared at her. Didn't break the eye contact. Knew she'd see it as another sign of weakness if he did. But she was right. He did hate her, and he did want to hurt her. Though what stopped him wasn't the fact she claimed she was his *matéras*. No, he stopped because the humanity left in him that she hated so much wouldn't break. Not while he breathed air in his lungs.

She rose to her full height, her red robes pooling around her feet, and glared down at him. One perfect hand lifted and pointed back toward the fortress across the barren field. "Leave me now before I change my mind and let Thanatos have a crack at you."

Though he wanted to run, Max turned and walked across the frozen ground, head held high, shoulders back. When he reached the massive log structure, he darted around the side to the servants' entrance at the back. He knew his place. Though the bulk of Atalanta's army was housed in the barracks nestled in the woods and steep-rising mountains behind the property, a few of her "chosen" resided with her in the big house. Thanatos, her archdaemon. A couple of servants. And him.

He went in through the kitchen and silently climbed the rickety back stairs to the fourth floor. This huge house, more like a wilderness lodge than anything else, was still an improvement over the Underworld. There he hadn't had his own space. Here, even though it was freakin' cold 24-7 and his toes were in a constant state of numbness, at least he had more than a corner to call his own.

After being banished from Hades for reasons he still didn't understand, Atalanta had moved her army to this barren wasteland deep in the forests of northern British Columbia. He knew why she'd brought them here. Because it was isolated. Just as he knew this house and all the land around it had once belonged to some old oil tycoon who'd struck it rich somewhere in Alaska. That man was now dead, the gruesome details of his mutilation alive in Max's mind thanks to Thanatos, but no one in the nearby community of Fort Nelson had any idea a demigod from the Underworld was living among them. None realized they would soon die. Or that the woman who now resided here plotted revenge and was formulating a way to take over the world.

His thighs ached by the time he reached the fourth level. He was so tired from the day's fighting he could barely see straight. At the end of the long hall that split the floor in half, he eased open the three-foot-high door and crawled through the small space. Inside, he grasped the rungs of the dusty, wooden ladder and climbed until he reached the attic. Then finally sighed in relief.

Across the dirty floorboards, his pallet beckoned. The filthy porthole-shaped window high on the wall looked out at the frozen gold-brown training field, but he didn't spare it a glance. He never did. Its only use was to let light into the dingy room, as it did now.

He was grubby, covered in blood and sweat, and he needed a shower in the worst possible way, but it could wait. Right now he wanted comfort. The kind he could only get from one thing.

He crossed the room. The blanket had already been removed from his pallet—by one of her minions in the house who'd watched the scene outside, no doubt. Punishment, he was sure, for not killing that daemon when he'd had the chance. If there was one life lesson he learned every day it was that in this world, everything had consequences. But today he barely cared.

Next to his pallet, a fresh bowl of water and a plate of bread had been left for him. Though his stomach growled at the sight, he ignored the pathetic food and instead continued on. To the fifth floorboard from the wall. To the one only he knew was loose.

He pried the board up with fingers still so cold he could barely move them. After lifting the corner, he reached underneath to draw out the glass.

It wasn't a mirror, but it wasn't clear either. The oval piece was frosted on both sides, rippled as if from the inside out even though it was smooth to the touch. Around the outside it was rimmed in what looked to be gold, though Max couldn't be sure, as he'd never seen real gold before. All he knew was that it was heavy, a solid weight in his palms, no bigger than a saucer, and it held a magic like nothing he'd ever known.

A window between worlds.

He cradled the glass gently against him, walked forward until his feet brushed his pallet, then sank down to his knees. He held the glass in front of him and whispered the words the little old lady who had visited him in secret both in Tartarus and here had taught him.

"Show me my heart's desire."

The ripples inside seemed to move. And then the glass cleared. Heat flowed from the object in his hands into his body, warming him from the outside in. And when he looked, he saw her face.

Excitement pumped through him because only rarely was she looking straight on when he peeked. And because it meant at this very moment she was gazing through glass somewhere herself. Maybe she was thinking of him right this second, as he was thinking of her.

Oh, she was beautiful. A smile spread across his face. She never aged, but then, being an Argolean, she wouldn't, would she? Not until the last few years of her life. To anyone else she would look to be in her early thirties, though he was sure she was much older. Her skin looked silky, her eyes a dreamy violet color, a lot like his own, or at the very least how he hoped his appeared. Her hair was a deep auburn, today falling to her shoulders in a silky drape he was sure was as soft to touch as it was to look at. But as he peered closer, as he drank her in inch by inch, he realized her features were set, that her jaw was locked, her mouth a slash across her pretty face. And though he'd seen her take on many expressions, this was one he didn't know. Today she looked . . . upset.

A protective urge bubbled up in him. A need to find who had hurt her and why and then make them pay. But before he could read anything else in her features, she turned away and the image faded. The glass once again became the same frosted, rippled and cold piece it had been before.

"No. Wait. Come back." He shook the glass. "Show me my heart's desire. Come back!" He said the words again. And again. Only nothing happened. The heat that had been there only seconds before was now gone. Right along with her.

Knowing it was all he was going to get tonight, he stretched out on the pallet, closed his eyes and cradled the glass against his chest. Tears burned the backs of his eyes. His stomach rumbled again. Never before had he felt as dirty and gross as he did at this moment.

Maybe she could see back through the glass. Maybe that's what had upset her and why she'd turned away in disgust. But even as the thought hit, he knew it wasn't true. The little old lady in the white robe had told him it only worked one way. And yet that was small consolation when just thinking of her reminded him of everything he couldn't have.

He liked to imagine she would be proud of him. For standing up to Atalanta, for staying true to what he knew he was deep inside. But the reality was, maybe she wouldn't be. Maybe all she'd see when she looked at him was the same thing everyone else saw. A grimy, ten-year-old boy no one wanted.

He rolled away from the food his body desperately needed, fought back the tears that were now sliding down his cheeks and held on tighter to the glass. The warmth that had flowed into him before still resonated in his chest, so he clung to that feeling. And to the hope that someday she'd come for him.

He didn't care anymore why she'd let him go. He only wanted her back. If the gods could see their way to send her to him, he would be the best son any mother ever asked for. He promised.

Sleep pulled at him. He saw her face again. Only this time she was standing in a field of white, her beautiful features lined with worry as she looked, searched. For him, he hoped. And though he knew it was only a dream, he ran to her.

Because even just the dream of her was better than anything else in his miserable life.

As an Argonaut, Zander had never been one to just "go with the flow." It went against his nature. If someone said sit, he stood. If he was told to go one way, he went the other. The only person he took orders from was Theron, and then usually grudgingly, so listening to Callia boss him around right now didn't just set him on edge, it sent every single hair on his body standing at attention.

However, he wasn't stupid. He knew there were times when it was better to bite your tongue rather than let the rage rumble through. And right now—though he hated it with a passion—this was one of those times.

But there was still no way in Hades he was getting naked in front of her.

He crossed the room without looking at her, dropped onto one of three velvet couches in the sitting area and reached forward to unlace his boots. Too late he realized the couch he'd picked was the same one he'd bent Callia over one dark and sultry night nearly eleven years before.

Blood pooled in his groin. His skin grew hot and damp. Her words, the words she'd whispered to him the night he'd intercepted her after she'd been to see the king, echoed in his head.

Take me, Zander. Fast. Before someone gives me a reason to say no.

Thirteen simple words. That was it. She'd known exactly what to say to turn his entire world upside down in the span of a heartbeat.

Perspiration dotted Zander's forehead as he remembered the feel of her silky smooth skin, the taste of her wet heat, the way she'd come apart around him right in this very spot. He reached up to wipe his brow. Dropped his arm. Then scowled, because that was a memory he *so* fucking didn't need in his head while he sat here unlacing his boots so Callia could do her little "examination."

And—dammit—the rod of steel now nestled between his legs was an in-your-face reminder she, and not the *gynaîka* he was about to marry, was his soul mate.

He let the boot in his hand thunk against the floor. Looked up and glared across the room. Callia had finished setting up and was now looking out the tall windows toward the countryside beyond, her arms folded across her chest and her jaw locked and tense.

His chest pinched as he watched her. Gods, he'd been a fool. Back then there hadn't been a single thing about her he hadn't needed. Hadn't *wanted*. He'd been so blinded he couldn't even comprehend a time when she *wouldn't* be exactly what he needed and wanted most.

But that was then, wasn't it? Before he'd realized what she really was deep inside. Before he'd discovered Hera had been absolutely correct in picking Callia as his soul mate because she was the epitome of everything he hated most. That past? What he'd done with her in this room? That really was a fantasy. This—he stared at her cold indifference and saw her as she really was and not as he'd wanted her to be—this was reality.

The erection he'd been fighting since he stepped in the room faded. He dropped the other boot, locked his jaw and stood as he lifted the shirt over his head. He'd removed his weapons before coming into the castle, as was protocol, so he didn't have to worry about his parazonium or any of the other gizmos Titus was always cooking up. And he was glad. Fiddling with his weapons would mean more time in this room with her alone.

"Where do you want me?"

She turned away from the window without meeting his eyes, dropped her arms and pointed toward the end of the king's now-empty desk. "There. Sit."

He crossed the floor silently in bare feet and eased a hip onto the end of the king's long desk. He tested the piece of furniture for stability, and when he was sure it wasn't going to collapse under his weight, scooted back until his legs were hanging over the edge and his bare feet dangled inches above the floor.

She didn't say anything about the fact he wasn't completely naked, and he wasn't about to bring it up again. To distract himself, he stared down at his toes while she moved around the room. She pulled a small side table with her supplies next to her. Seconds later he felt her hand land on his back and couldn't stop the way he arched in response. When she said, "Deep breath," he forced himself to relax as she moved the stethoscope around, obviously listening to his lungs.

The metal against his skin was cold, but her fingers were warm and silky—too warm and silky. His blood was already heating just from being this close to her, and every time she brushed his skin, it set off tremors deep in his body. He focused on his breathing, on the steady in and out, in an attempt to stay calm. When she moved around to stand in front of him, repeating the order, he averted his eyes from her face and focused on the fitted white sweater she wore instead.

Her gasp brought his head up. "What happened to you?"

"Nothing. I'm fine."

"That's not nothing." She focused on his shoulder as she looped the stethoscope around her neck, reached for her bag and came back with gauze and supplies.

"Leave it," he said before she could touch him. "It's just a flesh wound."

She dabbed at the dried blood with a wad of gauze. "The muscle's torn. You need this stitched closed before infection sets in."

"It's already healing."

"I see that, but—"

He grabbed her wrist, stilling her motion. A jolt ran through him at the connection, but he ignored it. The last thing he needed was her hands on his body more than was already necessary. "I said leave it."

Her eyes slid from the wound to his face and held. And before he realized it, he was staring into eyes like a Caribbean sunset in the human world. Eyes he'd looked into countless times before as they'd made love. Eyes he'd dreamed about numerous times in the years since, until he'd woken in a cold and aching sweat.

Thoughts vanished from his mind. The connection they'd had from the first sparked deep in his chest, burned in the bottom of his soul. Tempted him to reach for her and find out if she felt it too. He couldn't be the only one who remembered, could he? She had to feel something when she saw him. When she stood this close. When she touched him.

Thoughts, memories, feelings he'd kept buried for a long time pushed in as he stared into her gemlike eyes. A movie of their time together flickered in front of his face. And then, when he got to the part where she betrayed him, that blaze went out. Leaving behind nothing but charred ash and ruins.

It didn't matter what she felt. Their past was over and done with. The Fates had screwed him in more ways than one. There wasn't anything about her now that could change what had happened back then.

He dropped her hand as quickly as he'd grabbed it. Then glanced back at her sweater. "Finish the exam."

Which—dammit—didn't do shit to cool him down because her breasts were now all he could see. Oh, man, they were as round and plump and gorgeous as he remembered, and he was almost sure he could see her nipples straining against the soft cotton. If he lifted his right arm, just a little, he could touch one. Could feel the nub swell and harden beneath his fing—

She stepped back slowly. Set the supplies and her stethoscope down. Cleared her throat. The sound brought his thoughts back where they should be. But the quiver to her voice when she spoke told him his harsh command had gotten through loud and clear. And why that made him feel like an ass, he had no clue.

"We'll just go on with the brunt of the exam then. There's no need for the standard poking and prodding."

Relief swept through Zander. That suited him just fine. He only wanted out of this room. Preferably sooner rather than later.

"Sit up tall," she said. "And close your eyes." He did as he was told, gripping the edge of the desk with his hands and straightening his spine, thankful her voice was once more level and direct and that now, at least, he didn't have to look at her. "Good. Now, you'll likely feel warmth as I search for any abnormalities, maybe a pinch there in your shoulder, but for the most part this shouldn't be painful."

Maybe not for you.

He drew in a deep breath, tried not to frown, and though Callia didn't touch him, he felt her hands hovering mere centimeters from his bare chest. As a healer, she had the ability to seek out problems within the body and focus her energies to restore balance and health. Argoleans were less susceptible to disease than humans and healed faster, but at the core they were still mortal. Though Zander knew she wasn't going to find anything wrong with him.

"Easy," Callia murmured. "Breathe slowly, in and out. That's it. Just let your mind wander and your body relax. Good. That's . . . good."

There was something oddly calming about her voice—always had been—and the heat radiating from her fingers warmed first his skin, then seeped deep into his muscles, and finally, his bones. She was probing his body, searching for ailments, but it almost felt as if she were reaching inside him with her bare hands, crawling into his skin and making herself at home. Warmth slid through his chest inch by inch as her fingers shifted and her hands moved over him. And oh, man, he liked it. Liked the way she filled him. It felt good. Calming. Complete. The way he imagined the Elysian Fields probably felt when one passed to the afterlife.

Out of nowhere the pain in his shoulder jackknifed, sending sparks to his brain as if he'd been sliced all over again. He gasped, tensed, dug his fingernails into the wood of the king's desk

His eyes flew open. He stared at her as he gritted his teeth in pain. Her face was scrunched up as if she felt it too, but her eyes remained closed and she didn't pull her hands away.

"It's deep," she said. "Are you sure you don't want me to fix it?"

The wound. She was in the fucking wound. "No," he rasped between clenched teeth, fingers digging deeper into the wooden desk. "It's . . . fine."

"Ilithios." Ever the professional, she left it at calling him an idiot and didn't push again. Soon her fingers were moving once more, sliding away from his wound until the pain lessened and warmth returned to his chest.

Holy Hades. He blew out a ragged breath. That was most definitely not a pinch. If she'd ever wanted to hurt him, she could have done it with barely a flick of her finger.

"I need you to focus again, Zander," she said firmly. "Relax. Close your eyes."

Relax. Yeah. That sounded possible.

He took another deep breath. Tried to think about . . .

nothing, like she'd suggested. And succeeded, for all of two seconds. Until her hands started moving south. Down his rib cage and abdomen, and stopped to hover right over his belly button.

"Lie back," she said. "And spread your legs slightly."

The command was enough to send the blood straight to his groin. His cock strained against his pants. And oh, yeah, this was wonderful. He was going to have a hard-on in a matter of seconds, and she was telling him to lie back and spread his legs.

He gritted his teeth again, did as she said and prayed her eyes were still closed. She didn't touch him, but he sensed her move closer. Felt the heat between his legs as she eased nearer and leaned over his groin, her hands millimeters above him now, moving slowly lower, now over the waistband of his pants, down the zipper, lower still. His skin tingled in the pressure points between his hips and torso. Warmth continued to move south. He held his breath and waited, even as he felt himself grow impossibly hard beneath the fabric of his pants.

Her hands hovered over his lap. Warmth turned to heat to a white-hot burn in his groin he knew all too well. And oh, fuck, that was her breath against his belly button. She was leaning way over him. Her face so close. Images popped into his mind: Her succulent lips. Her mouth against his skin. Running lower. Her tongue . . . Her doing this exam and whatever else she wanted to him, naked, with him laid out before her like an offering.

His breaths came deep and ragged as he fought the arousal. If she so much as bumped his cock accidentally he knew he'd go off, right here on this makeshift examination table. And would that not be mortifying or what? He told himself it wasn't her. It was what she was doing to him. *Any* healer doing this exam would have the same effect on him. It was the energy rushing through him that was juicing his libido, not *her*.

Yeah, right, dumbass.

It felt like an eternity before she moved on, down his right leg, and he finally drew a full breath when he felt the warmth spread out of his groin and down his limb. She was now quick and efficient, examining one leg and then the other. And there was only a tiny twinge of electricity in his groin again when she moved back to start at the top of his left leg.

All that warmth seemed to rush out of the big toe of his left foot, and he heard her push up from the floor, sigh and finally say, "You're done."

She turned away from him, replaced the tools she'd used earlier in her bag. Almost afraid of what he'd see, he opened his eyes, stared up at the three-story-high ceiling with its gilded ceiling plates and tried to calm himself. Didn't work, though. Yeah, that heat was now gone, but his cock was still stiff as a board and there was no way she'd missed that when she'd opened her eyes.

Fuck it. She was being professional about this, and that meant he should be too. After all, there was nothing left between them, right? He pushed up with his elbows.

He shifted to find a more comfortable position—as if there were one. She had her back turned to him and she didn't look up, not even when she crossed the floor, grabbed his shirt from the couch and tossed it his way. "Everything seems fine. I'll tell the king you're able to . . ." She stopped herself. Seemed to think twice. Then finally said, "That you're healthy. So long as the sample comes back normal, there's nothing else you need from me."

"Sample?" he asked, catching his shirt in his lap and shifting it to hide his still-raging hard-on. "What sample?"

She recrossed the floor, reached into her bag and handed him a small plastic cup and lid. "You'll need to provide a sperm sample for lab analysis." She set a brown paper bag beside him on the desk. "Leave it in the bag on the desk when you're done." Then she lifted her bag and headed for the door.

Too stunned to move, he only stared at the plastic cup in

his hand as she reached the door. She wanted him to . . . ?
With her waiting outside this door while he . . . ? Right *now*?

His gaze shot to her, and though he most definitely wasn't
a prude, something about this felt wrong. Really freaking
twisted wrong.

She stopped with one hand on the knob, but she didn't
turn. And there was no way he could read her expression
when she said, "I wish you and Isadora . . . much happiness, Zander. Yeah, I . . . May you and yours flourish in the
tradition of the great heroes."

The congratulatory words traditionally offered to an *ándras* and his bride wedged their way into his head, then
slinked down to his chest. Where they settled. Cold. Heavy.
Dark. The arousal he'd been fighting since he'd stepped
into the room slid out the door right along with her, leaving
him unsatisfied and edgy. And irrational as it was, his temper flared as the door clicked shut behind her and silence
settled over the room.

He didn't want her good wishes. He and Isadora didn't
need her approval. Growing more pissed off at her words,
his reaction and what had and hadn't happened in this
room, he glanced down at his lap, where his cock was now
fairly shriveled.

He was over her, dammit. He didn't need her. And he
knew one very clear way to prove that fact once and for all.

Except . . . before he went looking for Isadora to do just
that, he apparently had to jerk off on command. Or stay
locked in this room for the rest of his immortal life.

Shhhhhiiiiiiiiiiiiiiiiiiiiiittttttt.

Muttering curses at Callia, the king, this whole damn situation, he grabbed the cup and his shirt, tossed both on the
couch, then sank down into the cushions. It took several
minutes for his heart to stop racing and his thoughts to quit
swirling, and when both did, he let his head fall back
against the headrest, closed his eyes and pictured Isadora.
Pale, petite, pretty, perfect. It was no great secret she was
one of the most attractive *gynaíkes* in all the land. And

wouldn't you know it? His cock didn't even twitch at the thought.

He blew out a long breath. Tried again. This time palmed his groin. He could do this, *dammit.*

Except . . . nothing happened.

Frustrated, he mentally undressed Isadora in his mind as he stroked himself, hoping that would do the trick. He pictured her in a long flowing skirt and a sleeveless top. Her pale hair fell all the way to her hips. She skimmed her fingers over her throat, slid them lower, around the outside swell of her breasts, down her sleek rib cage, to finally land at the hem of her coral top. Her milky white hands crossed in front of her, tugged at the fabric, and he caught a flash of sleek skin, the soft indent of her belly button and her toned upper abs as she drew the top higher. He held his breath and waited, watched as inch by inch she revealed herself until she was pulling the garment up and off, and her high, firm, *very* naked breasts were all he could see.

And oh, yeah. They were perfect. Pink. Tight. Just the right size for a guardian's hands. For his mouth . . .

She whispered something. His name? He wasn't sure. Before he could figure out what she'd said, she was leaning forward, her hair coming down to hide her face as she slid her fingers into the waistband of that long, elegant skirt and pushed it down her curvy hips.

His mouth ran dry. He waited. Couldn't see anything but all that silky hair and the fabric of her skirt sliding low . . . lower. And then . . . all that was left was a mound of satin pooled on the floor at the base of two of the sexiest legs he'd ever seen and a river of auburn hair he wanted to part with his fingers and dive into.

His dick tingled. He felt the blood flow south. He rubbed himself through his pants. Silently cheered because . . . *Yes!* . . . this was finally working.

Only . . . when she eased back upright and all that glorious flesh came into view, he realized the *gynaíka* suddenly naked before him was no longer petite and perfect. She was tall and voluptuous, with silky red hair and eyes the color of amethyst. And she was smiling, just for him, like she had hundreds of times before. That one look brought his cock to instant alert, sent every last drop of blood to his groin. And he grew impossibly hard. Harder than he'd been in years. Just that fast.

Callia turned away, giving him a clear view of her toned ass and legs, braced her bare knees on the seat of the couch, inched them wider until he could barely breathe. She shifted around to glance over her creamy shoulder with a sultry come-get-me look that grabbed hold of his chest like a vise and wouldn't let go.

And then she threw the death blow. The one that crumbled him from the inside out. She whispered, "Take me, Zander. Fast. Before someone gives you a reason to say no."

Ah, gods, he was lost. It wasn't even worth fighting anymore. His seed boiled deep at the remembered feel of thrusting hard inside Callia and giving her exactly what they both wanted. And even before the first twinge shot up from his balls, he knew he was royally fucked.

Only problem was, it wasn't in any way, shape or form the way the king wanted.

CHAPTER FIVE

Isadora stepped from the shower and tugged a plush towel around her body. After the scene in her father's chamber, she'd felt dirty. Had needed to wash off the stain the entire ordeal left behind. The way they'd all stared at her. The things Demetrius had said . . .

She grabbed another towel and wrung the water from her hair to keep from focusing on his words again, then tossed it on the counter.

In her bedroom she eyed the heavy full-length gown that Saphira, her handmaiden, had left hanging on the closet door. Her stomach pitched. She couldn't stand to look at that dress. Hated covering her skin with it. Despised the weight and texture. Sickness welled in her stomach at the thought of doing one more thing someone else wanted her to do. Instead she ripped the towel from her body, tossed it onto the bed and took a deep breath.

Pants. She wanted pants. But where would she get them? She lifted her thumb, gnawed on the tip of her nail. She could ask Casey. Her half-sister would jump at the chance to help her out on this one. Of course, if her father saw her dressed in anything other than a gown it might shock him into cardiac arrest.

"Isadora?"

Zander's voice in the anteroom hit her a microsecond before the door to her chamber pushed open and he stepped inside. Where he stopped. Dead in his tracks. And didn't move.

And oh, shit. Heat rushed to her cheeks at what he—the first male ever—was seeing. She scrambled for the towel and wrapped it tight around her body, wishing she'd thought to grab her robe from the bathroom.

Good gods, why was he here? And why in the name of all things holy was she freaking out like some spineless virgin?

Because, technically, you are one, Isa.

"I, uh . . . I'm sorry," he muttered. "I didn't realize you weren't . . . decent."

Obviously. But now that he knew, why wasn't he making any attempt to leave?

"It's . . . it's all right," she said, searching for composure. "I just didn't expect you . . . anyone . . . to come barging in."

Where in the blazes was Saphira?

He didn't respond. And when she finally turned to face him, she found he was staring at her with a blank expression she couldn't possibly read.

Which, okay, shouldn't surprise her. She knew she wasn't a hot commodity. She was too pale, too thin, bony where she should be curvy. So it was no surprise he didn't look overly pleased by what he'd seen. But this . . . this was just . . . awkward. She'd barely said ten words to him in all her life, and now they were standing here face-to-face, her nearly naked, with the weight of a marriage looming between them and the knowledge that in a matter of days they'd be having . . . sex.

When he still didn't say anything, just continued to stare at her with that stone-faced expression, she dug down deep and pulled up her courage. "Did . . . did you want something, Zander?"

Nice one, Isa. He's male. He's an Argonaut. He just barged into your bedroom like he owns the place. And you're practically naked. What the hell do you think he wants?

Or did before he saw you . . .

She tugged the towel closer. Curled her bare toes into the thick carpet. Waited.

Finally, after what felt like an hour, he opened his mouth as if he were going to say something, then closed it just as quickly. His head lowered, and he rubbed a hand across his brow. "I'm not quite sure what I'm doing here," he muttered. Then louder, "No. I do know." He looked up. "You're father's forcing this marriage on you. You don't want it, do you?"

"I . . ." Isadora didn't know what to say. If she agreed with him, he'd know how she truly felt, and their binding would start off with animosity between them. But if she wasn't honest, they'd never be on equal footing. And though her father didn't yet realize it, she didn't intend to let any *ándras*, this one included, bully her again. "No," she said firmly, straightening her spine. "I do not."

"I didn't think so." He dropped his hand, locked his gaze with hers. He was truly handsome, bronze and buff and blond, but she didn't feel even an ounce of attraction toward him. Never had. "I'm glad you told me. But as archaic as I know it is, in this situation, your father has the final say."

Yeah, she knew that too. And she didn't like it. Her jaw clenched.

"However," Zander said, glancing down at his hands, "I don't like the way this was forced. So . . ." He paused, seemed to gather his words. "What Demetrius said, back in the king's chambers." His gray eyes lifted to hers again. "That was wrong of him. And I for one apologize if he upset you. There are facets of Demetrius even the rest of us don't understand."

Isadora didn't answer, but her blood pressure shot up at the mere mention of Demetrius's name. For the first time in weeks—since returning from Hades, where she'd sacrificed her soul and a great deal more to save Casey—she felt something other than numb. Bitter hatred burned in her veins. The kind she thought she'd been saving only for Hades himself for what he'd put her through in the hours she'd been in his realm. But no, this burst of emotion was centered directly on Demetrius.

"I'm sure you would not choose Demetrius if you could," Zander went on. "But if there's another Argonaut . . . one of the others, whom you'd rather have fill this place . . . I'd like you to tell me now."

Isadora's eyes narrowed. "You do not want to marry me either."

"No," Zander said quickly. "It's not that. I do. I mean . . . I wouldn't have volunteered if I didn't. I . . ." He shifted his feet, rested his hands on his hips and blew out a breath. "I just think you should have a choice in this matter. A female should always be able to choose who she wants to be with."

This was not a conversation Isadora had ever expected to be having. Not with him. Not with anyone. He was offering her a choice. Him or one of the others. Unlike her father, he wasn't going to force her to marry him. And though she had a feeling binding himself to her was not his first choice either, for whatever reason, he'd committed to this. And yet . . . he was leaving the final decision up to her.

She thought about him. What little she knew of him. Years ago he'd had the reputation of being a player, but lately that had waned, for reasons she didn't quite understand. It was rumored his tastes ran more toward human women, and he hadn't been seen with any Argolean *gynaíka*, at least not that she knew of. And she was usually kept up to speed on what the Argonauts were up to, at least personally, because Saphira and her horde of friends liked to gossip. But he was always polite. He didn't seem to care much about the Council or their rumblings, and he was a fierce guardian. One who, rumor had it, couldn't be killed.

Those were good traits to pass to a child.

She thought about the other Argonauts. Cerek, with his friendly smile and stormy eyes that hinted of secrets she wasn't sure she wanted to know. Titus, who she'd never seen look anything but stoic and whose knowing glances put her on edge whenever he came near the castle. Gryphon's piercing light eyes that screamed of conquests near and far—and several inside this very castle. And Phineus, Mr. Adventure, rebel without a cause, the one rumored to breathe fire.

She definitely didn't want to wake up charred in her own bed. Or know the *gynaíka* who served her at the castle had also served her spouse in private. Or have her own secrets pulled from her mind without permission. And she definitely didn't want to be privy to the darkness her spouse held that could threaten to drag her deeper into an abyss she already wasn't sure how to crawl out of.

She looked back at Zander. And knew he was the best of the worst. At least, for her sake, she hoped he was. "I choose . . . you."

For a heartbeat, he didn't say anything. And then, he motioned with his hand. "Come to me."

She pulled the towel tighter around her breasts. Slowly, she crossed the floor, her bare feet silent as she stepped from carpet to solid wood. When she was a foot from him she stopped and had to tip her head back to look up. He was taller than she'd realized. And bigger. Everywhere. In fact, from her vantage point he seemed . . . downright huge.

He closed the distance between them. Heat from his body encircled her where she stood. She smelled sandalwood and something citrusy. And though her pulse kicked up at his nearness, there was no excitement rushing through her veins. Not even a flicker of arousal.

He tipped her chin up with his finger. Warmth flowed from his hand into her cold skin. "I will never intentionally hurt you, Isadora. If you are honest with me, I will be honest with you in return. Do you understand?"

She nodded once.

"Trust is all that I ask of you. Nod so I know you believe me."

She did.

"Good." His gaze ran over her face. "Now, kiss me and show me you are as committed to this binding as I am."

She didn't move. But neither did she fight him. Not even when he lowered his head and brushed his lips over hers.

The sensation was . . . soft. His lips were supple, yet firm, and when he skimmed them over hers again, she felt herself respond. Felt her mouth move beneath, not in approval but in . . . acquiescence.

It was over quickly. He eased back and stared down at her. Neither of them seemed to know what to say. There was no heat burning in his eyes. No flash of desire. He didn't appear to be holding back his passion, and, she supposed, that was a good thing. Because that kiss hadn't done anything for her except check off a box in the life column of things she'd never done.

"I'll return in six days for the binding ceremony." He left the room quietly, the door clicking softly at his back.

Alone, Isadora walked to the vanity and sank onto the plush-covered stool to stare at her reflection. That numb feeling had washed back over her sometime during her conversation with Zander. In a matter of days she'd be his *syzygos*. His wife. And that kiss? It was only a hint of what he would do to her when they were husband and wife.

No excitement, apprehension, not even worry ran through her at that thought. She let the towel fall to her waist. Slid her fingers through her long blonde hair from root to tip. The thick mass hung to the middle of her back. As heir to the throne, and female, she was held to the traditions many Argoleans had given up long ago, much to the disapproval of the Council. Her hair was to remain long, she was to wear only full-length gowns that covered her limbs in their entirety and she was to be untouched. In every sense of the word.

Was that still true?

She dropped her hair. Pushed away memories from her time in the Underworld that tried to creep in. Tried to settle the unrest that grew deep in her soul with each passing day. She would be two hundred years old in a few months. Two hundred years and never been kissed. Until now.

With hands steadier than she expected, she pulled open the drawer of the vanity and fished around until she found scissors. They glimmered in the early evening light as she thought about who she had been before and who she was now.

Her father expected her to bind herself to Zander and

produce an heir. To cement the monarchy so the Council could not overthrow her reign once he was gone. And she would do exactly what he commanded, because her life, now, was sacrificed. But that's where it ended. There would be no follow-up "spare." No matter how nice or agreeable or handsome Zander was, she would not take him into her bed again once her pregnancy was confirmed. And oh, she would rule. Much to the dismay of the Argonauts, and the Council, and most of all, her father.

She had five hundred years before she passed from this life into the next. And once she did, her soul no longer belonged to her, but to Hades. It was way past time she stopped living for everyone else and finally started living for herself.

She opened the blades of the scissors and captured a clump of hair near her temple. Then, without hesitation, she sliced.

Zander paused on the other side of Isadora's closed bedroom door, took a deep breath and rubbed a hand over his brow. He wasn't sweating. If anything, his skin was cold and clammy, much like Isadora's had been.

Not important. He headed out of the anteroom toward the grand marble staircase. Walking in on a very naked Isadora had not been what he'd expected. Or planned. Or, *skata*, wanted. But now that he had, he couldn't get the memory of her out of his mind. Bare as the day she was born. As perfectly formed as any Argolean male hoped. The female that would very soon be his for the taking. And why the hell that didn't excite him, he didn't know.

Before he could stop himself, his thoughts were skipping back, comparing Isadora's body to the heady fantasy of Callia he'd conjured up in that damn study. Only one got his blood going. Only one shot his body temperature into the out-of-this-world range. Only one made him hard with just a thought.

Shit. He stopped with one hand on the banister. Forced out a breath, drew another one in.

Isadora is not the one.

His heart rate kicked up, but he worked to keep it steady. Told himself, okay, so his body wasn't reacting the way his mind wanted, but that didn't mean he couldn't still make this work. There were Argolean aphrodisiacs he could take that would help with his libido. And if those failed, he could always cross into the human realm, knock over a pharmacy and lift some Levitra or Viagra or Cialis. He'd used human drugs before. He knew they'd work in his system. He could use them again for the sake of his marriage and their people.

You never had to use them with your soul mate, dipshit.

"Whatever," he muttered, picking up his pace again. "It's just biology, dumbass."

"Talking to yourself again, old man?"

Zander pulled up short at the base of the stairs on the second floor, one hand on the newel post, as he peered into the shadows.

Near the far wall, Titus stepped out from behind a column he'd obviously been leaning against, waiting. "I always suspected you were a little senile."

"Hey," Zander said. Because, yeah, this was awkward too. "What's up?"

Titus crossed his arms over his broad chest. Stood with his legs shoulder width apart. The stance was defensive, but not aggressive, and Zander was glad. He wasn't in the mood to get his ass handed to him anymore today.

"Theron told me to wait for you. He got a message from Nick. Daemons hit a village somewhere near the North American colony. Seems there was a mix of half-breeds and humans living there. Nick's asked for help locating survivors. Theron already sent the others out. He wants you ready to roll."

Excitement pricked Zander's skin. Theron was letting him fight? He'd expected to be sidelined from now until the time Isadora produced an heir. But maybe since they weren't officially bound yet, Theron was giving him one last job. "Yeah. Sure. I just need to grab some weaponry. Then we can go."

"One thing first." Titus stepped in front of Zander, blocking his path to the next set of stairs, and Zander's back tightened in anticipation of what would come next. Retribution was a bitch, but Zander had it coming.

"What you did before . . . in the king's chamber. That was . . ." Titus lifted his hand, looked at it. Seemed to debate whether he was going to reach out and touch Zander's shoulder or plow his fist into Zander's abdomen. Zander stiffened, but then Titus dropped his arm. "That was heroic, Z. I just want you to know all of us . . . especially Demetrius . . . we won't forget this."

That pride returned, swift and consuming, to smack Zander in the chest all over again. And yeah, he may be fighting his own personal demons where Isadora and Callia were concerned, but this was why he was making the sacrifice. For Titus, who couldn't touch anyone except in anger; for Demetrius, who was so screwed up no one knew what the hell was wrong with him; for Cerek, who kept his distance from all females. He was doing it for all his guardian brothers who couldn't make the same sacrifice for a thousand different reasons.

"Demetrius forgets everything. Guarantee by next week he won't give a shit about the whole thing."

A smile cracked Titus's usually somber expression. Or at least, what could be considered a smile for Titus. One corner of his mouth quirked. "Probably. That, or he'll come up with a reason you did this to screw the rest of us over somehow."

Zander shook his head. Smiled himself and followed Titus as the other guardian turned and headed for the stairs.

"And just so we're clear on something else," Titus said as he walked. "No way in hell I'm gonna start calling you Your Royal Highness just because you're binding yourself to Isadora. Your Royal Heinie, maybe."

Zander's smile widened as they turned the corner and headed for the Undercroft, the room on the lowest level of the castle where the Argonauts stored weaponry and any other gear they might need. This was more like the Titus he knew.

"Or Your Majesty," Titus went on. "More like Your Major Dumbass. Ooh, wait. Better yet. You know how the Council always addresses the king as His Most Faithful Serene Highness? We'll call you His Most Fucked-up Sperm-donating Heinie." Titus seemed pleased with his own joke. "Yeah, that one fits."

Zander's smile faded as Titus pushed the heavy door to the Undercroft open with his shoulder. Yeah, that one totally fit, didn't it? His future had just been summed up in one lame-ass title.

He grabbed a new scabbard and parazonium, draped the strap across his chest and positioned the weapon at his back, then slid into his jacket and pushed all thoughts of the king, Isadora and, especially, Callia out of his head. "Let's make tracks, Titus. No sense letting Demetrius have all the fun."

"That's the best plan I've heard all day." Titus grabbed his own gear and nodded toward the door. "I'm ready to kick some daemon ass."

So was Zander. In a way Titus or any of the other Argonauts would never understand.

CHAPTER SIX

Max jerked awake, drenched in a cold sweat and shaking from head to toe.

The air caught in his lungs, stifling, stagnant. He sat up quickly, staring into the dark as his heart raced and his senses slowly righted themselves.

He was in his attic, on *his* pallet. Moonlight streamed through the high, dirty window on the far wall, illuminating the layer of dust on the barren floorboards until the room looked like it was covered in snow.

Not the training field. He glanced down. There was no blood on his hands. He hadn't just killed in a rage like he'd seen in his dream.

A dream. Just another useless dream.

He took a deep breath. And another. Closed his eyes and worked to slow his racing pulse. The dream had come, just as it always did. And as always, he had trouble separating it from reality. In this one he'd seen his mother—again— looking for him. Only, when she saw what he'd become, what he'd done, a horrified expression had crossed her delicate features and she'd turned her back and fled.

Not reality. Just a dream. Just a stupid, stupid dream . . .

Feeling steadier, he opened his eyes and glanced around. As his pulse settled and his eyes adjusted to the dim light, he realized this dream must have been a doozy. The bread that had made up the dinner he hadn't eaten was strewn across the floor, most of it smashed. The plate was broken into at least three pieces and his water was nothing more than a damp circle on the hard, cold wood.

Strange.

With a shrug he shook off the thought and lay back down. He wasn't sure how long he'd been asleep, but it must have been hours, judging by the light. Outside and down below, he could hear Atalanta back at work after the dinner break, training her daemons. Luckily, she'd left him alone to sleep, obviously too disgusted with his humanity to look at him. The clash of weapons, cries of defeat and Atalanta's bellowing rage rang up through the air to pound at his brain.

He tossed his forearm over his eyes and tried to block out the sounds. Shivering, he wished for his blanket, though he knew how useless it was to wish for anything here. He wasn't getting that back tonight, so he'd just have to get used to it and suffer.

To keep from thinking about the cold, he rolled to his side, drew his knees to his chest and pictured his mother's face again. He breathed deep. If he focused hard enough, he was almost sure he could feel the warmth of the glass in his hands earlier.

The glass.

He sat bolt upright, very much awake now, his heart racing once more. Only this time it wasn't a dream that haunted him, it was reality.

He jumped to his feet, dropped back to his knees, searched every inch of his pallet for the glass, only to come up empty. His hands shook, and tears blurred his eyes. Why hadn't he hidden it again before falling asleep? *Stupid, stupid Max!* Where was it?

His hands rushed over the pallet again and again, more frantic with each pass as he searched, but when his fingers finally caught something small and round and metal, he froze.

He lifted the coin into the moonlight so he could see it. Then went cold all over as he stared at the letter *A* stamped into the gold.

Atalanta's coin. Her marker. She'd been in his room. She'd seen him with the glass. And now it was gone. The ruined food, the spilled water, the broken plate . . . it all made sense now.

He was on his feet before he could stop himself, fueled by some building rage he'd never experienced. He backtracked down the ladder, hit the fourth floor and raced down the back stairs toward the kitchen, his temper and anger growing with each step he took.

Mine. Mine. Mine.

He ignored the kitchen workers and their growls of warning as he raced through the room. A blast of frigid air hit his face when he thrust the kitchen door open, but he ignored that too. Out across the training field he caught sight of the group of daemons huddled around Atalanta and one of her minions.

"Weak!" Atalanta bellowed. "If I wanted spineless maggots in my army, I'd replace the daemons with humans. Put your back into it!"

Max's feet moved with their own purpose. His vision blurred and darkened. Before he knew it he was pushing his way through the crowd and stopping in the center of the ring.

Atalanta caught sight of him out of the corner of her eye. The daemon she was fighting—Phobi?—took the opportunity to get the upper hand. But she was quicker than he was and a thousand times more deadly.

Her sword arced out just before Phobi struck, and with a scream that echoed through the frigid night air, his head flew from his body and thumped hard across the frozen ground. His body fell seconds later.

It was a sight Max had witnessed a hundred times before, and every other time a part of him had cried. Death was death, no matter the creature. But this time, he didn't even care. All he saw in his line of sight was Atalanta and his last breaking point.

"Maximus," she said as she wiped the dripping blade against her bloodred skirt. "How nice of you to join us."

"I didn't come to join you," he barked as he threw the coin at her. "I came for what you stole."

The coin landed with a soft thud against the earth at her

feet. She glanced down, but not even a flicker of recognition passed across her face. Her features remained as cold and blank as always.

She looked at him, stuck the tip of her blade into the ground so the weapon stood straight and without so much as flinching extracted the glass from the pocket of her robe.

Max's breath caught when he saw his treasure in her hands. Fear pushed its way up his throat. He knew without even asking what she wanted. For him to beg. To show his weakness in front of the others. And he would. For that glass and his one connection to his mother, he'd do anything.

"Is this what you want?" she asked in a sickeningly sweet tone. "This . . . trinket?"

He didn't answer. Couldn't. Words lodged in his throat.

She turned the glass slowly in her hands, but her eyes never wavered from his. "It's so pretty, Maximus. I wonder . . . Wherever did you get it?"

He knew better than to tell her a lie. The way she was staring at him, it was obvious she already suspected it had come from the gods. But he also knew better than to tell her the truth too.

She gripped the glass in her hand and tossed it to her right. Max gasped, his gaze following the glass as it hurtled through the air. Twisted and gnarled fingers caught it before it smashed to the ground. Zelus chuckled with amusement.

"Gorgeous, isn't it, Zelus?" Atalanta asked, still staring at Max.

"Yes, my queen," he growled.

A slow smile spread across her features. "It's yours, then." Zelus lifted it over his head.

"No!" Max screamed, every muscle in his body coiling tight.

Zelus's arms moved so fast, Max barely tracked them, but his heart lurched in his throat, and when the glass shattered against the frozen ground with nothing more than a soft, tinkling sound, every one of his dreams shattered with it.

She'd never be able to find him. Not now. Not ever.

Max's vision turned red, and he charged without thinking. His hand darted out, and he snagged Atalanta's blade before she could kick it from his grasp. A roar echoed across the training field, but he didn't look to see where it had come from, didn't even realize it had erupted from him. He felt something strike his face, but he ignored it. The blade in his hand swiped out, connecting with Zelus's flesh, dug into bone. The daemon howled, tried to fight back, but Max was too quick. He darted close and away before Zelus could react, and when Zelus was finally on his knees, Max didn't even hesitate.

Behind him he heard Atalanta whisper, "Yes."

His blade pulled back. The need to destroy overrode every one of his senses. Even that of morality.

A slicing sound echoed in the wake of his swipe. Zelus's head rolled across the ground to land next to Phobi's. His body landed with a thud seconds later.

Long, rolling, female laughter erupted behind him. "Yes, Maximus. *Yes!*" Atalanta clapped her hands together and then slapped them against his upper arms, jostling him in exuberance.

Sweaty, breathing hard and staring at his carnage, Max expected to feel remorse. But he didn't. Not a thread. This time what he felt was victory. And instead of the decapitated daemon what he saw was every one of his stupid and useless hopes and dreams ripped apart at his feet.

He let her pull him back to hug him against her body. Didn't fight her touch or tense like he normally did. "I knew you had it in you!"

She let go as quickly as she'd grabbed him and gestured to the others. "Hybris, quick. Go tell the cooks to prepare a feast. Tonight we celebrate my *yios*'s victory!"

Hybris rushed off toward the lodge. The other daemons broke up, heading toward their barracks across the field at the edge of the woods, grumbling words Max couldn't hear and didn't care to know. He still didn't move.

Feel something.

But he didn't. He didn't feel anything. Only a whole lot of . . . nothing.

Atalanta stepped in front of him. Her robe blocked his view of the headless daemon, but he didn't need to see the destruction to remember. He could call it up in his mind anytime he wanted.

She knelt until they were at eye level and stared at him with irises the color of coal. The kind that could spawn diamonds. If only it wanted to.

"You have just taken your first step toward me, *yios*, and I know how hard that is for you. I was once like you. Fighting what I was meant to do and be." Her voice was soft, not condescending as it usually was. And for reasons he couldn't explain, he found himself listening, falling into the lilt of her words. "You and I, Maximus, together we have the power to do anything. Together, we're strong enough to rule the world."

The metal disk she always wore around her neck slipped free of her robe to hang in front of him. He'd seen it before, but tonight it glowed as bright as the moon.

She cupped her hand against his cheek. "You do believe me, don't you, Maximus?"

He stared at the disk with its four empty chambers and tried to remember what he'd heard Thanatos, the archdaemon, tell the others about it. *'Tis the key that opens the doors of the world. Forged by the gods. Stolen by her.*

It didn't look like much of a key to him, but what did he know?

"Maximus?" One red-tipped fingernail tilted his face up toward hers.

"Yes?" he whispered, refocusing on her irises. Circles. Just like the medal at her chest.

"Yes, what?"

"Yes, *matéras*." The word was so ingrained, he didn't even

hesitate to say it anymore. Or maybe he was just finally willing to accept it.

She smiled then—a real smile, one he'd never seen before—and her startling beauty stole his breath. "Tonight, I am proud to call you son. Come, and celebrate with me. And when it is time for bed, you shall sleep on the softest feathers surrounded by nothing but luxury. For with me, you will never want again."

Somewhere in the back of his head a tiny voice screamed, *No!* But the sound was so faint, so muffled, he barely heard it.

She stood and held her hand out to him. "Come, *yios.*"

He glanced at her long fingers in the moonlight. Along the ground behind her, he could just make out the shattered glass beneath her feet. Surrounded by blood and death.

This is your reality. The rest . . . it was never real. Just a dream . . .

He dropped his sword. And as he slid his fingers into hers, he let go of the fantasy he'd held on to for so long. Of his mother, of his father, of the silly notion someone would come and rescue him. They wouldn't. Not now, not ever. Because Atalanta was right. He was just like her. A killer. An outcast. Nothing more than an unwanted hero . . .

His eyes flicked to the markings on his forearms standing out in dark contrast to her pale flesh. He focused on the ancient text as her fingers tightened around his, on the lines and swirls branded into his skin and missing from hers. And staring at their joined hands he saw then what he'd missed so many times before. They might be one and the same, but unlike her, he was blessed by the gods. Even in this place of horror.

His heart started to pound. Slowly at first, and then with more ardor as the realization sank in. And as he lifted his eyes to hers a new dream took the place of the old. Only this one wasn't warm and safe, it was dangerous and electrifying and all-powerful. It churned and swirled and exploded in his head until he was no longer numb. Until that part of him that had been fueled by rage only moments before became all he could see and feel and know.

"Yes, *matéras*," he whispered. He glanced back at the metal disk, for the first time in his young life believing what she said was true. With her, he could have anything he wanted. And through her, *he* could rule the world.

Her smile widened, though she had no idea what he was thinking. But one day soon, she'd know.

One day, she'd regret what she'd just created.

Callia sat in the chair behind her desk in the corner office of the clinic and stared out at the steadily fading image of the Aegis Mountains in the distance. As Argolean seasons coincided with those in the human realm, they were now deep in autumn, and today a low layer of clouds had descended on the valley that housed the city of Tiyrns. Those clouds were moving quickly now, blocking her view of the majestic purple spires and snowcapped peaks that were so often Callia's only source of peace.

There was an old myth that said the gods had long ago hidden something of great value in the Aegis Mountains when they'd bestowed Argolea upon her people. Something no one could keep in their possession for fear of one using it to the detriment of all. Callia had heard the story hundreds of times as a child. Had often looked out at this same view and wondered just what that something was. But today the myth was nothing but a flicker in her mind. Something of great value? She'd already lost everything she'd ever truly valued. And now—even though she hadn't quite believed she'd been holding on to him somewhere in her heart—she'd lost Zander too.

A knock sounded at her open door, just before a familiar voice called, "Callia?"

Her father, Lord Simon, second highest ranking member of the Council of Elders, stuck his head inside her office. "Am I disturbing you?"

She shook her hair back, adjusted in her seat. Any other

day, she wouldn't relish his company, but today wasn't exactly a normal day, and anything that kept her from thinking about Zander was probably a good thing. "No. I was just mulling over a case. What are you doing here? I thought you had Council business today."

"I do." He stepped into the room, wearing perfectly tailored slacks and a traditional Argolean crisp white shirt buttoned up to his throat with a long collar that looped from one side around his neck to drape over the opposite shoulder. He was close to four hundred years old, but he didn't look a day over forty. Tall and trim, she'd always thought he was handsome, with those green eyes and that black hair. She liked to think her mother had thought so too, and that it was part of the reason she'd bound herself to him. Not because she'd been forced to.

Inwardly, she shook her head as she took in his appearance. Conservative for their race, but relatively modern. Most half-breeds, or Misos, thought Argoleans ran around in Greek togas with grape-leaf wreaths in their hair. They had no idea how similar their worlds were.

"I took a break to bring you a surprise," her father said. "Thought you could use one. You've been preoccupied with work lately." The disapproval in his voice when he said the word *work* was more than clear, but she ignored it, as she always did.

When he glanced toward the door, her gaze followed. What was he was up to?

Seconds later another head appeared, only this one she most definitely hadn't wanted to see today of all days.

Loukas smiled, gleaming white teeth flashing against his tanned skin as he straightened and stepped into the office as if he owned it. "Surprise, Callie."

Callia rose slowly out of her chair, stiffened, though she tried not to show her reaction. She'd always hated the way he took the liberty of calling her Callie, as if he didn't approve of her real name and was trying to make her into something of his own. "Loukas. What are you doing here?"

His amber eyes flicked over her attire with disapproval; he didn't like the fact she wore pants. A lock of sandy brown hair fell over his forehead. As far as males went, he was attractive. Average height, fairly good shape, sharp features— but physically or emotionally he'd never done anything for her. And seeing as how she was betrothed to the *ándras*, that wasn't exactly great news.

He was also dressed in the same conservative *chison* as her father, but then, being as he would soon be *Lord* Loukas, the newest elected member of the Council, that wasn't a surprise either. "I came to invite you to dinner. Tonight. Your cleansing period is almost up. I—" Her father cleared his throat, and Loukas glanced his way. "*We* thought it might be a nice treat for you."

Callia couldn't speak. Had it really been ten years already? Mentally, she ticked through time and realized—oh, gods—it had been. Ten years next month. Her stomach tightened. "I . . ." She cast a quick look at her father, then back to Loukas. "I have a few more weeks, I believe."

"We know," her father said, drawing her attention once more. "But it's been long enough." He nodded toward Loukas and smiled with pride. "And Loukas happens to have the ear of the Council Leader. Lucian has agreed to this, so long as your binding ceremony doesn't take place until after the full cleansing cycle is complete."

Her stomach rolled as she slowly shifted her gaze back to Loukas, standing before her desk looking smug and victorious. He'd been rightly pissed at her after everything that had happened all those years ago, hadn't really said more than a handful of words to her since the cleansing ceremony and all during the cycle. And secretly she'd hoped maybe he'd decided another *gynaíka* was better suited for him. But that obviously wasn't the case now. Because here he was, swooping back in to claim his prize. As if she were nothing but a trophy. Exactly as the Council expected Argolean females to be. His by right, not by merit.

"So, dinner tonight, Callie," he said as if it had all been

decided. "Seven o'clock. My house. We have a lot to discuss. Plans to make." He glanced around her office and didn't hide his disgust. "I'm sure you're as eager as I am to get on with the future. Don't keep me waiting."

He didn't even wait for an answer, simply left the room. And what little bit of independence she'd gained these last ten years seemed to drift out with him.

"Lucian is very excited about your upcoming binding," her father said with eagerness as Callia sank into her chair and tried to breathe. "He's planning a big celebration." Simon glanced toward the still-open door and the empty hallway beyond. "Between you and me, I think Lucian's going to announce his retirement from the Council shortly thereafter and appoint Loukas as his replacement. Loukas has a head full of good ideas. I can't even begin to tell you how beneficial this will be for our people."

Callia's stomach rolled. Yeah. Good ideas. She knew all about Loukas's *ideas*. Like pushing females into the Dark Ages, taking away their independence, their jobs, stressing that a *gynaíka*'s only worth was to serve the *ándras* in guardianship over her and to produce offspring to populate their race.

"Callia? What's wrong?"

"Nothing. I . . ."

Tell him no, Isadora. Stand up for yourself. Prove him wrong. Prove them all wrong.

Callia's temple throbbed as her own words from earlier ran back through her mind. Gods, she'd given Isadora advice about the king? What a joke. Callia couldn't even stand up to her own father.

She closed her eyes, braced both elbows on her desk and rubbed her forehead. She didn't want to bind herself to Loukas. Didn't want to bind herself to anyone, for that matter. The only one she'd ever wanted didn't want her back. And the thought of being intimate with Loukas . . . Oh, gods, she couldn't do it.

She dropped her hands, looked up at her father and

opened her mouth to tell him just that. Then stopped short.

He was staring at her with those green eyes that had seen so much and expected even more. Her mother's death had wounded him badly, and he'd never remarried. Callia's affair with Zander—and everything that had come after—had nearly broken him. He'd put his reputation with the Council on the line for her. He'd tended her broken body when no one else would. He'd made sure she didn't die on that Greek mountain. And when it was over, when she had nothing else to live for, he'd arranged a way for her to come home to Argolea. So she could be protected from the dae-mons in the human world, so she could work at the clinic she'd always loved, so she could have some sort of purpose and life, even if most days she didn't understand what that purpose was anymore.

He could have turned his back on her like everyone else—Loukas included—but he hadn't. He'd stayed with her. And ultimately, that was why she'd stayed with him all these long years as well.

A true leader sets aside his personal wants for the good of the whole. And he makes sacrifices. Ones that, in the end, justify all that came before.

The king's words hit her hard, making sense in a way she'd never expected.

"Callia?" her father asked again. "What's happened? You looked distraught when I walked in here. Did you come from the castle?"

She nodded, unable to lie to him, at least about this. "Yes. The king called a meeting while I was there. He . . ."

"What?"

She faltered, unsure she should tell him, then figured, what did it matter? He'd find out on his own soon enough. "He announced the princess's engagement."

His mouth closed, and darkness crept over his eyes as realization dawned. "Another Argonaut." Disgust filled his voice. "Which one this time? Demetrius?"

She shook her head, glanced down at her hands. "No. Isadora is marrying . . . Zander."

His silence finally pulled her gaze up. Surprise lit his features as dusk settled over the room.

"I see," he said finally.

A lump formed in her throat. One she couldn't get rid of no matter what she tried. "I thought the news would please you."

He took her hands and pulled her from her chair. Warmth flowed into her arms and the familiar scent of sandalwood assailed her senses. "Nothing that causes you pain pleases me, Callia. Contrary to what you might think, my biggest objection to your relationship with Zander was not simply that he was an Argonaut, but that he used you."

She blinked as he reached out and tucked a strand of hair behind her ear, shocked he was finally discussing Zander with her after all these years, even more shocked he was touching her. She couldn't remember the last time he'd touched her. Not since . . . not since Greece.

"You may not want to hear it, but the Argonauts will do anything to undermine the workings of the Council. And you, my daughter, were a way to do just that."

"That's not true. Zander would never—"

"He would. And he did. I don't for a minute doubt that was the motivation behind his seducing you. It worked too, didn't it? Your . . . situation . . . drew attention away from the important social issues the Council had been working on at the time. They had to deal with you and the Argonauts, me and the fallout. Even the king's sudden interest in Council workings. It's taken years for them to regain the headway they lost because of your scandal."

The king had known? The blood drained from Callia's cheeks. He'd never said a word to her about it. All these years, she thought her history with Zander had been private.

"But besides all that," her father went on, his voice softening just a touch. "Even if Zander's intentions had been honorable, which they were not, he could never appreciate you for what you are, because he does not come from the same background you do. It's in his genetics not to care about females or family. His own parents didn't want him, for gods' sakes. All he knows is fighting. And doing what he damn well pleases. You can't fight bloodlines, Callia. His are too strong. His link to the gods too close. He never needed you. Not really. And I never wanted you to fall victim to the rage that's from his line. I suppose for Isadora, he's a good match, but not for you. I want more for you."

Tears burned Callia's eyes. Tears she definitely didn't need today on top of everything else. Why did he have to sound so damn rational when what he wanted was so wrong?

"Loukas," he went on, "now, he understands where you come from. He understands our history and he's dedicated to rebuilding Argolea into what it once was. He will cherish you in the way you should be cherished. This binding with Loukas, it's a good thing for you. It's a good thing for us. You know that, don't you?"

As her father waited and his words sank in, the scars on her back tingled. The ones she didn't think of most days because their pain had faded so far in her memory. But now they stood out in stark contrast to the rest of her skin. And she remembered why she had them. How she'd gotten them. And what they represented.

Sacrifices. That's what life came down to. Not happiness. Not completion. Not love. Life kept going because there were those in the world willing to sacrifice their wants and needs for the good of the rest.

I am not a leader, your majesty.

Not yet. But maybe one day . . .

Her heart thumped hard in her chest as she thought about the road behind her and the one ahead. No, she didn't want to bind herself to Loukas, but maybe the king was right. By doing so, perhaps she could figure out a way to help the females of their world. Or at the very least, find a way to keep Loukas from oppressing them the way she feared he would, with no one else to challenge him.

She looked up at her father. And knew she was doing the right thing, even if it hurt her heart. "I realize it's . . . what must be done."

A smile spread across Simon's face, a victorious grin so like Loukas's, it chilled her blood. He gripped both of her arms at the shoulders, squeezed gently. "Perfect. You'll see, Callia. This is the start of a whole new life for you. With your cleansing period over, there's no reason to even think about the past again."

The singsong tones of his words seemed to hang in the air, even as he said good-bye and left the room. And alone, Callia turned to look out the window again toward the Aegis Mountains, which were now completely hidden by clouds.

Something of great value. The myth drifted into her mind again. That past her father was so ready for her to forget was the only thing left that she valued. That and the memory of a love she'd once known and the child she hadn't. She could sacrifice a lot of things, herself included, but never the memory of either of those. And not her father, not Loukas, not even the reality that Zander was marrying another could ever convince her to do so.

"Holy fucking Hera." The air seemed to leave Titus's lungs on a gasp as he and Zander stood in the center of what used to be a small town high in the Cascade mountain range and stared at the destruction.

One dirt road led into the isolated settlement. No cars or vehicles could be heard through the trees. Around them everywhere, dead bodies littered the ground. But they weren't just Misos. There were humans, half-eaten and mutilated, scattered throughout the carnage as well.

"Fuck me," Zander said as he took it all in. The rotting carcasses, the blood-stained ground. The stench of death.

This was much worse than any scene he'd come across in over eight hundred years.

Atalanta's wrath was growing—and innocent lives were paying for it. When she'd still been confined to the Underworld, her daemons had hunted Misos to send their souls to Tartarus as payment to Hades for Atalanta's immortality. But thanks to Casey and Isadora, Atalanta was no longer immortal. Now she was determined to create as much suffering as possible in her need for vengeance against the Argonauts. All because she'd been banned from the group millennia ago.

Zander thought the body near his feet had at one time been a human woman, but it was now nothing more than mangled flesh and organs. His stomach rolled. The daemons also killed to feed. Theron had warned that the daemons would become more aggressive and start hunting humans as well as Misos in their need to regain the strength they were no longer getting from the Underworld.

Now, as he looked out at the gruesome sight around him, Zander believed it. He also knew the war had shifted for good. For hundreds of years he'd roamed this earth *thinking* he was protecting humans. Now he was doing it for real.

Across the bloodied field, he spotted Theron talking with a man as big as he was, waving his hands and pointing off toward the tree line. Nick, Zander realized as he and Titus drew closer, the leader of the half-breed colony in this part of the world. Zander had met Nick before, a week ago, when he'd been sent to the Pacific Northwest with Titus to run patrol in these mountains. So far his interactions with the half-breed had been limited, but there was a whole lot about Nick that just didn't add up.

His size, for one thing. He was bigger than all the other half-breeds, and definitely far more aggressive. He was never seen without fingerless gloves and he also had a long scar that ran down his left cheek and disappeared into the crease of his mouth. The jagged ridge wasn't the result of a claw or even a blade like the daemons used. It had come from something else. Some kind of weapon Zander had never experienced before.

But that wasn't the strangest thing about Nick. There was something about him that screamed human and Argonaut all at the same time, something not even Theron seemed to know how to explain. And since that combination was completely impossible, it made the situation that much weirder.

Theron motioned over Zander and Titus. Nick didn't bother to glance up or acknowledge them, just smoothed a map out on what looked to be a door strung between two sawhorses. The muffled cries of Misos checking for survivors floated on the air. "There's a path that runs through the mountains here. On the other side it opens to a canyon. A river cuts the terrain, but this time of year, with the rain we've had recently, they wouldn't be able to cross."

Theron skimmed his finger along the map until he came to a point farther downstream. "What's on the other side of this river?"

"Another mountain range. Though the ones on that side have extensive cave systems that run for miles."

"Someplace they think they can hide," Theron mumbled as he stared at the map. "This bridge. Is it usable?"

"Yeah," Nick said, rubbing a gloved hand over the top of his close-shaved head. "Last time I was up there, at least. It's a pretty far trek, though. We're talking women and children. And that bridge wasn't in the best of shape the last time I used it." Unlike Theron, Nick didn't seem to have on any protective gear aside from grimy jeans, a long-sleeved black Henley and work boots. He didn't seem to notice the cold as he looked up and around what was left of the town; he was too juiced on endorphins to care. Strapped to his hips were two semiautomatic pistols and several blades of various sizes.

At least the half-breed came prepared.

"I've got men scouring the hillsides along with your guardians to see if they're close by, in hiding," Nick said. "Odds are good we'll find—"

"They're not here," Theron cut in, his eyes never leaving the map. He pointed toward the canyon and the rickety bridge. "They're heading here. Thinking it's their best means of escape. And the motherfuckers are herding them."

"Demetrius!" Theron motioned the other Argonaut from the far side of the devastation, where he'd been examining something on the ground. As Demetrius came over, Nick casually pushed away from the map, said something quietly to Theron and turned to leave, heading in the opposite direction toward a group of angry Misos searching a pile of rubble. He didn't utter a single word of thanks to Zander or Titus for coming to his aid, didn't even acknowledge that they were there. And he didn't once look at Demetrius.

It was pretty obvious Nick had only asked the Argonauts for help as a last resort, and that several in this community were resistant to their presence. But still . . .

Zander refocused as Demetrius joined them.

"I want the three of you to head toward this canyon," Theron said. "The daemons have got a four- or five-hour head start on us, so you'll need to make tracks. The group that's missing is made up of six females and fourteen young, ranging in age from two months to ten years."

"Christ," Titus said. "They're about to get slaughtered."

Not if Zander had anything to say about it. Didn't matter if some in this village didn't want their help. His blood pulsed as he listened to Theron rattle off the coordinates for what could be his last mission for quite some time.

"Take extra precautions," Theron advised. "We need those survivors brought back alive so we can figure out how and why they hit this village and what Atalanta's planning next." He handed them each a satellite phone. "These are programmed for the colony. When you locate the survivors, use this and someone will come pick them up."

As they each pocketed the phones, Theron glanced from

Demetrius to Titus, then finally nodded Zander's way. "And don't let him get dead. Especially now."

"I don't need a bodyguard," Zander grumbled.

"Too bad," Theron tossed back. "You've got two."

Titus clicked his teeth as Theron rolled up the map. "I got this homeboy's back, pa. Don't you worry none. We'll kick some daemon ass and get him to the chapel on time. Guaranteed."

Zander glared over his shoulder. "Oh, you're a real comedian."

"Just remember what you need to do," Theron said, the seriousness of his tone reminding each of them this was no joking matter. "Do you have your transmitters?"

When they each nodded, Theron said, "Good. Now go with the power of the blessed heroes as your guide."

They turned and headed for the trees, but Theron's voice stopped them on the edge of the village. "Guardians," he called. His tone was crisp and clear, and Zander had no doubt he used it now for a purpose. Sound ceased behind Theron in the ruined village. Several heads turned in their direction—Misos, Argolean and human alike, all working for one common cause now, regardless of how they felt about one another. Even Nick stopped what he was doing and looked up. "The Argonauts are these people's last hope. The entire world's last hope at this point, whether they want to believe it or not. You are needed now more than you or anyone else could ever know. Don't *any* of you get dead."

Theron headed back into the melee, and that, Zander realized as he watched his friend walk away, was the standard against which all leaders should be measured. Theron not only knew how to take a stand, but where and how to draw the line so others knew as well. He might not always want to lead, but he didn't back down. Not from anything. Not even his destiny.

"Come on, Z," Titus said. His eyes flared with the thrill of the battle that lay ahead. "Let's hunt some daemon."

Beside Titus, Demetrius grunted his approval.

As Zander followed his guardian brothers deep into the woods, he knew he wouldn't back down from his destiny either. It was laid out before him now like a gleaming path. The only thing left to do was bloody the ground at the threshold with the bodies of a few daemons he was more than willing to send back to Tartarus for good.

CHAPTER SEVEN

"My patience grows thin with your lack of progress, Thanatos." Atalanta drummed her fingers on the thick wooden table. "The North American Misos colony should be extinct by now."

Thanatos fought from growling in response. They were seated in the dining room of the Canadian lodge that was now their headquarters, at opposite ends of the fifteen-foot table. Between them, spires of candles perched within twisting arms of metal illuminated the room and cast flickering light over Atalanta's pale, disgusted features. Outside the dark windows, clouds moved over the waxing moon, and in the distance a lone wolf howled.

To his right, *the boy* cleared his throat and reached for his goblet.

Thanatos glanced sideways, hatred brewing in his veins. Oh, yeah, the kid may be enjoying his little reprieve from that dungeon he called a room, but he'd be there again soon enough. Thanatos would make sure of it.

"Do you have nothing to say to me?" Atalanta asked, her icy voice cutting through the fantasy taking root in his mind.

The daemon imagined all that creamy flesh melting from her bones. She was mortal now, which meant she could be killed. But she still had godlike powers, and there was nothing she didn't see or control.

His eyes slid down the long, slim column of her throat and hovered on the heavy chain around her neck. The gold links disappeared into the vee of her bloodred robe, but Thanatos knew what rested between her flawless breasts.

He'd seen the pendant once when it had slipped from her cleavage.

"Maximus," Atalanta said firmly. "Leave us now, *yios*. The servants have prepared a room for you in the west wing."

"Yes, *matéras*." The boy pushed back from the table, wiped his mouth and walked toward Atalanta. Slowly, he leaned down and kissed her cheek.

Thanatos's hatred burned hot and vile all over again. He could move quickly. Before either realized it, he'd be at the other end of the table and their fragile bodies would be in those flames. Burning, their bones splintering until they were nothing but ash . . .

"Thanatos!"

His gaze jerked back up. Atalanta was on her feet and moving quickly around the table, straight for him. The boy was nowhere to be seen.

Thanatos stiffened and pushed to his feet.

She stood almost as tall as he did, at nearly seven feet, and she loathed weakness in her soldiers, which was why he'd learned never to show even a hint of fear in her midst. "I will not tolerate insubordination!"

He spread his feet in a defensive move in case she attacked and tried to keep the contempt from his voice when he said, "The North American Misos are getting aid from the Argonauts. One of our hunting parties decimated a key settlement just yesterday, and any stragglers are being rounded up and disposed of as we speak."

She stopped a foot from him. "How many half-breeds were killed?"

"At least sixty."

"Sixty is nothing. There are three times that many hiding in the mountains there."

"We'll find them."

She walked to the fireplace and stared into the writhing flames. "You said the Argonauts came to their aid?"

"Yes."

"Then they're searching for those stragglers as well. Such a bunch of do-gooders, those repulsive Argonauts. No," she said, her voice growing oddly calm. "This is your chance to take several of them out."

"Me?"

She glared at him over one bare shoulder. "Yes, you, Thanatos. Are you not my archdaemon? Are you suddenly too good to fight?" Her voice hardened in a way that sent a warning flash to his brain. "Find the stragglers and you'll find the Argonauts. Use the half-breeds as bait if you have to, but kill the Argonauts. And then destroy what is left of their miserable colony."

A strange sense of foreboding settled in Thanatos's chest. She was eyeing him as if he were nothing. Like any ordinary daemon. Like he was . . . expendable.

Him? Expendable? Daemons were a dime a dozen. He should know. He killed the weak ones himself before they could get him killed in battle. But he was the archdaemon now, not simply a grunt. As they stared at each other, his mind skipped to the training field today, and the way she'd been whispering with Phrice on the sidelines, like the shit-for-brains daemon had anything worthwhile to say. Then to the scene with Maximus, and the ease with which the puny boy had bested Zelus with only his blade.

Had she been interviewing Phrice to be his successor? Were they scheming against him? As disturbing as that thought was, though, it wasn't the one that concerned Thanatos the most. The question suddenly pinging around in his mind was one of much greater importance. Namely, were they all ultimately dispensable once Maximus relinquished his humanity and finally took his place at her side?

He eyed the chain around her neck again with a growing sense of doom and thought of the pendant. Of the circle. About his future. Or what little he instinctively knew was left of it.

Atalanta turned to face him. Behind her, flames licked up the massive stone fireplace, backdropping her in a sea of orange and red and blistering blue he wished would devour her whole.

"I've reached the end of my patience with you, Thanatos. Kill or be killed. That is our motto."

Kill or be killed.

She would kill him first chance she got, he realized as he stared at her. He could read it in her black-as-night, soulless eyes. To her, he was already dead.

He bowed his head slightly even though the monster in him despised the weakness it portrayed. But he was already planning. Planning how to mete out his justice and win.

"As you command, my goddess."

Zander rubbed a hand over his wet hair as he peered into the forest with its towering spires of Douglas fir and Western hemlock.

Demetrius, crouched on the forest floor where he'd been studying prints left in the soft earth, looked up and pointed. "They've turned north."

A light rain fell, steaming off their heated bodies, their breaths like smoke in the damp air. The three of them—Zander, Demetrius and Titus—had been running for the last four hours, trying to catch up with the daemon party stalking the band of Misos who had escaped the destruction of their village. So far they'd come across nothing but tracks. But they were fresh, and Demetrius, known for his tracking skills, was sure they were closing in.

"They've gone off the fucking path," Titus said.

Demetrius pushed up on his knees, the long duster he always wore flapping in the slight breeze. "All that will do is slow them down." He gestured to the thick underbrush, a dense mass of Oregon grape, salmonberry and saplings all struggling for light. "They'd need a hatchet to cut through that shit. And every broken limb and downed seedling just screams, 'Here we are, come and get us.'"

Other than the water dripping from leaf to leaf in the

thick canopy above, the forest was silent. Eerily so. As if it too knew the evil sweeping through it.

Zander looked through the trees toward the mountains beyond. "They're heading that way for the caves, right? Maybe they've already reached them."

Demetrius scowled. "At the speed they're traveling, and with young, they'll never make it. The daemons are almost on top of them. They'll catch them by the bridge for sure."

Zander's stomach pitched at Demetrius's blunt revelation. This was war. He knew that. There were always casualties. But children . . .

Titus studied his handheld GPS. "If we swing around to the east and head back at the fork in the next trail, we might be able to cut off the daemons before either party reaches the bridge." His gaze lifted, locking first on Zander, then on Demetrius. "I know, probably for shit, but unless either of you has a better idea, it's our best option."

Zander checked the extra knife he kept strapped to his thigh, and then they set out again, picking up their pace and streaking through the forest. Demetrius led the way, with Zander in the middle and Titus at the rear. It was nearly an hour later when they made the turn at the trail fork and headed back north. In the distance, the sound of rushing water filled the silent void of the forest, which meant they were getting close to the ravine and the lone bridge that crossed it. They pushed on, picking up their speed.

Don't let us be too late . . .

A shrill scream sounded through the trees. Demetrius, the fastest of the three, tore off the path and sprinted into the woods. Zander and Titus followed. As they drew near, roars drowned out the crash of waves against rock. Followed by the horror-filled shrieks of females and young alike.

Demetrius was already engaged by the time Zander and Titus reached the edge of the trees. His weapon clashed against flesh and bone. Snarls and snaps and more screams rose in the late afternoon air as he sliced out with his blade and decapitated one daemon, then moved on to the next.

The forest opened up to a wide bank of sedimentary rock that seemed to tumble off into nowhere. Far below the ledge, a river swirled and twisted. On the opposite side of the ravine, the mountains rose in all their splendid glory, a promised hiding place for the Misos, linked only by a rickety wooden footbridge missing planks and supported by decaying rope.

Zander counted at least eight daemons advancing on the group, not including the two Demetrius had already taken out. Six Misos females shielded at least a dozen young in a semicircle, their backs to the ravine. Their only weapons were rocks and twigs, except for one gun—though even that was useless against monsters like these. And the female holding the gun was shaking so much she was more likely to hit one of her friends than the daemons themselves.

And then there was the fact no one was protecting all those young from the ravine mere steps away at their backs.

"Get back from the edge!" Zander yelled.

"Zander!"

Zander whipped around at the sound of Titus's urgent voice and realized he was the only one not kicking ass. Adrenaline surging, he yanked his parazonium from the scabbard at his back and ran toward the seething daemon closest to the group.

He sliced, kicked out, swiveled to avoid claws and teeth. Around him snarls and screams filled the air, mixed with the clap of blades striking flesh and bone. But the daemons were relentless. When they fell they got up; when they took a blade they kept going. The only thing that stopped them was decapitation, but it had to be done at just the right angle. And cutting the head off a seven-foot monster with the strength of Heracles wasn't exactly easy.

The daemon he was fighting swiped at him with razor-sharp claws. Zander twisted out of the way. The daemon swung again, this time catching the edge of his jacket. A ripping sound echoed, and fire crept across Zander's back. Zander reached for the knife strapped to his thigh and threw it end over end. It plunged deep into the daemon's chest. The beast howled. With his blade in the other hand, Zander swung out and around, slicing into the daemon's side.

The beast stumbled but didn't go down. With a roar, he backhanded Zander across the face, sending him to the ground. Zander hit the rocks hard. The wind left him on a gasp. Sweat and blood dripped down into his eyes.

Screams echoed behind him. He turned his head just enough to see another daemon advancing on the group. A child, no more than eight or nine, stood shaking, clutching the leg of one of the females, blue eyes wide with fear.

Zander scrambled to his feet. "Titus!" he hollered over the fight. "Get them across that bridge!"

Titus, ten feet away, swung his parazonium from the daemon he'd just decapitated and paused to look toward the group. His eyes grew wide, as if seeing the young for the first time.

"Go! Now!" Zander yelled as he charged the bloody daemon seething in front of him. This one was too close to the children. He couldn't risk getting them across himself.

The monster's claws caught Zander's arm, but he barely noticed. He thrust his parazonium out and around. The blade met soft flesh and sank in deep. When the daemon roared and fell to his knees, Zander popped the unholy with his elbow to knock him back. In the split second the monster swayed, dazed, Zander swung and sliced, sending the beast's head rolling across the hard ground.

"Everyone across the bridge!" Titus yelled, his boots eating up the distance between the fight and the group's only path to safety. "Right now. Hustle already!"

Zander swiped at his eyes with his forearm and took one quick look toward the group to make sure they were safe.

The females' eyes were all wide with fear, but they urged the young toward the bridge. All but the one with the gun. She stood still as stone, the whites of her eyes visible all around her irises, the weapon in her hand shaking as if she were in the middle of a magnitude-ten earthquake.

Skata. Zander didn't have time to worry about her. Three more daemons had emerged from the woods and saw their victims' impending escape. Instead of attacking Demetrius, engaged in battle with another daemon and closest to them, they changed direction and charged.

"Demetrius!" Zander yelled. The Argonauts were outnumbered, outmatched, and there was no way they could protect the Misos unless Titus got them onto the other side of the ravine and cut the bridge's ropes. Which then left two against one, two, three . . . *seven.*

Holy fucking Hera.

"Titus! Get them across *now!*" Zander wrapped both hands around his weapon, drew in a deep breath and put himself between the advancing daemons and the bridge. If he made it out of this—*when* he made it out of this—he was never taking life for granted again. He'd seen the future in those eyes a moment ago. A future that wouldn't exist for any of them unless he and his warrior kin did their job right here and now.

"Go back to hell, you motherfuckers!" He lifted his blade high over his head and coiled to pounce.

A scream echoed behind him, followed by an odd popping sound. Before he could strike, fire rushed through his shoulder and lower back. He had a moment of *What the . . . ?* then the parazonium flew from his hands and clattered on the cold rocks, out of his reach. His hands jerked out to catch it, but they seemed to be moving in slow motion. Then he was falling, falling . . . going down face-first even as the daemons were closing in.

"Zander!"

"Zander! *No!*"

He wasn't sure why everyone was suddenly screaming his name, but he didn't really care. As the ground rushed up toward him at light speed, he had only one last thought.

Just when he'd finally decided he had something to live for, it looked as though the gods had granted his death wish.

CHAPTER EIGHT

Callia paused at the top of the staircase outside the king's chamber and rubbed her throbbing temple. It wasn't the king and his failing health that had given her this massive headache. It was what she knew she had to do next.

A true leader sets aside his personal wants for the good of the whole. And he makes sacrifices. Ones that, in the end, justify all that came before.

Maybe if she repeated the king's words enough, she'd start to believe them.

Shaking off the woe-is-me attitude that wasn't going to do her any good now, she headed down the stairs, her bag in hand. She checked her watch as she rounded the newel post on the third floor and hit the next flight of stairs. She had roughly thirty minutes before she was due at Loukas's house. She needed to run home, shower and change. While she wasn't about to get gussied up for the *ándras*, she wasn't in the mood to antagonize him either. At least not until they were . . . bound.

Just the thought sent her stomach swirling, but she ignored that too. She'd spent a long time thinking about her life after her father had left her earlier in the day, and she knew only one thing for certain. If she was serious about instigating change in this country of theirs, then it had to start with her. And she wouldn't be able to do that until she was Loukas's . . . wife.

She was so wrapped up in her thoughts, she almost didn't see Isadora until it was too late. The princess rounded the newel post on the second floor, heading up. Callia stopped mere inches from running the *gynaíka* over. Then did a double take.

"Isadora. My gods. What happened to you?"

Isadora reached up warily and rubbed a hand down the back of her pixie-short hair. Her once-long blonde locks now flared out all over her head in a messy but flattering way. The cut made her eyes look bigger, her face more prominent. It drew attention to her high cheekbones and a mole on the left side of her mouth Callia had never really noticed before.

But the hair wasn't the only change. The princess was not wearing her traditional attire. Instead of a long gown, tonight she was decked out in sleek black pants, a fitted red sweater and sandals that showed off red—bloodred—painted toenails.

Her father was going to shit bricks when he saw her.

"Nothing happened to me," Isadora said, stiffening her spine. "I'm fine."

Realizing how admonishing she must sound, Callia gave her head a shake. "I—I didn't mean it like that. I think you look wonderful, it's just—"

"Callia!"

Callia and Isadora both peered over the edge of the banister to the lower level below, where Titus was shouting and running across the marble floor at a dead sprint.

He took the stairs four at a time until he was in front of both of them. His rugged face and Argonaut clothing were smeared with blood and dirt and something . . . green. Locks of long wispy brown curls had pulled free from the leather strap at his nape to brush across his cheeks, and he was breathing like he'd just run a marathon. "I need you to come with me. Right now."

"What happened?" He'd obviously been fighting. Where and with whom, though, she didn't know.

"There's been an accident."

"Who?" Callia and Isadora asked together.

Titus seemed to suddenly realize they weren't alone. His

gaze swung to Isadora, but if he noticed a change in her appearance, he didn't show it. "Zander. It's bad."

For a soul-searing second, time stopped for Callia. Her chest squeezed tight until it was hard to get air. She'd just seen him. She'd *just* had her hands on him. He'd been alive and well and *whole* earlier today, just like every day. He was invincible. Immortal. Nothing could hurt him.

"Is he going to be okay?" Isadora said next to her. "Who's with him now? Titus, how bad is bad?"

But Titus's attention wasn't focused on the princess. When Callia finally pulled it together and looked up, she realized he was staring at her with an all-knowing and pitying expression.

"*Skata,*" he whispered. "I didn't know you were the one."

Callia drew in a breath. Froze. Then whispered, "What are you talking about?" though she had a good feeling she already knew. Too late she remembered that Titus could read minds.

He shook his head slowly. "I knew it was a female who'd hurt him. I just didn't put two and two together. He was careful never to think about you in my presence."

Silence settled like a heavy weight in the air around them. At her side, Callia could feel Isadora's eyes boring into her with a million questions. Her heart pounded in her chest, so loud she was sure the other two could hear it.

Hurt him? Hurt *him*? He'd been the one to walk away from her and their . . . She swallowed hard, unable to even think the word. Her heart beat faster as she tried to keep herself calm.

"I don't understand what's going on here," Isadora said.

Titus ignored her. "You have to come with me, Callia. Now."

"I—I can't go anywhere." Callia did *not* want to relive the pain of those memories. "I'm supposed to be at Loukas's in . . ." She glanced at her watch, seeking something familiar. Normal. Predictable. ". . . ten minutes."

"Fuck Loukas!" Titus took a step closer, and Callia's eyes

grew wide. "Zander is going to die. I can't save him. If you won't do it for him, then do it for the king."

"I . . ." Her head was in a fog. She was having trouble focusing. "He can't die. He's immortal."

"No, he's not," Titus said quickly. "He just thinks he is. Please." He reached toward her, but stopped short of touching her, instead curling his fingers into a fist before they made contact. "Please." The pleading in his voice cut through her shock-infested haze. "He needs you."

He never needed you. Not really.

Her father's words from earlier in the day echoed through her mind. And for reasons she couldn't explain, she had a burning urge to prove him wrong. Even if in such a miniscule way.

She stared into sea green eyes flecked with shades of golds and browns. Eyes that saw way more than she ever wanted them to see. "Where?" she whispered.

"The human realm."

Slowly, Callia nodded even as a frisson of fear whipped through her. "I'll need supplies."

"We'll run by your clinic before we go back."

"I'm coming too," Isadora said quickly.

"No," Titus stated firmly, his eyes swinging toward the princess. "It's too dangerous for you. Callia and I will handle it." He focused on Callia once more, effectively eliminating Isadora from the conversation. "Thank you. I promise this will be over quickly."

Callia's stomach knotted. For her, where Zander was concerned, it would never be over.

Zander tried to open his eyes, but there was something sticky keeping them glued together. Something cold and goopy and . . . wet?

He was lying on his side—that much he knew for sure—but when he tried to roll to his back he couldn't make his body obey.

Where the hell was he?

He tried again with the eye thing and managed to break the seal. Through hazy, murky vision he saw the tips of his eyelashes, covered in—yep—some kind of sludge. The ground beneath him was cold and hard, but he wasn't out in the elements. He was inside something—a building, a barn, a cave?

A cave. Yeah. That had to be it. His head was in a fog, but he knew he'd been fighting. That explained the goopy shit in his eyes. Daemon slime was hard to get rid of. He'd obviously been injured, but he couldn't get his brain to click into gear on how or where or when that had happened. Why wasn't his brain working?

He closed his eyes tight, tried to clear the haze. Faintly— and with great effort that sent pain thrumming through his skull—he remembered the fight with the daemons. The cliff. Demetrius and Titus. The frightened females and all those screaming young. And he remembered falling . . .

"I can't. Oh, gods, Titus, did you see? I'm not strong enough for this."

Whoa. Wait. He knew that voice.

Callia. Here in this cold place. Where she never in a million years should be.

His eyes popped open again as far as the goop would allow and he let go of his surroundings to focus on the voice.

"You have to." Titus's voice now. Firm and harsh and as focused as Zander had ever heard the guardian. "I can't do it. You're the only one who can."

Can what?

"What if I'm not strong enough?" she whispered. "Titus, what if . . ."

What were they talking about? Again Zander tried to roll to his back, but still he couldn't move. Growing more frustrated by the minute, he settled for shifting his head on the rocks, then regretted it when pain stabbed at his skull.

He was sure he screamed like a little girl, but Titus and Callia didn't stop their bickering and no one seemed to care that he was in agonizing pain.

"It can't get any worse than this, Callia. You have to do it."

Zander moved his head again, enough so he could finally see the two of them where they stood a good distance away. Though his vision was murky, he saw he'd been right. He was in some kind of cavern. A lantern in the center of the room cast shadows over their bodies and illuminated the rock walls and stalactites hanging from the ceiling.

Callia lifted her hands to her cheeks. "One bullet is imbedded in his spinal cord. Titus, do you know what that means? If I try to dislodge it, I could make it worse. He won't just be paralyzed from the waist down, he'll be paralyzed everywhere. It could cut off his breathing. The consequences could be much worse—"

Paralyzed? Whoa. Wait a minute . . . Zander tried to move his legs again, only nothing happened.

"You don't have any other options!" Titus barked.

Okay, this didn't sound so good.

Callia glanced around the barren room. "I could go back. We could get someone else. Someone stronger. I've heard of witches in the Aegis Mountains who—"

"There's no time for that."

"Then we'll make time! Zander is—"

"Not gonna last that long!" Before Callia could protest once more, Titus slapped his hands on her shoulders to hold her still. His eyes widened, his body stiffened and something like agony flashed across his rugged face just before he swayed.

"Titus! Oh, gods, not you too." Callia clutched his forearms. "Are you okay? Titus, talk to me. What's happening?"

Titus staggered but caught himself. His head seemed to loll on his shoulders. Somehow, Callia kept the massive Argonaut from going down. Seconds ticked by before he lifted his head and peered down at her.

Zander squinted, tried to move again to get a better view at what was happening, but he was pinned, frozen . . . paralyzed?

Shit, that couldn't be right. He was an Argonaut. Argonauts couldn't *be* paralyzed. And he was immortal.

Callia gasped, drawing Zander's focus back to her.

Titus's grip tightened on Callia's shoulder and as Zander watched, some sort of connection flared between the two. They stood locked in each other's gaze, neither moving, neither speaking, neither trying to break free.

And an emotion Zander hadn't felt in far longer than he could remember flared hot in the center of his chest, pushing out all that panic and replacing it with something much, much darker.

Get your hands off her, you motherfucker. She's mine.

Long moments passed. Electricity crackled in the air. Finally, Titus sagged. His eyes rolled back in his head and his grip loosed on Callia's arms. He slumped to the floor on his knees at her feet.

"Titus?" She reached for him. "Please don't fall apart on me."

He shook his head slowly back and forth. "I'm . . . I'm okay. I'm not . . . hurt." But he didn't sound okay. He sounded totally rattled.

And no one was supposed to be rattled around Callia but Zander.

That rage wedged itself tighter in Zander's chest. Rage and an instinctive need to annihilate that seemed to come from somewhere outside himself. *Right now you're okay, you SOB, but just wait until I can move my legs again.*

"What happened?" Callia asked.

When she tried to touch him, Titus blocked her with his forearm. And the way Callia flinched like he'd hurt her sent Zander's already amped-up adrenaline shooting into the out-of-this-world range. He tried to move again. Failed.

Zander ground his teeth together and glared at Titus. *Try that over here, dickhead.*

Neither paid him any attention. Why couldn't they fucking hear him?

"You have to tell him," Titus muttered.

"How . . . how can you know?" she whispered.

"Because I experienced it. Through you. And I guarantee he doesn't know half what you went through."

Callia's face paled.

They were whispering now, and it was hard for Zander to hear, but he almost thought he heard Titus say, "And once he does know, if he's still an asshole, then I'll kick his butt into the next realm myself."

Zander's temper flashed. *I'd like to see you try it, dipshit.*

Titus reached out, hesitated, then laid his hand on Callia's cheek and whispered something Zander couldn't hear but which brought tears to Callia's soft violet eyes. Then he added louder, "It's gone on too long, Callia. You have to put him out of his misery. But know this. If you can't do it, I will."

And that was as much as Zander could take.

He shifted, rolled, screamed every vile word he knew at Titus. And that was saying a lot, considering who he hung out with. But he didn't hear the words. All he heard was a loud keening sound echoing through the room around him. And not until both of their heads jerked his way did he realize the sound had come from him.

"He's coming around," Titus said.

They were both at his side in an instant. And lucky for him, that was just about the time Zander figured out how to make his arm work. He swung out, hoping to nail Titus in the jaw, but even he knew the motion was stilted and weak. This was supposed to be his kinsman, but right now Titus looked more like the enemy than any daemon Zander had ever encountered.

"Shh, don't try to move too much, Zander." Callia's soft fingers closed over his arm and she easily replaced it against his side. "Titus, get me my bag. I'm going to need that syringe."

"About damn time," Titus muttered. His footsteps sounded across the floor.

Zander hoped the piece of shit wasn't coming back. One good hit, that's all he needed . . .

He tried to breathe, in and out, and closed his eyes, focusing on Callia's hands and the way she was freeing him from his clothing.

Oh, man, this was not right, but it felt good. Sinful. Erotic. Like it had in the king's study when she'd had her hands over his naked flesh for that little exam. He didn't even care what was wrong with him anymore. He just wanted her to go on stroking him like she was doing now.

He wasn't paralyzed, dammit. He could *feel* her.

She ran her hands up his bare chest and down again, around the shoulder he'd injured earlier and then down his right arm. Electricity shot through his skin. He groaned—from pleasure or pain, he wasn't sure which—and reveled in her touch.

This was all he ever wanted. Why couldn't he have this for the rest of his life?

"That's it, Zander," she whispered. "Just relax and don't fight it."

"Here it is," Titus mumbled somewhere close.

Something sharp pricked his arm. His eyes flew open. His upper body tensed, then in a rush all of it—the pain and jealousy and rage—seemed to leak out of him through that one spot. He saw her face above him, calm, collected and comforting. Her heat encircled his body like a wreath. Her scent so strong, he inhaled it all the way to his soul. And he knew if she was really putting him out of his misery as Titus had suggested, then at least this was a pretty awesome last image to take with him to the other side.

"Yes," Callia whispered as darkness pushed in and he floated. "That's it. Just let go."

He was powerless to do anything else. The cave grew dimmer until the picture of her faded. Until he could no longer hear her sweet voice. Until there was no sound at all. Not even his beating heart.

CHAPTER NINE

"Here's your dinner, my lady."

Isadora looked up and smiled, though the grin wobbled just a touch as Saphira set a tray of food on the ottoman.

"I had Cookie whip up your favorite. Roast lamb with potatoes."

Isadora closed the book in her lap and set it softly on the settee next to her in the sitting area of her suite. Outside, the sun was just setting to cast an orange glow over the Aegis Mountains. By some supreme force of self control she kept her hand from shaking. "Thank you, Saphira." Then she did her best to lie. "Mm, it smells delicious. I'm starving."

Her handmaiden obviously wasn't buying it. She cocked her head and pursed her lips in disapproval. "You look sickly. Perhaps you should eat and go right to bed."

Going right to bed most definitely wasn't on Isadora's to-do list tonight. And she wouldn't call her new hair and clothes "sickly."

But instead of arguing, Isadora faked a yawn, covered her mouth with her hand and said, "You may be right. My eyes are suddenly very tired."

Saphira's dark gaze narrowed, but it didn't waver from Isadora's face. "Hm."

Not to be deterred, Isadora lifted her spoon, leaned over the tray and took a bite. "Mm. I was right. Delicious."

When the plate was half-empty, Saphira finally sighed. "I suppose I should let you finish your dinner in peace."

Finally. Isadora smiled.

"Would you like me to turn the bed down?"

"No need. I'm going to let my dinner settle and read a bit more before I turn in."

The answering harrumph told Isadora loud and clear the *gynaíka* didn't approve of that either. "You'll need all the rest you can get before the binding ceremony. The king will be most disappointed if you're not one hundred percent."

Binding ceremony. Yeah. Right. Like she'd almost forgotten all about *that*.

"Good night, Saphira."

"Good night, my lady."

Isadora waited until the outer door to her suite clicked closed, then flipped the book open to the page she'd kept hidden from Saphira's probing eyes.

> *Ὧραι. The Horae. Three goddesses of balance controlling life and order. They bring and bestow ripeness. They come and go in accordance with the firm law of the periodicities of nature and of life. They are, by essence, the correct moment.*

She ran the palm of her hand over the fabric of her new black slacks covering the marking on her inner thigh. She didn't need to see it to know it was there. The image was emblazoned in her mind. The omega symbol with wings. By definition, omega marked "the end." All other Argoleans carried the alpha marking, yet she and Casey were different. As the Chosen, theirs signified the prophecy regarding the end of Atalanta's immortal reign. But the wings had always confused Isadora. Why wings? They weren't random markings. They had to have a meaning.

Damn, but she wished she'd regained her power of foresight already. Her half-sister, Casey, could see into the past of others, and she herself had always been able to glimpse shots of the future. But during her illness mere weeks ago, just before she and Casey had been united as the Chosen, she'd lost her powers, and they had yet to return, for reasons she didn't understand. If she had them now, maybe she could get some idea what this all meant. And how and why she felt so unsettled now.

She'd been poring through her books for hours. And though she couldn't explain it, she needed to know the answer to her questions before she was forced to bind herself to Zander. Something in her gut told her this was important not only to her future, but to his as well.

She looked back at the text with a mixture of dread and foreboding. There was one person who knew what this all meant. One person who could fill in the blanks. Only he was the last *ándras* she ever wanted to be indebted to.

Before she could change her mind, she jumped to her feet and rushed to the massive walk-in closet on the far side of the room. The invisibility cloak was hidden all the way in the back, hanging underneath the full-length silk cloak she wore to formal palace affairs. She pulled it from the hanger and stared at the lightweight black fabric between her hands.

Please let this still work.

She turned out of the closet, slipped her feet into the black flats Casey had been more than eager to provide her and buttoned the cloak around her shoulders. On a deep breath, she pulled up the hood and headed for the door.

Standing in the Grand Hallway of the castle for a moment, she listened to the early evening sounds. Somewhere close a bell chimed. A door opened and closed. Footsteps padded softly away.

She headed for the back stairs. At the base of the stairwell laughter and the sounds of dishes clinking in the kitchen drifted her way. She paused in the shadows just outside the doorway and held her breath. This was it. Time to see if the Fates had decided she was worthy of a crown or not.

She stepped into the kitchen. Three cooks filled plates with steaming meat and potatoes. A handful of servants were refilling glasses and gathering silverware. Dishwashers stood at the massive sinks, cleaning pots and pans and cooking utensils. At the long wooden table on the far side of the room, six members of the Executive Guard were taking their dinner break, telling stories and laughing as they spooned food into their faces.

No one looked her way.

Holding her breath, she took a step toward the back door, past Cookie, the oldest member of the kitchen staff. Still no one paid her even one iota of attention. She wrapped her hand around the back door handle, pulled slightly. Behind her she heard someone yell, "Who didn't latch the door? The wind's pushed it open!"

Before someone could close her in, she slipped out through the narrow opening. The door slapped closed behind her. Fresh evening air filled her lungs and a smile she just couldn't contain swept across her face.

She'd done it. She was outside and no one even knew.

Confidence growing, she breezed past the four guards at the main gate without so much as a backward glance. She didn't stop until she reached the road at the bottom of the hill and stood staring at the city of Tiyrns.

Massive buildings made of marble filled the skyline. The city fanned outward from the castle, most of the businesses and shops close in, the residential areas and seedier neighborhoods farther out. And though she could have flashed to the section of the city she intended to visit tonight, she didn't, instead reveling in the fact she could walk wherever she wanted and no one could see her.

Her. The future queen of Argolea. Outside the castle walls. Beyond her father's heavy hand. Away from everything that was slowly killing her.

Don't dawdle, Isadora.

Right. She wouldn't. If she was gone too long, eventually someone would miss her and then all hell would break loose.

Remembering the map she'd studied earlier today, she imagined Corinth Avenue. Her eyes slid closed, her limbs grew light. And then she was flying.

Flashing was a strange sensation, and one she didn't get to experience all that often, because she was usually confined to the castle. One of the benefits of living in Argolea was the fact its residents could flash from place to place simply by envisioning a location in their mind. Way faster than walking through a city of two million. Much safer than the unpredictable cars and trucks Isadora had seen in the human world. Of course, you had to be outside to flash, and you couldn't go through walls and buildings, but tonight that wasn't a problem.

She slowed, then halted and opened her eyes to exactly what she'd imagined when she'd overheard the description of this area of the city. Darkness had completely pressed in, and streetlamps every ten yards illuminated the dreary cobblestone road. The shops here were run-down, their glass fronts dingy, some missing lettering that had been stenciled on far too long ago. Most were already closed. A trash can was overturned on one sidewalk, leaking garbage and day-old food. A trio of grubby young who looked like they hadn't seen a bath in days and who couldn't possibly be more than ten rifled through its contents.

She avoided the bar to her right, walking quickly past the open door. Rowdy shouts drifted her way, followed by a female's laughter and chairs scraping the wooden floor. Ignoring what sounded like a party inside, she made for the lone shop on the corner of the barren street. The one marked HELIOS.

Light burned at the back of the store. Though the sign out front said CLOSED, Isadora placed her hand on the door handle and pushed.

The scents of incense and herbs used in ancient ceremonies burned her nose. Candles flickered here and there on tabletops and from a chandelier over a counter near the far wall. Tables covered in a variety of colorful fabrics held polished stones, dried flowers and herbs, crystals and beads. And throughout the entire space, human trinkets were scattered like gold dust in a flowing river.

A four-inch replica of the Statue of Liberty, a cell phone, a book called *Twilight*. Women's heeled boots, a shirt with the word *Abercrombie* emblazoned across the front. Everywhere you looked you could find something not of this world. And everywhere you looked, you were drawn deeper into the store.

Isadora slid the hood off her head and glanced around the cluttered shelves, the busy displays. *My gods. He's been smuggling human relics back for years.* Part of her wasn't sure how the Council turned a blind eye and didn't shut this place down. Another part smiled because its existence was exactly what she'd hoped to find.

She took a step farther into the room and bumped into a table. A picture frame teetered, then clattered to the table with a clank.

"We're closed," a voice called from the back room.

Carefully, she replaced the frame on the table. And swallowed in the silence that followed.

She'd never been good at blackmail, and she'd already played this card once. She wasn't sure how long she'd be able to use it. But she needed him now—maybe more than she had then.

Footsteps echoed behind the far wall. She stayed where she was and waited. And hoped she hadn't interrupted him in one of his . . . moods.

Sound ceased. Though she'd heard his steps, he didn't come through the dark and open door at the end of the long room. Where was he? She squinted to see clearer.

"How did you escape your playpen, Isa?"

Isadora jerked at the rough voice behind her, whipped around and tipped her head back to look up at Orpheus.

Her pulse pounded under his glowing green gaze, but she held her ground. He stood as tall as the Argonauts, was as big and brawny and just as menacing, with his rugged features and broad shoulders. But that's where the similarities ended. While the Argonauts were dangerous in their own right, Orpheus was downright disturbing. The way he could poof through walls wasn't normal, and when his eyes flashed green in that daemon way, as they were doing now, they made Isadora want to run screaming for the hills.

She slapped a hand against her chest. "Gods, Orpheus, you scared me."

"I should," he said without humor. "Right now, Isa, you're on my turf. You would be wise to be very scared."

She didn't move. He was waiting for her to tuck tail and run. He wanted her to be afraid. And she was. The half of him that was daemon—which he wasn't hiding from her now—was unpredictable. But instead of giving in to the fear, she clung to the vision she'd had of him before she'd lost her powers. To the one that had pushed her here tonight. To the one of him saving her.

He edged closer until she felt his hot breath on her skin. "Haven't you heard the rumors? Daemons eat virgins for supper." When she didn't answer, he reached out and fingered her newly shorn hair. "This, I like. Don't tell me the king banished you from his playground because you cut your hair, and a sinner is the only one you can turn to now."

The amusement in his voice brought her chin up. Fear and ridicule, that's how he worked. That's how he'd always worked, but she wasn't going to fall for it. "Don't flatter yourself. And don't get your hopes up. My father is sicker than a dog. In mere weeks you'll be bowing down and pledging your allegiance to your new queen."

"Don't count on it, virgin. I pledge my allegiance to no one." He let go of her hair, walked past her and around the shop's counter.

She turned, her gaze following his fluid movements. To the average person, he looked like everyone else: an Argolean, albeit a big one. But he wasn't. He was what everyone feared and hated most. "How about to the one person who knows your secret?"

He glared at her over his shoulder. And those eyes, which had slowly faded to black when he'd touched her hair, flashed green all over again. "You would be wise not to threaten me, Isa. I guarantee you won't enjoy the consequences."

She lifted her chin again. *Screw him.* She'd been through much worse than he could dole out. She'd tangled with a god and lived to tell about it. "I need your help, Orpheus."

He frowned. "I should have destroyed that damn invisibility cloak as soon as we left Olympus."

"That's not what I meant."

He braced both massive hands on the counter that ran along the wall and leaned back. "Do tell then, what could you *possibly* want from me? I'm all ears."

"I need . . ." She hesitated, because even to her this sounded stupid. "I need you to teach me."

"Teach you what?" A bored expression raced across his features.

"To fight."

He scoffed.

"I'm stronger than I look."

"You're pathetic."

"I want to learn." He opened his mouth, but she cut him off. "There are factions that do not want to see me rule and will do whatever it takes to undermine my authority. Weakness is not an option for me. You *will* teach me to fight so that when the time comes—and it will—the first person who challenges my rule will realize I'm not just a patsy."

He glanced away with a "yeah, right" look. But he didn't say no, and she took that as a subtle yes. Anything that undermined the Council or the Argonauts pleased him, and she could practically see the wheels turning in his brain, imagining her taking down Lucian, the head of the Council, with her blade.

The image nearly made her smile before she remembered death wasn't always the answer. "I also want you to teach me something else."

"Lara Croft fighting tactics aren't enough?"

Lara Croft? She shook off the question. Pulled the slip of paper from inside her cloak and set it on the counter in front of him. "I want you to teach me about this."

He went still as glass, and for a split second, those eyes flashed green again. "I don't know what you're talking about."

"Yes, you do," she said slowly. "I'm not clueless, Orpheus. I've done my research. The omega symbol was the marking of the prophecy. These hatch markings here . . ." She pointed to the wings around the omega, the ones found in the first symbol of the translation of the Horae and on her skin. "They mean something else."

He rolled his eyes. "You are higher than a—"

"No," she said forcefully, refusing to let him sway her. "I'm not. Something's building. Has been building for weeks, since the moment Casey and I united. I can feel it. Only it's different from before, and I don't know what it means."

She stepped forward and pointed to the text she'd copied. "The omega with wings, that's the symbol for the Horae, and there weren't two, there were three. Goddesses of balance, half-sisters of the Moirae, or the Fates. Three is a powerful number in science, religion and mythology. The third dimension, the triangle. Beginning, middle and end. The three Fates, the Trinity—"

"You're suddenly religious?"

She scowled. "The Triad, the three phases of the moon, the three Muses—"

"I thought there were nine."

"—the three Furies, the three faces of Hekate—"

"Stop." His humor faded. "Witchcraft is not something to joke about, Isadora."

Her mouth closed. The green glow was back to his eyes. And the tense line of his shoulders told her she'd just hit on something big. "I'm not joking."

"Leave well enough alone, Princess."

"I can't. The buzzing in my head won't let me. You know what it means, don't you? This isn't just about me and Casey anymore, is it? There's someone else."

His jaw flexed. And in the silence she knew she was right. Just as she knew she'd been right to come here. Her adrenaline surged.

"What do you want from me?"

"What are you offering?"

"You . . ." Her mind spun. "I'll make sure you live the way you always have."

He frowned. "Not buying it. If you'd wanted to out me, you'd have done it a long time ago. You're too softhearted for that and we both know it."

"Fine. I won't tell anyone about this little shop. You can go on smuggling materials and people to and from the human realm and no one will be the wiser."

"No one *is* the wiser. You saw what I let you see. Try again."

He had the power to alter perceptions? Wild.

"Gold," she said quickly.

He harrumphed. "I don't need your money, Isa. Look around you. This place is a gold *mine*."

Glancing around, she realized he was right. "Fine then, what do you want?"

His eyes flashed green one more time. Only *this* time it wasn't with malice. It was with heat. The kind that burned into the middle of a female and told her loud and clear what was on an *ándras*'s mind.

Daemons are impotent. The widely known fact floated in her brain even as her eyes ran over him from head to toe. Only he wasn't just daemon. He was Argolean too. And if he'd been sired by a daemon after all, it meant that little fact was null and void.

"I think you know what I want," he said in a low, rough voice.

She swallowed even as her heart hammered against her ribs. "You want me to . . . to sleep with you."

"No, Isa," he said, those burning eyes roaming over every inch of her skin. "I don't plan to sleep. What I want is your body. Every inch. Mine to do with as I please. Whenever and wherever I choose. For as long as your training lasts."

"Training?"

He nodded toward her right thigh, where her marking was hidden behind her slacks. "What you've got there is more powerful than you or your sister realize. It didn't end with Atalanta's immortality. It began. But to tap into its powers, you've got to learn how to wield it. You're right. I can help you. But it'll cost you."

Her stomach churned, and an image from the Underworld popped into her brain.

"Don't look so repulsed, Isadora," he said with a hint of humor. "Something tells me you may just enjoy it."

Her body.

It wasn't really her body anymore, was it? In a matter of days it would belong to Zander. When she passed from this world into the next, it would belong to Hades. In the meantime, shouldn't she have a say in what she did with it? This was her choice, no one else's. And if it got her to her ultimate goal, then it was worth it.

Shaping her own destiny and not letting others do it for her was worth her virtue.

She lifted her gaze to his. Didn't even flinch. "Yes."

His eyebrows lifted in surprise. He was still leaning against the back counter, and it was obvious from his shocked expression he'd expected a different answer.

"I said yes," she repeated. "For as long as my training sessions last, my body will be yours. But you will teach me everything, Orpheus. Everything I want to know and more. And if you don't know it, you'll find it for me."

She took his silence for a yes. Turned for the door. "We'll start the first session tomorrow. I'll be here at the same time."

"What about your husband?"

She paused but didn't turn.

"Yes, Isa," he said. "Even I know you're to be bound to the Argonaut Zander. Word spreads all the way out here, *virgin*."

She turned slowly and met his gaze. Level, cold, as hard as the one he was giving her. "Zander is injured. I'm fairly certain the binding ceremony will be postponed. Which means we have time to get started before then."

"And your virtue?"

"Is mine to do with as I please."

He whistled low. "Hubby's not gonna be pleased to find out you broke the seal without him."

Her jaw clenched. "Then he'll just have to get used to living with disappointment. I sure have."

She headed for the door.

"Isadora," he called, this time in a softer voice.

She hesitated with one hand on the doorknob.

"There are severe consequences for adultery in this culture. Especially for a female of the monarchy. Are you sure you want to do this?"

She thought of the females who had been punished. Though many thought the archaic chastisements of the past were over, Isadora knew the Council was pushing to have them reinstated. Orpheus was right. They would come down hard on her if she was caught in a compromising position, but not on him. Males had always gotten off scot-free. Until she could rule and set things right, their . . . relationship . . . could be deadly. Especially for her.

The marking on her inner thigh tingled. No, it was still worth it. She'd rather die at the hands of the Council than never take a chance on something she knew in her soul could change the shape of her future.

She pulled the door open with one hand and lifted the cloak's hood over her head with the other. Renewed determination flowed through her veins like sweet, rich wine. "I'll see you here tomorrow night, Orpheus. Don't keep me waiting."

CHAPTER TEN

Someone was singing. And it definitely wasn't him, because he couldn't carry a tune for shit.

The sound was sweet to Zander's ears, the voice relaxing. He didn't recognize the song, couldn't really make out the words, but he didn't care. It sounded much too good just the way it was, even jumbled and muffled to hell and back. Something brushed his forehead. A hand? Then his shoulder, now his hip. Soft fingers moved to his leg. He breathed deep and relaxed further, listening to the velvety sounds of the voice as it grew stronger, clearer, and felt the silky smooth hand running over his skin.

His leg . . .

His eyes flew open. He could feel his leg. Only . . . shit . . . why was everything black?

"My eyes . . ." Whoa, was that his voice? It sounded way too thick and raspy to be him.

The singing cut off abruptly. "Zander?"

Callia? What the heck was she doing here? He searched his memory, tried to connect dots that didn't want to go together. Came up empty. "I can't see anything."

"It's okay." Her hand brushed his forehead again. And oh, shit, her fingers sliding against any part of his bare skin felt *really* good. He tipped his head toward the sound of her voice and drew in a deep whiff of her scent. As sweet as summer roses. Oh, yeah, that was definitely her. "It's a side effect from the drugs. It'll wear off."

Well, that was a relief. But why would he need drugs?

And then, like a light switch flicking on, he remembered.

The daemons, the fight, him getting hurt and waking up in that cave with both Callia and Titus.

If she was with him it meant he wasn't dead. But—His brain flashed to the way Titus had been touching her, and just that fast, his blood turned to a roar in his head.

"Relax, Zander." Her hands pressed down on his shoulders. "I don't want you getting up yet."

Her voice calmed him. He stopped fighting. And wasn't that weird? Until he'd heard her, he hadn't even realized he was moving.

"That's better," she said.

He squinted because things weren't quite so black anymore. A shadowy figure hovered over him. The edges of his vision were blurry but growing brighter. "Where's Titus?"

"He went to find Demetrius."

Probably a wise choice on the guardian's part.

"Demetrius lured the daemons away after you got hurt," she said.

He did? Zander's brow creased. "What about the Misos?"

She let out a weary sigh, and he felt her hands on his leg again. Unwrapping bandages? He wasn't sure. But she was slowly coming into focus. "A few . . . didn't make it."

"The young?"

"Lie back, Zander." She pushed on his shoulders again.

She went back to whatever she was doing to his right leg. And her voice was soft when she said, "Six of them . . . They . . . There were just too many daemons and not enough . . ."

She didn't finish. But he didn't need to hear the words to know what she was thinking. *Not enough Argonauts.*

He let his head fall back and closed his eyes as nausea churned in his stomach. "There was a boy. No more than eight . . ."

"I don't know what happened to him," she said softly.

Silence settled between them as she worked. He thought about the boy with the blue eyes. This war was getting bloodier by the minute and he was about to take himself out of service until Isadora produced an heir. How many other young would die because there weren't enough Argonauts fighting for them?

His mind skipped to Demetrius, and he wondered if the guardian had been injured and if Titus had been able to find him. And if so, would the guardian be able to get Demetrius help in time? There'd been at least seven daemons in the fray when Zander went down. Seven against one—even two—were tough odds. And if there was one Argonaut who even came close to Zander's recklessness it was Demetrius.

Shit. Demetrius wasn't immortal like Zander. He didn't stand a chance.

Zander needed to go find them. To help instead of lying here like a frickin' invalid. It was the least he could do until the king pulled him out of the rotation. He pushed up to his elbows.

"No," Callia said quickly, her hands once more at his shoulders, pressing down. She wasn't half as strong as he was on a good day, but for some reason she was able to keep him from getting up now. "You're in no position to go anywhere just yet."

"I'm fine," he said, glancing past her to see where the hell he was.

They were in a cave, that much he could see. The same one as before? It didn't look like it. This room seemed bigger than the last, the ceiling at least thirty feet above, nearly invisible in the dark. Water slapped and gurgled somewhere close, but he couldn't see more than a few feet in front of him. A couple of lanterns had been set up, one near his feet, another somewhere behind his head, their soft lights casting shadows across both the rock floor and Callia's face.

He tried to look away but couldn't completely tear his gaze from her features. Her auburn hair was pulled back into a tail at the nape of her neck, and the lanterns highlighted the curve of her cheekbones, the long supple line of her throat and the gentle swell of her lips. She didn't look at him, had gone back to work on his leg while he'd taken stock of the room, but she knew he was watching. He could tell by the way she avoided his gaze.

What was she doing here? And why hadn't she left yet? Even if he'd been injured badly, he was all right now. She could leave anytime she wanted.

His eyes narrowed with suspicion as he watched her, as gorgeous and perfect as she'd been every other day of her life, and so totally *not* his it made his chest ache and reignited the resentment he always struggled with whenever she was close.

But there was something more. Something not quite right about her. Her skin was pale. Dark circles marred the skin under her eyes. The way her shoulders tensed, she looked like she carried the weight of the world and more.

Not your problem.

"I need to go find Demetrius and Titus."

"No, you don't," she said without looking up, her hands continuing to rewrap his leg.

"If Demetrius is injured—"

"Then you'll be no help to him. Just sit back and relax."

Irritation growing, he moved to sit up. "This is bullshit."

She dropped her hands from his wounded leg and pushed him back down to his elbows. "Bullshit is you thinking you're invincible. You're not. So just lie down and stop acting like a five-year-old."

His temper flared. "I don't need you to fix me, Callia. I'm already healing, in case you haven't noticed. I don't even know why the hell you're here. I'm immortal. I don't need you or anyone else to heal me."

"Ilithios." She pushed to her feet so fast his head snapped back. And when she glared down at him there was a fire in her eyes he didn't remember seeing before. "Six hours ago you had a bullet lodged in your spinal cord. Do you *get* what that means, Zander? It means I had to cut you open and take it out. Then heal you all over again. It wasn't just a

simple procedure. You might be immortal, but without me right now you'd be paralyzed. And you're not going anywhere until I'm satisfied I didn't fuck up and injure you worse than you were before."

She stepped over him and disappeared into the dark. And alone, he stayed right where he was, his weight perched on his elbows, his mouth hanging open, his eyes staring after her. It wasn't so much what she'd said that had stunned him speechless—though he couldn't remember ever hearing her swear before—it was the look in her eyes when she'd been saying it.

Anger, sure. Frustration, yeah, that was obvious. But overriding all of that was fear. True fear. The kind you experience when you think someone you care about is on the verge of dying.

She was afraid. For him.

His heart rate kicked up in his chest. He closed his eyes, drew in a deep breath as he lay back down on the pallet and told himself it didn't matter. But it did. He wasn't such a jackass that he couldn't see that it mattered. A lot.

Fuck. He was supposed to bind himself to Isadora in a matter of days. He didn't need his soul mate finding a way back into his life. Not after all this time.

Callia came back into the room, her footsteps echoing across the hard ground. She'd unbound her hair, and now those red locks partially shielded her face. She was careful not to make eye contact, just stepped around him, knelt down again and went back to work on his leg.

And though he didn't like it, he felt like a prick. Especially when her fingers brushed his leg again and sparks of electricity rushed across his skin at the simple contact.

He didn't talk while she wrapped a bandage around his thigh. Tried like hell not to react to every graze and tug and sweep of her flesh against his that seemed amplified now, after his little realization moments before. But when her hands stopped moving and she glanced up toward his chest, he drew in a breath and waited—for what, he wasn't even sure.

"You're shivering. Are you cold?"

He was? Okay, now *that* was weird. He hadn't even noticed.

"No, I'm fine," he said. But even before the words were out, a shiver racked his body and knocked his teeth together.

"Ilithios," she whispered again, rising and crossing the room. She came back with a blanket and proceeded to wrap it around his body. "I've had senile patients who were easier to deal with than you. Even the king isn't this much of a pain in the ass."

He couldn't help it; one corner of his mouth curled. She'd always been able to make him smile, even when he'd been in a pissy mood.

She felt his forehead, cursed, then knelt near his head. Her scent surrounded him like a wreath of roses. Leaning over, she lifted at his shoulders. "Sit up."

"What are you doing?"

She pushed him up gently, shifted around and moved behind him. "You're obviously freezing. Until we get your temperature regulated I'm going to use my body heat to warm you."

Her body heat? Oh, man, *no.* "Look, I don't need—"

"Shut up with the 'I don't need' crap, Zander. Right now I don't really give a rip what you think you need."

Her blunt words cut off his protest. What had happened to the agreeable *gynaíka* he'd known all those years before? That one had been pleasant and proper. This one didn't take crap from anyone. Especially him.

She eased back to sit, slid one leg on each side of his and pulled him back against her. And oh, sweet goddess, there was a reason he hadn't let himself get near her in ten years. When she was close like this, he forgot everything, including his own name.

Her perfect breasts pressed against his back. Her hips cradled his like they were made just for him. Her arms wound around him, and she tucked the blanket in tighter, locking her heat against his. He could feel her heartbeat against his spine, feel the warmth between her thighs near the wound on his lower back. And when she exhaled, her silky, hot breath ran down his neck and made him shiver all over again.

"Just relax," she said near his ear, obviously misreading his reaction. But yeah, like he was going to correct her now? Not a chance. The blood was already pounding in his veins and that tingling in his groin felt way too good to ignore.

"That's better," she said softly. "I don't know why males have to be such babies when they're hurt."

He closed his eyes, rested his head back against her shoulder and told himself this wasn't sexual. It was . . . medicinal. Yeah, that was it . . .

"You say that like it's a bad thing," he muttered. Her hands rubbed up and down his arms, and that tingle grew with every brush of skin against fabric.

"It is," she answered. "I'm just trying to help you here."

Suddenly, he could think of a number of ways she could help. And they all started with her hands rubbing those sinful circles on his naked flesh, not the blanket covering his skin.

When he realized where his thoughts were headed, his eyes popped open and he tried to refocus. But he didn't move away from her body. Couldn't. "Where is 'here,' anyway?"

"Somewhere in the Cascade mountain range. I'm not sure exactly where. Titus brought me here. After he hid you in that cave, he went back to Argolea to get me."

"How did we get in this cave? It looks different from before."

"You remember that?" When he nodded, she sighed and lifted her left leg so her knee was pointing toward the ceiling. The motion eased him further into the warmth of her body, distracting him from his question. "That was this same cave, just nearer the opening. It was too cold, though. A storm's moved in and I was worried about infection and keeping you warm."

Oh, man. She felt so good. Too damn good. He cleared his throat. "How . . . how far in are we?"

"About a hundred yards or so, I'd guess. I thought you'd be warm enough this far in, which is why I didn't have a blanket on you earlier. These mountains are volcanic and there's geothermal activity underground."

For the first time he realized there was no breeze blowing through this cave, and though he was cold, the air wasn't nearly as chilly as the interior of a cave in the middle of the mountains should be. "That's why the air isn't frigid."

"Yes. And because the hot springs are heating it."

"Hot springs?"

She nodded and pointed to the right, into the dark. "There are at least four pools over there. We lucked out because there's no way we could have built a fire in here."

And that explained her short-sleeved shirt and the fact he thought he'd seen a drop of perspiration on her brow earlier.

They sat like that a few minutes in silence, and he could feel his body warming from the heat of hers pressed against his. That tingling continued to grow little by little with every stroke of her fingers against his arms and chest.

Jeez, of all the healers Titus could have gone to for help, he had to bring her. Her skills were rare, but there were other healers in the city of Tiyrns who could have been just as helpful. Though none were as closely linked to the king and the Argonauts as she was.

Warmth gathered in his chest under the motion of her fingers. Reflexively, he quivered, and she pulled him tighter, again misreading his body's reaction. If he were smart he'd pull away right now. He wasn't going to die—he knew that for sure now—and whether she wanted to believe it or not, he didn't need her. Not to save him, at least. But he did want her. As her hand slid over his chest, brushing the rough fabric of the blanket against his nipple and sending sparks of desire shooting to his groin, he knew he wanted her more than he had during the king's little exam. More than he had that first night in the castle, more than he could ever remember wanting anything in his long-ass life.

Which was wrong, wasn't it? He was binding himself to Isadora, and Callia . . . she was still betrothed to that SOB Loukas, though he had no idea why they hadn't finalized the union yet. It was wrong to be thinking about sex with her now, especially here, when she was simply being a Good Samaritan.

Her hands brushed over his chest again, the fabric tweaking his other nipple, and he drew in a sharp breath. Her hand stilled, and at his back he felt her heartbeat kick up. He waited, unsure what to say or do. Then she brushed her fingers over his nipple again, almost as if she were experimenting with his reaction to see what he would do next.

And either that was totally twisted and sick or . . . or it meant some part of her was as turned on as he was right this minute.

Whoa. Wait. That's wrong too, isn't it?

Questions, options, answers he wasn't sure he was ready for pinged around in his brain. But no matter what he told himself, it didn't feel wrong. Right now it felt . . . pretty damn right.

You can't do this. End it before it begins. She's not yours.

But technically she was his, wasn't she? Regardless of how they felt about each other deep down, she was still his soul mate. And they had a physical connection he'd never experienced with anyone else. He knew she felt it too by her shallow breathing and the increased pulse at his back. The question was, what was he going to do about it?

His mind spun with possibilities too wicked to put into words. She lifted the other leg so he sank deeper into the vee between her thighs. Heat gathered there, pressing against his lower back, shooting erotic flames from her body to his until blood pooled hard in his groin.

He closed his eyes, tried to slow his breathing. It had always been like this with her. This instant arousal whenever she was close. Would it be so horrible to act on it here and now? Once he was bound to Isadora, that was it. Her forever and no one else. He intended to live up to his vows, which meant once the ceremony was complete he'd never again have the opportunity to feel Callia's body pressed up against his like this, never again get to marvel at the softness of his soul mate's skin sliding against his or taste the sweetness of her on his tongue.

And oh, yeah, he could still remember that honey-sweet taste sliding down his throat . . .

His eyes popped open. Screw remembering. He could have that now. She was here. He was hard. And judging from the way she continued to rub his chest and arms, she wanted him too.

One night. No strings. He was strong enough for sex, that he knew for sure. His cock jerked as erotic images of the two of them together flashed in his brain. His erection grew even harder. He sucked in a breath even as a little voice deep inside cautioned, *You're playing with fire.*

Her hands stilled against his chest. "Are you still cold?"

His throat was so thick he couldn't answer. No, he was hot. Burning, just for her.

She lifted her hand, ran it across his brow. "Your skin is clammy. *Skata.*"

She pushed him up quickly and slid out from beneath him before he could protest. And he was just opening his mouth to tell her he was fine and convince her to come back when he caught sight of what she was doing.

She gripped the bottom of her T-shirt and tugged it up, revealing the nearly sheer cami underneath. He sucked in a breath and held it while she yanked the T-shirt up and over her head as she had in his fantasy, then tossed it on the ground. She toed off her shoes and quickly reached for the button on her pants.

"Wh-what are you doing?" Holy Hades, was that his voice? He sounded like he had when he'd first come to, all wasted to hell and back. Belatedly he realized he was braced on his elbows, watching her with rapt attention. Like a man starved. Unable to look away if his life depended on it.

"I'm taking you into the hot spring," she said matter-of-factly as she popped the button on her jeans and pushed them down her long, luscious legs. And oh, shit. If he thought he'd been hard before, he was seriously mistaken. His cock *throbbed*.

"Callia—"

"We have to get you warmed up *now*," she said firmly. The fabric hit the ground around her ankles, and then she was wiggling out of the jeans, kicking them to the side and standing over him wearing only the cami and panties that made his mouth water, looking like a sex goddess come to offer herself as a sacrifice.

There she was. His soul mate. Practically naked and his for the taking. He'd have to be a fool to refuse her now.

She eased down, wrapped both her bare arms around his chest and eased him up to sitting. And the scent of her . . . it broke through his last defense.

"Come with me, Zander. This will feel good. I promise."

He had no doubt about that. What little blood was left in his limbs shot right into his cock as she helped him to his feet. And with it, every protest he'd ever had where she was concerned slipped right out of his head.

CHAPTER ELEVEN

Callia hauled Zander to his feet. He swayed, but she caught him and managed to brace her feet on the rocks to keep them both from going down. Didn't need her help? Bullshit.

"Hold on to me," she said. She wrapped her arms up under his and around his back, supporting his weight. And holy cow, he weighed a lot.

He perched his palms on her shoulders. "I got it." But he didn't. Not even close.

She shifted under his left arm, slid her hand around his waist and grabbed his on her opposite shoulder to steady him. The blanket she'd tucked around him earlier slid to the ground and in the dim light she saw a flash of very male, very naked skin.

Ignore it.

She would. She was a professional. She'd seen plenty of naked bodies over the course of her career. And none—not even the really gorgeous ones—had ever turned her on.

None were Zander.

She shook off the thought, gripped his hand tighter at her shoulder. "Just a few feet to the pool. It'll be hot."

He didn't say much as they moved slowly toward the water, and she was grateful for that. Even though the temperature in this section of the cave was like a sauna and perspiration slicked her skin, she was very much aware that she was wearing nothing more than underwear right now. But what were her options? She was obviously going to have to get in the water with him to hold him up, and she hadn't brought a change of clothes. Wet undergarments were a small price to pay for making sure her patient lived and she didn't freeze to death in the process.

They made it to the edge of the first pool. As she eased him down to sit on the rock ledge, she wished she'd thought to bring the lantern. It was darker on this side of the room. Shadows played across his skin as he dipped one toe into the water and pulled it back quickly.

"*Skata.*"

"I told you it was hot."

She'd tested it earlier, just to make sure, and knew it was right around a hundred and four degrees, which wasn't that bad except when you were already freezing. While he was preoccupied with trying to ease his feet into the steaming liquid, she slid into the pool and sucked in a breath as the hot water surrounded her legs and torso.

The bite was a shock to the system, but after a few seconds, her muscles began to relax. The water hit just below her breasts, the bottom of this part of the pool one continuous long flat rock that was smooth beneath her bare feet. She walked to where Zander was sitting on the edge of the pool, his feet now submersed in the water, his hands in his lap as he acclimated himself to the temperature.

Gods, he was really beautiful. For a moment, the look of him there, totally naked with the light from the lamp across the room highlighting the angles and planes of his very chiseled body, stole her breath. She'd seen him naked before, many times, but she wasn't sure she'd ever stopped to appreciate his body aesthetically. Now she did.

His shoulders were broad, his chest muscular and defined, the play of muscle over bone so smooth it was as if he'd been carved from marble. His abs were taut and ripped, his arms as thick as her legs. And that thin line of hair that ran from his chest to his navel, then lower, was like a blinking arrow, urging her to keep looking.

She drew in a breath and told herself to wise up. He was her patient, she was his healer. Their past was so over and done with it wasn't even funny.

Refusing to look down, she leaned into him and once again wrapped her arms under his and around his torso. His legs immediately opened, and within seconds she found his bare chest pressed up tight against hers. And other things. Most definitely where she didn't need them.

Her heart rate kicked up being this close to him, just as it had in the king's study, just as it had when she'd worked on him earlier. She had to grind her teeth together to keep her voice even. "Come on. We'll go slow. It'll feel good once you get used to it."

He muttered something that sounded an awful lot like "I thought that was my line," but then she didn't care, because he was sliding into the water and she was focused on making sure his legs didn't go out from under him.

He hissed in a sharp breath, let it out slowly. She kept a hold of him as they slid in deeper and the water rose up to their shoulders. His breathing slowed and he closed his eyes, but he didn't make any attempt to push away, and she figured he either knew he needed her help right now or he was oblivious to the fact she was still holding him.

The water made him virtually weightless and easy to maneuver. Slowly she walked them to the side of the pool, where the rocks were smoother and more comfortable to lean against. Bracing his back against one very flat rock, she continued to keep her body tight against his so he wouldn't slide under and drown.

Steam rose around them. The tips of her wet hair slapped against her shoulders. With a groan he rested his head back on the rocks behind him. Beads of sweat popped out on his forehead, so she lifted a hand from the water, shook the droplets from her skin and wiped his brow.

"Hmm," he said as her fingers ran across his skin. "That feels good."

A half smile curled her mouth before she could stop it. He'd always loved it when she massaged his forehead and ran her fingers through his hair. "Better?"

"Way better."

"I told you you were cold."

"Not anymore. I think I feel my toes again."

Her smile widened. That was definitely good news. She continued to rub his forehead, his temples, trail her finger down the bridge of his nose and up again. Had he broken it at one point? She didn't remember the small lump there in that spot. She glanced at his throat, at the long jagged scar he'd gotten in some fight. This one she remembered well. Remembered running her fingers and tongue over it as they'd made . . .

Dangerous, a little voice warned. *If you don't stop touching him, you'll cross the healer-patient line . . .*

She frowned. She was part human, wasn't she? Didn't she deserve a few minutes of downtime herself? After the last few hours—days, for that matter—she deserved more than a few minutes. Hell, after the last ten years she deserved a lifetime of peace. Why couldn't she relax and enjoy these few stolen moments with Zander, free from the animosity and anger that had ruled them both for so long? Was it too much to ask for just a handful of minutes to remember why she'd fallen for him in the first place?

Yes. Definitely yes. Getting close will only end badly.

As she sat there stroking him, arguing with herself and feeling guilty, she found she wanted this moment to last. Needed it to. For reasons even she didn't understand.

Almost as if he heard the voices in her head, his eyes popped open, shattering the serenity. She stilled when she realized he was completely focused on her, the blue-gray pools of his irises as clear as she'd ever seen them. "What?" she asked hesitantly.

"Why did you come?"

"I . . ." Okay, yeah. Damn those superhero healing properties. He was definitely lucid now. "Because Titus asked me to."

"You could have said no."

True. And she'd considered it. For all of two seconds. But

like a fool, she'd never been able to turn her back on him. "I made a vow to help those in need."

"Even me."

It wasn't a question. They both heard it. Instantly she remembered all too well how he could turn a blind eye to those in need. And just like that the peaceful moment passed.

She dropped her hand back into the water and focused on that scar on his throat to avoid his gaze. Water droplets glistened on his naturally tanned skin, ran over the puckered surface.

"Even you."

Silence settled between them. His breathing and the lap of water against rock was all she heard.

"Where did you go?" he finally asked. "After?"

Shock registered. That he was asking. That he even cared. After all this time, did it even matter anymore? She thought about not answering then figured, why not? "I . . . I needed some time. I stayed where I was. In Greece."

He nodded. And she couldn't help wondering whether he'd known where she was all along. "I heard a rumor you went to a human medical school."

He had? News flash to her. Why would he even care? She could ask. She wanted to. But ultimately decided against it. She didn't want him becoming agitated in his state, and if he was trying to satisfy some morbid curiosity, then she'd just let him. For now. "I did. I studied at the Aristotle University of Thessaloníki."

He lifted a hand from the water to scratch his stubbly jaw. "Weren't you afraid? In the human realm, alone? Argoleans are prime targets for daemons."

She shrugged, stared at a droplet of water that ran from his cheek, down across his strong, square jaw and under, to trail down his scar. "At first, a little. But Thessaloníki is a big city. I made sure I was never really alone. Daemons don't like to make a scene in front of humans if they can avoid it."

"They used to avoid it," he said quietly. "Things are different now."

Yeah, they were, weren't they? Now that Atalanta was mortal again her daemons didn't care who got in their way. She'd been so lucky the day . . .

Her stomach churned, but she forced the memory back. "My father was also with me for a while. That made it easier at the start."

"Oh, right," he said with very clear disdain. "Your father. Why does that not surprise me?"

She lifted her eyes to his and saw in his chiseled features that the contempt he'd had for her father was very much alive and kicking today, though why it mattered to him now she'd never know. He'd once accused her of letting her father rule her life. And for a long time, she had. But when it came down to the most important decision, she'd gone against what her father wanted. And paid dearly.

She looked back at the water curling softly around Zander's skin and tried not to remember the pain. But it never really went away. "Do you really want to talk about my father?"

"No."

His immediate answer was no real surprise. So why did the blunt word make her chest ache?

"I just want to know one thing," he said. "Why did you come back? If the human world was so great, why return to Argolea at all?"

What answer could she give that would make sense? She didn't want to tell him her father had begged her to return. Or that the increase in daemon activity in the area had scared her enough to make her consider returning to a world that devalued its females. And she definitely didn't want him to know about the daemon she'd run into one night walking home from class. That had definitely been a sobering experience, especially after the way the creature had stared at her like he recognized her. She'd been lucky the group of humans had come by when they had and she'd escaped unscathed. But she definitely didn't want to tell Zander about it now or see his I-told-you-so smug expression.

So instead she shrugged and simply said, "It was just the right time to come back."

He studied her with intense eyes, as if he knew she was omitting the truth. She averted her gaze and stared at his throat again, but her adrenaline pulsed, and her heart rate kicked up under that ruthless stare.

At some point during their conversation she'd let go of him, but he seemed to be supporting his own weight just fine now, and the conversation was already too intimate for her liking. She didn't need to add physical proximity to the mix.

Just about the time she was going to tell him he was being rude and ask him to stop staring, he shrugged. His features relaxed as he slid farther into the water. "Must be nice having an in with the Council so you can come and go as you please. Most Argoleans aren't so lucky."

Lucky? The scars on her back tingled. And her mind skipped over the first few months she'd been home. She wouldn't call that luck. Not by a long shot. She'd call it . . . misery.

Before she could think of an answer, his head disappeared under the water.

And all of it—the irritation, anger, even the misery—poofed right out of her head.

"Zander!" She braced her feet on the bottom of the pool and swept her arms through the water to find him. Only he was gone. Vanished. Right out from under her.

Panic closed her throat. It was so dark she couldn't see him, the water nothing but a glassy black oil slick. Why had she let go of him? Why hadn't she thought to bring the lantern closer?

"Zander!"

His head popped back up out of the water, and he gave it a shake, sending water droplets raining down around her. "Man, that's hot."

She nearly screamed with the mixture of relief and anger bubbling through her veins. Her eyes grew wide and she clenched her hands together in front of her in fists. Then she punched his good shoulder with what little strength she had left. Water sprayed up into his face where she'd slapped at the pool. "Oh, my gods, you scared the crap out of me. Why did you do that?"

He had the audacity to look confused. "Do what?"

And that's when everything—his agreeing to bind himself to Isadora, his injury, being here with him like this, so close, their conversation and his disappearing under the water to scare her—coalesced in her brain until it was too much. The air whooshed out of her lungs on a groan and she let herself fall back into the pool, let it cradle her exhaustion and, for a second, take it all away.

Far, far away, where she didn't have to think of any of it.

"Callia? What are you . . . ? *Skata.* Come back here."

His hand wrapped around her ankle. She felt him pulling her, but she didn't fight the gentle tug, not even when water rushed over her face, cutting off her air. She was so tired. Emotionally wrung out and at the end of her rope. He was right. Coming here had been a major mistake. Had she thought she could handle being around him? She couldn't. She needed to leave now and get back to her clinic, where things were normal. And predictable. And, dammit . . . safe.

Her feet bumped into his rock-hard chest, then her knees. She sensed him leaning over her, and then his arms wrapped around her waist. She still didn't fight him, didn't have it in her, not when he hauled her up out of the water, not even when they were chest to chest and she was sliding down the long plane of his body.

She sputtered, coughed, sucked in a deep breath as water ran down her face.

"What the hell were you thinking?" he asked in an irritated voice.

She coughed again and tried to shake the water out of her eyes. "Me? You're the one who pulled . . . the disappearing act."

"I was getting my hair wet, not sailing out to the open ocean for a midnight swim. You have no idea where this pool leads or what's out there in the dark. First Titus, now this. Are you *trying* to punish me here?"

She stilled in his arms. Slowly looked up at his now-frustrated face. Tiny lines cinched his eyebrows together and creases marred his perfect forehead.

What did Titus have to do with anything? And why on earth would Zander think she was trying to punish *him*?

Water ran from her hair down her face to drip onto his broad chest. She stared at his bewildered expression, gave her head a small shake. Told herself she was seriously hearing things. "Are . . . are you still loopy from the meds I gave you? Or am I?"

He frowned. "One of us is."

"Why—?"

"Because, dammit, I think I'm about to kiss you."

That jumpstarted her muscular system. She pressed her hands against his shoulders as her eyes grew wide all over again. "Why in Hades would you—?"

He was so close she didn't have time to brace herself. His mouth captured hers in a searing kiss that radiated all the way to her toes. His lips were hard and unforgiving and he tightened his arms around her as he crushed her to him, pulling her in until she had no choice but to grab on for dear life or slide under the water and drown.

Their attraction had always been combustible. Insane. Definitely unhealthy, when she thought of everything that had resulted because of it. Gods knew, she didn't need a repeat of the years of pain she'd already endured. So why wasn't she pushing him away?

He slid the tip of his tongue along the seam of her mouth. "Open for me, Callia." His tongue made another long lingering sweep. "Let me in."

Oh . . . she shouldn't. One taste and she knew she'd be a goner. He'd nearly ruined her once before with his wicked promises of pleasure. If she let him in now . . .

His hands shifted on her back, slid lower. When he cupped her ass and lowered her so the hard ridge of his arousal brushed the cleft between her legs, she gasped.

He didn't wait for an invitation. Or give her brain time to catch up with the moment. His tongue slid deep into her mouth without hesitation, and he kissed her, taking exactly what he wanted while she went a little mad at the feel of him after so very long.

Ten years. Had she so totally forgotten what he tasted like in that time? What he felt like? She groaned as memories of yesterday converged with the reality of today. Sweet, like honey. Dark, like danger. Mysterious, like the ultimate forbidden fruit. He was all of that wrapped up into one sinful concoction, enticing her to let go. But she'd been here before. She knew what would happen if she did.

Her fingers dug into the flesh of his shoulders. Her entire body tensed. She knew this was the jumping-off point for her, that if she didn't end it right this second there'd be no turning back.

Something finally clicked in her brain. She pushed against his chest. Reared back. Somehow managed to break free from his wicked and talented mouth. "I can't. Zander. I—"

"You can. I've seen it." His lips were pink and close and way too tempting. She swallowed hard. "And I'm not giving you time to think of a reason to say no."

His mouth covered hers again, with a little more urgency and a lot more forcefulness. She moaned at the way he nipped at her lip, at the way he changed the angle of the kiss, at the way he dipped his tongue inside to slide over and around hers until she felt drugged from the dark taste of him. But when he pulled her hips tighter against his, brushing the hard, bare length of him against her most sensitive spot, whatever bit of self control she'd been hanging onto evaporated right out of her grasp.

She melted. Groaned. And latched on to the unbridled ecstasy she knew only he could provide.

Her hands found their way up into his hair. She wrapped her fingers around the golden strands and kissed him back. He groaned his approval, stroked deeper with his tongue and lifted her up and down in the water to rub harder against her, right where she wanted it most.

Electricity zinged along her nerve endings. Water from the pool slapped the rocks at his back as he moved. She inhaled the sweet male scent of him and reveled in the taste on her tongue.

He turned her easily, as if she weighed nothing, and then she felt the smooth rocks behind her. But all she could focus on was the hot, hard Argonaut at her front. His mouth slid to her ear, her throat, down to the hollow indent near her collarbone in a way that had always driven her wild. Fleetingly she wondered if he was strong enough for sex, but then she dismissed the thought. His wounds had already sealed shut. And in the water she was nearly weightless.

"Zander . . ." She tipped her head back, closed her eyes, lifted her hips to rub in time with his. "Oh . . ."

"Gods, you taste good." He hefted her higher in the water, until the surface of the pool hit at her lower ribs. "I need more."

Desire burned in her center. He had the straps of her camisole down before she could protest. The cool air of the cave and the water droplets sliding down her chest puckered her nipples into stiff peaks, but it was the way he groaned his approval at the sight that supercharged her blood and sent her libido into overdrive.

"Taste me," she whispered.

The arm around her waist tightened. The heavenly erection pressing into her panties throbbed. He cupped his free hand around her breast and squeezed, then lowered his lips to draw her deep into his mouth.

And the feeling . . . oh . . . better than she remembered. Hotter. Wetter. His tongue was on fire and so much more erotic than she'd dreamed. Her whole body contracted as he laved her nipple, ran his teeth over the point and sucked deep all over again.

He hitched her over to the side, moved to the other breast and laughed against her straining nipple. "Oh, yeah. Do it. Come for me."

She was about to. She'd heard of females who could orgasm simply from nipple stimulation, but she'd never been one. She lifted her chest higher, pushed against him. And then realized she was rubbing against his thigh like a dog in heat.

Embarrassment burned her cheeks. She hesitated. But his mouth was on hers before she could say anything, and he shifted her back so his cock once more pressed against her satin-covered slit.

"That's right. Stay with me," he whispered.

She groaned. Kissed him back. Shivered when his fingers found their way to the edge of her panties to follow the line of silk from her hip to her inner thigh.

"Do you want me to touch you?"

She could barely form a coherent thought, let alone answer. Desire clogged her throat as she tightened her arms around his neck and lifted her hips, granting him access. Somehow she managed to nod.

His smile was a little bit smug and completely delicious as he took her lips again and slipped two fingers beneath her panties to run along her folds.

"Oh, man, you *are* wet," he said as his mouth moved to her ear and his hot breath wound down the sensitive skin of her neck. His fingers stroked up and down, over and around, until she was moaning and riding him all over again.

"Do you want me inside?" She nodded. Grabbed tight to his hair. Nearly came when he circled her clit again. "Say it."

"Yes," she gasped. "Inside."

He pushed in one finger. "Like that?" Pulled out.

Tension gathered. She could feel it building. Needed him to keep going. "Oh . . ."

"More?"

"Yes . . ." She groaned when he did it again, this time using two fingers to fill her. "Zander, oh, gods . . ."

He stroked her deep, just the way she liked. His lips found hers again, his tongue dipping inside to stroke her mouth like he was doing with his fingers. She was already so close she knew it wouldn't take much to push her over the edge. She tightened around him, enjoying every slide and tug but wanting so much more. Her arms pulled him closer; her mouth gave exactly what he took. And she relished the groan that tore from his chest when she sucked on his tongue and wouldn't let him go.

His fingers left her heat abruptly and she moaned in protest when he tore his mouth from hers. But then his hands were pushing and pulling and her moan turned into a *yes* when she realized he was stripping her of her panties.

"No more games," he growled.

Her underwear flew by her head to land somewhere behind her on the rocks. His eyes burned into hers as he moved closer. She was so hot and needy she didn't even mind that her camisole was around her waist or that if she wasn't careful he'd see the scars on her back. Right now the only thing that mattered was him and what she desperately needed him to do to her.

"Tell me you want me," he whispered as his hands wrapped around her waist and he lifted her in the water all over again.

She gasped as he pushed his way between her legs. He braced her back against the flat rocks, leaned down and drew her earlobe into his hot, wet mouth. Between her thighs, his hard thickness pulsed as it slid up and down her naked slit.

"Tell me," he insisted, this time sucking hard on her lobe

until a shot of pain licked its way up her skin. But it didn't hurt. If anything, it felt good. He lifted his hips, rubbed up and down, found the apex of her opening.

The last ten years of wanting condensed into this one moment. "I do," she whispered. "Oh . . . Zander . . . yes . . ."

His hips surged, and she sucked in a breath as the tip of his erection wedged its way inside her. She groaned. Found his mouth. Kissed him hard. It had been so long, she'd forgotten how big he was, how much strength was gathered under those corded muscles, how insanely wicked he felt between her legs.

He pulled all the way out, pushed in just a bit more. Groaned himself as his tongue stroked hers. "Callia. Gods. You're so fucking tight. I won't be able to last if you don't ease up. You're protected, right?"

She was quaking. So close to coming herself, and he was only an inch inside her. She quivered at the thought of the full length of him thrusting deep into her body.

He pulled out again, reached down and pinched her nipples. She gasped as electricity shot between her thighs and breasts. "What kind?" he asked.

"What kind of what?" she muttered as she tried to pull him back. Why was he bothering to talk when all she wanted was him?

"Protection," he said as he lowered his head to stroke his tongue over her nipple. "I can't chance you getting pregnant again, not when Isadora and I are about to be bound." He drew her breast deep into his mouth, licked and sucked like he had before.

Only this time his mouth at her breast didn't have the same effect. Something went cold inside her. Something that only moments before had burned red hot. "You're still"—she swallowed hard—"binding yourself to Isadora?"

"Of course." He moved to her other breast. Licked the nipple. Squeezed with his hand as his cock found its way back to her crease. "I gave the king my word."

He was serious. There was no humor in his voice. And like a bolt of lightning, reality hit.

This wasn't a reunion, as she'd foolishly convinced herself earlier. While she was totally wrapped up in the emotions of being close to him after all this time, for him this was nothing but sex. And he didn't have any qualms about fucking her right this minute while his fiancée waited for him back at the castle.

Callia's stomach pitched. And a thousand different I-told-you-so's hit her from all sides.

She braced her hands against his shoulder and shoved. Hard. "Zander, stop. Wait. There's something you need to know."

CHAPTER TWELVE

Callia pushed hard against Zander's shoulder, but it was like trying to move a building. "I'm not protected. I've been in a cleansing period for the last ten years."

He stilled against her while she went cold all over. Her heartbeat hammered so loud in her ears she was sure he had to hear it. He stared down into her eyes, and she waited for him to say something, to acknowledge the fact she'd just told him she hadn't been with anyone since him or take some kind of ownership over the fact *he* was the reason she'd had to be cleansed in the first place. But he didn't do either. He just studied her with those cold, intense eyes as if he didn't believe her.

Silence settled between them. An eternity seemed to pass. The water suddenly felt cold and tainted.

Finally, he shrugged. And her heartbeat kicked up when he dipped his head and nipped her earlobe. This time hard enough to hurt. "I still want to fuck you." His hands found her hips and he pulled her close to rub against her swollen tissue all over again. "If you get pregnant you can always get rid of it again like you did last time."

Her eyes flew wide. *"What did you say to me?"*

"You heard me. And we both know you, of all people, know how that's done." His voice hardened. He reached down to maneuver his cock into position. "No more talking now, Callia. Let's fuck like we both want."

Callia could barely see straight, but with his hand beneath the water she didn't even hesitate. She lifted her leg, braced her bare foot against his rock-hard stomach and pushed as hard as she could. "You son of a bitch! How dare you!"

He stumbled backward in the water, his face full of shock and irritation when it lifted to hers. "What the hell?"

She was shaking as she jerked her camisole back up and shoved her arms through the straps, then hauled her naked ass out of the water. Only this time her tremors had nothing to do with arousal. They were spurred on by contempt. And bone-jarring anger, the kind she'd never given herself over to. Not even after he'd left her.

"Fucking A," he muttered in the water behind her as she searched for her underwear. "You're gonna get all pissy *now*? Can't you wait ten fucking minutes until we're done?"

"Go to hell!" A red haze covered her vision, but she finally spotted her panties three feet across the damp rocks. She crossed to them and pulled them on, then moved back to the bedroll Titus had set up for Zander before he left, and yanked on her pants.

She should have let him die. She never should have let Titus talk her into coming here . . .

He was out of the water and at her back before she ever heard him move. One strong hand closed around her upper arm and jerked her around to face him. "You selfish little bitch. Don't go getting all high-and-mighty on me."

"Let go of me." She braced both hands against his chest and pushed hard. Only it did little good. He was like a granite statue. Immovable. "How dare you say something like that to me!"

"How dare I what?" he mocked. "Tell the truth?" He dropped her arm as if she'd burned him, shook his head. Whatever arousal had darkened his features before was long gone. Disgust now etched its way clearly across his chiseled features. "I could have called a spade a spade and told you what you really are, but I didn't."

"Because you wanted to fuck me," she tossed back. "Not because you *care* about me."

"I stopped caring a long time ago. You made sure of that." His gaze took a heated stroll across her body, as if he had the right. As if he *owned* her. The need to cover herself swept over her, but she resisted the urge. "But I've wised up. You're the last female I'd ever want to fuck. I don't know what the hell I was thinking."

Her jaw clenched at the disdain in his eyes and the way it made her skin crawl as if *she'd* done something wrong. "And what am I?" she asked, lifting her chin in a clear shot of challenge.

His eyes narrowed to menacing slits. "A murderer."

Her mouth dropped open. She was too shocked to whisper more than "What did you call me?"

"I asked you for one thing," he growled as if he hadn't heard her. "One fucking thing. Just to wait a few days so I could work things out with Theron. But you couldn't do even that much for me, could you? You ran right off to your father and did exactly what he wanted. You got rid of my child like it meant nothing!"

Something clicked in her brain as she glanced around the dark cave, tried to reconcile what he was saying with what had happened nearly eleven years before. "Are you saying you think that I . . . you think I had an abortion?"

"I know you did!"

Her anger ebbed as ten years of confusion and hurt finally made sense. "Zander, I didn't . . . couldn't . . ." She shook her head. "I never—"

"Don't try to lie to me," he ground out. "I went to that human clinic."

Slowly, she lifted her eyes to his. Only the Argonaut standing in front of her was not the hot and bothered almost-lover she'd shared that pool with. He wasn't even the injured and battered one she'd saved from paralysis. This one was a warrior tensed for attack. A threat. A killer. One who could rip her to pieces with his bare hands if he wanted.

She swallowed hard, took one step toward him and tried

to defuse his rage. He'd warned her once it was in him, that as he hailed from Achilles's line, it was his curse to bear, and that he always fought against it so it didn't control him. But she'd never seen it full force. At least not until now.

"You were there?" she whispered.

"Oh, yeah, I was there."

"Then you know—"

"I saw the chart. Talked to a nurse. By then you and your *father* were long gone, hiding somewhere because of what you'd done. Did you think I wouldn't find out? It was all right there. In black and white." His voice lowered. "You didn't even have the decency to tell me. You just ran off in the night like the murderer you are."

"Zander." She took a deep breath, tried to calm herself because one of them sure needed to be rational here. "I didn't run off. After you left me to take care of whatever it was you needed to do, there were complications. I was bleeding. I thought I was having a miscarriage. I couldn't go to an Argolean healer because then they'd have known about . . . us."

"Liar," he whispered.

"I'm not lying. I was scared. My father found me. He took me to the human realm so I could get help. I didn't abort our baby, Zander. I tried to save him."

"Liar!"

"You have to believe me." Panic closed in as she stepped closer. The menace in his eyes was something she'd never believed possible in anyone—especially him. "I would never have hurt our child. I loved our baby. When he was born . . . you don't know what I went through for him."

"Liar!" he screamed again. "I've heard enough lies from your mouth to last an eternity."

"I wouldn't lie. Not about this—"

His hands closed over both her arms and squeezed hard. "I said enough!"

All her life she'd been a healer. Even as a child she'd known she was special, that while other Argoleans had powers that benefited themselves, hers benefited others. But when Zander grabbed her, forcing her palms to push against his chest to keep him away, the only thing she could think of was defending herself against someone who so obviously hated her with every fiber of his being.

Power rushed into her hands as if she was pulling it from some unseen force, and without thinking, she directed it right back at the threat in front of her. It flowed out of her body and she pushed it with her mind as hard as she could, without even realizing she was doing it.

Zander's eyes grew wide. He barely made a sound as he crumpled to the ground at her feet, then gasped in several breaths as if his lungs suddenly weren't working.

Her hands vibrated from the raw power that had just rushed through her, and Callia stumbled back, shocked and repulsed by what she'd done. Remnants of a rage she'd never experienced trickled through her body, leaving her nauseated and unstable. Her vision blurred, darkened, but she shook her head to clear it. Not once had she purposely hurt someone until now. Never had she known she had it in her.

Her adrenaline surged and her airway constricted. She backed up until she hit the rock wall of the cave.

"Callia . . ." Zander tried to push up on shaky hands and knees but couldn't make his limbs work. He hit the ground with a thwack.

Holy Hera. What have I done?

Terror closed in around her. She had to leave. She had to get out. She couldn't stay here. Couldn't breathe . . .

She whipped around and frantically searched for her coat. Spotting it ten feet away, she scrambled for it and the boots Titus had convinced her to wear when he brought her here in the first place.

"Callia," Zander rasped again. "Wait. I didn't . . ."

She took off running, heavy coat flapping behind her as she sprinted for the mouth of the cave and the exit toward fresh air.

Tears burned her eyes as she ran. She choked on emotions long buried but kept going, the need to get as far away as possible the only thing she could focus on. Her lungs burned, and her leg muscles screamed in protest, but she ran on.

Finally, when the pain was too much to bear, she skidded to a stop and sucked in a deep breath. Silence met her ears as she tried to slow her racing heart. Adrenaline still surged through her body, but the panic had thankfully subsided. Slowly, as her pulse came down, she became aware of her surroundings and turned a slow circle.

She was in a forest, how far from the cave she didn't know. It was dark, but enough moonlight filtered through the tall pine trees above to illuminate the frosted boughs, the snow-covered ground and the dense underbrush. Wind whistled past her face, and a shiver ran down her back. Suddenly aware of the sweat from her sprint now chilling her skin, she pulled the thick coat closed at her front and cursed her stupidity.

An owl cried somewhere above. Dried leaves and branches crackled off to her right. Callia whipped around as her heart rate rocketed, and the reality of her situation sank in deep.

She didn't know where she was. Pulse pounding, she tried to figure out which direction she'd come, but everything looked the same.

Dammit, dammit, dammit.

Dread bubbled up in her chest. The wind howling through the trees was an ominous reminder she was alone. She shivered again and pulled her coat tighter around her. Every crackle of twigs and brush, every shadow moving over the forest floor from trees swaying above, sent her anxiety spiking.

Relax. Think. It's just your imagination.

The logical side of her brain took over—the side that had saved her numerous times before. Okay, so she couldn't stand out here in the open like this for long. She'd have to wait until morning, when it was light, so she could see which way to go. Titus had mentioned a ravine and a bridge. If she could find those tomorrow, she could find the trail that would lead her back to the half-breed settlement he'd told her about. In the meantime, she'd have to find a place to hunker down out of the elements and out of sight from any predators.

She cringed, knowing she never should have let her emotions get the better of her. She should have stayed in that cave. Even if it meant staying with Zander. Damn, who was the idiot now?

Feeling marginally better, at least with a plan, she squinted through the trees and tried to figure out which way to go. The darkness was so thick, it was virtually impossible to see anything but tree trunks that all looked like gray mirror images of each other. She turned a slow circle as she searched, then swung her gaze back to the left and froze.

Could it be . . . ? Was that . . . ? She thought she'd seen something flash orange. Like a flame or a . . . campfire.

A campfire? Out here?

There it was again! She looked harder. Or could it possibly be the glow of lights through a cabin window?

Her adrenaline pulsed at either prospect. Both meant humans or half-breeds, but definitely not daemons, as they didn't need heat or creature comforts to survive. And that was enough to bring a breath of relief into her chest. Because either way it meant she wasn't alone after all. And, thank Zeus, she'd take her chances with humans over daemons any day of the week, day or night.

She took steps—slowly, because she was still unsteady— toward the light that continued to flicker far off through the trees. And told herself though the last hour had been pure hell, one good thing had come from it. She was done with Zander forever. He'd made it perfectly clear how he felt about her: he didn't. And that was all she needed to know.

There wasn't a single thing in the world that could ever draw her back to him.

The lodge was silent as Max pushed out of the gigantic featherbed he'd been given in the west wing of the mansion and landed soundlessly on the hardwood floor.

He half expected someone to come running with a club and beat him, but nothing happened. He was careful as he crept across the floor and pulled the heavy door open. A chill slid down his back from the cool night air, but nothing creaked. For a moment, he imagined some faceless god was on his side for once, then dismissed the thought. No one had ever been on his side. The only person who cared what happened to him was him.

He inched his way out of the room. The hallway was dark, only a smattering of moonlight from a window at the end of the corridor lighting his way. Since he'd been given pajamas for the first time—blue flannel checked pj's that felt like heaven against his sweat-damp skin—he was warm enough. And he knew he could get used to this kind of life. A warm bed, clean clothes and enough food to fill his belly so nothing hurt. But he was smart enough to realize this wouldn't last. Atalanta was baiting him. For what, he didn't know, but there was no way this would end well. At least for him.

Nothing moved around him. No sound met his ears as he rounded the corner and headed up the grand stairs toward Atalanta's chamber. His heart pounded hard and steady in his chest, but it wasn't fear shooting adrenaline through his body. It was excitement. And the knowledge the tide was about to shift.

He reached the top level and moved like a ghost across the hardwood. A balcony overlooked the grand staircase and the four floors below. Two massive double doors straight ahead opened to Atalanta's suite of rooms, which occupied the entire floor.

She never locked the doors. Why would she? No one dared come up here. Pulse pounding with anticipation, Max laid his hand over the doorknob and slowly turned.

No squeak, no groan, not even a whoosh of air as he pushed the door inward. Could luck really, finally, be on his side?

He moved quickly toward the bedroom. As his attic was above this level, he knew the layout of her suite better than anyone. He'd gotten used to her life drifting up to him the last few weeks. To the muffled sounds of her voice, to the rush of water from the bathroom, to the measly heat radiating upward from lamps and the furnace system that ran throughout the lodge.

He stood in the open doorway staring into the room, breathing slowly through his nose so she couldn't hear him. As a god in the Underworld, she'd never truly slept. Sure, she'd needed rest now and then, but it was nothing compared to what she needed now. Ever since they'd been in the human realm, she'd slept more and more, reinforcing what he'd already figured out: she was like him. Mortal, though somehow she still retained powers like those of the gods.

He watched the slow rise and fall of her chest. Focused in on the chain around her neck. Held his breath and waited to see if she sensed him. When she didn't move a muscle, he took a step forward.

"Think carefully before you act, young Maximus."

Max's head whipped to the side, toward the ethereal woman standing silently in the shadows beside him. His mouth dropped open at her sudden presence, and panic filled his chest.

The old woman who'd given him the glass. He'd recognize her anywhere. Tonight she seemed ghostly, almost as if she were an image and not real, her diaphanous robes as sheer as her iridescent skin. But her face was the same. Her flesh still wrinkled from time, her hair as white as snow, and her eyes . . . just as focused and intense as they'd been the first time he saw her.

"Yes," she said softly, "I am the same. And this does not concern you."

He knew no one could hear or see her but him, but it was still weird to hear her voice so clear in this silent room. He chanced a look at Atalanta, afraid maybe her godlike powers would make her aware of the woman, but she slept on silently.

Excitement pulsed all over again at that realization. Didn't concern him? No, it didn't concern *her*. Or her useless glass.

He ignored the old woman as he moved to the edge of Atalanta's bed. The pendant lay exposed above Atalanta's cleavage. Her head was tipped to the side, one arm up by her face. Her other arm was draped across her belly. The closer he got, the stronger his confidence grew.

"Maximus . . ."

He reached out a hand.

"Maximus, don't!"

His fingers grazed the pendant. Heat rushed into his limb at the first contact, and he sucked in a breath, not expecting the metal to be anything other than cold. Atalanta startled, and his gaze rushed to her face, his fingers frozen to the disk. For the first time, fear and the repercussions for being caught became very real in his mind.

An eternity seemed to pass. Sweat broke out on his skin, but he dared not move. Atalanta's eyelids fluttered but stayed closed. With a soft grunt she shifted her head in the other direction and fell back into rhythmic breaths.

And Max felt like his heart started in that moment.

Wasting no more time, he leaned over and examined the clasp of the chain.

"You do not know that with which you tamper," the old woman said, now at his side. Her voice vibrated, as if she were restraining her emotions. He continued to ignore her and used his other hand to help push in the heavy clasp. It opened with a soft click. When Atalanta still didn't move, he slid one side free from her neck and gently tugged.

Atalanta grunted, shifted her head; then the chain was free and he was holding the disk in his hand.

"Maximus, this is not a mere trinket. It never should have been in Atalanta's care, but it most definitely should not be in yours."

The hollow disk radiated energy in his hand. It slid through his fingers, into his limbs and down into his chest until it reverberated through every muscle in his body. A sense of power washed through him, and he felt like he grew three times his regular size in the seconds that followed, even though physically nothing changed.

Cool.

A smile slid across his face. Moving past the old woman, he headed back through Atalanta's sitting room until his hand landed on the outer door.

"Maximus." The old woman appeared at his side again, almost as if she'd floated through air to join him. He didn't look at her, his eyes still glued to the pendant. But from the edge of his vision, for the first time he realized she stood no taller than him. "It's not too late. There's still time for you to put it back. No one will ever know what happened here."

"Why aren't you afraid for her to have it?" he whispered, not looking away from the four empty chambers that were obviously meant to hold some kind of stones. He turned the disk in his hands. Each chamber was slightly different. One was round, one was oval, one diamond shaped. The last was triangular.

"Because she cannot wield its power."

"But I can."

The old woman didn't answer, and in her silence, Max knew the truth. Yeah, this was what Atalanta was afraid of. And he had been smart to come here and take it. His smile widened as his fingers curled around the smooth edges.

"Maximus—"

"What is it?" he asked, finally looking up. Stark fear registered in the old woman's eyes when his gaze met hers, and wasn't that interesting? She was some ancient godlike creature, and she was suddenly afraid of him. A ten-year-old boy no one wanted.

"It is"—her voice lowered—"death and destruction in the wrong hands."

His smile grew even wider. "Perfect."

"Maximus—"

Max flew down the stairs as silently as he could and into his room, where he tore off his pajamas and threw on his clothes and boots. A pang of regret zipped through him when he glanced at the warm, soft bed, but he pushed it aside. When the hollow disk was safely hidden inside his shirt, its energy radiating across his skin, he finally turned to grab his coat.

The old woman stood inside the door of his room, but this time her eyes weren't scared, they were filled with sadness. "She'll hunt you," she said quietly.

"It's better than staying here. We might not be in Tartarus anymore, but this is hell just the same. And you know it."

She shook her head slowly, that sad look still in her eyes. "You are so much like your father."

His back tingled. "An asshole?"

Her eyebrows lifted in surprise, and something like amusement crossed her face. But after everything that had been done to him, shocking some ethereal old lady with blunt language didn't even register on his I-give-a-rip chart.

"I meant—"

Oh, yeah, he was *so* not going there. "Save it. We both know I don't have a father."

"You do," she sighed. "And regardless of what you think now, there is still hope."

At her words, hatred for Atalanta's torture, for the old woman's meddling, for the parents who'd left him to rot in this hellhole whipped through him and condensed in the center of his chest, right where the pendant lay against his skin. And a rage, the kind he'd always tried to hold back, simmered right beneath the surface of his control. "There's no such thing as hope. There's only this." His hand closed over the pendant beneath his shirt. "And right now, this is mine."

He moved past her and out into the hall, almost as if the pendant were leading him, giving him strength and courage he'd never had before. And wasn't that even more cool?

"Remember your humanity, Maximus," the old woman called after him.

He nearly laughed as his feet hit the first floor and he headed for the hidden entrance he came and went through when he didn't want the house servants to see him. His humanity hadn't ever done shit for him. And it sure as hell wasn't going to save him now. He didn't need it. He didn't need anything or anyone for that matter.

He only needed himself.

Thanatos stood in the center of the run-down cabin high in the Cascade Mountains and glared at the two daemon warriors in front of him: Dumb and Dumber. "Explain how the Argonaut got away from you."

The two daemons looked at each other.

"We . . ." The one to the left shifted his gaze Thanatos's way. "When the second Argonaut showed up to aid the first, we retreated. We knew we had to report back to you about the loss of the others."

Thanatos's jaw clenched. This was why the Argonauts still lived. Because Atalanta filled her army with brainless cowards. There was a reason these morons had been in the Fields of Asphodel, awaiting sentence in Tartarus, when she'd found them. Because they were too stupid to live.

And she blamed *him* for the fact the Argonauts outsmarted them at every turn?

He rested his hand on the hilt of his sword. "And was the first Argonaut injured in battle? You said he killed six daemons. He couldn't have done that much damage unscathed."

"Well . . ." The daemon dumb enough to start this discussion looked at his pal, then at the ground where the two hunters' blood seeped into the dirty floorboards. Hunger showed clearly in their glowing green eyes. "He was still fighting."

"We wanted to make sure you didn't walk into a trap," the other daemon piped in.

The two looked at each other and nodded, like they'd just covered their asses well.

"Thank you." Thanatos gripped his sword. "You've both proven your worth."

Both daemons had the bad sense to glance at each other again and smile, their twisted lips curling over stained teeth. And Thanatos figured that was as much relief as they deserved. He drew his sword and sliced through both their necks in one fell swoop.

Their decapitated heads dropped to the ground with a smack, followed by their twitching bodies, to land on the human hunters they'd planned to feast on only moments before.

Disgusted, Thanatos slid the sword back in his scabbard and turned to look around the decrepit cabin.

Things were not going at all as he'd planned. Now, not only did he have Atalanta breathing down his neck, but he didn't even have a platoon in this region to command. He was going to have to hunt the Argonauts on his own. That or hightail it out of this forest for good and spend the rest of his life running.

Options swirled in his mind. Could he survive on his own? Atalanta would come after him. But he was smarter than the average daemon. And he still had his archdaemon powers. At least until she caught him. And killed him.

If only he'd figured out a way to get that damn disk from around her neck . . .

A sharp knock at the door of the cabin brought his head around. Followed by a voice. A soft female voice.

"Is anyone in there? I'm sorry to bother you, but I saw your light on. Hello?"

Thanatos drew in a deep breath and caught her scent. Yes, definitely female. And Argolean. And . . . special.

Now this was interesting . . .

"Hello?" She knocked again. "Is anyone there?"

How had someone of royal ancestry wandered into these woods? As questions swirled in his mind, a way out of this mess he'd created for himself condensed into a plan. A plan that didn't involve Atalanta's pendant but was just as good.

Without hesitation he jerked the door open. The female's eyes grew wide with shock, and she opened her mouth to scream, yet no sound came out. When she turned to run, he easily grabbed her arm and stopped her.

The scream that finally tore from her chest reverberated through every cell in his body. His feral smile widened.

He pulled her inside the cabin with one easy yank. "We haven't officially met, Princess. I'm the archdaemon. And right now, I'm your worst nightmare come true."

CHAPTER THIRTEEN

Zander pushed himself up to his hands and knees and took a deep breath. Okay, this time he was pretty sure he could do it without . . .

Nope. There it went.

His head spun like he was on the mother of all benders. Sonofabitch. What the hell did she do to him? She was a healer, for crap's sake.

The sound of heavy footfalls reached his ears, echoing down the long tunnel. For a second he held his breath and listened, then exhaled when he realized who it was.

Titus.

He'd know the sound of the Argonaut anywhere. They'd spent enough time together wandering backcountry and hunting daemons for Zander to pick Titus out based on his clod-stomper footsteps alone. Sure enough, the scents of pine and fresh blood wafted on the air, followed by Titus's gravelly breath.

"Callia? I'm back."

Zander eased back to rest on his heels but kept his head down. Man, when he saw her again . . .

"Z," Titus said as he came around the corner, surprise in his voice. "You're up."

Zander focused on the rocks in his direct line of sight and worked on knocking back the motherfucking migraine.

Titus chuckled. "I woulda thought by now you'd be almost back to normal. Brother, you don't look so good."

"I'm fine."

"Oh, yeah, I can see that." Titus chuckled again, "By the way, you're butt-ass naked."

Zander thought about flipping Titus the bird, but that would take too much energy.

Titus's feet shuffled on the rocks to Zander's right. "Where's Callia?"

"Gone."

"Gone? Gone where?"

"Away, I guess."

"Away? What the hell happened?"

"Nothing." Zander pushed to stand, irritation fueling him, then had a moment of *Oh, shit* when the room spun. He reached out a hand to steady himself on the rock wall. "It's none of your damn business anyway."

"Tell me you at least sent her home." When Zander didn't answer, Titus added, "Zander. Tell me you fucking opened the portal and sent her back to Argolea."

"I might have," he mumbled. "But she didn't give me a chance."

"Fuck me," Titus breathed. "You let her leave, in the middle of the night?" He pointed down the dark tunnel. "It's twenty degrees out there. And snowing. Not to mention there are daemons roaming this area. You know she has to find holy ground to open the portal on her own. She's not an Argonaut. She can't open it from anywhere. And we're on the top of a fucking mountain."

"Wait." One hand braced on the rock wall, Zander lifted his head. "You and Demetrius didn't take care of the rest of those daemons?"

Titus ran a hand through his wavy dark hair, frustration radiating off him in waves. "By the time I found Demetrius, he was so bloody and banged up he could barely lift his parazonium. The two fuckers he was fighting didn't look much better, and when they saw me, they bailed. I got Demetrius home, then came back for you and Callia. But sure as shit, those daemons didn't get too far away."

Skata. A rush of adrenaline speared Zander's chest and spread beneath his ribs. He scanned the cave floor, seeing it clearly for the first time since he'd awoken and found Callia leaning over him. He spotted fresh clothes—ones Titus must have hauled back when he'd brought Callia to heal him—and stooped to pull on the pants. "She can't have gotten far."

How long had she been gone? Ten minutes? Fifteen? Panic edged its way in. Shit, why had he let her leave?

"What the hell did you say to her, Zander?" Titus quickly checked his blade and shoved it back in its scabbard.

"Nothing. I . . ." He jerked on his shirt, dropped to the ground and shoved his feet into fresh boots as the conversation with Callia replayed through his mind. Every goddamn word of it.

"Fuck," Titus whispered. "You dumb shit."

Zander clenched his jaw and went back to lacing his boots. Rage pushed its way up his torso. Rage over Titus's suddenly protective nature where Callia was concerned—who the hell did he think he was anyway?—and the way Callia had flat out lied to his face in this cave minutes ago. And about something so precious, so important too. But he fought it back, pushed it down, breathed deep so he could stay in control. Regardless of the things she'd done, he didn't want her dead. And he needed Titus's help right now if he was going to find her before she got herself into serious trouble.

He rose to his feet, threw on his jacket and lifted his bloody weapons from the ground. "Let's just go fucking find her, all right?"

Zander took off at a jog down the darkened corridor, not caring about the supplies they'd left behind. Ahead, moonlight illuminated the opening of the cave and the snowflakes falling in a sea of white from the sky. At least two inches of fresh powder had accumulated recently, and there were tracks in the snow. Boot marks that had to be Titus's from where he'd stepped through the portal right outside the cave, and smaller ones. Ones that were already filling in.

"There," Zander said, pointing to what had to be Callia's footprints leading away from the tunnel.

"She was running." Titus squatted on his haunches, examining the tracks.

Zander frowned. Yeah, well, no shit, Sherlock. She'd wanted away from his ass as fast as possible, hadn't she? He rubbed a hand over his temple, the lingering effects of the energy she'd so easily inflicted on him still hovering behind his skull.

Titus pushed up on his thighs and stood. "She's not that far ahead of us. We should be able to catch her if we hustle."

Her footprints were easy to follow until the snowfall increased and the forest turned into a sheet of white. They tracked her for a least a mile through the trees before the snow covered her prints. Zander stopped and turned a slow circle as big, white, chunky flakes fell all around him and clung to his hair, eyelashes and the stubble on his jaw. Dammit, where was Demetrius when they fucking needed him? "There's nothing out here."

Titus scanned the eerily dark forest. His mustache and soul patch were white with ice crystals. He squinted and pointed through the trees. "There. A light."

Zander held up a hand to block the snow from slapping him in the eyes. "What is that? A fire?"

"A house of some kind. There's nowhere else to hide out here, and contrary to what you think, she's not stupid. She wouldn't stay out in the open, no matter how pissed at you she is."

Zander ignored the jab and picked up his pace. He made it another fifty yards in the trees before pain exploded behind his eyes and radiated through his skull all over again. Only this time it was a hundred times worse than what Callia had thrown his way.

"Mother . . . fucker." He grabbed for a tree trunk, swayed but caught himself before he went down.

"What the hell's wrong with you now?" Titus asked, stepping up beside him.

Zander pressed his fingers against his temples, leaned his shoulder against the Douglas fir at his side. "I don't know." Another sharp pain gouged out the area behind his eyes. "Son of a fucking bitch."

"Is it your back?"

"No." He cringed as the pain knifed him again. "It's my fucking . . . head."

"When did you hit your damn head?"

"I didn't." He leaned forward, tried to give gravity a chance to ease the throb. "What the hell did she give me?"

"Nothing that would have fucked up your head. Holy crap, Zander. Eight hundred years with barely a scratch, and in the span of two days you're about to keel over. Old age has finally hit you, moron."

That couldn't be it. This was something else, but Zander didn't know what.

"Come on, old geezer," Titus said, tugging at Zander's sleeve with his gloved hand. "We gotta find Callia. Then we'll have her take a look at your pathetic head."

"She'll probably bash it in," Zander mumbled. But he let Titus pull him along and tried not to think of what might happen when they found her, only focused on finding her before it was too late.

Fear drowned out the scream in Callia's throat as her body sailed through the air. She smacked into the far wall of the cabin and slumped to the ground. Pain ricocheted off her forehead where she'd hit the hard wood, a stabbing sensation behind her eyes. In a daze she tried to get up, but her head spun, and stars fired off in her line of sight.

"You make this too easy, Princess," the daemon growled behind her. "Get up."

She shook her head, rolled to her back and pushed up on shaking hands. Then wished she'd kept her back turned. The monster coming toward her was straight out of a nightmare. Seven feet of quivering muscles. His catlike face didn't mesh with the sharp pointy ears, the goat horns sticking out of his head or his human body. But his fangs were a clear reminder he was anything but docile. She'd run into a daemon once before—in Greece—but that one hadn't been nearly as large as this one. And he definitely hadn't been as menacing.

Adrenaline spiking, she scooted backward, but hit the wall. She glanced right and left, desperately searching for a way out. The cabin was small, nothing but a main room and a doorway that led to what looked like a tiny kitchen. A table blocked her path.

She wished beyond wishing she could blend into the wall or flash herself somewhere else like she could in Argolea. A piece of broken porcelain from a bowl he'd thrown at her earlier caught her eye. She picked it up and heaved it toward the daemon.

"I see you want to play." He deflected the shard and stepped over—oh, gods—what looked like a pile of bloodied, decapitated bodies. Her stomach roiled. She scrambled to her feet and darted toward a wooden table, putting it between her and the monster.

The daemon chuckled. "Imagine my surprise, running into you here, of all places." A menacing smile slid across his gnarled face, his sharp teeth glinting in the low light from a lamp above. "I have to be the luckiest archdaemon ever."

Terror made it hard for her to latch on to coherent thoughts. But two got through. One, for some reason this beast thought she was Isadora. And two, from her schooling she knew the archdaemon supposedly had powers none of the other daemons did, though just what those were, she couldn't remember.

She was dead if she stayed put. In hopes the cabin had a back door, she turned and ran through the kitchen. She made it two steps before he grabbed her from behind. Claws raked across the top of her chest and lower abdomen, and she screamed in pain as he dragged her back into the main room.

"A fighter, I see." The daemon threw her onto the table. Her back and skull hit the old wood with a deafening thwack, though the pain was nothing compared to the fire burning in her torso. The massive hand holding her down was like ten tons weighing on her chest. "Do you know, Princess, what the biggest perk is to being the arch-daemon?"

She struggled, tried to roll off the table, but couldn't move more than a few inches. Blood soaked through her shirt, and the burn intensified.

"No?" he answered for her. "Then I'll tell you." He leaned over, so close the vile stench of his breath triggered her gag reflex. She tried to turn her head but his other hand caught her face. She looked up into glowing green, soulless eyes. "I'm not impotent like those other fuckers."

Terror turned to bone-melting horror. She struggled harder. His foul laughter echoed all around her as she fought against his rock-solid hold.

"Ah, Princess," he growled. "This is going to be fun."

"What have you found, Thanatos?"

Callia froze at the sound of the sharp female voice. The daemon loosened his grasp enough to allow her to look to the side. A woman dressed in red stood on the far side of the cabin as if she'd appeared from thin air. Her robe draped over one elegant shoulder, the waist cinched in tight. The long, flowing fabric pooled on the ground at her feet. Her skin was like alabaster, her hair a long fall of black silk, and though she was easily as tall as the daemon, she was a thousand times more graceful. But her eyes . . . her eyes were just as dead and soulless as his.

Atalanta.

Though pain still seared across her abdomen, Callia sucked in a breath and held it. Evil—true evil—swirled in the room as Atalanta moved forward.

The daemon let go of Callia and straightened at the side of the table. He bowed his head. "My queen. I—I did not expect you."

"Of course you didn't," Atalanta said. "Which is why I'm here." She moved closer. "Why have you not killed this Argolean?"

The daemon's glowing eyes darted Callia's way and back again. "She . . . My queen, she is of royal blood."

Atalanta's dark eyes narrowed as she moved closer. A spark of recognition crossed her flawless face as she studied Callia. "Why, Thanatos," she said in a somewhat shocked voice, "she is." Her gaze slid down the length of Callia's body and back up again, and she drew in a deep breath, closing her eyes in the process.

Callia didn't move. She wasn't sure what was happening, but she sensed there was some kind of power struggle going on between these two. The daemon was all but vibrating at her side, and as her eyes darted his way, she saw the way his clawed hands clenched and unclenched at his sides, a very clear indication he wasn't happy with Atalanta's interruption.

Panic clawed its way up Callia's throat. Her gaze darted back to Atalanta, who still had her eyes closed and seemed to be focusing on . . . something.

This was not good at all. Callia's muscles went rigid. Her situation had not improved.

Atalanta's eyes popped open, and she focused in on the daemon. "You've done well, Thanatos."

He breathed a sigh of relief. His hands unclenched.

"This time," Atalanta added. She nodded down at Callia. "She's not just royal. She's the boy's mother."

The daemon's jaw dropped open. He looked down at Callia, then back at Atalanta. "The—"

"Bring her. If the boy doesn't cooperate, she might become useful after all." Atalanta turned for the door.

The daemon hesitated, seemed to debate his options, but then he grabbed Callia's arm and pulled her up.

Fire erupted in Callia's abdomen all over again, and she cried out as the daemon jostled her into a sitting position. Blood spurted from the gash across her chest and torso.

Atalanta whipped back around and for the first time focused in on the bloody wounds. Her gaze darted toward the daemon. "You weren't going to kill her."

"I . . ." The daemon shifted his grip so he was behind Callia. "She fought back."

Atalanta's eyes burned to sharp points of light. "You were going to use her as a bargaining chip." She advanced. "Were you planning to create your own heir?"

The daemon let go of Callia's arm and took a step back. He held up his hands in front of him. "No, my queen. Of course not. I was going to bring her to you."

Alarm rang through Callia's mind.

"Liar!" Atalanta's hand shot out. Callia ducked down on the table and covered her head. A beam of energy blasted from Atalanta's palm and hit the daemon square in the chest. His body sailed back and crashed into the pantry on the back end of the small closet-sized kitchen. The shelves splintered and collapsed. Pots and pans, jars and cans rained down around him. He groaned and tried to get up but couldn't.

"I am the only ruler in this world. Not even the gods can touch me." Atalanta skirted the table and shot another blast at the daemon.

He moaned and writhed. "My . . . queen."

She stood over him, menace washing her face white. "I am the only queen you will ever know. My mercy saved you, Thanatos. And your quest for power just condemned you."

She blasted him again, and Callia covered her ears and curled into herself to block the nightmarish screams from her mind. Burning flesh scarred the air. It wasn't until smoke drifted out of the kitchen that she realized that with Atalanta distracted, this was her one shot to get away.

Callia dropped her hands. Pain radiated across her torso. Sweat slid down her temple. Before she got a foot on the floor, Atalanta was in front of her.

Atalanta reached out a hand. Callia tensed, half expecting

another pulse of energy to split her in two, but there was nowhere to go.

Atalanta's hand hovered directly over Callia's wounded stomach and chest. And as Callia had done to her own patients too many times to count, she felt the wounds closing from the inside out. Sharp sparks of pain pulsed all around the gashes, and she hissed in an agonizing breath. The pain condensed until it was drawn out like a needle pulling thread, leaving behind only a mild sting. Bewildered, she stared down at her stomach as the twinges prickled her skin, and the slashes in her flesh sealed themselves right before her eyes.

Slowly, she looked up. Atalanta's eyes were closed as Callia's often were when she provided a healing treatment. And though it was completely insane, a strange sort of communion passed between them. Healer to healer. Female to female. Mother to . . .

Suddenly the demigod's face contorted and she jerked her hand back. Her coal black eyes flew open and zeroed in on Callia's. "I see what you and the others have planned, Eirene."

"What?" Instinct told Callia whatever the demigod had seen was not good. "I . . ."

Atalanta took three frantic steps back, reached for something at her chest. Her face darkened as she grappled against the fabric of her robe. She froze. Fury raced across her features, colored her pale skin red. "Maximus!"

Her bellow shook the small cabin.

Atalanta jerked toward Callia again. "Killing you solves two problems. You and your guardian will pay for Maximus's treason." The demigod held out the hand that had burned the daemon into dust and started toward Callia. Only this time there was no healing in her expression. There was pure, unadulterated murder.

Oh, shit.

Callia braced herself. Wished like hell she'd stayed in that cave with Zander after all. And then she screamed.

* * *

The light grew stronger. As they came to a break in the trees, Zander realized Titus was right. The glow was coming from the windows of some kind of cabin. He squinted to see clearer. Would Callia be desperate enough to turn to humans for help?

"Depends on how bad you pissed her off," Titus said at his side.

Zander cut his gaze to the guardian beside him, not for the first time hating the fact Titus knew every one of his goddamn thoughts.

Titus frowned. "For the record, I'm not wild about it either." He nodded toward the run-down cabin. "You wanna knock or go balls-in?"

Zander was just about to tell Titus where he could stick his balls when a roar shook the trees, followed by a sharp, shrill, bone-chilling scream. His muscles tensed. The headache he'd been battling the last five minutes dimmed to a passing throb. Instinct ruled as he reached for his blade. "That was Callia."

Titus grabbed for his own parazonium. "You sure?"

Hell yeah, he was sure. He'd know the sound of her voice anywhere.

"Zander, wait!"

Zander charged the front door of the cabin and kicked it in with his boot. A blur of red whipped his way. The eyes of the female peering back at him grew so wide he could see the whites all around her black irises. Behind her, Callia lay faceup on a table, her shirt ripped open, blood staining her skin and clothing.

He lifted his blade, let the rage consume him and charged.

Atalanta flicked her hand his way.

"Zander!" Callia screamed. "No!"

Energy shot into his body and threw him backward, a lot like it had in the cave when Callia had attacked him, only this was ten thousand times worse. He hit the doorjamb hard. Wood shattered around him as he fell out of the cabin and landed with a brutal thump against the frozen ground.

Wood rained down from above. Pain ricocheted through his torso and stole his breath.

Voices echoed from inside. Callia's? Titus's? Screams followed by more shouts. Growls and roars erupted from behind the building, followed by the clank of weapon against weapon.

"Zander! Get the fuck in here!"

Zander pushed up on shaky hands and knees. Ground his teeth against the pain and hauled his ass forward. He wobbled, caught himself, lurched for the doorway. When he finally got there and looked inside, the scene was something out of a nightmare.

Titus faced off against two daemons, his blade arcing out and around. Callia darted under the table to get away from a third. Her arm was bloody, her face ashen and bruised. Atalanta was nowhere in sight.

"Zander!" The daemon advancing on Callia caught her foot and hauled her back and out from under the table. He flipped her to her back. As he brought his blade back, she leapt to her feet and thrust her hands against the monster's chest.

The daemon howled in relentless pain but was strong enough to backhand her across the room. She hit the far wall with a deafening thwack and slumped to the floor.

Sharp points stabbed into Zander's head all over again, but he charged anyway, swinging his blade out and around to nail the fucker in the side. Blood spurted from the open wound and sprayed over him and the floor.

The daemon stumbled, righted himself. He swung with his left hand, caught Zander's shirt with his claws and tore through his flesh. A sword followed, barely missing Zander's arm.

"I won't let you take the princess, Argonaut," the daemon roared. He arced out again with his blade.

Zander tried to swivel, but his body wasn't moving at the speed of his brain. It was like trying to fight in water. The daemon lifted his sword for the killing blow. A growl erupted from the other side of the room. The sound distracted the daemon for a split second, and Zander ducked beneath the monster's arm. He stumbled out from behind him, lifted his own blade high with both arms. "Go back to hell, mother-fucker." He swung hard, though it took every ounce of energy he had, slicing deep into the daemon's side.

The monster shrieked, fell to his knees. Zander struck again, slicing into the beast's arm, his back, his other side. Blood spewed in every direction, most of it hitting Zander in the face. The daemon dropped to the ground, but Zander kept attacking. Rage consumed him, the kind he never let free, and each time he struck, he saw Callia as he had when he'd stepped into the cabin, laid out like an offering to Atalanta.

His parazonium stabbed the creature's back, a sickening sucking noise echoing through the small cabin when he pulled the blade free and attacked again, never once aiming for the daemon's neck. It was too soon to end the SOB's suffering. He struck again and again, his vision blurring in a sea of red.

Someone plowed into Zander's side, knocking him off balance. Zander hit the floor with a sharp thunk. Surprise widened his eyes as he looked up at Titus, then morphed quickly to fury. "You motherfucking son of a bitch!"

Titus knocked the parazonium out of Zander's hands. Zander snarled and tried to push himself up, but he was weaker than he thought, and whatever was affecting him was kicking in good now. He tried to get up but fell right back on his ass.

The daemon behind Titus rumbled and made a move to initiate round two, but Titus didn't give him a chance. His blade arced out to sever the creature's head from its body with one fell swoop. Then he swung back toward Zander. "Rein it in, Z."

Struggling, Zander made it to his feet. Sweat and blood

slid down his face to drip onto his chest as he narrowed his eyes. His heart pounded hard against his ribs. Menace rolled off him in waves. One word echoed through his mind: *Kill.*

Titus widened his stance. "Think this through carefully, Zander. I don't care if you're fucking immortal or not. I'll cut you if I have to. And trust me, it'll hurt."

Zander sneered and crouched down ready to strike, his focus zeroed in on the body and blade in front of him.

"Fuck, me," Titus whispered. He gripped his blade tighter. "That daemon's dead, Zander. They're all dead. And Atalanta's gone. I'm not the enemy here. I'm your friend. Your brother. Trust me, man. You don't want to do this."

It was like looking through a tunnel, with sound and sights on the periphery blacked out. But as Zander focused on Titus, on the way the guardian's chest rose and fell with his labored breaths, on the sweat pouring down his face, on the way he was fixated on Zander like *he* was the enemy, a strange sort of realization dawned.

Slowly, Zander's eyes swept the room, first landing on the daemon he'd been fighting, dead on the ground beside him, then to the pile of bodies across the floor and finally to where Callia lay slumped unconscious against the wall. Awareness flickered through his head, shifting the boiling darkness consuming him into something softer and far more familiar. And like a balloon suddenly popping, air whooshed out of his lungs.

"Callia," he whispered. Eyes locked on her, he rose from his crouch. His energy flagged as he brushed by Titus and dropped to the floor next to her. "Callia? Oh, shit."

Titus's blade clattered to the floor behind him. "Holy Hades," he muttered.

Zander tore Callia's shirt the rest of the way open, saw nothing but faint white lines against her chest. He felt for a pulse at her neck, found a weak thump beneath his fingers. He cradled her head in his hands. "Callia, wake up."

She didn't move. Her head lolled to the side like a rag doll.

"Callia?" Zander said louder. "Wake up. Shit. Titus!"

"*Skata.*" Titus pushed Zander's hands out of the way and felt for himself. "Her pulse was low but there when I checked a minute ago." He moved his fingers against her throat. "There. It's there. She's alive."

Alive. But not for long. Now that the rage had passed, Zander's brain was working. But that was about it. "I can't get her back to Argolea." Panic clawed its way up his chest. "I'm too weak to open the portal."

Titus's intense gaze focused in on Zander. Quickly he pulled something from his pocket, chucked it at Zander. Zander caught the satellite phone with both hands while Titus shifted his arms under Callia and lifted her from the floor. "I can't take her back to Argolea either."

"What? You have to. Look, if this is about earlier, I—"

Titus headed for the door. "I can't take her back and leave you here. You look almost as bad as she does. There'll be more daemons coming."

"I can take care of myself." Zander pushed up, stumbled, would have gone down if the wall hadn't been there to break his fall. What the hell was happening to him? He paused, sucked in a breath. He'd been through countless battles before, and none had ever left him as weak as he was now.

"Do you have your tracking medallion?" Titus asked from the doorway.

Zander reached for the small round medallion all the Argonauts wore that was their one beacon for help when they were in trouble. "No. Shit. I must have lost it somewhere near that ravine. Or in the cave."

"I lost mine too." Titus hitched Callia higher in his arms. "Call Nick."

"Nick?" Zander darted a look at the satellite phone in his hand. The one Nick had given each of them before they'd left on their hunt from the half-breed settlement days before. The one he'd thought was useless.

"Tell Nick how to reach us." Titus headed out into the snow with Callia. "And haul ass, Zander. Atalanta didn't just poof out of here for no reason. She wants your girl, and I guarantee she'll be back. With an army this time."

CHAPTER FOURTEEN

"There's nothing wrong with him."

"What do you mean there's nothing wrong? He looks like he's about to kick it any minute."

Voices drifted to Zander's ears, rousing him from the blackness surrounding him like a shroud. He felt like he was pushing his way through a thick, soupy haze that didn't want to clear and was fogging both his vision and mind.

"Physically," the female voice said again, "there's nothing wrong with him. I can't find a single thing that explains his deterioration. But I can tell you this. Every time her vitals dip, so do his."

"What are you saying?" a male voice asked. Unfamiliar. Deep.

"I'm saying," the female said on a sigh, "they're linked. In a way I've never seen before. Nothing we do to him affects her, but that's definitely not the case the other way around."

Zander strained to listen through the fog.

"Are you telling me there's nothing you can do for him?" a male voice asked. This one Zander had heard before. But where? He struggled to make the connection but couldn't. And why wasn't his brain working?

"That's exactly what I'm telling you," the female said. "We have to focus on her."

"Then focus, dammit," the familiar male voice said again.

"We are." This time the female's voice held an edge of frustration. "The problem is, you're not hearing what I'm saying. It's not the injuries that are killing her."

"Then what is it?" another female asked. This one too was familiar, calm where the others were frustrated, and Zander found himself struggling to bring his eyes open so he could make the connections he knew were right on the tip of his mind. He squinted but couldn't see more than a hazy film.

"She doesn't seem to have a will to live."

"*Skata.*"

Okay, that voice was clear as a bell. Zander knew Theron's voice anywhere.

On a groan, Zander rolled to his side and pushed himself up to sit. Pain stabbed every inch of his body, but he ignored it. The bed beneath him was firm, more like a gurney than a mattress. He looked up and around as his vision came and went, took in the white walls and bandages and tape on the long counter to his right and realized he was in some kind of medical facility.

The half-breed colony. Which meant Titus had gotten him and Callia here after all.

Links, memories, flashes of what had happened in that cave, in that cabin, hit him from all sides. *Callia.* His feet hit the floor. Almost went out from under him. To keep from sliding to the ground he braced a hand on the bed behind him until he was steady, then slowly followed the sound of voices toward the hall.

Shit. He was weak. Weaker than he'd been his whole life. Just crossing the room made him feel like he'd climbed Mount Olympus.

He gritted his way through the pain. When he rounded the corner and looked down the long narrow hall, he discovered he'd been right. A small group was huddled deep in conversation. Theron, Casey, Nick and a female who wore blue scrubs and held a clipboard.

"Zander, oh, my God." Casey rushed to his side and tried to take his weight by slipping an arm around his waist, but he brushed her off and leaned one hand against the wall near her head instead. "You shouldn't be out of bed."

He ignored the king's daughter, the one who would never

be queen because her mother had been human, and looked at Theron. "Where's Callia?"

"She's being monitored," the female said before Theron could answer.

The woman was average height for a half-breed female, average weight. Her dark hair was pulled back into a pony-tail and she had *nerd* written all over her plain-Jane fea-tures. She also obviously didn't think much of him, because the scowl on her face was anything but friendly.

Zander dismissed her and looked over her head toward Nick, standing on her other side, looking like he had a mi-graine the size of Mount Rushmore. *Join the fucking club.* Nick dwarfed the woman in both size and confidence. "I want to see her."

"Zander," Casey cut in with a hand on his arm. "That's not a good idea."

Zander glanced down at Theron's wife, his eyebrows drawn together, while a strange feeling brewed in his chest. They were keeping something from him. "Why not?"

Theron pushed away from the wall where he'd been leaning to stand at Casey's side. "Because she's not doing well. And neither are you. You're in no position to . . ."

Zander's gaze jumped to Theron, and warning bells went off in his head. What was Theron doing here? If Titus had gone to Argolea and brought him back, and Casey had come with him, it meant something wasn't right. These days Casey stuck close to the castle for Isadora's sake.

"Don't fuck with me, Theron. Did she wake up? How long has it been?"

"It's only been twenty-four hours," Theron sighed.

Zander cut a look at the healer, then refocused on Theron again. And he knew his temper flared in his eyes, but he didn't give a rip. "Twenty-four hours? Why the hell haven't you taken her back to Argolea if they can't do shit for her here?"

"Watch it, hero," Nick mumbled from across the narrow hall.

Zander's eyes whipped to the leader of the half-breeds.

"Don't piss him off," the female muttered to Nick. "You saw her scars."

"What the hell are you mumbling about?" Zander glared down at her. "And who in Hades are you anyway?"

"Lena," Nick said behind her, straightening from the wall himself. "One of our best healers. So ditch the attitude, or I'll put your ass back in that bed myself."

Zander's jaw ticked, and that familiar feeling of rage pushed against his chest. The only thing that kept him from losing his cool was the palm of Theron's hand now pushing against his sternum.

"Everybody chill out for a few minutes," Theron said. He glared down at Lena. "And cut the digs. Tell him what you just told us."

The female heaved out a breath like she didn't want to tell him anything, but finally said, "Do you know anything about daemon poison?"

"Daemon *what*?"

"Poison," she said louder, challenging Zander with her eyes in a way that made him wonder what the hell he'd ever done to her. He was 100 percent sure they'd never met. "An archdaemon's claws are filled with a poison. Even if the wounds heal, the poison destroys healthy tissue one cell at a time. If it gets into the bloodstream, it travels to the organs and does the same, though at a much slower rate."

"What are you saying?" Zander asked.

"She's saying Callia's infected, Zander," Theron said. "Titus told us what happened in that cabin. Atalanta sealed Callia's wounds, trapping the poison inside."

Zander looked from face to face, trying to make sense of what they'd just told him. "I've been cut, bitten. All the guardians have been wounded. You—"

"You've never been cut by an archdaemon," Theron said.

"Odds are good none of you have tangled with an archdaemon," Nick cut in. As Zander glanced his way, Nick frowned, the expression doing shit to settle the unease in

Zander's gut. "The archdaemon doesn't usually fight. He commands. We've seen this before. Certain victims my scouts have come across have had the festering type of wound Lena described. We didn't know what it was until we found a female, alive, with a similar wound on her leg."

Lena looked down at her feet, pursed her lips as if she'd heard it all before, but Zander didn't miss the revulsion sliding over her features or the way she refused to meet his or any of the others' eyes.

"She was pregnant," Nick went on. "In a great deal of pain. She'd been raped. Repeatedly." Casey gasped, and Nick rubbed a hand over his forehead, like just the thought sickened him as well. "We tried to help her, but she wouldn't let us. She begged us to kill her."

"From what we can tell," Lena finished for Nick when it was clear he didn't want to go on, "the archdaemon is the only one who can reproduce. We think he uses this poison to immobilize his victims and keep them alive long enough to give birth."

"Dear God," Casey said, covering her mouth with her hand. At his side, Theron slipped an arm around her waist and drew her close.

"The rate of gestation seems to be severely amplified for daemon offspring," Lena continued. "A month, maybe two. We're not entirely sure. We haven't been able to study it."

"Study it?" Zander snapped. "Like a science experiment?" His thoughts ran back to Callia. To the way she'd been laid out on that table before Atalanta.

"We did find one of these offspring shortly after birth," Nick said, flicking Zander a warning look before focusing on Theron. "Dead. Its body looked human, but there was something about the eyes that wasn't right. And the internal organs—"

"When we did an autopsy," Lena cut in, "we found it wasn't like us at all. Six-chambered heart, three lungs, two sets of kidneys. Imagine a race of these half-breed daemons living among us. It would be like—"

"The ultimate new weapon," Theron finished for her, his jaw flexing.

Zander barely caught what they were saying. His stomach rolled, and he kept seeing Callia, bloodied and bruised. Heard her screams in that cabin before they'd gotten there. He pushed his hand against the wall to give him something solid to focus on so he didn't lose it right there and then. "Is she . . . ?" Gods, he couldn't even say the words. "Was she . . . ?"

"No," Lena said quickly. "There's no sign of sexual assault to the female you brought in. We think you got there right after he infected her. The other guardian who came in with you explained what you found—we think some kind of power struggle between the archdaemon and Atalanta. Maybe he was going to impregnate her, but Atalanta had other plans? We just don't know."

Relief was quick and consuming, but as fast as it hit, it faded. Zander ignored the half-breed healer's babbling. "What did you do for the others? The ones you found who were infected?"

"Nothing."

"Why—?"

"They all died, hero," Nick said.

Zander's gaze jumped back to Theron, now holding Casey tight at his side. Tears brewed in Casey's eyes. Sympathy stretched across Theron's face.

"No." Zander turned his back on Theron and refocused on the healer. Panic and urgency rushing through his veins. "There has to be something you can do."

Lena sighed and dropped her crossed arms. "There's nothing. I—"

"Zander," Theron said, reaching for his arm.

Zander shook off Theron's hand. Fuck that. They were all acting like this was a lost cause, and it wasn't. It couldn't be. "Callia's a *healer*."

"So am I," Lena said, frustration edging her voice higher.

"But it doesn't matter. She can't heal herself, and my powers aren't strong enough for this."

It did matter. Callia was all that mattered right now. Zander's eyes slammed shut. His mind spun. Images of Callia over the last few days whipped behind his eyelids like a movie. Her taking care of him, her cradling his body in that cave, warming him with her heat, enticing him with her essence. Hurting him. His disjointed thoughts stopped spiraling long enough to latch on to that moment. To what she'd done to him. To what she'd almost done to that daemon who'd tossed her across the cabin.

His eyes popped open. "Her powers are transferable."

"What?" Lena asked. "How do you know that?"

How did he know? Because he'd seen it with his own eyes. And felt it in his own damn body. "Because she showed me. Her gift is being able to draw pain and illness out of the body. She can also throw it back. You can tap into that. Use your powers to harness hers and extract the poison."

Lightbulbs flashed on behind Lena's light brown eyes. "Theoretically, that might work. But how would I trigger it? She'd have to push pretty damn hard for me to pull out the infection. And she's unconscious. We have her sedated right now, but even without the drugs, mentally she's out of it."

"You get her off those drugs," Zander said, "and I can get her to do it."

"You?" Lena asked with disdain. "You can barely stand up straight yourself."

Zander edged away from the wall, swayed, caught himself. A renewed sense of purpose pulsed in his veins, giving him the strength he needed to get through whatever happened next. "I'm fine."

Lena shook her head, and the contempt Zander had sensed in her before came back full force. She crossed her arms over her chest, dangled the clipboard from one hand. "I really don't care if you pass out, Argonaut. But I'm curious how you, of all people, can trigger her powers."

"She has to be good and pissed."

Lena's eyes narrowed. "You don't say."

"Lena," Nick murmured, a warning in his voice.

She brushed Nick's hand off with a flick of her wrist, her gaze locked on Zander. "And I suppose you're the one person in the world she's got reason to be pissed at."

It occurred to Zander this little half-breed was gunning for him, but he didn't know why, and honestly, he didn't fucking care. The only thing he cared about right now was getting to Callia and getting her the help she needed. "Yeah, that's right. No one pisses her off more than me. Now are we going to do this or what?"

Lena's eyes tightened to thin slits, and she clenched her jaw so hard, Zander was sure her teeth ground together. "Yeah, we'll do this. But get one thing through your head, *Argonaut*. When she wakes, she's not leaving here with you." Her gaze cut to Theron. "She's not leaving here with either of you."

Confused, Zander looked to Theron, who'd let go of Casey and now stood at Zander's side in a very clear, very defensive posture.

"Lena," Nick said firmly. "That isn't our concern."

"Too bad, Nick," the female tossed over her shoulder. "I'm making it my problem. I saw the scars on her back. I know what they mean. And I know you of all people know what they mean too."

"Scars?" Casey asked. "What scars?"

Lena's fiery gaze swung Casey's way. "The ones she got when she was punished."

"Punished?" Zander's brow wrinkled. He didn't remember scars. Not anywhere on Callia's smooth, creamy skin.

"Nick," Theron warned in a low voice, "put a leash on your female."

"I'm not of your world, *Argonaut*," Lena spouted before Nick could stop her. "And no one 'puts a leash' on me." She turned fully to Casey. "Did your Argonaut here tell you how they treat females in his world?"

"Lena—"

"You should know," Lena said, ignoring Nick again. "Seeing as how you live there now."

"Nick—" Theron started.

"She's got every right to speak her mind, hero." Testosterone all but bounced off the hallway walls. Nick moved in to stand directly behind Lena in an offensive move none of them missed. "Especially on this. And we both know she's right."

"What is everyone talking about?" Casey asked. Her violet eyes searched the group with a level of frustration Zander felt all the way to his bones.

Lena's features settled into a smug expression. "Males in their world"—she gestured toward Theron and Zander with her chin—"can do whatever the hell they want. But females? They're under a whole different set of rules."

"Theron," Casey said cautiously, looking toward her husband. "What is she talking about?"

Theron's jaw visibly twitched as he stared at the healer. "It's an archaic tradition. One that's not practiced anymore. The cleansing ceremony hasn't been used in ages."

Cleansing ceremony.

The blood drained from Zander's face.

"Tell that to the female in that room with lash marks embedded in her skin."

Casey gasped.

Lena took one seething step toward Zander. "I don't care if she screwed around on you or humiliated you in front of the whole kingdom. No woman deserves to be whipped like a dog. Not for infidelity and definitely not for something as sacred as giving life. I'll help you save her, but after that you're not touching her. Not ever again."

Voices kicked up in the corridor as Zander watched the healer head up the hallway and disappear through a door, but he barely heard the arguments swirling around him. Because suddenly the blood screamed in his ears and Callia's words from the cave—words he thought had been a lie—were all he could focus on.

I've been in a cleansing period for the last ten years.

No. No, no, no . . .

Zander's stomach rolled and pitched. The hallway spun and tilted. He needed air. Fast. Turning, he ran his hand along the wall, but didn't feel the wood and stone. He swung out and grasped the first arm he caught. "Air. Surface. *Now.*"

Voices around him went silent, and he felt Theron's big hand close around his upper arm. "Zander. *Skata.* You don't look good. You—"

"Air!" he roared. Couldn't they fucking tell he couldn't breathe?

"Nick," Theron said quickly.

"Down the hall. End of the corridor. There's a stairway that will take you to the surface of the colony. But—"

Zander didn't wait to hear the rest. He was weak, and he was fading fast, but his legs moved as if his life depended on it.

Somehow he made it to the surface, pushed the heavy sealed door open and stumbled out onto the ledge of a great canyon.

The door whooshed closed behind him as he gasped air into his shrinking lungs. Pebbles crunched beneath his feet, skipped over the edge and tumbled below where the ground dropped at least a mile and a stream meandered like a writhing snake. Ahead and to the right the hillside climbed, covered in dense underbrush and spires of pine trees, but he didn't see the beauty. He barely saw any of it. All he saw and heard and felt was Callia's face, Callia's screams, Callia's pain.

Ah, gods. What had he done?

He dropped to his knees as his vision blurred. Rocks and twigs impaled his knees, his shins, his bare feet. He barely registered the bite and sting, because his mind was a thousand miles and ten years away.

"Damn Hera."

The voice, female and elderly, was not a complete surprise to Zander, not now, not at this moment when nothing else in his never-ending life seemed to matter except how badly he'd fucked up. He turned his head and looked toward a group of boulders where a slight woman dressed in diaphanous white sat perched on a rock, staring down at him. Her hair was pale, her features sharp, her skin wrinkled yet luminescent. Power radiated from her, the kind of power he'd never had, and he knew in an instant just who she was.

"Lachesis."

Her brow lifted. "Why the hell don't you think I'm Atropos?"

He refocused on the pebbles in front of him, tried to breathe through the pain, but it stabbed him from all sides. "Atropos wouldn't waste her time on me."

"Why not?"

He didn't answer. Couldn't. His mind raced, swirled, replayed every conversation, every moment since the day Callia had told him she was pregnant.

"Because you can't be killed?" the Fate asked.

Silence met his ears. And for a split second he thought he'd imagined her. Then she said softly, "You are not immortal, Guardian."

Lachesis slid off the boulder and came to stand in front of him. Hot pink slippers peeked out from beneath her flowing robe, looking ridiculous and real all at the same time. Just like his life. "You're right. I can't snip the thread of your life, I can only spin it. But even I can't see how far it will stretch. The distance of your life depends on two things: Her. And what you do now."

Slowly, Zander's head came up, and as the Fate's words sank in, little links clicked into place in his mind. He wouldn't have died in that cave. He might have been paralyzed if Callia hadn't removed that bullet, but even when he'd come to, he'd known his body was working hard to repair itself. The only other time—besides now—when he'd known death was waiting to claim him had been ten years ago. When he'd been alone. At home. Uninjured. And Callia had been in the human realm.

"She's my weakness," he whispered.

Lachesis knelt in front of him, and though she didn't touch him, he felt the heat from her hand as it hovered over his cheek. "A heart is never a weakness, Guardian. It is a gift. A blessing even Hera could not keep from you. Many were the guardians from your line who wished for such a treasure. Your vulnerability isn't one to be feared. It should be cherished."

He closed his eyes against the pain. So much pain. All because of him. "I . . . hurt her."

"Yes," she said softly.

"When I think of what she went through . . ."

"She's resilient. Stronger than you or her father think. And there is power within her yet unharnessed. Things are never as black and white as they seem. Sometimes pain is the catalyst to our destiny."

At the mention of Callia's father, anger wedged its way into Zander's chest. He looked up. "Why didn't you come to me sooner? Why now, after ten years, when she's dying?"

Lachesis sighed, stood, and though she was no more than four feet high, seemed to tower over him. "Because that's not the way it works, Guardian."

"And how does it work?"

"I cannot tell you anything you don't already know. I can only lay out your options before you. Nothing in life is static. The course your life takes depends on the choices you make."

"And what are my options?" he said, pushing to his feet and pointing toward the rock formation behind him and the hidden door into the colony even he wasn't sure he could find anymore. "She's dying in there and it's all because of me. It's all because . . . of . . ."

The air whooshed out of him along with his adrenaline even though he fought it. Fought it with everything he had in him. But still he wasn't strong enough to stop it. Just as he hadn't stopped any of what had happened.

". . . me."

"Yes," Lachesis whispered, stepping closer. "I would take your pain if I could. But I can't." Her arms came around him and though he didn't actually feel her, her strength eased him down to sit on the hard ground. "Use it, Zander. Use it and that purpose you've been seeking for over eight hundred years. Give her a reason to live. The story of your life, of hers, doesn't end here. Not unless you let it."

Zander stared past Lachesis, toward the edge of the cliff and the canyon beyond. Days ago he'd stood on the ledge of a cliff much like this one and wished for death. Now . . . ? Now it wasn't about him anymore. He didn't care if he lived or died, but he couldn't let Callia die. Not knowing everything she'd been through because of him. Not when he hadn't had a chance to set things right.

His gaze refocused on Lachesis. And questions, suspicions he needed confirmed filled his mind. "She gave birth to a son."

"Yes."

"Her father knew."

"Yes."

"All these years, no one ever said a word."

He watched something wary pass over the Fate's features. "Things aren't always what they seem. The web of deception spins strongest near those we trust the most."

His eyes narrowed at her strange words.

"The truth will come in time. But you have to heal her first."

He took a deep breath. Knew she was right. With Lena's help, he could do it. He could piss Callia off to the point where she channeled her powers and fought the infection. He could try to make up for at least one part of his horrible mess. And then . . .

"And then nothing is guaranteed." Lachesis hovered over the boulder he'd initially seen her sitting on, a strange glow behind her. And she was fading.

"Wait," he said, holding out a hand.

"The thread is thin, warrior." She faded before his eyes. "Yours, hers, the offshoot. It grows thinner by the hour. The future hinges on the present. Before the end, remember that she is the constant."

Then she was gone.

CHAPTER FIFTEEN

Reality was a funny thing. As Callia lay staring at the ceiling, she tried to piece together images in her head. She knew she'd been injured badly by that daemon, but the details of the attack were fuzzy. She also knew she was in a bedroom—not a medical facility—and that the bed was soft, the room plush, and that she was obviously healed enough to be away from major medical intervention. But she wasn't sure how that was possible or who was responsible for her miraculous recovery. And she didn't know where the hell she was.

Frustrated when her mind wouldn't stop spinning, she sat up and swung her legs over the side of the bed. She pushed up and wobbled on legs weaker than she expected, but caught herself on the edge of the mattress. The pink hospital gown fell to her knees. Her bare feet sank into plush cream carpeting. A lock of hair swept past her vision and she pushed it back with her hand. Thankfully, someone had washed her hair. The thought of what had been in it . . .

Don't go there.

She shuffled across the floor toward a small round window. When she reached the rock wall, she cupped a hand against the glass and peered out into the darkness. Stars met her line of sight but nothing else. No ground, no trees, no mountains. Nothing.

The door behind her creaked, and she turned.

"You're awake." Zander ducked under the doorway and frowned. "Should you be out of bed so soon?" He closed the door and crossed the floor in three long strides. "You look pale."

Yeah, well, no shit. She'd lost a lot of blood. What the hell was he doing here?

His gray eyes searched every inch of her face. "How do you feel?"

How did she feel? Confused. Surprised. And not entirely sure she wouldn't pass out. "What . . . are *you* doing here?"

He tipped her chin up with his finger, continued to look her over as if she were a science experiment. "Your eyes look good. Way better than before." His brow creased. "Are you hungry? I bet you're starving. They brought food up earlier, but you were still sleeping." He turned his head toward the door. "I could go get you something if—"

"Brought food up earlier? Whoa." The last time she'd seen him, in that cave, they'd argued. "Zander. What the heck is going on?"

A knock sounded at the door. They both looked over, but Zander was the first to speak. "Come in."

A female with dark hair pulled into a ponytail stepped into the room. She wore black slacks and a sweater and she shot a cautious look at Zander before focusing in on Callia. "You're up." The female's features softened just a touch. "How are you feeling?"

The voice was familiar. Callia narrowed her eyes. "Um. Better."

"That's good." The female's gaze shot to Zander.

There was no missing the tension in the room or the sparks shooting between Zander and this female. Zander glanced back at Callia. "I'll step out for a few minutes so you can check her over."

"That would be good," the female said drily.

"I'll be right outside if you need me."

The door clicked closed behind him. And in the silence Callia didn't know what the hell to think.

"Why don't you have a seat here on the end of the bed," the female said.

Her heart rate definitely higher than it had been before, Callia slowly moved to the bed.

"My name's Lena," the female said as she tipped Callia's chin up and flashed a penlight in her eye. "We didn't officially meet before."

"Your voice is familiar."

Lena smiled. She was a pretty girl, not breathtaking, not beautiful, but pretty, especially when she smiled. Her brown eyes almost sparkled. "It should be. We've spent quite a bit of time together these past few days. I'm a healer. Do you know where you are?"

"Um . . . You're not Argolean."

Lena put the penlight away and reached for Callia's neck, feeling her way down to the top of her chest and across her collarbone. "No. I'm Misos. And you are—"

"In the half-breed colony," Callia breathed, as it all started to make sense. "You're a healer? You're the one who treated me?"

"Yes and no."

Lena must have read the confusion on Callia's face because she smiled again. "My powers aren't nearly strong enough for this kind of healing." She focused in on Callia's skin. "This is amazing. You're going to end up with nothing more than a faint white line. You'll probably be the only one who notices it. Imagine what we could do if we put our powers together more often."

Callia reached her hand up to run her fingers over the smallest ridge. "Wait. Are you saying I did this?"

"You helped." Lena smirked. "Quite a bit. But I'm not willing to let you take all the credit." She unsnapped the shoulder of Callia's gown. "Let's take a look at your abdomen. Lie back."

Callia leaned back on the bed and let the female draw her gown down so she could look at the wounds on her stomach. "Wow. These are healing just as well. In a few days there won't be anything left."

Callia shifted up enough to glance down at her stomach. Two thin pink lines marred her abdomen in a downward angle toward her right hip. But the healer was right. In a few days they'd be gone.

Her mind flashed back to the cabin. To that seething daemon. To his claws slicing across her stomach and chest. There'd been blood. So much blood. She'd known she had mere minutes before she bled out. "How did I get here?"

Lena helped her sit up again and repositioned the gown so it shielded her breasts, but drew it open at the back. "Two guardians brought you in."

"Two?"

Lena reached for something behind her. "Yes. One was called Titus. He left shortly after you arrived. I think he went back to destroy the cabin where you were found and eliminate the evidence. This is going to be cold."

Before Callia braced herself, something small and round and metal touched her back. She flinched before she realized it was a stethoscope, then took a deep breath on instinct.

"Good," Lena said. "Again." She moved the stethoscope around Callia's back, listening to her lungs, then repeated it on her chest. Satisfied, she looped the instrument around her neck then rebuttoned Callia's gown. "Your lungs sound great. No sign of the infection either. You really are a medical miracle." She spread Callia's hair to the side. "Though this is an interesting mark here on your neck." She brushed at the base of Callia's hairline. "Is it a birthmark?"

"I . . . I don't know. I never . . ."

"It almost looks like an omega."

Callia didn't care about any of that. She was still stuck on the how-she'd-gotten-here-and-who'd-found-her mystery. "Who was it?"

Lena's eyebrows drew together as she dropped Callia's hair and came around to stand in front of her. "Who was what?"

"The other guardian," Callia said, frustration growing. "You said there were two."

"Oh." Lena frowned. Glanced toward the door and back again with disapproval evident in her eyes. "That one."

Callia's heart rate kicked up. "Why . . . why didn't he leave with Titus?"

Lena's frown deepened. She stuffed her hands into the pockets of her slacks. "That's the million-dollar question, isn't it? He keeps hanging around even though neither of us wants him to. He hasn't left your side for more than ten minutes, and he's a complete bear to anyone who tries to get near you besides me. I mean"—she glanced toward the door again—"he was right. I did need him at the beginning to jump-start your healing, but not anymore. I don't know why he won't leave. Maybe if you—"

"What do you mean you needed him to jump-start my healing?" Callia's pulse pounded in her veins and a strange tightness condensed in her chest. "Lena, I can't heal myself. I've never been able to."

Compassion softened Lena's brown eyes. "I don't know a healer who can. Me included. I didn't believe him myself when he said your powers were transferable, but he was right. I guess in this instance, the fact you hate him worked to your advantage."

Strange memories, visions, sounds clicked in Callia's brain. She saw smoke, fog, a burning light that looked as if it came from a ship. She heard voices calling, drawing her in, familiar ones from days gone by but which she couldn't quite place. The scene was peaceful and she remembered wanting to go, had some uncontrollable urge to step onto that boat and sail through the murky waters to lands unknown. But in the background, growing louder by the second, had been another voice. A male voice. Zander's voice.

I didn't believe you. I never believed you. Why would I? I left you. Did you hear me, Callia? I left you when you needed me most. And I didn't even look back.

A lump formed in Callia's throat. Those words had been real. That voice had been his. He'd stirred emotions in her she'd kept buried for years. The same emotions he'd dug up in that cave when he called her a liar.

Transferable.

"He purposely made me angry so I'd force my pain out on him," she muttered, staring across the room. Dear gods, she really could transfer her powers. That moment in the cave with Zander hadn't been a fluke.

"Yeah," Lena said. "And it worked. With you pushing most of the infection out, I was able to extract the rest. It explains your amazing scars. The force of our combined power is incredible. I only wish . . ."

"What?" Callia's eyes darted up to Lena's.

"I only wish you'd known about that when you got the other scars. The ones on your back."

Callia's chest went cold. Of course Lena would have seen the scars on her back. But Zander . . . "You didn't tell Zander about them, did you?"

"No." Lena crossed her arms. "Not exactly."

"What do you mean, not exactly?" Callia rose slowly to her feet.

Lena dropped her arms in a huff. "It's really a moot point, don't you think? We both know he saw them before."

Oh, shit. Callia dropped her head into her hands. Oh . . . *shit.*

"Why are you so upset he saw them again?" Lena asked in a sharp tone. "You got them because of him."

Callia rubbed both hands over her face. Oh, gods, he'd seen the one part of her she always kept covered. Knowing about the scars was one thing. Seeing them was something else entirely. "It was my choice," she said quietly. "You wouldn't understand."

"No, I would understand."

At the ice in Lena's voice, Callia glanced up. Hatred and contempt creased the half-breed's face. "My mother was Argolean, like you. Eighty-four years ago she was betrothed to an *ándras* she didn't love. Her parents arranged the marriage because she was already a hundred years old and hadn't found a mate yet. I guess you could say she had cold feet. She ran away, accessed one of the secret portals in the

Aegis Mountains and came to the human realm. Where she met my father. A human. They fell in love and she got pregnant with me. But females in your realm aren't safe anywhere, not even here."

Secret portals? Callia had thought they were fiction.

"Her father tracked her down," Lena went on. "My *pappous*. He found her, and he took her back. And he had her whipped, just like you. They called it a cleansing ritual, but there was no cleansing about it. It was punishment, clear and simple. Because she dared go against what the males of your world deem right."

The bite in Lena's voice made Callia swallow hard. She didn't doubt the half-breed's story. But she forced herself to ask the question burning on her tongue, even though a part of her already knew the answer. "What happened after?"

"She escaped again and went back to my father. I was born not long after." Lena dropped her arms and glanced down at the bed. "They were on their way to this very colony when a group of Argolean males tracked them down. When my mother refused to go back with them, a fight erupted. They were both killed."

Callia's eyes slid closed. She eased to sit on the bed again. "How did you . . . ?"

"Nick and a few of his soldiers came across the fight. They killed several of the males. The others ran off. He brought me here, to the colony, and a woman took me in. I was two weeks away from my second birthday, but I remember bits and pieces of that fight. Of my mother. And I remember the scars on her back, just like yours."

Callia's heart broke for Lena, but her own situation was so different. She shook her head, opened her eyes. "I'm sorry. I'm so sorry that happened. It's horrible. You have to know that isn't normal in my world."

"Not normal?" Lena's eyes grew wide. "Look at your back."

Callia shook her head. "No one tracked me down or forced me to submit. It's not like that anymore."

Fire erupted in Lena's dark eyes. She pointed toward the

door. "That so-called guardian out there is responsible for the marks on your back. He's here to take you back. You know that, don't you?"

"It's not like that. He didn't—"

"He did. I saw the guilt in his eyes. I saw the way you reacted when he whispered in your ear. And now he's waiting until you're healthy enough to take you back so he can punish you all over again. Well, I won't let him. You're not leaving here with—"

"He doesn't know, Lena." Callia pushed to her feet again, her own temper and voice rising. "He doesn't know what happened to me because I never told him. It was my choice." When Lena's mouth snapped shut, Callia softened her voice. "Don't you see? I could have stayed in the human world, but I chose not to. I wanted to go home. I wanted to be with my father. The cleansing ceremony . . ." She lifted her hands, dropped them. "It's not practiced anymore. My father is one of the Twelve and I . . . I was betrothed to a future elder. My relationship with Zander—" She looked toward the door, swallowed the lump of remorse suddenly thick in her throat. "It hurt my father, in ways you—no one—can understand."

She glanced back at Lena. "I knew what I was getting into with Zander from the very beginning. I made my own choices. Zander has his faults, but he's not like your *pappous*. He'd never intentionally hurt a female. And if he'd known what I'd chosen, he never would have allowed it to happen. No matter how he felt about me at the end."

"Then why?" Lena asked, her voice barely above a whisper. "Why would you let them do that to you?"

Callia looked down at her bare feet, her toes all but buried in the thick carpeting. What answer could she give that would make even a lick of sense? It hadn't entirely been for her father, to save face, to restore his name within the Council. It hadn't been so she could marry Loukas down the road either—that hadn't even been a thought in her mind. Part of it had been . . . for her. Her power was all about balance, about restoring order to the body, but she couldn't heal herself. And crazy as it sounded, physical pain, though it hurt, could do that. It could ease some of the anguish in her heart and give her something else to focus on. And in some small way, it had been a step toward making things right.

"Because," she said softly, "I needed my own sense of peace." She shook her head again. "I know you can't understand that. But this was not his fault. It wasn't ever his fault."

Lena glanced toward the door, and though there was still disapproval in her eyes when she looked back to Callia again, at least there wasn't contempt. "I'm protective. It's in my nature."

Callia kept her distance from people, primarily because she'd learned to keep things to herself, but this was the kind of female she could see herself being friends with. "It's a good way to be. For a healer. But Zander's not the enemy. He never was."

"What is he then? To you?"

The question threw Callia off-kilter. He was . . . the guardian who had turned her world upside down. The one person she'd never gotten over. And . . . the love of her life.

Her heart pinched at that realization, but she pushed the emotion away, like she'd gotten good at doing over the years. "He's . . . Zander."

Lena stared at her for a long minute, then finally sighed. "I guess this means you want me to be nice to him."

One side of Callia's mouth turned up at the edge. "Maybe not nice. Just not mean."

Lena headed for the door with a roll of her eyes. "Not mean. To an Argonaut. It goes against my better judgment. I'll tell him he can come in now." She stopped with one hand on the doorknob. "I'd like you to stay another day and get some more rest. But I know you'll do whatever you want. Regardless of what I think."

"Thank you."

Lena hesitated. "I've harbored resentment against your

world for a long time. I'm not entirely ready to let go of that. But I may be ready to see another side. Maybe." She opened the door. "Good luck to you, Callia."

The door clicked shut softly in Lena's wake. Out in the hall, muffled voices drifted to Callia's ears. Lena's, Zander's. She wasn't sure what was said, but the conversation was over quickly; then soft footsteps faded away.

Questions swirled in Callia's mind as she sat on the edge of the bed again and tried to make sense of this crazy day. Lena had said he hadn't left her for more than ten minutes since he'd brought her here. Was he gone now too? A small part of her hoped so. An even bigger part hoped not.

Gods, she was a mess.

She gripped the edge of the bed and drew in a deep breath that did little to calm her racing pulse. A soft knock sounded at the door, bringing her head up. She waited. When it happened again, she managed a weak "Come in."

CHAPTER SIXTEEN

Callia's stomach pitched as Zander stepped into the room. The always-confident guardian looked like death warmed over. Not physically—physically he was as strong and healthy as ever, his wounds from that cave nothing but a memory—but emotionally. His eyes were flat, his step heavy, his blond hair disheveled as if he'd run his fingers through it numerous times. An unseen weight seemed to press down on his shoulders and permeate the room around him, one Callia felt all the way to her bones.

She'd never thought of him as old. To the average human he looked like a sexy, rugged thirty-five-year-old in the prime of his life. But he wasn't. He was 829 years old. And today—right now—all those years seemed to flicker in his stormy gray-blue eyes, reminding her of everything he'd done and seen and been.

"Lena said you checked out fine."

Callia's pulse pounded as she studied him. He was wearing the traditional black fighting pants—the same ones Titus had brought for him in that cave. The long-sleeved white Henley showcased his muscular arms and pecs and shielded all but the tips of his Argonaut markings down his fingers. Light stubble covered his square jaw, as if he hadn't shaved in days, and the faint scars on his knuckles, his throat, the little bits of skin exposed here and there only added to his mystery and intrigue.

Gods, he really was beautiful. Even scarred from all those years of fighting. She remembered the first time she'd seen him. Nearly eleven years ago. She'd been thirty—adulthood for a human, a mere child for an Argolean. The king had specifically asked her to take over as royal healer, a position her mother had held years before, until her death. She'd been at the castle, overwhelmed yet trying to look like she had a clue, when she'd passed Theron and Zander in the hall on their way up to see the king.

Her heart had stuttered then—much as it did now—and she'd felt like she couldn't breathe. He'd always had that effect on her. And it had only intensified, building until the night he'd pulled her into the king's study and she'd thrown aside everything she'd ever learned about balance and order and given in to desire.

He stuffed his hands into the back pockets of his pants but didn't move. It was clear he didn't know what to say or do, and in the silence, Callia's pulse picked up to the beat of a marching band. She wasn't sure why he was still here, but one thing was clear: he felt guilty. And that was something she couldn't deal with.

"Zander, you don't need to stay. I'm fine. You don't owe me—"

"Did I ever tell you about my mother?"

The strange comment cut off Callia's words. The intensity of his gaze told her whatever was on his mind was important, and maybe she should listen. "No," she said slowly. "I don't think so."

"She worked at the castle." He crossed to sit next to her on the bed, though he was careful not to touch her. "This was the twelfth century, so things were quite a bit different. Archidmus was king and the Council had way more sway over the monarchy then—over the population in general." He leaned forward to rest his elbows on his knees and kept his eyes downcast. "Her name was Khloe and she was a teacher. She taught the king's children and some whose parents worked in the castle. She was bound to a scholar named Alastor. His older brother served as the family's representative to the Twelve.

"They had no young, and had only been bound for a

handful of years when my father, Nikator, came across her in the castle one day."

The way he said the Argonaut's name sent a shiver down Callia's spine. She knew he thought little of the *ándras* who had given him life, but he'd never talked much about him, and she'd never asked. The rumors about Nikator were well-known throughout the kingdom, though, and those rumors were part of the reason her father had objected to her relationship with Zander in the first place. Nikator had lived up to his name—the conqueror—in every aspect imaginable. He'd been a brutal fighter in and out of battle, an *ándras* who lived outside the law and took what he wanted without remorse. Often by force.

Suddenly, she wasn't so sure she wanted to hear the rest of this story.

Zander clasped his hands, and though he looked down at the floor, Callia was sure he was seeing hundreds of years into the past, not the thick cotton threads of the rug beneath his feet. "I like to think that it was consensual. That they met and had a connection." *Like us,* she knew he wanted to say, but didn't. "But I know that wasn't the truth. She wound up pregnant, and knowing how the Council would view"—he swallowed, visibly sickened—"her rape . . . as adultery and not the crime it was, she did the only thing she thought she could do.

"She found a witch in the mountains who helped her get rid of it. Get rid of me." He held his hands out in front of him, palms down so the ancient Argolean text that ran down his fingers was visible. "Only it didn't work. Even back then, in the womb, I couldn't be killed."

Callia's breath caught. And she remembered his words that day she'd told him she was pregnant. *Do not hurt my child. If you don't want him, I'll take him. But whatever you do, promise me you will not do something drastic.*

He'd seemed so angry. So untrusting. And his words had stung, because yeah, she'd been freaked by the news herself, but she'd been so over the moon in love with him then, she hadn't understood how he could jump to conclusions she hadn't even yet contemplated.

"Three times," he said, still staring at his hands. "Three times she tried to get rid of me, but it never worked." He reached up and ran a finger down his neck where the long jagged scar puckered his skin. "I was born with this."

Callia's stomach rolled. She closed her eyes as their conversation in the cave came back like a slap in the face.

And what am I?

A murderer.

"She ended up having me in secret," he went on. "The witch who delivered me saw the markings on my arms and hands and alerted the Argonauts. And though none of it was her fault, my mother knew the Council was going to punish her, badly, because of her link to them." He hesitated, stared down at the carpet, then quietly added, "She killed herself a week after I was born."

"Oh, Zander—"

The bed moved, and the brush of his fingers against her cheek brought her eyes open. He was kneeling in front of her, his handsome face marred with lines of worry and regret, and the sheen of tears she saw in his eyes nearly broke her. "I didn't know. I thought . . ."

He paused, swallowed hard, seemed to gather his thoughts. His hand slid down to cover hers in her lap and his eyes followed. "I never wanted to be an Argonaut. These damn markings, they've dictated my life from the start. And I've served with so many. Some who were complete asses like my father and made me wonder what the hell I was even fighting for. And then Theron's father came along—Solon—and things started to change. The guys I serve with now are decent. They're not like the Argonauts of the past. Even Demetrius isn't half as bad as some. When you told me you were pregnant, I couldn't just leave Theron in the lurch. I owed him too much. I left you to make arrangements so another could be chosen in my place. But it never got that far."

She dreaded what he would say next but needed to hear it.

"Your father found me at the castle and told me you'd changed your mind and that you'd gone to the human realm to end your pregnancy."

Callia's eyes shot up to his, and she watched slowly as he shook his head. "I didn't believe him. So I tracked you down. I found the clinic. A nurse told me it was already done and that you were gone. Your records confirmed it."

"I never—"

"I know," he said. "I know now. I should have known then that you wouldn't do something like that without talking to me, but I was filled with so much"—he looked around the room—"rage." He ran his free hand over his scalp. "Sometimes it controls me. And when you didn't come back, when weeks stretched to months and then to years, I let that belief sink in. I figured you really had wanted something else after all."

All these years he thought she'd been the one to walk away. When that was the farthest thing from the truth.

Tears burned her eyes. Tears she thought she was done crying. "I went to the human realm to try to save our baby, Zander. I didn't . . . I wouldn't . . ."

He squeezed her hand. "I know."

Emotions flooded her, overwhelmed her, pinched her chest so hard it was tough to get air. She let go of his hand and pushed up to stand, needing to do something physical before the pain and disbelief pulled her under. She crossed to the window, reached out and rested her hand on the cool rock wall. "My father told me about that meeting between you two. But he said you were the one who changed your mind. That you decided you didn't want to leave the Argonauts after all."

Dear gods, she'd believed her father. *Believed* what he'd said. Even begged the *ándras* to tell Zander where she was in Greece in case he realized he'd made a mistake and wanted her or their child after all. No wonder he'd never come for her.

"He never wanted us to be together," he said quietly behind her.

No, he hadn't. Simon hated the Argonauts with a vengeance. So much so, Callia often wondered where the vehemence came from. It wasn't just Zander as a person her father disapproved of. It was his link to the Argonauts and what they stood for.

"He . . ." Anger burned hot behind her eyes, as hot as the deception she felt in her heart over what her father had done.

She felt Zander at her back, even before his hands settled on her arms and he turned her to face him. But she didn't look up. Couldn't face what she knew was in his eyes. When he pulled her close, she rested her head against his chest. Didn't even try to fight the gentle embrace.

"If I had known," he said in a voice thick with emotion, "I would have been there with you. Every second. Nothing would have kept me away. And no one . . ." His muscles tensed against her. "No one would have ever hurt you."

She didn't know what to say. Wasn't sure she could have this conversation now. Didn't know if she ever could.

"Callia." His fingers slid into her hair and he tipped her face up to his gently. But it wasn't anger that plagued his features. It was regret. And sorrow. And a grief only she could understand. *"Thea."*

The use of the nickname he'd given her all those years before touched a place deep inside she'd closed off from the world. *Goddess.* He'd told her once he considered her his own personal goddess. She'd believed him. Then hated him. And now . . . didn't know what to think.

When he eased down to brush his lips over hers she froze. Didn't pull back. Wasn't sure if she even could. This—as crazy as it was—this felt right. They'd both lost so much, and she'd been grieving for years, never knowing until now that part of the reason she continued to hurt was because she'd never shared that grief with him.

His hands slipped down her hair to her shoulders, around

to pull her closer. The brush of skin against cloth vibrated through her body. She sighed against his mouth, tipped her head and opened for him on reflex.

The kiss was slow and gentle. He slid his tongue into her mouth, stroked hers leisurely, like he had all the time in the world, as if tasting her for the first time and savoring every moment. And she found herself responding, bringing her arms up to his chest, giving him whatever he asked for, telling herself in the back of her mind this wasn't rekindling something that never should have happened in the first place. This was closure. Consoling each other. Finally letting go of the past once and for all.

His lips moved languidly over her jaw, to her ear, and she shuddered at the warm breath blowing across her skin and down her throat. "You're so strong, *thea*," he whispered in her ear. "Such a fighter. When I think about what could have happened to you . . ."

His words pinged around in her brain as she breathed in his scent. And then, as if they found their mark, a memory lit off in her mind. A memory from that hunting cabin with the daemon who had nearly killed her.

A fighter, I see.

Followed by Atalanta's voice.

She's the boy's mother. Bring her. If the boy doesn't cooperate, she might become useful after all.

Her chest squeezed tight all over again. Only this time it wasn't with grief and pain, it was with shock and a really bad feeling. It couldn't be . . .

"What?" Zander asked. He pushed her back, his eyebrows drawn together to form a crease between his stormy eyes.

The explanation her father had given her after the birth joined in the chaos. An earthquake in the Peloponnese. The doctor unable to make it to her cottage due to the destruction. Complications with the delivery. Her, unconscious. A stillborn child. Aftershocks so strong they crumpled the house.

Her father had told her he'd only had enough time to get her and himself to safety. He hadn't been able to save her son's body from the rubble. She'd never even seen his face.

"No." She whispered the word, covered her mouth with her hand. Stared at Zander as links fell into place.

"Callia?" He gripped her shoulders, the questions in his eyes turning to dread. "What's wrong?"

"I . . ." She swallowed hard, dropped her hand. Barely believed what she was about to say. But somehow, in some way, it felt like the truth. "I think my father lied to us about everything. Zander, I think our son might still be alive."

Max knew Fort Nelson was the first place Atalanta would send her monsters to look for him, so he stayed in the woods and crossed the river well downstream. It had snowed recently, but the Fort Nelson fork wasn't yet frozen, though the water was colder than Atalanta's bitter wasteland.

The metal disk warmed his chest as he moved, and though he couldn't be sure, it almost felt like that warmth was trickling down into his limbs as well.

Super cool.

He climbed out of the river on the other side, shivered and ducked into the trees. He couldn't wait too long—he had to keep moving—but he needed a minute to catch his breath. Sitting near the base of a tree, he pulled his knees up to his chest, wrapped his arms around his legs and tried to warm himself. A water droplet dripped down from the top of his head. He watched it splash on his forearm, then evaporate into the air.

He looked closer. Watched the next droplet hit and disappear as well.

Freaky.

Easing back, he glanced at his arms. They were already dry. Then at his legs, where his jeans were nearly dry as well. Against his chest the disk burned hot but didn't sear his skin. His sweatshirt was now only slightly damp and his coat was wet just at the sleeves. He reached up and touched the disk with his fingers, smiled and knew then it really did have magic inside.

He scrambled to his feet with a burst of energy he'd lacked before. Then he hiked another mile to the Alaska Highway and hid out in the brush until he saw the head-lights of a semitruck far off in the distance.

Confidence breathed new life into him, and he stepped out onto the side of the road, waving his arms.

The lights barreled closer. With the layer of ice covering the road he wasn't even sure the truck could stop. But then the whine of gears shifting down met his ears, and the truck slowed to stop twenty feet in front of him.

He ran toward the cab, around to the driver's side. Slowly, the window lowered. Max squinted to look up at the human face peering back.

"You lost, boy?"

"Um . . ." Now what? "No. Not exactly."

The man perched his arm on the window ledge and leaned over to get a good look at Max. "That coat won't keep you very warm out here. Temps are droppin' like twenties in a strip club. Where you come from, boy?"

"Uh . . ." He couldn't say Fort Nelson. He thought about what little he knew of this area. "Alaska."

The man's eyes narrowed. "Alaska, huh? How'd you get all the way out here?"

"I walked."

The man looked him over again, seemed to focus on his face. And the hair on the back of Max's neck stood straight under that scrutinizing gaze. "You runnin' away from some-thin'?"

Sweat broke out on Max's brow. "No."

"Uh-huh," the man said, unconvincingly. "How'd you get that bruise?"

Max ran his fingers over his left cheekbone. The only thing he could think of was when he'd attacked Zelus ear-lier. "I . . . I don't know."

The man harrumphed. Then finally nodded toward the passenger side of the truck. "Get in."

Max's eyebrows shot up. He stood frozen for a split second before racing around the front of the truck and climbing up the tall steps. Once inside, the heat of the cab instantly warmed his last cold spots.

The trucker stared over at him. The man was probably in his fifties, with thinning hair on top, a round belly and callused hands that had seen a lot of work. "Name's Jeb. I run the West Coast route for a small company in Vancouver. Where you headed, boy?"

Max twisted his hands in his lap. He hadn't thought too far ahead. Where could he go? He'd heard Atalanta and Thanatos talk about a half-breed colony down south. "Oregon."

"What's in Oregon?"

Max knew not to be too secretive. But he wasn't about to give anything away. "I have relatives there."

Jeb studied Max closely again, then finally said, "I'm on my way to my base in Vancouver. Have to pick up a load, then I'm heading to Las Vegas. You don't cause too much trouble, you can ride along."

"Th-thanks." Max leaned back in his seat. But he didn't relax. Something warned him to be on guard. This guy might just be human, but Max had learned long ago not to trust anyone.

Jeb shifted. The gears whined and echoed as metal scraped metal and the big rig picked up speed. "Yeah, I never liked my old man much either. Mean cuss. I sure the hell hope you're runnin' somewhere better than that, boy."

So did Max.

Callia bolted as soon as they came through the portal in the Gatehouse.

Zander reached for her, but she slithered out of his grip and sprinted for the door. "Dammit, Callia. Wait!"

The two Executive Guards stationed at the portal exchanged bewildered glances. Zander searched for the Argonaut on duty training the newest recruits. None of the Argonauts were thrilled with the Council's decision to turn monitoring of the portal over to their guards, but babysitting rankled even more, and Gryphon—the lucky guardian this time—looked ready to beat his head against a wall.

"Zander—what the hell?"

Zander ignored the question and moved toward the door. "Get Theron and the others and get to the Argolion," he shouted.

Gryphon's light eyebrows drew together as he pushed up from his chair. "Why in Hades would you be going to see the Council?"

"Just do it!"

He raced out the door of the Gatehouse and stopped on the sidewalk outside the building. The city of Tiyrns sparkled in the fall sunlight. A crisp breeze brushed past his face. He searched the busy street for Callia but didn't see her. Closing his eyes, he envisioned the Argolion—the ancient building that housed the Council gatherings and the council members' offices. In seconds he flashed to the steps outside the massive building and darted inside.

Rows of columns lined the inner corridor. Not seeing Callia anywhere in the great lobby, he headed toward the Council chambers and prayed they weren't in session. The marble floor gleamed before him as he moved. He cursed himself for not planning this better.

He rounded the corner and spotted her ahead, about to open the double doors into the Council chambers. "Callia! Wait!"

She turned, looked at him, and the torment in her eyes all but killed him. "I have to see my father."

He grasped her arm and gently turned her toward him. "He may be in session. Wait until Theron gets here and we'll question him then. He—"

"I don't care, Zander. Ten years. It's been ten years!"

She pushed the door open before he could stop her,

ducked under his arm and disappeared inside. He moved to grab her but drew up short when he stepped inside and all sound ground to a halt.

Twelve Council members sat in high-backed chairs in a circle around the Great Alpha Seal carved in marble in the middle of the floor. Behind the circle, on a raised platform, Isadora, the royal representative for the meeting, sat in a regal chair, overseeing the proceedings. To her right, Casey stood watching, and standing on both sides of the sisters, alert and armed, were two members of the Executive Guard.

All eyes turned their way. Tension permeated the air. Zander cast a quick glance around the room and found two, three . . . five more guards stationed at the exits to the circular chamber.

Skata, they should have waited for Theron and the others.

"What is the meaning of this disruption," Lucian, the leader of the Council, said, brow furrowed as he rose to stand in front of his chair. The *rompa*, or ancient red robe each Council member wore during proceedings, draped around to pool at his feet.

"I need to speak with my father," Callia announced, her gaze zooming in on her father, seated to Lucian's right.

"Callia," her father admonished, rising himself. "This is uncalled for."

"You lied to me," she said.

Her father's shoulders tightened. Zander watched Lucian shoot Simon a questioning look. From the corner of his eye he spotted Loukas—Lucian's son and the *ándras* Callia's father had betrothed her to as a child—push to his feet from his seat near the wall on the far side of the room.

Oh, yeah, this was an ideal clusterfuck. All the major players were here, and from the tension suddenly thick in the room, Zander had a feeling things were going to go from bad to worse in no time flat. Three guards he could take and still protect Callia. But not seven. And definitely not on top of the twelve sets of glaring eyes zeroed in on him.

"Callia," he said quietly as he took a step toward her and reached for her arm.

She shrugged out of his grip and moved inside the circle, coming to stop in the center, just above the great Alpha seal. "You said Zander left me, but he didn't."

"Callia." Her father's eyes darted from her to Zander and back again. "This is highly inappropriate."

She ignored him, advanced until she was but a few feet away. And even though Zander was ticked at the way she didn't listen to him and had bolted without thinking, a small part of him couldn't help being impressed by her strength and courage. She was surrounded by twenty *ándres*, the twelve strongest politicians in their society and their guards. The ones who had forever scarred her with their twisted cleansing ritual and had the power to destroy her career and everything she'd built for herself over the years. And yet she wasn't backing down.

"You told him I never wanted to see him again," she said to her father, "but you lied about that too. You know I would have left here forever with him if I could have."

Zander's chest ached at that revelation, but the way Loukas stiffened on the other side of the room drew his attention. No one else seemed to notice. All eyes were glued to Callia.

"What else did you lie about?" she asked. "What else have you been hiding from me all these years?"

"Callia," her father said gently, reaching for her. Zander tensed, ready to lurch to her rescue, but she moved out of her father's grasp. Simon dropped his hand, flustered. "You're obviously not thinking clearly to come here and say these things to me. I think you need to go back to your clinic and—"

"Let her speak," Theron announced from the doorway.

The Council turned in unison toward the arched doorway where Theron stood, flanked by the remaining Argonauts save Demetrius.

Zander breathed out a sigh of relief, turned back to the circle and moved inside to stand behind Callia.

Simon glanced from her to him and back again, then turned to Lucian, the stress of the moment clearly visible in his eyes. "Lord Lucian, I apologize for my daughter's interruption. May I request that the Council be adjourned until I can deal with this . . . disruption?"

Lucian's jaw clenched, irritation evident in his jade green eyes. "So be it. The Council is adjourned until tomorrow."

Whispers floated on the air as the other ten Council members rose and took their leave, shooting Callia, Zander and the Argonauts questioning looks. But Lucian didn't move. And neither did Casey nor Isadora, who had joined her sister to stand behind the circle. Out of his peripheral vision, Zander saw Loukas inch toward his father's side.

Dumbass. The prick needed to get fucking lost, once and for all.

"Callia," her father admonished when the others were gone. "This is completely uncalled for. I'm not going to—"

"I want to know what happened on that mountain in Greece," she said, rolling over him. "I want to know what else you lied to me about. I want to know what you did with my baby."

Isadora gasped and covered her hand with her mouth, but the princess's shock was the least of Zander's worries. Simon's suddenly wide eyes and pale face triggered a conversation in Zander's mind.

Things aren't always what they seem, Guardian. The web of deception spins strongest near those we trust the most.

"What happened to him?" Callia demanded. "What happened to my son?"

Simon's terror-filled eyes darted from Callia to the Argonauts near the door, then finally to Zander, and held. He ignored Lucian's muttered questions at his side. Sweat broke out on his forehead. The *ándras* started to shake.

"Make her leave," Simon said to Zander.

"*What?*" Callia turned to look at Zander, then back to her father. "I'm not going anywhere. If you think after all this time I'm—"

"I'll tell you," Simon said to Zander again, ignoring Callia. "But not her. I can't tell her."

"Simon," Lucian hissed. "You are forbidden from speaking!"

A familiar hum lit off in Zander's blood, a warning that what he was about to hear was anything but good. But he tamped it down and put himself between Callia and her father before she could tear into him again.

"Zander, get out of my—"

He gripped her arms. "Wait outside."

"No way."

"I won't cut you out," he whispered. "I promise. But for whatever reason, he won't tell us with you here. You have to go outside."

She stilled. Stared at him. In the instance of silence that followed, the connection they'd always shared flared deep in his soul. There was a world of hurt and lies between them, but on this they had to be united. On this she had to trust him.

Her jaw clenched, but the muscles in her arms relaxed against his hands. "If you lie to me too—"

"I won't," he said softly, hoping she heard the truth in his words.

When she nodded, he glanced over his shoulder at Casey. Without being asked, the king's half-breed daughter stepped quickly from the raised platform and hustled to Callia's side. "We'll wait outside." She took a step toward the door. "Callia?"

Callia stayed where she was, staring up at Zander. And in her violet eyes he saw clearly for the first time in years. He saw everything she was to him, everything she'd been. Everything he'd done before and during and after their time together, and so much he wanted to do over. He saw . . . his soul, as clearly as if he were looking inside himself. And he saw his life. Not ending like he'd thought when he'd spoken to Lachesis on that mountain cliff, but continuing on, through her, because of her, with her.

"I promise," he said again.

She took a deep breath. Then turned and walked out of the circle toward the door.

Pain lanced through Zander's chest as he watched. Pain and a renewed sense of fury that even now the truth had to be hidden. But it wouldn't be for long.

When he heard the outer door click closed, he turned and glared at Callia's father. Even though he didn't want to, he capped his rage. Knew losing it now would do no good. At his back he heard Theron and the other Argonauts step in behind him. "No more lies," he told Simon. "This time you tell the truth. What did you do with my son?"

Simon glanced once guiltily at Lucian, and then he started talking. But what came out of his mouth wasn't anything Zander had ever expected to hear. And the cap on his rage blew free to boil up and over before Simon paused to take his first breath.

CHAPTER SEVENTEEN

What was taking so long?

With one arm wrapped around her waist, Callia chewed on her thumbnail and paced the corridor outside the Council chambers. Her nerves were in high gear. Sickness welled in her stomach. There'd been some kind of commotion in the chamber just after she'd left the room, but Casey hadn't let her go in and now she was going out of her mind wondering what the hell was happening.

Just when she was ready to plow through the wall to see what was going on, the chamber door pulled open and Titus stepped through the small opening.

He closed the door quickly at his back. Didn't look happy. If anything, he looked pissed and . . . seriously disturbed. He moved to stand in front of her, but he didn't speak.

"Where is Zander?" Callia asked.

"Inside. He can't . . ." Titus paused. "I don't think it's a good idea for you to talk to him just yet."

What the hell did that mean? Callia's nerves jumped. "Titus, what did my father say in there?"

He looked down at her hands, now hanging by her sides, hesitated, then reached for them. He winced when he touched her, and she remembered the way he'd gone down to his knees in the cave when he'd touched her then. He never touched anyone—not on purpose—so the fact he was initiating contact now sent her anxiety into the out-of-this-world category. "Titus?"

He drew in a deep breath and focused on her hands. "Callia, he made a deal to save your life. You . . . There were complications during the delivery. He says if he hadn't done it, you would have died."

"What kind of deal?"

His eyes came up level with hers. Hazel eyes that saw so much and yet not enough. "Your life for your son's."

Her life. One for another. The truth she'd dreaded was real. "So he really is dead."

"I . . ."

The unease across his face drew her eyebrows together. "Titus, what?"

"Simon doesn't know. The child was . . . alive . . . when the god left with him. He hasn't seen either since."

Her chest squeezed so tight she gasped. Her baby had been alive. He hadn't died on that Greek mountain, in the middle of an earthquake, as she'd been led to believe. How could she not have known? Why hadn't she felt it? And what would any god want with her child?

"Who?" she asked. "Who was it?"

"Callia—"

"Don't placate me, Titus." She wrenched her hands from his grip. "Tell me who it was."

His jaw twitched, and she saw in his eyes that he didn't want to tell her, but finally he said, "Atalanta."

Her vision turned red and her pulse pounded in her veins. Before he could stop her, she flung the double doors open and spotted her father, still standing in the center of the circle, eyes wide and afraid as she advanced on him.

"Callia," Titus called at her back. "Wait—"

"Callia," Simon said, holding his hands up. "Just listen to what I have to say."

"You son of a bitch. How could you?"

Voices echoed around her. She was aware there were other people in the room and that they were shouting, but she couldn't make out their words. All she felt was pain. All she saw was betrayal. All she knew was the one person she'd trusted had done the unspeakable.

Arms locked tight around her waist and pulled her back.

She struggled, but they were made of steel and unrelenting. The buzz in her head made it hard to hear, but the haze over her vision was dimming, and slowly she realized her father was on his knees, his face red and scratched.

"Calm down, Callia," Titus hissed in her ear. She zeroed in on her father's face. She'd hit him. Hard, from the looks of it.

Her father lifted his head. Guilt and remorse reflected deeply in his eyes. "You have to understand, it was the only thing I could do."

She braced her hands against the arm wrapped around her waist and tried to push free. "You gave my son to a monster!"

Her father shook his head. Dropped it. "I know. I know. But you would have died otherwise. And the child. I thought he was dead."

"He was alive!"

"I . . ." He cringed. "I didn't know that until they left. You have to believe me."

Disgust roiled through her. Contempt for his words. But as she stared at her father, kneeling on the Alpha seal in the center of the circle with Lucian behind him and all of the Argonauts watching, the red haze dissipated. And her image of him as the honorable and unbreakable lord dissolved too.

Her body still vibrated, but she stopped fighting Titus. He whispered something in her ear, something she didn't hear, then slowly eased her to the floor. But he didn't completely let go of her, and from the corner of her eye she saw Theron was holding Zander back in the same way. And she realized that was why he hadn't come out to talk to her as he'd promised.

"Why?" she asked, focusing on her father once more. "Why didn't you ever tell me?"

Simon shook his head. "I couldn't. It was part of the agreement. She put a curse on you that limited your lifespan if I ever uttered a word to you about it."

She glanced at Zander, who still looked ready to commit murder. Zander was the only other one who'd known she was pregnant, and her father had effectively separated them so no one would know what had happened.

The rage washed out of her, leaving behind pity and disdain.

"Let go of me, Titus," she mumbled. "I'm not going to attack him again."

Titus let go and stepped back, but he didn't go far.

"Why me?" Callia asked her father. "Why my child? The Argonauts have been reproducing for thousands of years. What was so special about my baby?"

Her father sat back on his heels, reached up and rubbed two shaky hands over his face. If it was possible to look more guilty, he did then. But he didn't answer. And in the silence dread pooled in Callia's stomach.

"What else aren't you telling me?" she asked hesitantly.

"I loved your mother," Simon muttered. "When she died . . ."

Callia had been only seven when Anna had died. The Royal Healer had succumbed to something as ordinary as pneumonia. And her with a stronger immune system than most. It had never made sense. But looking back, a lot then hadn't made sense. Something had happened between her parents. Something that had broken Anna's will to live and tainted their marriage.

She stared into her father's sad eyes as her mind spun. Why would Atalanta want her son over the hundreds of other Argonaut offspring over the years? Only one answer made sense.

"You're not my real father, are you?"

Simon's eyes fell closed. She ignored the pain in his features because right now she didn't care. Right now there were more important things to discuss.

"Who?" she asked. "Who did she have an affair with?" She glanced around the room. "One of the Argonauts? You've hated them for so long. Was that why you didn't want me to be with Zander?"

Unease churned in her stomach as her gaze settled on Zander, still being restrained by Theron. He was the oldest of the Argonauts, and he had probably known her mother, but her instinct said it hadn't been him. She glanced at the others. They were all at least two hundred years old. She was only forty. It could be any one of them. It made sense. Argonaut lineage from both sides. Would that give a child enhanced powers?

"I . . ." Her father's broken voice pulled her attention his way again. He sniffled. Swiped his forearm over his face. "If Anna hadn't been a healer, none of this would have happened."

Callia froze. And links, connections, threads she'd had no idea were entwined became crystal clear. The skin on the back of her neck, right at the base of her hairline, tingled.

She ran her fingers up under her hair, over the marking Lena had pointed out when she'd been at the colony. The one that was oddly . . . like the one on Isadora's thigh.

"She had an affair with the king," she whispered. Her gaze shot to Casey, standing at her right. Then to Isadora, across the room.

"Callia." Her father pushed up to his feet. Held his hands out toward her. "I'm still your father. What she did . . . that doesn't change anything."

Didn't change anything? Um, yeah. It changed everything. Panic pushed its way up Callia's chest. Panic and a sense that everything was about to crash down around her.

She turned for the door before anyone could stop her. She needed air. She needed a second to herself. She needed . . . shit . . . she didn't know what she needed.

"Callia!"

She wasn't sure how she made it out of the chamber, but she was sprinting when she hit the corridor. She paused to get her bearings, spotted a sign halfway down the hall and was inside the plush female sitting room before she even realized her feet had moved.

One whole wall was filled with floor-to-ceiling mirrors. She stared at her reflection, then whipped around and lifted her hair, tried to peer over her shoulder at the marking on her neck. The small but unmistakable winged omega.

The door to the bathroom pushed open. In the reflection Callia caught Casey's gaze fixed on her neck. She dropped her hair and turned.

"Are you okay?"

Was she okay? Yeah. Not likely. "You tell me. I just found out a demigod with a bad case of revenge kidnapped my son because he's the heir to the throne of Argolea. Would you be okay?"

Casey's expression softened. Dark hair fell over her shoulders, but her violet eyes were very clear and very familiar. "I know what you're going through."

Callia huffed. "Yeah, you know? I don't think so." It wasn't that she didn't like the half-breed, it was that right now she had a thousand other things to deal with besides getting chummy with her long-lost half-sister.

The bathroom door pushed open again and this time Isadora came inside. Only she didn't look half as concerned as Casey.

"Lovely," Callia said as she took in Isadora's tense face. "We might as well just have a party." Her headache kicked up and she rubbed at the spot between her eyes.

Casey looked toward the princess. "She's got the mark. On her neck."

"Let me see." Isadora stepped closer.

"Sure, why not?" Callia mumbled as Casey lifted her hair like she was nothing more than a lab rat. "This day can't get any weirder."

The two inspected her neck; then Isadora eased back and Casey let Callia's hair down again. A deep furrow marred the princess's pale face, and oh, yeah, it was obvious Isadora was not happy about this little bit of news. But what daughter would be? She'd just found out her father had yet another illegitimate child. Gods, the king had taken Zeus's "go forth and multiply" decree to the extreme.

Isadora finally sighed. Glanced between the two. "The least one of you could have done was be male. Then I wouldn't still be forced to marry Zander."

Zander. *Skata*. Callia clenched her jaw. How had she forgotten all about the fact Zander was set to bind himself to someone else? At what point had *that* turned into the least of her worries?

"What does the marking mean?" Casey asked Isadora. "I thought you and I were the chosen pieces of the prophecy. But Callia has the mark too."

Isadora pursed her lips, and from the tense expression on her face, it was clear she knew something and didn't want to elaborate.

"Isa?" Casey asked.

"I'm not sure," Isadora finally said. "I've been doing some . . . research, but I haven't come up with anything concrete yet." She focused on Callia. "Have you always had it?"

Callia really didn't have time for this—or care much at this point—but she sensed these two weren't going to let her leave until they got some answers, so she cooperated because truthfully, she wasn't quite calm enough to face her father—Simon . . . *Holy shit*—again.

"I didn't even know it was there until today."

Casey's gaze jumped to Isadora.

They both stared at Callia, and Callia's stomach did a slow roll. "So that means . . . ?"

"I don't think any of us know," Casey said. "But it means something."

Callia's gaze strayed to Isadora, whose jaw was clenched so tight the sharp slash of bone beneath the princess's pale skin was visible. Isadora knew something. Something she wasn't telling her or Casey.

Yeah, well, screw that. Callia didn't really give a flying rip right now.

"Have you . . . ?" Casey asked, not seeing the look on Isadora's face. "Has your head been bugging you lately? Like when we're all in the same room. Earlier, when you stepped into the chamber, I felt—"

"A buzzing," Callia finished. "Yeah, I felt it."

"Me too," Isadora said. "I felt it that day in my father's room as well. When the Argonauts were there and . . ." *Zander volunteered to marry me.*

Isadora's unspoken words hung like a weight between them, reminding Callia once more what else was wrong with this whole fucked-up situation.

Okay, screw this chitchat. Callia moved toward the door. "I need to talk to Zander."

"He left," Isadora said.

Callia turned slowly, one hand on the bathroom door. "What do you mean, he left?"

"Left, as in walked out the door. Right after you did." Isadora studied her nails. "I heard Theron mention something about the colony. Nick has information about recent daemon activity in the area. My guess is they're going to try to locate Atalanta's base."

No way.

A renewed sense of brutal betrayal welled in Callia's chest. He'd left. Hadn't said a word to her. Hadn't kept another of his promises. *I won't cut you out . . .*

She'd just been shuffled off to wait. Again. The Argonauts were doing what they always did, and she was the female who had nothing to offer. The harsh reminder of the way she'd been treated by her father, by Loukas, by every male in her godforsaken life, stabbed deep and twisted hard. "Where is my father?" she asked through clenched teeth.

"Simon's been put under house arrest by Lucian. I imagine they're together."

Callia imagined that as well. Like she even cared what happened to either of them at this point.

Fury filled her thoughts. She wasn't about to sit back and do nothing. If Zander thought he could push her around . . .

"You won't be allowed to cross the portal," Isadora said when Callia moved for the door again. "The Executive Guard will never let you through. By now Lucian's already sent word that you'll be trying to cross. The Argonauts too."

Callia's frustration grew to explosive levels. She turned on Isadora. "Damn them. I won't just sit back and—"

Casey's hand landed on Callia's forearm, and warmth spread up her skin at the contact. "No one expects you to." She glanced at the princess. "There's always the other way."

Isadora pursed her lips.

"What other way?" Callia asked.

"The secret portals," Casey said.

Callia's gaze jumped from one sister to the other. "You know where they are?"

Isadora didn't answer. And in the silence, Callia realized the princess wasn't going to share the information. Callia's eyes grew wide with disbelief.

That anger intensified to draw every one of her muscles tight and rigid. She and Isadora had never gotten along, and now Callia understood why. Had Isadora known the king was Callia's father? Was she hoping this would never come out?

"Isadora," Casey prodded.

Isadora sighed and shrugged. "I don't know where they are . . . exactly. But I have a . . . friend . . . who does."

Rage colored Callia's vision but she forced herself to stay calm. She needed the princess's help right now, more than she'd ever needed anyone's help before. "Then what are we waiting for? Let's go see your so-called friend."

Isadora didn't move, and that dead look Callia had noticed days ago in the king's study when she'd tried to convince Isadora to stand up to her father came back with a vengeance.

"Your son won't rule. The Council will never recognize him as an heir, because your mother committed adultery." She glanced at Casey, then back to Callia, and oh, yeah, the bitterness got through loud and clear. "It doesn't matter

what any of us want. It doesn't even matter that you're Argolean. All that matters are the rules. And the traditions."

It was all Callia could do not to wrap her hands around
Isadora's throat. Was the princess honestly as heartless as
she sounded? She was talking about her nephew. Flesh and
blood. Even if she didn't want to recognize Callia's son,
that's exactly what he was. As Callia fought the rage, faintly
she wondered if this was what Zander battled on a daily
basis, but the thought dissipated as she narrowed her eyes
on her new half-sister.

"I don't care about any of that right now. I just want my
son back."

"Well, I do care," Isadora said. "Your son's father will sire
the heir to the throne. There's no going back on that now.
Zander made a commitment to the king. And the king is not
going to change his mind simply because the truth of your
parentage finally came out. He'll acknowledge you, but he'll
bury the fact Zander is your son's father. Mark my words. No
one but us and the Argonauts will ever know the truth."

That was it. As much as Callia could take. She lunged for
Isadora.

"Oh, my God!" Casey gasped, grabbing Callia around the
middle and tugging her back. "Stop it! Both of you."

Isadora didn't flinch. And she didn't look fazed, even as
Callia struggled against Casey's hold. "Take a close look,
Callia. I don't like this situation any more than you do. If it
were up to me, none of this would be an issue. But I don't
have a say in it and neither do you." She stood rooted in the
same place, her eyes hard, unreadable stones. Eyes that
said she'd been beaten down more times than Callia could
even imagine. Eyes that seemed brutally resigned to her
fate as nothing but property. "I'm not trying to piss you off.
I'm just telling you the way it is."

Though she didn't want to, some part of Callia softened
toward Isadora. Just enough so she didn't tear the princess's
larynx out. She stopped struggling against Casey.

"This situation isn't going to miraculously fix itself when

you find your son," Isadora added. "You need to be prepared for that."

Callia's chest rose and fell as she tried to regulate her heart rate. And even if she didn't like it, she heard clearly what Isadora was saying. Even if they got her son back from Atalanta—and that was a big *if*—Zander's binding to Isadora was still on. Once an agreement was made with the king, it was final. And no matter what she or Isadora or even Zander wanted at this point, it was moot because it was all out of Isadora's hands. Out of all their hands.

It wasn't right. It would never be right. But at this moment . . . Callia didn't give a flip about politics and what was wrong with their world. "I'll deal with it. All I want is my son." She zeroed in on Isadora's tense face and though it nearly killed her, gentled her voice. "Please. Help me get to the human world so I can find him."

Isadora sighed. But it wasn't with relief. It was with resignation. Resignation and indifference. "Fine, then. I'll take you to the secret portal."

"Where is she?" Zander twisted the daemon's arm so far up the monster's back, bones cracked.

The daemon growled, tried to wriggle out from under Zander's hold, where he had the motherfucker pinned to the snowy ground. Around them, blood splatters stained what used to be pristine white.

"Zander," Theron said behind him. "Enough."

Zander twisted harder, ripping the daemon's arm clear out of his socket. The beast howled in pain. Beside him on the ground, two decapitated daemons lay steaming in the frigid night, their bodies illuminated by the moonlight filtering through the tall Douglas firs.

Covered in blood and sweat and other revolting viscera, Zander ignored Theron and leaned down so he was right at the daemon's good ear. The one he hadn't yet ripped off. "I'm gonna gut you like a pig if you don't tell me where Atalanta is."

"Zander," Theron said again, grabbing his arm. "I said that's enough. If you keep this up he won't be able to talk."

The daemon coughed. Blood sprayed over a fresh patch of powdery snow. He lifted his head inches off the frozen ground. "Go to hell," he rasped.

Zander's vision blurred. He shook off Theron's hand. Reached for his knife. "You go first, asshole." In one swift move she sliced the Daemon's jugular. Blood spurted over him and the ground. The daemon gagged and struggled.

"Fuck," someone whispered behind him.

Zander pushed up from the ground, every muscle in his body vibrating. He looked over what he'd done. Two mutilated daemons and the third choking on his own blood. Not a single one had told him where Atalanta was hiding out. Where his son was now.

He shoved the bloody knife into its holster at his thigh and turned away from the group. Behind him he heard one of the Argonauts decapitating the last daemon.

Pussies. Let the motherfucker bleed for a while.

He pulled out the GPS from his pocket and stalked across the snow. North was his best bet. Nick had mentioned the attacks were stronger father north. He wouldn't be so gentle with the next daemon he found.

"I said, hold up, Guardian." Theron stepped into Zander's path.

Zander halted. Flicked his eyes up. "Move."

"Where do you think you're heading?"

"Where do you *think* I'm heading? Get the fuck out of my way."

Theron squared his shoulders. Cerek and Gryphon took up space next to him.

Slowly, Zander lowered the GPS and looked at his kinsmen. Titus moved up on his right. Phineus on his left. They were boxing him in. "What the hell is this?"

Theron moved forward. "Look at you. You're covered in shit. Your shoulder's bleeding like a sieve and you're on the edge of an eruption. You didn't even give that last daemon time to answer before you ripped his ear off."

Zander looked into the trees.

"You're going back to the colony," Theron said. "You're getting that shoulder patched up, your ass cleaned off and your head cooled out. You're no use to anyone like this. And we're never going to find the boy unless you chill it down a notch."

The rage bubbled up and over. Zander dropped the GPS, had Theron by the front of his jacket and was up close and personal before any of the other Argonauts saw him move. "Try and make me."

"No!" Theron barked when Titus and Cerek moved to pull Zander back. He didn't pry Zander's hands off or move to get out of Zander's hold, even though they both knew he was ten times stronger than Zander. Instead he focused in on Zander's eyes and lowered his voice. "I don't know what you're going through. None of us do. But this isn't the way, Zander. I'm trying to help you here. We all are."

Zander's jaw ticked. Through a tunnel he heard Theron's words. But the rage was right there. Thrumming to be released. Coloring his vision and actions and thoughts.

"Do the smart thing, Z," Theron said. "We need to regroup. Come up with a plan. Nick will have information about where the most recent strikes have been. And you need that shoulder cleaned up before infection sets in. You won't be able to find your son if you've got gangrene."

Zander breathed deep. Once. Twice. Again until the haze started to clear.

"That's it," Theron said.

Slowly he let go of Theron's jacket and eased back. But his muscles were still coiled tight. And he felt like a rubber band, ready to snap any second.

"Cerek, Gryphon, Phin," Theron said to the guardians. "Take care of the bodies. Titus?"

"Yo," Titus said.

"Get Nick on the horn and tell him we're coming in."

As Titus moved off to get a signal on one of the satellite phones Nick had given them, Theron put a hand on Zander's shoulder. "You okay?"

Zander glanced at the hand, then at Theron's face, and though he still wanted blood, he knew Theron was right. "No."

"You were smart to leave Callia at home."

The image of Callia standing up to her father and the entire Council flickered through his mind. "She'll be pissed."

"She'll be alive." Theron glanced to the side. "And she doesn't need to see this shit."

Titus stepped up again, phone at his ear, mouthpiece tipped away. "Nick's got a scout out this way. He'll be here in twenty to pick us up."

Theron nodded. "Good."

Zander's jaw flexed and that familiar, all-encompassing rage pushed in again. Twenty minutes to wait. Another thirty back to the colony. Who fucking knew how long until he got stitched up and they put a plan together. The need to annihilate overrode everything. Even common sense.

"Hold it together, Zander," Theron said. The leader of the Argonauts turned to the others piling the mutilated daemons in a small clearing. "Let's ignite these motherfuckers."

Zander stayed where he was. On the edge of the group while they all worked to clean up his mess so no humans accidentally came across the bodies. The heat from the fire singed the hair on his face and arms. A foul stench filled his nose and lungs, but he didn't move away. He'd done this thousands of times, killed and watched the remains go up in smoke. But then he'd always had a sense of victory. Now he felt nothing but the urge to kill again. And a rage he was only barely keeping bottled inside.

Sooner or later it was going to explode, and he wouldn't be able to hold it back. He only hoped Atalanta was around when it happened.

CHAPTER EIGHTEEN

"You brought friends, I see. Yum."

Isadora turned at the sound of Orpheus's voice. He was decked out all in black—black boots, black pants, black sweater, black trench coat—and his eyes were as black as she'd ever seen them. Standing in the wind, near the base of Mount Parnithia, in the Aegis Mountains, with his long coat flapping behind him, his hair tousled and dark stubble covering his jaw, he looked formidable and menacing. And just a little bit ticked at having to meet her out here in the wild.

"Don't get any ideas, Orpheus. They're off limits."

Orpheus lifted his brow, looked over her head and zoomed in on Casey. "Are you sure? That one looks . . . tasty."

"That's Theron's bride. I don't think you want to tangle with him."

"Your half-sister?" Orpheus's eyes narrowed. "Now this is interesting. Who's the redhead?"

Isadora glanced at Callia, talking quietly with Casey near the trees. They were both roughly the same height, both had long hair, though one's was dark and one's was auburn, but their build was the same. Their mannerisms similar. Why hadn't she noticed that before? And wasn't it just fitting that she was the one out of three that didn't fit in?

She shook off the thought, pursed her lips. Since she wasn't ready to call Callia her "sister" yet, she wasn't entirely sure how to answer his question. Not when she and Callia were obviously still spitting nails at each other. "The king's healer. She needs to get to the human realm. That's why we're here."

Orpheus's gaze swung back to Isadora. "How did you get past the castle guards?"

Isadora crossed her arms over her chest. "There was a commotion at the Council meeting today. We slipped out then."

"We?"

"The three of us."

His eyes sharpened. "Interesting."

Isadora tried to read his expression as he studied Callia, but couldn't. A little of the jealousy she'd always harbored where Callia was concerned trickled in.

He stepped around Isadora toward the other two. "This must be my lucky day. Three pretty females and no Argonauts for miles."

Callia ignored his comment. "Isadora said you know the location of the secret portal."

"Portals," he corrected. "There are several. And you, Healer, don't mince words, do you?"

"Not anymore. Where are they?"

He glanced toward the hills. "The witches who live out here keep them mobile so the Executive Guard can't close them down."

"Fine," Callia said. "Take us to one, then."

"Nothing's free, female." His gaze roamed over her. "It's going to cost you."

Callia opened her mouth but Isadora cut her off. "Add it to my payment plan."

Orpheus looked her way with a smirk. "I've yet to collect the first payment, Princess. You sure about this?"

Isadora saw Callia's perplexed expression from the corner of her eye. She thought of her father, the king, and all the trouble he'd caused because he just couldn't leave well enough alone. She thought of Callia's lost son. Of Zander. And of what Callia had already agreed to give up. Though Isadora and Callia weren't close, it wouldn't be fair for Callia to be indebted to Orpheus the same way she was. Especially when the female was the victim in this whole mess to begin with.

"Yes," Isadora said before she could change her mind.

"Isadora . . . ," Casey started.

Orpheus clucked his tongue. "Okay, Isa, in that case—"

"Wait." Callia zeroed in on Isadora. "What does he mean by payment?"

"It's nothing." Isadora turned toward Orpheus. "The secret portal. Take us to the nearest one."

Orpheus looked from one to the next, then finally shrugged and headed east into the trees without another word. As Isadora made a move to follow, Callia stepped in her path. "Hold on. I don't need you paying anything for me."

Isadora heaved out a breath. "I know you're mad at Zander right now, but don't take it out on me. Orpheus and I have . . . an agreement."

"What kind of agreement?"

"One that doesn't concern you."

"Isadora—"

Isadora was seriously losing her patience with this. "Do you really want to spend time arguing or do you want to get to the human realm and find your son? Because all you're doing is wasting time."

Callia's jaw tightened. "I don't need your pity."

"Don't worry. I'm not doing it for you. I'm doing it for your son. And Zander. And because helping you bugs the hell out of the Council. And right now I'm enjoying making waves."

Callia's violet eyes searched Isadora's face. Eyes, Isadora noticed for the first time, that were just like Casey's. Just like the king's. And nothing like hers.

"You've changed," said Callia.

"You have no idea."

"Ladies," Orpheus called from the trees. "Either we go now or we're going to miss it. When I said these things were temporary, I wasn't kidding."

Callia stared at Isadora a beat longer before turning to follow Casey into the woods. They walked for roughly twenty minutes before they came across a small tent city. Orpheus left them and headed for a female sitting on a stool outside a neon green tent. She rose, wearing a long red, flowing skirt, a white sweater, and a purple scarf wrapped around her neck, and greeted him with a pat on the arm and a smile like they were old friends.

They spoke for a few minutes, then Orpheus pointed their way and the female looked over. Long snow-white hair curled around her shoulders. Her wrinkled brow said she wasn't thrilled by their arrival.

As they approached, the witch zeroed in on Callia. "The king's daughters I know. This one is a mystery."

"I—"

"She's the king's healer," Isadora said.

"More than a healer." The witch took a step toward Callia. "Why do you seek passage into the human realm? Danger lurks there. You know that to be true. You've experienced it. Do you seek something of value? Is personal gain your goal? Power? Is that why the three of you have come here today?" Her gaze swung over them. "Do you expect me to help you with that goal in mind? That which you do not understand cannot be made to—"

Frustration bubbled through Isadora. "She doesn't want—"

"I can speak for myself." Callia shot a warning look Isadora's way, then refocused on the witch. "Yeah, I am looking for something of value. My son. He was taken from me and I need to get to the human realm to find him. These two"—she nodded toward Isadora and Casey—"offered to help me. But if that's not a noble enough cause for you, then so be it." She glanced at Orpheus. "You said there are several secret portals, right?"

"Um." Orpheus looked down at the witch. "Yeah."

"Fine. Take me to the next one."

Orpheus hesitated, then spoke to the witch in a language

Isadora didn't understand, a language that definitely wasn't ancient Argolean.

The witch searched each of their faces while she listened, and something in her expression shifted. She said something back to Orpheus, but before any of them could ask what was happening, the witch stepped forward and held up her hands, palms out.

"I bind thee, the Hours, from doing harm unto yourselves or others." Then she closed her eyes and chanted. "Goddess divine, now bring me power that grows with every passing hour. Bring control back unto me. As I will, so mote it be." She opened her eyes, dropped her hands. "You may pass." She called over her shoulder, "Isis!"

A female with red spiked hair, wearing leggings, a military jacket and hiking boots ducked her head out of a purple tent behind the witch. "Yeah?"

"These three are to receive safe passage through the portal. Take them there."

Isis hustled out of the tent and looked them each over. "Seriously?"

"Isis—"

"Yeah, yeah," Isis said with a scowl, motioning them on. "Well, hurry it up. These things wait for no female, and I don't have all day, you know."

Casey and Callia exchanged bewildered glances but did as the second witch prodded. The first turned to follow. Before Orpheus could do the same, Isadora grabbed his arm. "What was that?"

"What, Isa? You don't speak Medean?"

She narrowed her eyes. "Don't play games with me, Orpheus. She called us the Hours. I was right about the Horae, wasn't I? And what was all that 'binding' crap?"

Orpheus glanced around to see if anyone was watching, then reached down and patted the outside of her leg where her mark was located. "I told you what you've got there is a powerful weapon," he whispered.

She gritted her teeth so she wouldn't pull away from his shockingly intimate and revolting caress. At some point she would have to pay him back. Thankfully, that wouldn't be today. "And that scared her."

"Yes. Because she knows what you could do with it if you wanted."

"And what is that?"

A slow smile spread across his face. "Oh, Isa. Do you really think I'm going to lay all the cards on the table for you right now? Before you've given me what I want?"

She drew in a breath, tried to keep herself calm. With Orpheus, it was always a game. But at least he'd confirmed her speculations. Callia—her half-sister—was as linked to her and Casey as they were to each other. The question was, just what did it all mean?

"No, Orpheus. I don't think you'd ever do anything for anyone but yourself."

She turned to follow the others, but this time he caught her arm, spinning her around to face him. The humor was gone from his face when he said, "Be careful in the human realm, Isa. There are evils there you can't begin to imagine. And where you're concerned, they're amplified. A thousand times."

"Are you trying to scare me?"

"Yes. And you'd be smart to be scared. Even though I've been training you, your new powers will be unpredictable. Even more so with those two." He nodded toward the tent Casey and Callia had already disappeared into. "Do not think this so-called weapon you have will protect any of you."

"Careful, Orpheus. In a minute I'll think you actually care."

"I do. I have a vested interest in you, Isa." His eyes sharpened. "And when someone strikes a deal with me, I always collect."

He held her gaze until she wanted to scream. Held her arm until sweat pooled at the base of her spine and she fought the urge to struggle free. Her stomach churned with apprehension and doubt. And not for the first time, she questioned that vision she'd seen of him saving her. The last one she'd had before she'd lost her powers. That little voice in the back of her head screaming *Devil!* grew louder with each passing day.

Finally he let go, but he didn't break eye contact. And the warning she saw flash in his dark eyes sent her nerves spinning all over again. "You'd better go, before the others start to wonder. But don't worry, Isa mine. I'll be waiting for you when you get back."

They'd driven twenty-four hours straight, stopping only to gas up.

In Vancouver Jeb dropped the load he'd hauled down from Alaska and picked up a new one. He hadn't asked Max a ton of questions, and he hadn't cared when Max had stayed in the truck out of sight during the switch. At first it had seemed weird. What kind of guy didn't wonder about a homeless ten-year-old? Then Max decided Jeb's lack of interest was a good thing. He might just make it through this yet.

They'd taken off again, heading south. At the border Max crawled into a compartment behind the driver's seat when they'd gone through customs. Not that he knew what the big deal was, but Jeb had told him it was either that or get tossed out in the cold, so he'd listened.

Jeb was quirky but, Max decided, harmless. Sometime after passing through Seattle, Max finally relaxed and drifted to sleep. He wasn't sure how long he was out—a couple hours? more?—but when he came to, there was a jacket covering him and the truck wasn't moving.

He pushed up, groggy and out of sorts. The jacket fell to his shoulders. Anxiety pricked his skin, sent sweat to his brow. It didn't matter how far he'd come; as far as he was concerned he'd never be far enough. Rubbing his eyes, he glanced through the big rig's windshield and realized they were at some kind of truck stop. Bright lights beat in from the outside, and Jeb was outside talking to a middle-aged woman with a cap covering most of her gray hair. She wore snow boots and a thick winter jacket zipped over her middle.

Jeb handed the woman something—money?—waved and headed toward the truck. The woman turned and went inside the small building.

The driver's-side door groaned open and Jeb pulled himself up into the monster vehicle. He flicked one look at Max before pulling off his coat and shoving it into the compartment behind his seat. "Thought you'd done died, boy. You been out goin' on seven hours."

Seven hours? Max peered through the windshield to get a better view. Dusk was just settling in, but he could see the landscape here was different from the Seattle area. Thick pine and fir trees surrounded them, a thin layer of snow covered the ground and city lights were nowhere to be seen. "Where are we?"

"Just past Mount Hood. About eighty miles north of Bend, Oregon. We ran into some heavy snow near Government Camp. Had to chain up. Thought fer sure that'd wake you. But nope. You sleep like the dead, boy."

Max barely heard the man as he rambled. They were in Oregon. He knew from conversations he'd overheard that the half-breed colony was somewhere in the mountains of Oregon. And the half-breeds were continuously outsmarting and outmaneuvering Atalanta and her daemons. Which meant he was as close to safety as this trucker was ever going to get him.

Jeb turned the key in the ignition and the big rig roared to life. As he put the truck in gear, Max said, "Aren't you hungry? I'm starving. Can't we stop longer so I can get something to eat?"

Jeb turned right around the back of the truck stop instead of left onto the road. "Already ate. Maggie's gonna let us park it here so I can get some shut-eye. You can go on in and get something if you're hungry. She made some elk stew that's the best thing since my pappy gave me my first can of Copenhagen."

They were stopping? For real? And Jeb was going to take a nap? This couldn't be any easier. Max fought a smile as he sat up in his seat. "Yeah. Cool. I'm so hungry I think I could eat a bear."

Jeb killed the ignition, tossed the keys onto the console between the seats and shot him a what-the-hell's-gotten-into-you? look. "You haven't strung more'n five words together since you climbed into my truck. What got stuck in your bonnet all the sudden?"

"Me? Nothing."

Jeb studied him closely. "You're not plannin' to run off are ya? There's nothin' good in these woods out here, you know. You'd just freeze to death. Or worse."

"Run off?" Max tried to brush off the worry. "Where would I go?" He reached for the door handle before Jeb could stop him. "I'll just let you sleep while I go eat. Thanks, Jeb."

Jeb harrumphed. "Okay, but don't wander. Be ready to go in two hours. I got a schedule to keep."

Max nodded as he jumped out of the truck. "Two hours. Got it."

Jeb was already leaning back in his seat and pushing the cap over his face as Max closed the door. The frigid air bit into his skin, but standing in the middle of the back lot of the small truck stop, Max took his first deep breath of freedom. He hadn't thought he'd make it this far. Couldn't believe his luck. He wasn't home free yet, but once he had some food, he'd snag a map and figure out where he was going next.

Against his chest, the disk warmed his skin, and he walked toward the building with a smile on his face and a spring in his step. A shadow moved behind the window. Squinting closer Max realized it was the woman from out front—Maggie. She lifted a hand and waved at him. Almost on reflex, his stomach growled.

He made it as far as the back door of the building before he heard the scream. A blood-curdling shriek that froze his hand on the door handle and sent his heart rate into the triple digits.

A roar echoed from inside. Something hit the door hard. Max jumped back and let go of the handle. The screeching stopped altogether.

Run. Go. Now!

His adrenaline surged as he took off toward the truck. Though there was no way the daemons could have found him so fast, the bone-chilling temperature told him otherwise. They were here. Somehow. They were here.

"Jeb!" *Hear me! Turn on the truck!* The door to the building behind him crashed open, followed by an ear-shattering roar, but he didn't look back. "Jeb!"

Twenty feet from the big rig, the driver's-side door popped open and Jeb dropped to the ground, muscles coiled tight, face white as snow. He didn't cower the way most humans would in the same situation, and the look in his eyes as he took in the monsters behind Max said he'd seen daemons before. "Come on, boy! Run!"

Max didn't have time to question the hows or whys of that. He sprinted as hard as he could toward the truck, his arms and legs pumping, his heart pounding in his ears.

"Run!" Jeb hollered, motioning with his arms.

Just as Max reached the tail of the semi, something caught his leg. He went down hard, face-first into the gravel. Snow and rocks impaled his hands and face. The daemon growled behind him, grabbed on to his leg and yanked.

Terror clawed its way up Max's throat as he dug his fingers into the frozen ground, tried to grab something to stop him from being dragged across the parking lot.

And then he heard a roar, only this one wasn't daemon, it was human. Something warm and fluid squirted across his neck. The daemon let go of his leg.

"Get up!" Jeb screamed.

Max pushed up to his knees, his ears ringing, his hands

and face a mixture of dirt and blood. Whipping around, he saw Jeb holding a hunting knife as long as his forearm. The daemon was on the ground behind him, blood spilling from a wound in his chest.

"Get up!" Jeb screamed again.

Max scrambled to his feet.

"Go! Go!" Jeb got a handful of Max's jacket and half pulled, half pushed him toward the cab of the truck. As Max skidded to a halt and reached up to grab the handle, he glanced back and saw Jeb standing with the knife in his shaking hand while the daemon pulled himself to his full height and glared down at him.

Max tugged himself up. Inside the cab he spotted the keys Jeb had tossed on the console. Could he drive this thing? He'd watched Jeb all the way down here. Hell yeah, he could drive it. And at the very least he could mow down some daemons while he learned. His hands shook as he found the right key and shoved it into the ignition.

"You made a foolish choice, human," the daemon outside growled. "Like the half-breed inside. The boy belongs to us."

Max's fingers froze on the keys. Maggie was a half-breed?

"I got a knife here that says different."

"You're no match for me, human," the daemon snarled.

"Yeah, prob'ly not," Jeb answered. "But I'm not about to make this easy for you. That boy's done nothin' to nobody."

Max hesitated. All he had to do was turn the key, stomp on the gas and take off. Never look back. But something stopped him. Something in the center of the chest that ached so bad, it wouldn't let him leave.

I grow tired of your humanity, Maximus. Kill or be killed. That is the world in which we live.

Never before had Atalanta's words been so true. If Max left, the daemon would rip Jeb to pieces. If Max joined him, even if he was able to overpower this one, the other two inside would be on top of them in minutes. And there was no telling how many more were out in those woods.

The disk burned hot against his chest. He looked down at the markings on his hands. What good was ruling the world if you lost yourself in the process?

The daemon growled outside. Max let go of the keys, whipped around and searched the storage area behind the seats for Jeb's toolbox. When he came up with a twelve-inch-long screwdriver, he figured that was as good a weapon as he was going to find, threw the driver's door open and leapt from the truck.

Jeb had circled around so neither he nor the daemon were looking Max's way. As Jeb lunged with the knife, Max tightened his grip on the screwdriver and inched closer. Jeb's knife only nicked the daemon's arm, didn't even draw blood. The daemon chuckled and swiped out with his claws, catching Jeb across the chest and abdomen.

Jeb howled and fell back against the ground with a thunk. Blood oozed from his torso, staining his shirt. The knife flew from his hand to land yards away on the cold ground. Jeb tried to crawl backward over the ground to reach his knife, but it was too far away. The daemon leaned down so he and the trucker were face-to-face. "I told you that you made a foolish choice, human. Say hello to Hades for me."

Jeb's eyes widened with horror as the daemon lifted his razor-sharp claws.

Max charged. Arm raised high, he shoved the end of the screwdriver deep into the daemon's neck. Immediately the daemon shot up, wailing in pain. He threw Max off. Max hit the ground hard, the impact stealing his breath, and rolled across the frozen lot. The daemon stumbled backward until he hit the side of the semi, shakily grabbed the handle of the screwdriver and pulled.

Blood spurted from the wound like a fire hose. It was clear the screwdriver had hit the daemon's jugular. The daemon fell to his knees on the ground, shrieking while his hand covered the wound and blood continued to pour through his fingers.

"The knife," Jeb croaked, still trying to crawl backward.

Dazed, Max slapped out, searching for the knife himself. Finally, his hand closed around the handle. Snow and gravel filled his palm. Adrenaline pumping, he pushed to his feet and stopped in front of the daemon, still on its knees, writhing in pain.

Kill or be killed.

Yeah, he'd learned that lesson well, hadn't he? Only it wasn't the way Atalanta had ever intended.

Adrenaline pulsing, he swung back and through, just like she'd taught him, decapitating the monster before it could regain its strength and kill them both.

He didn't dwell on what he'd done. Didn't even look down at the grotesque head severed from the daemon's body. Max turned and headed for Jeb. He dropped to his knees next to the man, immediately ripped off his coat and pressed it to the human's wounded chest.

"R-run," Jeb breathed.

"I'm not leaving you out here."

Jeb's hand closed over Max's wrist. "There are . . . more."

Yeah, Max already knew that. Atalanta's scouts traveled in threes. But that wasn't all. There would be more coming. Lots more. Especially when this one didn't check in.

Max stared down at the human, wondered how things had turned so bad so fast. He didn't want this. He didn't want any of it. He wasn't dumb enough to think Atalanta loved him and wanted him back. No, what she wanted was the disk he'd stolen from her. The key to controlling this world and the next. And she wouldn't stop until she found him and took it back.

Unless . . .

He reached down and palmed the disk against his chest. It still burned warm, giving him a strength he hadn't had before. It had gotten him all the way here when he should have been too tired to move. He didn't know exactly what it was, but it had power. Like the glass that old lady had given him. And instinctively he knew only bad things would happen if Atalanta got it back.

Remember your humanity, Maximus. Let it be your guide.

The old lady's words sifted through his mind. Maybe the disk could help Jeb, if only so the man could stay alive long enough to get out of this hellhole.

And if not, well, at least Atalanta wouldn't get it back.

He squeezed his hand around the disk, then drew the chain over his head with frantic fingers. While Jeb watched him, Max stuffed the disk and chain inside his coat pocket.

"Wh-what are you d-doing?" Jeb asked.

A roar echoed from the doorway of the building. Max's body stilled. They didn't have much time.

Quickly Max tucked his coat around Jeb again, pressed it into Jeb's wounds and placed Jeb's hand over the top for pressure. "Do me a favor and keep this safe. Do you think you can make it to the truck?"

Eyebrows drawn together in confusion, Jeb turned his head slightly on the gravel, glanced toward the truck. Nodded.

"Good." Max squeezed Jeb's hand. "The keys are in the ignition. Get in, lock the doors and go. And don't look back. You're right. More will come. But they're coming for me. Not you. I'm sorry I dragged you into this."

"Max?"

Max pushed to his feet and turned toward the daemons.

This was it for him. No way he could outrun two daemons. But maybe . . . just maybe he could draw them far enough away to give Jeb a fighting chance.

He sucked in a deep breath. The image of his mother—his real mother—passed before his eyes: her red hair, her violet eyes, her sweet and beautiful face. He'd hoped some day to meet her. To ask her why she'd let him go. Now it really didn't matter anymore. Funny that all that mattered was doing the right thing.

"You bastards!" he yelled. "I'm not going anywhere with you. Go back to hell, you freaks!"

The daemons growled in half warning, half anticipation of a kill yet to come.

His adrenaline surged, and fear raced up his spine. True fear, because he knew what was coming next. He'd seen it up close and personal. But Max didn't hesitate. He took off running into the trees as fast as his legs would carry him.

CHAPTER NINETEEN

The shower did little to chill Zander out. A frenzied storm bubbled beneath the surface of his control, and every second he spent here at the colony wasting time only energized the lightning inside him.

He wrapped a white towel around his waist without bothering to dry himself off. When he stepped into the bedroom Nick had told him to use to get cleaned up, he found Titus leaning against the wall and Lena already setting out scissors, needles and medical crap on the coffee table in the sitting area.

Lovely. Titus was here to make sure Zander didn't snarl at the half-breed and that the healer, who obviously didn't give a rat's ass about Zander, did her job.

He didn't bother arguing. Instead, he crossed the floor and dropped into the chair the healer nodded toward. The sooner he got stitched up, the sooner he could haul ass back to the hunt and find his son. Fear and dread spread through his chest, condensed into rage. This time he had very definite, very gruesome plans for the next SOB he found.

Titus didn't speak as Lena went to work, just crossed his arms over his chest and chewed on the toothpick sticking out of his mouth.

Lena pressed all around the edges of the wound with her fingertips. "It's not too deep. This shouldn't take long."

He kept his eyes on the pale yellow wall while she went to work.

She glanced at his face. "Nick mentioned what happened." When he didn't answer, she stuck him with a needle—not, he noticed, gently. "Is it true? Does Atalanta really have your son?"

Just the mention of his son sent the firestorm swirling all over again. He clenched his jaw, worked hard not to let the rage overtake him here, curled his hands into fists and tried to think about . . . nothing.

Except it didn't work.

She set the syringe on the table, reached for a needle and threaded it, her focus intent on the instruments in her hands. "Does she . . . does Callia know?"

He wasn't in the mood to talk. Especially about Callia. But he also wasn't in the mood to piss off one more person who could push him over the edge. "Yes."

"And you're here looking for him. Where is she?"

"Home."

"In Argolea. Where she's safe."

The disapproval in her words was more than evident. He clenched his jaw to the point of pain so he didn't let her have it.

She drew the needle into his skin and back up again, never meeting his gaze. "You underestimate her, Argonaut."

Like he gave a rip what she thought.

She continued stitching. He went back to watching the wall. Silence descended as she worked. Finally, she tied off the ends of the threads, snipped and covered the wound with a clean dressing, then said, "That's it. I'd tell you to be careful with it, but I have a feeling you'll just do whatever the hell you want, so I won't bother."

She packed up the rest of her things, flicked a look at Titus still leaning against the wall. "I'm done."

Titus nodded once and Zander had the distinct impression he was being babysat.

Which rankled. Big-time. That fury bubbled and swirled.

"I hope you find what you're looking for." Lena stopped with one hand on the door. "Just don't be surprised if it's not what you expected."

Rankled? Shit, forget Titus. The healer knew how to

irritate the fuck out of a person. He needed to get the hell out of here, like *now*, before he blew his lid.

Zander pushed to his feet.

"Hold up, old man."

Titus ambled toward him, shifting the toothpick to the other side of his mouth and shoving his big hands into his pockets. His shoulders remained relaxed, but the intensity in his eyes was a big ol' red flag that he had something on his mind.

I don't have fucking time for this.

"Well, make time," Titus muttered.

Zander heaved a sigh, because even in his mood he knew taking Titus on right now had *bad news* tattooed all over it. "What?"

"The healer had a point."

Zander shot his kinsman a bored look.

"Callia has a right to be here."

Not a fucking chance. "It's too dangerous."

Zander didn't make it a foot away before Titus stepped in his path. "Too dangerous for whom? Her or you?"

Zander narrowed his eyes. "What the hell are you getting at?"

"I'm just saying. It should be her decision, Z, not yours. To hell with how it affects you."

Zander's eyes widened. Titus knew Callia was his vulnerability? Fucking fantastic. His mind skipped back over the connection Titus and Callia seemed to share and that rage worked its way in again. He clenched his jaw to tamp it down. "Screw how it affects me. You know it'll be a thousand times worse if those daemons find her now. I'm not letting them touch her. Not letting anyone touch her. She's been through enough. You don't like my methods, don't agree with my decision? Too fucking bad. She's not your soul mate, so it's not your damn call."

One side of Titus's lips curled, just a touch. A lame-ass grin that made Zander want to shove his fist through the wall . . . or through Titus's face, he didn't care which.

"Suspicion confirmed," Titus muttered. Then louder, "Word to the wise, dude. You are officially fucked."

Zander glared at Titus as the other Argonaut moved toward the door. "Tell me something I don't already know."

"Do yourself a favor, Z. Before you fuck this up any more than you already have. Tell Callia the truth."

Zander stared after Titus as the guardian left the room, confused by what had just happened here. He'd never understood Titus, and now was no exception, but he had a strange feeling the guardian was trying to help him, not twist the knife. Outside in the hall, voices drifted to his ears, but he couldn't make out the conversation. All he heard were Titus's words pinging around in his head.

Tell Callia the truth? Yeah, right. That'd unleash a whole new set of problems he didn't need. Being honest—truly honest with her—meant opening himself up to his humanity, something he'd been trained not to do. Could he do it now? Let go of that self-control, tear open his soul and give it to her once and for all? Consequences swirled in his mind. History and stories of Argonauts from Achilles's line long dead. It would change him. Who and what he was. And the fundamental part of him that was a guardian. The immortal fighter he and the others had come to rely on. And then there was his son . . .

Footsteps drew close. A door slammed. Slowly his eyes lifted until he was staring at the very face he'd conjured in his mind. *"Thea."*

"I trusted you." Her eyes flashed. " 'I won't shut you out.' That's what you said to me. I trusted you and you left me there while you ran off to play god."

"Thea—"

"Don't *'thea'* me." Callia advanced on him, shoved her index finger into his chest. Was as pissed as he'd ever seen her. And more gorgeous than he could have imagined. "You don't ever get to call me that. He's my son, Zander. Do you get that? Mine. You didn't even know about him until recently."

"Callia—"

She swatted at his hands. "Go to hell. I don't need you, you know. I can get Theron or one of the others to help me get him back. I only came up here to warn you that you're not going to push me out of this. I won't let you." Her eyes blazed as she turned for the door. "Stay clear of me, Zander."

She had one hand on the door handle by the time he wrapped his arms around her waist from behind and lifted her off the floor. "Wait."

She struggled against his hold. "Let me go."

"I can't." He pulled her back against his chest as words he hadn't yet decided to speak bubbled up. "I've tried. Gods, I've tried but I haven't been able to. I need you."

"You never needed me. I was nothing more than a fling. A way to stick it to the Council. Something to pass your precious time."

"That's not true." She squirmed against him, and though it wasn't the reaction he wanted, he couldn't help it. His blood ran hot and went due south. Being close to her always electrified him, especially when she was grinding her sweet ass into his hips like she was doing now. "You were everything. *Are* everything."

"Liar." She pushed back, jammed the heel of her boot into his shin. He winced as pain shot up his leg. "You believed the worst about me without hesitation."

He had. She was right. And he'd never forgive himself for that fact. "I didn't stop needing you. I never stopped wanting you."

"Oh, yeah," she scoffed. "I can feel how much you want me. That's all you ever wanted from me, isn't it, Zander? Sex. Yeah, we were good at that, weren't we?"

A space in his chest went cold at the bite to her words. Instinctively, he let go.

She didn't flee like he expected. Instead, she turned slowly, the fire brewing in her rivaling the rage he kept locked inside. "Why don't you come and take me then, Zander? Since we both know that's all I ever was to you."

"Callia." Something had shifted in her. Something fueled by revenge and that wicked attraction that had drawn them together the first time. "Stop."

"Why?" One side of her mouth twitched, but there was no humor in her eyes. There was only anger and heat and malice. "I thought you said you *needed* me."

"I do." He backed up until he hit the couch. Held up his hands as she advanced, hoping to ward her off. Had no idea how things had turned so fast. "But not like this."

Her eyes narrowed. "I think *just* like this. Come on, Zander. I'm just a weak female. You have all the power here."

"No, I don't." Warning bells went off in his head. Even though this was wrong, even though he knew what she was doing had nothing to do with him and was all about making her point, he knew he wouldn't be able to resist her for long. Not when she was the one person he'd never been able to resist. "You do. You always have."

The muscles around her violet eyes tightened. She had her hand on the towel at his waist before he even saw her arm dart out. "You're right. I do."

She yanked the towel from his body and tossed it on the ground. Her eyes settled on his hips and his very—dammit—erect arousal. "You may be saying no, but your body is definitely saying yes." She lifted her gaze. Pushed her hands against his chest and moved closer until the long lean length of her body was pressed tight against his. "Come on, Zander. Show me how much you *need* me."

The blood pounded hard in his veins. Her sweet female scent surrounded him, enticed him, latched on and wouldn't let go. The tips of her breasts pushing into his chest and the soft sway of her hips cradling his erection drove him wild. But the callousness of her tone was the one thing he couldn't ignore.

"Callia," he gripped her shoulders. "Don't tempt me right now."

"Why not?" She resisted his push, sank her teeth into the base of his neck. "You said you wanted to fuck me in that cave." Her voice dropped to a husky whisper. "Now's your chance."

He closed his eyes, swallowed hard, knew he needed to get the hell out of here but couldn't seem to move. She was angry and hurt and feeling self-destructive after everything she'd learned today, which was the only reason she was here doing this to him now. But even though he understood that, it didn't change what he wanted. What he *needed*.

Heaven help him . . .

He let go of her shoulders, slid his arms around her waist. Tugged her close and buried his face in her hair. "*Thea . . .*"

"I knew it." She lifted her head, dug her fingernails into his chest. "You son of a bitch." As it had in the cave, an energy force shot from his body into her hands and straight back out again, hitting him square in the torso.

He gasped, the rush of power strong enough to knock him off balance. But this one wasn't nearly as powerful as the one she'd thrown at him before, and he didn't go down. Instead he reached for her shoulders again, but she twisted out of his grasp. "Go to hell, Zander."

She made it three steps before he snagged her by the arm. "I've been there way too long. And I don't want it anymore."

"Zan—"

He yanked her close, covered her mouth with his. The kiss was hard and pointed and left no doubt as to what he wanted. When she pounded her fist against his chest, he didn't let go. When she curled her fingers into his skin again, he drew her tighter, locked one arm around her waist and slid his other hand up into her silky hair so she couldn't throw his own pain back at him again. He walked her backward toward the door. Her spine hit the wood. She mumbled something against his lips, but he didn't loosen his grasp. Instead he changed the angle of the kiss, stroked his tongue over hers and pushed aside all the consequences of what he was about to do.

Her shocked violet eyes seared his when he pulled back,

but he didn't let it deter him. "You don't need me?" he said. "I got that loud and clear. But you get this. I didn't do anything to protect you when I should have, and I have to live with that, but I won't make the same mistake twice. And if that means leaving you a hundred times in Argolea where you're safe, then that's exactly what I'll do."

"You—"

"As for this?" He nodded down to where he still held her tight against him. "It's not at all what you think it is. Its eight hundred years of searching for you and ten trying to live without you. It's being close to you and wanting something I can't have. And that's not sex, Callia. That's you. Just you. The only thing I've ever wanted."

He let go of her and moved back, but he kept his eyes on her in case she came at him again. A storm brewed in her violet irises. One he knew all too well. Her lips were plump and pink from his kiss. Her hair a tangled mess around her shoulders. She glared at him as her chest rose and fell with her deep breaths. When she took a step forward, he braced himself.

"You don't fight fair," she whispered.

"I never claimed to."

"The soul-mate curse is bullshit."

His eyes ran over her face. Her perfect, familiar, gorgeous face. "It's my reality. Not yours."

"It's a cop-out. I don't belong to you, Zander. I don't belong to anyone." Her voice dropped to a whisper. "I make my own choices now."

She pressed her mouth to his so fast he barely had time to suck in a breath. Her kiss was as forceful and bruising as his had just been, and full of heat and passion and desire. And gods help him, it didn't matter if the move was made in anger or frustration or even self-destruction. Because this was her. His soul mate. His life. His heart.

"Callia—"

"Don't talk." She let go of him, grasped the hem of her sweater and pulled it over her head. The garment hit the

floor at their feet. He caught a flash of fabric and skin before she kissed him again and her hands slid into his hair.

Her full breasts pressed against his bare chest, her tongue
slid into his mouth. Her erect fabric-covered nipples abraded
his skin as he wrapped his arms around her waist and
kissed her back.

He wished she'd jerked the camisole off along with her
sweater, wished she'd ditched the pants at the same time.
Wished he weren't so delirious from the taste of her so he
could slow things down and savor this moment like he
should. "Callia—"

"Uh-uh." She let go again, popped the buttons on her
pants and shimmied out of them. Before he had a chance to
look, she was pressed up tight against him again, naked
from the waist down and his for the taking. "No talking."

Oh, holy gods . . .

Her tongue tangled with his and her fingers knotted in
his hair. She tugged his head where she wanted it and
kissed him deeper. Moaned into his mouth and pulled
harder. Drugged from the dark, erotic taste of her, he
groaned against her mouth and didn't realize she'd turned
him around until he pressed against her and found resistance where she hit the back of the couch.

"Pick me up," she mouthed against his lips.

He was powerless to do anything but what she wanted.
His hands rushed to her backside and he lifted her easily to
set her on the back of the couch, all the while stroking her
lips, her tongue, her mouth with his own. Her legs parted,
wrapped around his hips, pulled him in. When the tip of his
cock grazed her soft, wet slit, he realized this was going to
be over way faster than he wanted.

"Callia, I—"

"No talking, Zander." Her teeth latched on to his earlobe.
She bit down just as her hand found his cock. A lick of pain
shot across his ear, but he groaned when she closed her
fingers around his length. Slowly she drew her hand up, let
the hard cylinder of flesh glide through her grip. When she

reached the underside of the tip, she squeezed, drew his earlobe deep into her sultry mouth and sucked.

Every muscle in his body tightened. Rational thought flew out of his mind. He had one coherent need, and that was to get inside his soul mate *right now*.

A growl rumbled in his chest as he pulled his ear from her lips and drove his tongue into her mouth, kissing her with a rabid desire he hadn't felt in years. She mumbled "Yes" against his lips and drew his cock to her opening. Instinct ruled as her burning, slick wetness surrounded him, and he thrust hard at the first touch until he was seated deep inside her.

She moaned, shifted her hips and took him even deeper when he thought there was nowhere left to go. "Yes, yes, gods yes, Zander."

Frantic for more, he slid out and back in. Her arms locked around his shoulders, her legs around his back. Her silky camisole rubbed against his chest as she licked into his mouth, not the skin-on-skin sensation he wanted, but just as erotic when he thought of the fact she was still half-clothed and hanging on to him for dear life while he pushed into her and their coupling picked up speed.

Electricity shot down his spine. Sweat slicked his skin. She didn't stop kissing him, wouldn't give him a chance to talk. Every time he tried to slow down she held on tighter, pressed back, urging him faster. His breaths came fast and hard as he moved inside her and she tipped his head with her hands and kissed him crazy again and again.

He was pretty sure he could die right now and be happy for all eternity. The feel of her tight, moist sheath surrounding him, the taste of her dark, spicy essence on his tongue, the scent of his one perfect female aroused and wanting nothing but him . . . This was better than any heaven he could imagine.

She tightened around him, dug her fingernails into his shoulders, moaned against his lips. He moved quicker, kissed her harder, knew her climax was building—knew every one of her tells. Desperate to give her exactly what she needed, he plunged deeper, pulled her hips tighter to his, angled her body so the tip of his cock hit her sweetest spot over and over and over again.

She pushed against him, lifted herself in his arms, tore her mouth from his and groaned long and low as her body pulsed around him. And in that moment, he didn't hesitate. He latched on to her neck as she rode him, licked the sweet, tender flesh with his tongue and sucked. Then gave himself over to the sensations enveloping his cock and came harder than he had in his whole life.

Spent, she collapsed against his chest, rested her forehead on his shoulder. Her torso rose and fell with her rapid breaths, her pulse pounded in time with his. And his heart swelled as he drank her in inch by inch because this— *this*—was a moment he thought he'd never experience again.

"*Thea . . .*"

"I . . . oh, gods. I didn't mean for that to happen."

He slid his hands up in to her hair, massaged the nape of her neck, ran his fingers over the mark he now knew was there. "I don't hear anyone complaining."

"I . . ." She tipped her head so her temple rested against his chest. Was clearly trying to slow her own racing heart. "I won't get pregnant. It's not the right time. You don't have to worry."

Worry? How could she think that?

"I'm not worried," he said. "I'd love to see you swollen with my child. I missed it the last time. I . . ." He pressed his lips to the top of her head as his throat grew thick and that space inside him warmed with just the thought of a family. A real family. And when they found their son . . . "Tell me when and I'll make sure we hit the right time."

She stilled against him. Her head slowly lifted until her violet eyes rested on his, searching his face. In the silence he couldn't tell what she was thinking. Then she pushed against his chest and broke free. "I have to go."

"Callia—"

She maneuvered away from him and dropped to the ground, leaving him cold after the loss of her heat. She reached for her pants from the floor. "This was a mistake."

His chest tightened at her words. But before she could get away he wrapped his arms around her and lifted her from the floor. "It's not a mistake. You and I are never a mistake."

"Zander. Let me go."

Not a chance. Not ever again.

He walked them to the bed and laid her out on the comforter, covering her body with his. "I already told you, I can't." He lowered his head, pressed his lips to the hollow of her throat.

"Please don't," she whispered.

He shifted higher, kissed first her right cheek, then her left. "Do you remember"—his lips trailed kisses to her ear— "that night I waited for you in the woods behind your father's house?"

"Zander. Don't."

He kissed her earlobe, drew it into his mouth, breathed hot against her skin. "I didn't think you'd show."

She shuddered beneath him, and he felt the fight slide out of her body. Felt all those years of avoidance and misunderstanding shrink to this one moment. Felt that empty space in his chest fill to bursting.

"Your father wasn't happy when he saw me at the clinic earlier that day. But I had to see you. I needed you then, *thea*."

Her eyes squeezed tight, and he knew she was remembering that night. The same one that still played in his mind like a scene from a movie. One lone tear gathered at the corner of her lashes. "It . . . it wasn't you. He never wanted me helping the Argonauts or the king. I didn't understand then. But now . . ."

Now he understood too. "He knew about us then."

"He suspected," she whispered. "He didn't know for sure." He kissed her jaw, her throat, licked his way to that sensitive spot where her neck met her shoulder. She trembled at the touch, the reaction encouraging him, exciting him. "You were all I could think about. Do you know how hard it was not to tell the world you were mine? To keep what was happening between us secret? I wanted you in that clinic. I wanted to climb the trellis to your veranda and take you in your bed. I went a little mad that night when you didn't show."

She drew in a shaky breath when he kissed his way across her collarbone, when he slid the strap of her camisole down and pressed his lips to the rise of her breast. "I . . . I couldn't get away. He kept me up late, reading passages from Homer, talking about the Council. He suspected. I . . . I had to wait until he was asleep before I could sneak out."

He'd hoped that was the reason she'd kept him waiting that night. But hearing her say the words after all this time . . .

He slipped the other strap off her shoulder, drew the camisole down so her perfect breasts came into view. He cupped one heavy mass, breathed hot over the tip. "You have no idea how I felt when I saw you run through the trees toward me. Do you remember what happened that night, *thea*?"

"You . . . you kissed me." Tentatively, her hands slid up his shoulders, into his hair.

"Where?"

"Here." She arched her back and brought her breast to his lips. Whether the move was instinctive or persuasive, he didn't care. He drew her nipple into his mouth. Sucked until she quivered. A low moan escaped her lips, the sound so erotic he grew hard all over again. He moved to her other breast, repeated the stroke, the suck, the way his tongue traced the tip of her nipple and his teeth scraped the edge. She arched against him again, spread her legs. He sank down into the vee of her body until his heavy erection rested against her sleek, hot center.

"Then what?" he whispered.

"You . . . oh . . . ." She moved her hips so the tip of his cock rubbed against her tight knot. "You lowered me to the ground and pulled off my clothes."

He had. Right there in the small clearing. Hadn't been able to get at her fast enough. "What did you do?"

"I helped you," she whispered.

"You wanted me."

"Yes." She groaned as he trailed his mouth over the bunched-up fabric of her camisole.

"You wanted me to kiss you here, didn't you?" He pressed his mouth against her toned belly, slipped his lips lower.

"Yes."

"How about here?" He moved to the pressure point between her leg and torso.

"Yes," she groaned, straining against him.

"And what about here?" Gently, he kissed the top of her naked mound.

"Oh, yes."

"And now, *thea*? Do you want my mouth here now?" He brushed his fingers over her center, traced the line of her slit. Her body shook against him and the heady scent of her arousal drifted all the way into his soul.

"Yes," she breathed.

He made a long sweep of her cleft, settled on her clit, flicked the tip and sucked until she moaned and writhed beneath him. He didn't let up, taking her to the edge again and again. The sweet honey of her arousal made him light-headed. Shattered his resistance. Called to that part of him that was linked tightly to her.

His lips found her hip, her stomach, her breast. Her eyes were still closed tight as he sucked her nipple deep, as he pushed her legs wide with his knees and braced himself on his hands above her. His mouth moved back to her neck, and he latched onto her dewy skin, sucked, then lowered his hips so his pounding erection was cradled right where he wanted it most.

He lifted his head, pressed his mouth to her ear, pushed, gently, until he just barely entered her. She groaned. Her hands found his ass, tugged, tried to pull him in deeper, but he held back.

"Then was happened?" he whispered in her ear.

"You made love to me."

"No, *thea*. I loved you. Open your eyes."

Her dark lashes lifted, and her shimmering violet eyes focused on his. Eyes he wanted to lose himself in forever. Eyes that told him even if she never felt the same way about him, opening himself to her and his humanity was not a mistake.

"I loved you then, Callia. I knew that night in the meadow. When the rain fell around us. When you came apart in my arms. Only I didn't tell you because I was afraid it would push you away. That it was too soon. That you didn't feel the same. I thought . . ." Emotions closed his throat, but he gritted his teeth, knew he had to get this out. "I thought I had all the time in the world to make you fall in love with me. I was wrong. If I could go back and change one thing about the past it would be that."

Tears gathered in her eyes, and he lowered to his elbows, used his fingers to brush the wetness away from her cheek. Felt the last shred of his resistance melt away. "If I could go back, I'd tell you that I loved you. And it's not because you're my soul mate. If the Fates had pushed me toward someone else, I'd still have loved you."

"Zander." She closed her eyes tight, pulled his mouth to hers, lifted her hips and drew him in to her silky heat.

Their joining was slow and sultry. Not the frantic coupling of before, but deeper, hotter, a thousand times more intense. As he moved inside her, he threaded his fingers through hers, watched her face, kissed her lips, her nose, her cheeks, couldn't tear his eyes away as her pleasure mounted. He'd thought he was condemned to spending eternity without his heart, and here it was, beating inside him all over again. In her.

She moaned his name, arched her back. Her slick channel tightened around him, signaling her release was coming. He drove harder, pushed deeper, strained to give her what she needed. And when she peaked, when her body contracted with her release, he went with her. Let go of the battle he'd been fighting inside himself for so long. And finally turned everything over to her.

Max's legs burned. His lungs were on fire. He darted around and through trees, twisted his ankle on a root sticking out of the ground but kept running. Behind him he heard the daemons closing in, but he didn't turn to see how close they were. Knew if he saw them . . .

He hit a patch of ice and slid, arms darting out to the side to steady himself. Just before he went down, he slammed into the base of a tree. Pain shot through his torso and legs. He grabbed on and pulled himself up.

A growl echoed at his back.

Swallowing a gulp of frigid air, he pushed off the tree and tore off to his right, sliding down a snow-covered slope on his hands and butt toward what looked like a logging road below.

He slipped and slid to his side, righted himself with his arms, desperate for any way he could get to the bottom. A rush of water met his ears. If he could get to that stream and jump in, it could carry him away from this horror. He might freeze, but at least he wouldn't be lunch.

Heart pumping, he hit the bottom of the hill, jolted his legs. Above, thrashing and roars echoed in the trees. He scrambled to his feet and ran as hard as he could toward what he hoped was a big, swirling river.

Just as he reached the far side of the logging road, a daemon dropped in his path.

He tried to stop, lost his balance, fell back to smack his head against the hard frozen ground. Stars flashed in front of his eyes. He cried out in pain, but the face above scared the sound out of him.

Phrice. Only he was a helluva lot bigger than the last time Max had seen him, and way more powerful.

"That's right," Phrice said, leaning down. "I'm your own worst nightmare."

Max scrambled backward. Phrice was the archdaemon?

Panic and fear wedged their way into Max's chest. He crab-walked backward until he ran into a boot. Horror shook his body, made him lift his head. Dripping fangs and glowing green eyes peered down at him.

Phrice caught Max by the scruff of his shirt and lifted him high in the air.

Max yelped, kicked his legs. Claws punctured his shirt and dug into his skin. Pain shot through his torso.

"You've been a bad boy, Maximus. What should we do with him?" Phrice asked the other daemon.

"I can think of a few things," the second daemon said.

"So can I." Phrice pulled Max so close, the daemon's vile stench filled Max's nose and throat, causing him to gag. "Before this night is over, *boy*, you're going to wish you'd never been born."

Tears burned Max's eyes as he struggled. His humanity hadn't saved him like that old woman had implied it would, but he hoped at least it had saved Jeb. "Just make it fast," he whispered as a tear rolled down his cheek.

Phrice laughed. "That I can't guarantee." He hefted Max over his shoulder and stomped off into the trees with the other daemon on his heels. "Your fate is in Atalanta's hands now."

CHAPTER TWENTY

Callia's heart felt like it might sprout wings and fly right out of her skin. As Zander lowered his head to her chest and drew in deep, shattering breaths, she thought it just might.

Her body still trembled from the most delicious orgasm; her mind raced with the things he'd told her. In her heart she wanted to believe that even after everything that had happened between them, they might have a future to look forward to.

"Zander," Callia said gently, running her hands through his hair. "We have to get up."

"We will," he mumbled against her neck. "When I can move again."

Warmth trickled through her when she thought of the reason his body wasn't working. When she remembered what they'd done. How it had felt. How she wanted to do it all over again. Her muscles instinctively tightened around that glorious part of him still buried deep inside her, and he groaned in response.

"That's one way to get me moving again."

She smiled because yeah, sex had never been a problem for them. But even she knew this time it wasn't just about sex. It was more. She felt it, even if she couldn't bring herself to say the words.

Her smile faded. The real world and their multitude of problems beckoned.

The truth closed in around her, splintering the fantasy she'd been building. Their son was still missing. They'd wasted precious time here, making love, when they should have been searching for him. And to top it off, Isadora—Callia's half-sister and Zander's fiancée—was downstairs right this minute, probably wondering what the hell was going on in this very room.

She pushed gently against his shoulders. "I have to get up, Zander. I need to take a shower."

Slowly, he moved up onto his hands. When he lifted his head, his eyes were sleepy, his hair mussed. And though it made no sense, something about him looked . . . different. Calmer. More at peace than she'd ever seen him. "Trying to wash me off already?"

She stared at him, tried to pinpoint what it was that had changed in the last few minutes, but couldn't. They'd made love numerous times before, and yeah, sex relaxed him. But not like this. This was . . . something else.

When his brow furrowed, she gave herself a mental shake, refocused and slipped out from beneath him. "No, I'm just remembering why I came to the human realm in the first place."

He rolled to his side to watch her, perched his elbow on the bed and his head on his hand. "How did you get here, anyway?"

She turned a slow circle as she lifted her camisole straps back into place. "I came with Casey and Isadora."

"All three of you are here? How?"

"We came through a secret portal Isadora knew about."

"Where?"

"In the mountains."

His lips turned down. "There are witches in those mountains."

She caught the disapproval in his voice but somehow knew he wasn't going to lecture her about her actions. Which didn't fit. Because Zander always told everyone what he wanted them to do.

Weird.

She glanced around, again wondered what had changed in him and why, but was distracted when she spotted her clothes. She stooped to pick them up. "The others are probably wondering where we are. I don't think it would be a good idea to go back downstairs smelling like sex after they knew I was coming up to tear into you. And I especially don't want to smell like your sex in front of Isadora."

She spotted the bathroom and headed that way. "I'll be quick," she said over her shoulder.

She closed the bathroom door and took a deep breath. Her hands were shaking, her nerves a hot coil beneath her skin. Quickly she flipped on the shower, stripped the camisole over her head and stepped beneath the hot spray.

The heat immediately relaxed her. She closed her eyes, tipped her head back so the water hit at her chest. Tried not to let her brain wander, but even she knew it was inevitable. The pain at what her father had revealed stole her breath. She ducked her face under the water. The memory morphed into her conversation with Casey and Isadora, then coming here to find Zander, and her taking out all her anger and frustration over everything on him.

She wasn't going to do this again. Wasn't going to fall into the same mistakes she'd made before. He'd loved her? Did it even matter anymore? The only thing that mattered now was finding their son. The rest of it—her heart pinched— the rest was not important.

Cool air washed over her, and too late she realized the shower door had opened and closed while she'd been caught in her musings. She whipped around to see Zander moving under the spray toward her.

"What are you doing?" she asked.

"I decided your shower was a good idea."

Panic pushed at her chest. She stepped backward in an attempt to get away, but he seemed to eat up all the space in the small stall. "Okay, then wait outside. I'll be done in a minute."

Amusement crossed his handsome face. "Why are you all of a sudden shy? I've seen you naked before, *thea*."

"I'm not shy," she said, stepping back again. Her spine hit

the tile wall. "I just like my privacy, that's all. I said I'd be done in a minute. Then the shower's all yours."

"I like sharing with you." He reached for her arm.

She rolled her shoulder to avoid his grasp. "Zander, please." That panic clawed its way up her throat. She shifted her back more solidly against the wall. "Just wait outside."

His eyes narrowed. "What's wrong?"

"Nothing."

His fingers moved to her upper arm. "Callia, turn around."

She dug her heels in. Stared at his broad chest and the water running down his tanned skin in rivulets. "No."

He tugged on her am, and even though she knew it was useless, she resisted. He pulled her around easily, though, until her back was plastered to his front and his arms were around her, locking her in. "That's better, isn't it?" he whispered in her ear.

No. Water sprayed onto her chest and shoulders again. She closed her eyes. Wanted so badly just to forget the last ten years ever existed. But she couldn't. "Zander, please—"

"I saw the scars when you were injured," he said softly. "You don't have to be afraid for me to see them."

"I'm not."

"Then what's wrong?"

She squeezed her eyes, wished she could have avoided this conversation altogether. "They're . . . they're not something I like people to see. They're ugly."

He dropped his lips to her shoulder. Kissed her gently. "Nothing about you could ever be ugly." As he lifted his head, he loosed his grasp, eased back, and she knew by the way her skin tingled that he was looking at her scars. Even though they'd faded to nothing more than thin white lines, she still felt them. Every day. And she knew what they looked like. "When I think about what they did to you—"

"They didn't do anything I didn't ask for. It was my choice."

His silence confirmed what she knew he was feeling. And

okay, yeah. This was why she didn't want to be having this conversation. That pain she lived with every day, the pain she pushed down so she could get by, came thundering back.

"I— No one forced me, Zander." This, at least, she wanted to make sure he understood. "I volunteered for the cleansing ritual."

"Why?" he asked in a shocked voice.

It made so much more sense in her head than it ever would in words. "Because it seemed like the right thing to do. Because—I thought—I owed my father for risking his position to take care of me. Because . . ." She shrugged, looked down at the strong arms still wrapped around her. "I wanted to forget."

He was silent so long, she thought he hadn't heard her. Then he dropped his forehead against the side of her head and whispered, *"Thea."*

Thea. The word twisted the knife in her heart. Why couldn't she let him go? After all this time? Even now, when she was smart enough to know they had absolutely no future together and that this—them—was destructive, why wasn't she letting him go like she should?

"This," he said, letting go of her waist with one arm and drawing his hand to her back. "This is mine now." He laid his palm over her scars, and warmth gathered beneath his skin, spreading into hers as he spoke. "I can't make you forget, but I can take away the burden. It's mine, *thea.* Not yours."

His heat warmed the coldest space inside her, but she shook her head. "You don't understand. I didn't want to forget what happened, Zander. I wanted to forget you. I wanted to forget how I felt about you."

Silence fell between them. Tension turned the air thick.

"Is this your way of telling me you finally did?" he whispered.

"No. I didn't. I never have. That's the problem. It didn't work." Tears—hot tears she'd tried to keep back—burned her eyes. "Pain isn't freeing. It's just one more reminder of what you've lost. And now all I have are these ugly scars. That's what I'll have when this is all over. Whether we find our son or not. After you bind yourself to—"

She closed her mouth when she realized how bitter she sounded. Wished like hell she'd just kept her mouth shut. Or kept her camisole firmly in place.

He turned her in his arms until the water hit at her spine and his fingers ran through her wet hair, tipping her face up to his. "*Thea*, open your eyes."

She did, and saw all the same emotions she felt reflected back in his eyes. His silver eyes, no longer stormy and gray but shimmering and surrounded by a halo of clear blue.

"Zander, your eyes . . ."

"I'm not binding myself to Isadora. When this is over you'll have me. I'm yours, for as long as you want me. Even if you don't want me anymore, I'm still yours. I only volunteered to marry Isadora because I thought I'd lost you. If I'd known there was a chance we would end up here, do you think I would have made that agreement?"

He took her hand before she could answer, placed it over his chest until she felt the rhythmic thump of his heart beneath her palm. Then he took her other hand and placed it over her own heart. "Do you feel that?" he asked. "We're linked together, you and me. This goes deeper than the fact that I love you. It's more than just you being my soul mate. This is about us and the reason I've never been able to let go of you either." He moved in closer, and warmth closed around her as she felt her heart beating in time with his. "There's more, *thea*. No matter what happens today, tomorrow, there's more ahead for us. You are my life. This story doesn't end here. Not unless we let it."

His words touched her more than his earlier admission that he'd once loved her. Tears spilled out over her eyelashes, tracked down her cheeks before she could stop them. Gently, he lowered his head and brushed his lips over hers. Once. Twice. As softly as if he were touching the most fragile glass. *"Thea,"* he whispered against her mouth. "Don't let this end here."

Oh, gods. She'd always been powerless against him. He was right; the connection he spoke of was deeper than even she understood. And she was so tired of fighting it. Of fighting this. Them. What she'd always wanted.

Her lips moved under his as she kissed him back. And even though a small voice in the back of her head warned this was wrong, that eventually she'd get hurt again, that things never worked out for her, she couldn't help herself. She twined her arms around his neck, tipped her head, rose on her toes as she tasted him and he tugged her close so they were locked tight together, chest to hip. He groaned into her mouth, changed the angle of the kiss, nudged her back toward the shower wall. Water sprayed up around them as his hand ran down her backside to draw her closer still.

"Thea. I can't get enough of you."

She couldn't get enough of him either. She rose up, kissed his nose, his cheek, his mouth all over again. And though she knew the others were downstairs, that they were probably talking strategy, that she and Zander needed to be there, right now she just needed him.

She lifted her leg, slid her thigh up his to hook around his hip so he could settle between her legs. "Zander . . ."

The low growl in his throat told her he needed the same thing. He nipped at her earlobe as he pushed his hips playfully against hers. *"Thea . . ."*

The door to the bathroom opened with a slap of wood against wall. Zander stiffened, dropped her leg and moved his body in front of hers so whoever came through couldn't see her.

"Shit, Z. There you are."

Callia recognized Titus's voice even though she couldn't see around Zander's broad shoulders.

"Get the hell out of here, Titus," Zander growled.

"Oh, crap." Shoes squeaked on the tile floor, and then

Titus's voice came out muffled, as if he'd turned away. "I didn't expect you to be so, ah, dirty that you'd need more than one shower." Humor filled Titus's voice. "Hey, Callia."

Zander's scowl deepened as he looked down at her, and for some reason, the absurdity of the situation lightened Callia's mood. "Hey, Titus."

Zander rolled his eyes. "Okay, you've had your fun, Titus. Now get the fuck out."

Callia studied Zander, who still hadn't taken his eyes off her. Though he was clearly irritated with Titus's interruption, there was no heat behind the words. And that temper that seemed to come and go with him was nowhere to be seen.

She focused on his newly silver irises.

"I will," Titus said, sobering. "But I thought you both might want to know. Nick's scouts brought in a human. A trucker they found up in the northern country. Daemon attack. He's badly injured, but he's mumbling something about a boy who helped him get away. One he picked up hitchhiking in British Columbia."

Callia's smile faded, and a strange sense of foreboding raced through her chest. She knew Zander felt it as well, by the way his expression hardened.

Zander turned to look through the frosted glass toward Titus, careful to keep his body between hers and Titus's. And when he did, Callia spotted the scars on his upper back. Thin, faded white lines. Ones she was sure hadn't been there when she'd operated on him. Ones that were eerily familiar.

Wait a minute. What the heck is going on here?

"How old?" Zander asked.

"About ten."

Titus's answer was all she heard. Callia's eyes darted from the scars on Zander's back to his face when he turned. It couldn't be . . .

"And Z," Titus added, "get ready for this. The guy . . . the human? He says the kid had markings on his arms. Markings that look just like ours."

* * *

Urgency pushed at Zander as he and Callia headed down the long corridor. After Titus left, they'd quickly dressed. Callia hadn't spoken, but her nerves showed on her face, and he felt her anxiety all the way to his bones.

His boots echoed as they descended the stairs to the main level and turned to the back stairs that ran down to the medical clinic deep beneath the lodge itself. As the colony was built into large caverns hidden deep in the Cascade Mountains, the air was cool. Candles every ten feet lit the space to save power, and the rock absorbed all sound, making it seem deserted.

At the bottom of the stairs, Callia turned left toward the conference rooms where Nick plotted war strategy with his soldiers, but Zander tugged on her hand, still tucked tightly into his. "They're this way."

"How do you know? I left them down here."

"Because the medical facility is this direction."

Her expression was easy to read. The crease between her eyebrows said she didn't understand how he would know that. And when her face softened, he knew she'd figured out he'd been here when she was injured. And that he hadn't left her side.

Which was weird because she'd been a closed book the whole time they were together. He'd never known what she was thinking. What she was feeling. But now she was finally letting him in.

"I think," she said softly, "I never thanked you for saving my life."

He moved forward to brush the hair back from her face and press a kiss to her forehead. "I will make this right, *thea*." He tipped her chin with his finger. "No matter what happens, believe that."

Resolve settled in her eyes. She breathed deep. Nodded.

He squeezed her hand and led her to the medical rooms. Mumbled voices echoed their way as they turned a corner. Ahead a doorway to the left was open, fluorescent light spilling into the dark corridor. Theron's broad shoulders filled the space just inside the door.

The leader of the Argonauts turned when he heard their footsteps. "Z." His questioning dark eyes flicked briefly to Callia as Zander pulled her into the room after him, but Zander didn't let go of her hand. "We were just about to send a search party out for you."

"Where is he?" Zander asked, ignoring Theron's sarcasm. He looked toward another open door on the right wall. The sounds of machinery whirring and beeping met his ears.

"In the other room," Titus said. "The colony's healer is with him."

"I want to see him," Callia said. "Maybe I can help."

Zander glanced her way, then back at Titus. "Is he conscious?"

Theron nodded. "He was earlier."

Callia let go of Zander's hand and headed across the room. Zander followed through a doorway that led into a high-tech hospital room.

Wires and tubes ran from the man's arms to machines behind his bed. An oxygen mask covered his face, and bandages were wrapped around just about every exposed piece of skin on his body. Judging from the amount of damage, the guy was lucky to be alive.

Callia moved closer to the bed. Nick stood on one side looking down at the human while Lena checked the machines on the other side.

"How's he doing?"

Nick crossed his arms over his chest. "How would you be doing after being someone's lunch?"

Lena flicked Nick a withering look. Then glanced at Callia. "He's stable. For now. But I'm afraid you're not going to be able to talk to him. He just dropped off, and the drugs have hit him hard. Even if he could talk, nothing he has to say would be any help to you now."

Frustration washed over Callia's features. "What did he say happened? What about the boy?"

Pity crept into Nick's amber eyes. "He picked the kid up somewhere in British Columbia. They parked it at a truck stop just over the summit of Mount Hood." He glanced Zander's way. "There's a small Misos settlement there, so we patrol the region. Somehow it looks like they walked in on an attack."

"What happened to the boy?" Callia asked. "Was the boy with him?"

The panic in her voice clawed at Zander. He stepped up behind her, placed his hands on her upper arms.

"From what my soldiers got out of him," Nick said, "the kid told him the monsters were there for him."

Callia turned and shot Zander a look, and in her eyes he saw the same thing he felt. Fear. Urgency. The last threads of hope. Except he had a dark feeling he knew where this was going.

"So he got away," Callia said, twisting back to Nick. "The boy got free?"

"No," Zander answered before Nick could, his heart dropping. The feeling that Nick was more closely linked to the Argonauts than anyone understood washed through Zander as he read the truth on the scarred half-breed's face.

"You can't know for sure," Callia protested. "It's possible he escaped while the daemons went after this man."

"No," Zander said again, hating to hurt her more but needing—now—to be honest with her. "If it was him, Callia, if it was our son, he wouldn't have run. He wouldn't have left this human vulnerable."

She glared up at him. "How do you know? He's just a boy. He's just—"

"He's an Argonaut. It's bred into him." Zander glanced toward Theron and Titus, who had followed them into the room. Toward the doorway where Gryphon, Phineus and Cerek had gathered to see what was going on. And he thought of his own SOB father. To the way he himself had been as a child. To how he'd been raised. Trained. To that instinct he'd never been able to get away from.

"We were all more advanced than the average youngling. You can teach an Argonaut to be a warrior. You can beat out his emotions, take away his dreams and train him to be a killer. And if this was our son, if he was really with Atalanta, then I'm guessing that's exactly what she did. But she wouldn't have been able to alter his instinct. It's as much a part of him as his hair and eyes and skin. If he somehow got free from her, if he was with this human when the daemons attacked, he'd have fought. And he would have protected."

Tears gathered in Callia's eyes. She turned and looked at the human lying motionless on the bed. And the grief radiating from her filled Zander's head and heart and soul.

No one spoke as she looked around the room, as if in a daze. The only sounds were the beeps and whirs of the machines. Slowly she eased out of Zander's grip, moved across the floor and stopped at a chair where a small jacket was tossed over an arm.

"Is this . . . was this his?"

"The human was holding that when they brought him in," Lena said softly. "Whatever personal items we took off him are there."

Callia lifted the jacket to her face, drew in a deep breath. The jacket was ripped and shredded, covered in blood and grime and streaked with green, but she didn't seem to care. She closed her eyes, lowered it and clutched it to her chest. And that was all Zander could take. Because his heart was breaking too. Minutes ago they'd been so hopeful, and now . . .

He moved around the bed, turned her so he could cradle her against his chest while she cried. Whispered voices sounded behind him but he didn't care what the others were saying. Sobs racked her body as he pulled her close, the jacket pressed between them. He didn't even have the strength to pray this wasn't exactly what he thought. Because he knew. Some sixth sense inside him said this coat belonged to his son. And his son had somehow saved this human.

"Thea . . ."

Tear tracks stained her cheeks as she lifted her head. She opened her mouth to say something, moved the jacket between them. Then froze. Slowly, her brow furrowed.

"What?" he asked.

She pulled her hand from inside the coat. The fluorescent lights above reflected off a circular silver disk in her hand that looked tarnished from time and weather. A heavy chain attached to one side slipped through her fingers. Four empty chambers composed most of the body, but in the center was a small circle stamped with the seal of the Titans.

"Holy Hera," he whispered.

Her eyes widened. "That looks like—"

"The Orb of Krónos," Theron said in wonder from across the room.

Zander and Callia both glanced toward Theron, who was staring at the disk with wide eyes himself. Next to him, Casey and Isadora both stood silently, also transfixed by the medallion in Callia's hand.

Zander hadn't heard either of the females step into the room, but as he took in Isadora's new appearance—the short hair, the new clothes, the questions on her face as her gaze bounced between him and Callia—guilt snaked through him. He needed to talk to the princess, explain to her what had happened. Tell her he couldn't go through with the binding ceremony after all. And just where that would leave the monarchy, he wasn't sure. But if this—he glanced back at the disk in Callia's hand—if this was what he thought it was, then even that didn't much matter right now.

"Okay," Casey said cautiously. "You're all looking at that thing like it's the Antichrist. Could someone please fill in this clueless Misos?"

Theron pulled Casey to his side, shaken out of his trance by her voice. "Krónos was the father of Zeus, Hades and Poseidon. A Titan. The Titans were—"

"The ruling deities before the Olympian gods took over," Casey finished for him. "Yeah, I know my mythology. But that doesn't answer my question."

"It's just another myth," Nick said.

Theron shot the half-breed a look. "Myths are usually rooted in reality. And this—don't you think, warrior?—proves the point."

Nick frowned, shifted his legs wider in a defensive stance. Sensing the tension in the room, Zander said to Casey, "According to the legend, when Krónos realized Zeus and his brothers were going to overthrow them, he created the orb." He nodded toward the disk. "He poured into it the Chthonic powers, those of this world, and the four classic elements—air, water, fire, earth. Before the last battle of the Titanomachy, the war between the Titans and Olympians, he gave the orb to Prometheus for safe keeping. And he instructed him to use it only if the situation turned dire."

Casey's eyebrows pulled together. "But Prometheus was a Titan, wasn't he?"

"He was," Isadora said, speaking up. "But he didn't participate in the war, and he and a few others weren't condemned to Tartarus with the other Titans. When the war was over, Zeus had the losing Titans locked in the lower levels of Tartarus where they would be tortured for all eternity."

"And Prometheus didn't use the orb to unlock them," Casey guessed.

"No," Theron said to her. "Prometheus was a champion for humankind. He didn't want to see any of the gods with the orb. He scattered the four elements over the earth, and according to the legend, he hid the empty orb someplace where Zeus and his brothers could never find it."

"Something of great value," Callia muttered, looking at the disk in her hand. "He hid it in the Aegis Mountains. In Argolea."

Zander glanced at the disk in her hand. Even he could feel the raw power radiating from the ancient metal. If their son had had this when he faced the daemons, it was possible he would have had the strength to escape after all.

His eyes lifted to Callia's. And he saw then that she was suddenly clinging to the same hope.

"Okay, you lost me there," Casey said, letting go of Theron and moving to stand in front of Callia. "Why would Prometheus hide it?"

"Because, according to the legend," Isadora explained, "the person who wears the orb with the elements intact not only has the power to release the Titans from Tartarus, but he has the power to control this world as well."

Realization dawned over Casey's face. "She's using it to get around the prophecy." She looked at Isadora, then at Zander. "Is that what you're telling me? If Atalanta has this orb, and the four elements inside, she has the power to control the human realm?"

"Yeah," Zander said. "And the human realm is the one realm the gods haven't been able to control. The skies, the Underworld, the seas . . . those are theirs. But the human realm has forever been off limits. As long as she has the orb, she's immortal again, and more powerful than any of them. And if anyone challenges her"—he glanced at his guardian kinsmen, standing near Theron on the other side of the room, all tense because they knew just what this little thing could do—"she can unleash the Titans, which would then start a war like no one's ever seen before."

"Oh, God," Casey whispered, looking down at the orb. "So I guess it's a good thing she doesn't have it, huh? But I still don't understand how it got from Argolea to your son." She looked up and around, questions in her eyes.

Isadora focused on the orb. "It had to have been smuggled out. Someone must have found it." Her jaw clenched. "Orpheus."

"That little piece of shit," Nick muttered from across the room.

"It doesn't matter how it got out," Theron said. "If the boy had it, he must have gotten it from Atalanta."

"He stole it," Callia said softly, looking up at Zander. "That's why he was with this human. That's why the daemons were hunting him."

Yeah, he'd figured that out as well. And that's why they

would kill him as soon as they found him. If they hadn't already.

"Hold on." Isadora's voice drew Zander's attention. "There's a catch. Atalanta can't wield the orb on her own."

"Why not?" Casey asked.

"Because in her god form she's considered an Olympian, not a Titan. In order for any Olympian—even one of the Twelve—to wield it, they have to have a key. They have to have something from both the human world and their realm. They have to have—"

"They have to have someone who is half god, half human, perfectly balanced," Casey finished for her, eyes wide.

"Yeah," Isadora said softly, realization dawning in her eyes as she glanced at her half-sisters. "Now it makes sense, the markings we share. The Horae were all about balance and timing and order. Casey and I, as the Chosen, are that perfect half-god, half-human, but we're not balanced without you, Callia."

"So she needs one of us to wield the orb," Callia whispered.

"Yes," Isadora breathed. "Or one of our offspring. And since Casey and I don't have young yet . . ."

Callia reached up and touched the marking on the back of her neck. "She came after mine."

Isadora nodded. "Atalanta didn't steal your son because his father was an Argonaut. She stole him because she knew what you were before any of us did. Because our father, the king, is somehow linked to Themis, the Titan who spawned the Horae, and we are too. And she needs one of us"—she glanced at each of her sisters—"or one of our offspring to help her get what she really wants."

Callia's eyes darted to Zander. "Then she won't kill him."

"Wait," Zander said, sensing her excitement but not wanting to get their hopes up again. "If what Isadora said is true, if you three really are the modern-day Horae, Hours, *whatever*, and she needs you to wield the orb, then why didn't she just take you that day? And how did she even find you both in the first place?"

"I don't know," Callia said, shaking her head. "I don't know how she found us, but she wouldn't have taken me, because a child is easier to manipulate than a thirty-year-old Argolean who's dedicated her life to the monarchy. She'd have known I never would have helped her. I'd have chosen death first."

"And maybe she didn't have the orb at the time," Casey added. When they all looked her way, she said, "Ten years ago Atalanta was still immortal. She was still in Tartarus, building her army, right? You've all said she's a schemer, that she's constantly searching for ways to exact her revenge. If that's the case, then it makes sense she'd have backup plans. In case the prophecy did come to pass." She looked at Isadora. "In case we found each other and she was rendered mortal after all. She'd have been planning other ways to get exactly what she wants."

"Which is revenge," Theron said from across the room. His jaw hardened. "The females need to go back to Argolea. Now."

"What?" The sisters all turned to look his way.

"Theron . . . ," Casey started.

"I won't go back, Zander." Callia turned. "I have a right to be here."

She did. But Theron was right too. If Atalanta had lost his son, then she'd have no qualms about taking one or all of the sisters while she figured out a way to get the orb back. It wasn't safe for any of them to be in the human realm.

"The females have a point, hero," Nick said from where he stood near the bed.

Theron glared at the half-breed leader. "Stuff it, Nick. This doesn't concern you."

Nick's jaw twitched. "Actually, it does, smart-ass. Probably more than the rest of you, because my people fucking live here, while you all hide off in never-never land." He looked toward Callia, Isadora and Casey. "You ladies can stay at the colony for as long as you want. You have safe haven here."

"Sonofabitch," Theron growled. "Nick—"

Nick glanced at Isadora. "There's more to the legend, isn't there? Tell them the rest of it."

Isadora's eyes darted sideways. And in her irritated expression it was clear she didn't like Nick. Or the fact he was telling her what to do. "I don't know what you're talking about."

But she did. Even Zander could see that.

They didn't have time for this bickering. Zander turned his full attention on Nick. "Can you get me to the truck stop where your soldiers found the human?"

"Chopper will be the fastest way to get there," Nick said, rubbing a hand over his jaw. "We've got one at the airstrip, just outside Silver Hills. I can radio ahead and have it fired up."

"Good." Plans materialized in Zander's mind. From the corner of his eye he saw Callia's exasperated expression, felt her frustration. But he ignored it. He was heading into attack mode, and this time it wasn't just duty, it was personal.

"One question," Nick asked. "What the hell can one Argonaut do against a horde of daemons?"

"He's not just one," Theron announced. "If Atalanta's got one of our own, we're all going."

"And me," Callia said.

Zander didn't look over. "No."

"I—"

"Not this time, *thea*." Adrenaline pulsing with the prospect of what lay ahead, he focused on Nick. "We'll need maps of the terrain. Fresh weapons. And your best guess where you think she could be hiding out with my son."

"Done. But you're gonna need more than that, hero. Something tells me you're gonna need the favor of the fucking gods."

CHAPTER TWENTY-ONE

Callia crossed her arms over her chest and paced the length of the main living room in the lodge of the colony. Rustic tables and leather couches filled the space, making the room seem homey and inviting, but right now the last thing she could do was sit and relax. Every second that ticked by on the clock sent her anxiety into the out-of-this-world range and thoughts of murder spiraling through her mind.

It was close to ten P.M. Zander and the others had been gone almost thirty minutes. Only Gryphon remained, standing guard outside. Nick had insisted his soldiers could handle the babysitting detail, but Theron had been adamant the guardian remain. And Callia was still more pissed than pleased with the way she and the other "females" had been shuffled off to wait. Again.

"You're going to wear a path in the floor," Casey said from her seat on one of the couches. "Come over here and sit down."

"I can't." Callia chewed on her thumbnail. "Where do you think they are right now? If I had a map maybe I could—"

"Woe is the forgotten female," Isadora said on a sigh from the window where she was gazing out at the waterfall that spilled into a massive pool in the middle of the cavern. She looked over her shoulder at Callia and Casey. "Story of our lives, isn't it?"

"It's not like that," Casey said. "Theron does have a point, whether you two want to admit it or not."

Callia glanced at Isadora. "She really is a sappy newlywed, isn't she?"

"Yes," Isadora said, rubbing her forehead. "Disgusting,

isn't it? Makes my head pound worse than being in the same room with the two of you."

Casey crossed her arms again and leaned against the back of the couch with a huff. "I'm all for women's lib, you know, just not when it involves being stupid. And that's what going out there would be. Stupid." Her gaze shot to the orb resting on the coffee table in front of her. "If you two stopped moping long enough, maybe we could put our heads together and come up with a way to help."

"Like what?" Callia asked, exasperated.

Casey picked up a book she'd set next to her on the couch. "Do you both know the history of the Horae?"

"No," Callia answered. "Reading hasn't exactly been high on my priority list lately."

At her snarky remark, Isadora smirked.

Casey rolled her eyes. "Before Nick took off with the guys he gave me this." She gestured to the encyclopedia-like tome. "There were three. Sometimes called the Hours, or the Seasons. But mostly they were the wardens of the sky and Olympus. Eunomia was responsible for order in society. Dike maintained justice. And then there was Eirene—the peace and balance between the other two. And they all bore a mark: a winged omega."

"Eirene," Callia breathed, easing down to sit next to Casey on the couch. "That's what Atalanta called me in the cabin."

Isadora moved to sit opposite them on the other couch. "Our specific powers relate well to the Horae. My foresight, Casey's hindsight, your balance. It doesn't surprise me that Atalanta recognized you as Eirene."

"But I'm a healer. I don't—"

"What is a healer?" Casey asked. "Someone who restores balance to the body. Callia, you're the balance to us." She nodded at Isadora. "To the Chosen."

Callia glanced between them with the distinct feeling these two were tag-teaming her for something she wasn't sure she was ready for. She'd yet to adjust to the fact she was the king's daughter, and here they were throwing mythological bonds at her. "You know, that sounds all cool on the surface, but why do I get the impression there's more to this than nifty names and historic links?"

"Orpheus mentioned a weapon," Isadora said. "He told me that the three of us had something we wouldn't yet understand. I didn't believe him before, but . . . I know you both felt that electric shock when the orb was brought out." She held her hands over the orb resting on the coffee table between them.

"Um . . . what are you doing?" Callia asked. Sure, she'd felt the jolt Isadora described, but she still had no idea what it meant.

"Orpheus has been teaching me how to focus my abilities," Isadora answered.

"Wait," Casey said, holding up a hand. "What the hell do you mean, Orpheus has been 'teaching' you? And I thought you lost your power of foresight. Did it come back?"

Isadora's forehead wrinkled. "No, not yet. But this is different. This isn't looking into the future or the past. It's looking at the present. I'm curious . . . If we all focus on the same thing, maybe we can see an image. Or a location."

Callia's nerves hummed as realization dawned. She swallowed hard. "You want us each to focus on the guardians. See where they're going."

"No." Isadora's brow lifted. "Screw the Argonauts. I want us to focus on Atalanta."

Casey and Callia darted worried looks at each other.

"It makes sense," Casey said after a lingering moment. "We know a ten-year-old couldn't have outrun a daemon. Atalanta won't kill him. But she will hide him. If we can figure out where she's holding him, we could radio the Argonauts and tell them his location."

Hope, the first hope she'd felt since the guardians left, filled Callia's soul. Her palms grew damp. She rubbed them across her thighs. "What if she can see us? I mean, is it safe? If we can look at her, is it possible she can look back?"

"It could be, I suppose," Isadora said. "But what would that matter? She won't know where we are."

Callia looked from Isadora to Casey and back again. No one spoke. It made sense, but indecision roared within Callia. What if they were wrong? What if Atalanta's powers were strong enough so she could see them, what they were planning, read their thoughts or some—

Casey scooted forward. "So how do we do this?"

"Touch and focus is how I was always able to see the future," Isadora said.

"And I the past," Casey added.

Isadora looked to Callia. "Ready?"

No, Callia wasn't ready. But Casey was right. At least they were doing something, and the odds things could go wrong from simply looking were slim to none.

Tentatively, she lowered her hand onto the orb. The metal was cold beneath her fingers. Casey and Isadora lowered their fingers to touch the curved disk. As soon as all three made contact, heat flared up from the metal and shot through Callia's arm.

Callia sucked in a breath. The glow grew in intensity, changing from a soft pink to a bright red radiance that arced out all around their hands.

"That's it," Isadora whispered. "Now focus. Remember the goal."

Callia closed her eyes and pictured Atalanta. What she knew of Atalanta. Not so much the image of a deity, but the essence of her soul. Colors flashed behind her eyes. White, gold, blue, black. It was the black that stayed, like a stain, like the evil Callia imagined coursed through the demi-god's veins. A picture flickered. Fuzzy at first, but growing steadily clearer the longer she concentrated. Green rolling hills, a great river, cliffs, a winding road and domed building with three tiers that looked completely out of place perched high on a cliff overlooking the gorge below. And Atalanta, seated on a throne inside the building, dressed in bloodred robes, looking up at the circular balcony above and the twenty or so daemons from her army peering down, awaiting instructions.

This was not the mountaintop truck stop Zander and the Argonauts were heading for. This was somewhere else. Somewhere green and damp, not snow covered and cold. Voices rumbled but she couldn't make out the words. The daemons scattered until Atalanta was alone in the octagonal shaped room. She lowered her face and peered straight ahead. And seemed to be gazing . . . right at Callia.

I see you, Horae.

Callia gasped. Her eyes shot open. She looked from Casey to Isadora, neither of whom seemed startled at all. Their eyes were closed, their faces calm. They each breathed slowly, their hands resting gently on the glowing orb.

Yes, you, Eirene.

When Callia looked back, she didn't see the comfortable living room around her; she saw Atalanta once more, the throne she was seated on and the stone walls at her back.

I see into your mind. I know what it is you want. We are not that different, you and me. The ones left behind. The ones shunned by the mighty heroes. You know why he refused you.

Callia's heart picked up speed. She tried to pull her hand back from the orb but couldn't. It was cemented in place.

Because you are female. And to him that means weak. Do you honestly think he forbids you to fight because he wants to protect you? Because he loves you? She sneered. *An Argonaut does not know love. He is a product of the egotistical god from which he was spawned.*

"You lie."

He represses you because he can, Atalanta went on as if Callia hadn't even spoken. *Because his kind has been doing it since ancient times. And because you, Eirene, are his vulnerability. His weakness. His Achilles' heel. Do you think he cares if you live or die? He cares only for himself.*

"No," Callia whispered.

Ask him, female. And learn the truth. No male, especially an Argonaut, has honor in his heart. Not when his existence is on the line.

Thoughts of Zander ran through Callia's mind. Of their time together in the past. Of his admissions earlier today, here, in this very colony. Of his immortality. Of the fact he'd told her she was his life.

A feral smile crossed Atalanta's face. One that challenged and mocked. *Yes, Eirene. You know I speak the truth. He needs you only to live. And he and the others will go on repressing you for as long as they possibly can.*

No, it couldn't be true . . .

Your heroes walk into a trap. My daemons are waiting for them. Her voice dropped to a hiss. *And they will be slaughtered. Every one of them.*

Callia swallowed hard. "Zander can't be killed."

But he can be hurt. And my daemons will take great pleasure in torturing him until you die of old age.

Fear knifed into Callia's heart.

Of course, I may be willing to make a trade . . .

Atalanta gestured to her right, and that's when Callia saw the boy. Leaning against the wall, his head tipped to the side in sleep, his hands bound behind him and his legs stretched out on the floor. And that heart she thought had broken so long ago roared to life in her chest. He was a miniature version of Zander. With blond hair and bronzed skin and a face that looked like it had been kissed by angels.

I'm willing to spare young Maximus's life. For something of even greater value.

At the anticipation in Atalanta's voice, Callia's gaze shifted back to the demigod. And understanding dawned. "You want the orb."

Not just the orb, Eirene. I want you as well.

A voice in Callia's head screamed *No!* but the one in her heart told her this was her only option. She would do anything for her son. Even sacrifice her life to save his. And Zander . . .

She couldn't let Zander and the others walk into a trap. Not when she could do something to save them. Not when she knew in her heart Zander did love her. He hadn't left her here because she was his vulnerability, as Atalanta claimed. He'd left her to keep her safe.

"How do I know you'll keep your word?"

Because I give it to you as a hero. As a female. As a mother. Come now, Eirene. You must know once I have you and the Orb of Krónos, I won't need the others anymore.

Yeah, right. Callia wasn't stupid enough to buy that one. "And what about my sisters?"

I care not for the Chosen. This is between you and me. They cannot hear our conversation. Atalanta tipped her head. *Tell me, Eirene . . . just what are you willing to sacrifice for balance in this world and the next?*

Callia glanced at Casey and Isadora, both oblivious to what was happening right under their noses. All her life she'd sat back and done nothing while others made decisions for her. And in the end . . . what had happened? The ones she loved were hurt because of who and what she was. Now she understood why. And now she had the chance to change things.

She didn't believe Atalanta would keep her word, not for a second. And she wasn't stupid enough to take the demigod the orb. But if she could get away from the colony, if she could figure out where Atalanta was holding her son . . . Maybe she could alert Zander, and he and the others could reach the boy before it was too late. Atalanta only needed one blood relative of the Horae. Callia would gladly trade herself for her son. And she knew Atalanta wouldn't kill her if she truly needed her, which meant Zander would be safe as well.

She glanced at the satellite phone just out of her reach. At the one Nick had left for them in case there was an emergency. And before the half-breed leader's directions even passed through her mind, she had her answer. If she did nothing, Zander and the others were lost. If she took the deal, only her life was forfeit.

And that was fitting, wasn't it? Considering her life had brought them all to this point to begin with.

She refocused on Atalanta. "Tell me how to find you."

Simon sat in a high-backed chair in the formal living room of the home he shared with his daughter. On his lap he held a scrapbook his wife had put together before her death. On the table in front of him, the untouched glass of brandy reflected the low lights in the room.

He flipped the page and looked at a picture of Callia as a young girl, digging in the dirt behind their house. Another showed her with jam all over her smiling face. Yet another was of her opening gifts on her sixth birthday. Page after page of pictures of her life filled the book. Pictures of her with her mother. Of her with him. Of her alone.

She was alone now, wasn't she? And it was all his fault. Tears burned the backs of his eyes. Tears he had no right shedding. Because of his desire to make her his daughter by virtue, if not by blood, he'd taken away everything she'd ever cared about. A true father wouldn't do that. A loving father would have put her needs first.

A knock at the door brought his head up. But he didn't rise. He had no desire to move. The knocking turned to a rapid pounding.

"Simon, open this goddamn door!"

Lucian. Simon exhaled and closed his eyes. He had no interest in dealing with the Council right now. Didn't care what their punishment for his lies was going to be. Did it even matter anymore? He'd already lost the only thing that had ever meant anything to him. Every time he thought of the look of utter betrayal on Callia's face when she realized what he'd done . . .

"Have you gone deaf?" Lucian asked from the doorway.

Too late Simon realized Lucian was already standing in his living room. The blasted servants had left the door unlocked.

"You look like you've gone a round with Hades," Lucian

said. Still dressed in the traditional *chison*, he moved around the couch toward Simon. "Get up."

Simon leaned his head back against the chair and closed his eyes. "Go away. Whatever the Council has decided, I'll face it tomorrow. Right now . . . right now I just want to be alone."

Lucian's footsteps stopped in front of Simon's chair. "Loukas is missing."

"He's a grown *ándras*. I'm sure he'll turn up."

"No, Simon. You don't understand. Loukas disappeared after the confrontation in the Council chambers. A sentry with the Executive Guard told me he crossed through the portal shortly after the Argonauts. And he used the same coordinates."

Slowly, Simon's eyes came open and he stared up at the leader of the Council. "Why would he go to the human realm now?"

Lucian locked his jaw.

An odd sense of unease washed through Simon. He pushed up from his chair to stand before Lucian. "What aren't you telling me?"

Lucian was roughly the same height and age as Simon, but he'd always been more confident. A true leader who knew what their people needed. Tonight he seemed rattled. His thin lips pressed into a tight line. Finally, he said, "Ten years ago he passed through the portal much the same way. Only that time he followed you and not the Argonauts."

Little links clicked into place in Simon's mind. Questions he'd always wondered about but hadn't wanted to find answers to. "He followed me to find Callia."

Lucian nodded. "She was betrothed to him. He didn't believe your story about her being sick in the human realm."

Suddenly, everything made sense. "When he found out she was pregnant, he went to Atalanta. He brought her to that village in Greece."

"Yes. You have to understand that Callia's affair and pregnancy, with an Argonaut no less, when she was betrothed to my son and the future leader of the Council would have been an embarrassment none of us would have recovered from easily."

Fury filled Simon's veins. "You knew."

Lucian's spine stiffened. "Oh, get real, Simon. You're not blameless in this. You made the deal with Atalanta. You traded your daughter's life for that child's. No one forced you to do that. Don't pretend to be all high-and-mighty now."

"There never would have been a deal to make had Loukas not gone to Atalanta in the first place."

"That doesn't change the past. Nothing does. We can only worry about the present. I'm here because I think Loukas might have gone into the human realm again to find Atalanta."

Simon's eyes grew wide. "Why?"

"Because he didn't realize the child could possibly still be alive. So long as it lives, Callia will not bind herself to him. And that, I'm afraid, is the only thing my son wants." Lucian's shoulders seem to drop. "He believes it's what he deserves. He believes she's his by right."

Four hundred years. For most of his life Simon had gone along with the status quo. He hadn't questioned the customs and laws the Council said were beneficial to their world, because they hadn't pertained to him. And when he'd joined the Council, he'd turned a blind eye to right and wrong in favor of politics. His wife had challenged him on the laws more than once. Had told him progress and life would bloom from the *gynaíkes* in their land and not its leaders. But he hadn't listened. He'd scoffed at her ideas—at ideas he'd known she'd picked up from her time serving the king. They'd argued about it. And eventually the distance between them had driven her into the arms of another.

He'd been hurt and betrayed but—after her cleansing ceremony—had taken her back. Though their relationship had never been the same, the child she'd borne had become his whole life. The child he'd raised and molded and sheltered and repressed. The child he'd deserved. The child who had been his, by right.

Sweat beaded on his neck and slid down his spine. "You think he'll go to Atalanta and make her another deal? To kill the child? What could he possibly offer her in return?"

Unease crept over Lucian's face. "The Argonauts. And the half-breeds. If the Argonauts went to the colony, if Loukas followed them . . ."

"Dear gods . . ."

"Exactly."

Simon's eyes shot to Lucian's. "Why do you care? You worry not for the half-breeds, for the Argonauts."

"No, I don't care for either. But death is not the answer. My nephew, you remember, is an Argonaut. While I don't agree with what the Eternal Guardians do, I'll not have Gryphon's blood or the blood of the others on my hands."

Urgency pulsed through Simon's veins. Urgency and, he hoped in some small way, redemption. "We need to find Loukas and stop him."

"Orpheus is waiting for us at the portal. He knows where the half-breed colony is located. If we go now, we might get there before it's too late."

CHAPTER TWENTY-TWO

Callia's heart raced as she cleared the hidden tunnel that led into the caverns of the colony. Frigid air whisked across her cheeks as she pulled on her gloves. The nearly full moon illuminated the clearing and forest beyond with enough light to make her trek toward Silver Hills, where she hoped to find a means of transportation, easy to see.

She'd left Isadora and Casey sleeping. They'd both been exhausted and disappointed after nothing came of their "attempt" with the orb. Callia had been a wired mess until they both dropped off.

She pressed her gloved hand against the sat phone in her pocket. When she got close to town, she'd contact Zander. Have him trace her signal. He'd be pissed, but she was confident he'd be able to track her. And she was 100 percent certain Atalanta wouldn't kill her. Not if Zander found their son before the demigod decided she didn't need both her *and* Maximus.

Maximus. Max. Warmth rushed through her chest. Her son had a name. And now she had a face to go with that name. Renewed determination surged in her veins. She checked her compass once, then moved toward the trees.

She made it ten feet before an arm shot out of nowhere and snagged her by the neck. Callia gasped, tried to scream, but the hand clamped over her mouth prevented any sound from escaping her throat. One strong arm closed tightly across her middle and jerked her back against a warm, solid body.

Fear lurched up her throat. She struggled, but was held firm.

"You kept me waiting, *syzygos*," a voice breathed in her ear. A voice she knew all too well. "I warned you not to do that."

Syzygos. Wife.

Her heart rate shot up. Loukas. Here? Now? What the hell did he think he was doing?

"Did you think you could escape me?" he growled. "You tried once before, but I brought you back. And I'm getting really fucking tired of doing this."

Callia went still as stone, and for a second her brain flashed blank.

A roar sounded in the trees around them, bringing her mind back online like a power grid juicing up. Callia's eyes grew wide as a sea of daemons spilled out of the trees and charged the tunnels that ran into the colony.

No . . .

"They're going to die," Loukas breathed in her ear. "Every one of those vile half-breeds you seem to love so much. All because of your indiscretions."

No, no, no . . .

Callia struggled but couldn't break free of Loukas's grasp. On the far side of the clearing, Atalanta emerged dressed in the same bloodred robes Callia had seen earlier. At her side, she pulled Max along by a rope. When she reached the edge of the trees, the demigod stopped, looked their way and smiled.

Callia's heart lurched into her throat and she screamed beneath Loukas's hand.

"Did you really think she'd play by any sane rules?" he whispered in her ear. "She lured you out for me. The princess, the Argonauts, your *lover* and that stain you call a son will all be annihilated in one fell swoop. But not you. No, you're going to live. With me. Where you belong. And trust me, *syzygos*, this time, you will remember."

Zander stopped midstep on the frozen path. A searing ache lit off in his chest, drawing his focus and shutting down his other senses. Theron and Cerek's conversation with Nick drifted out of earshot. His vision dimmed until he no longer saw Phineus and Titus in the trees to his right and left scouting the area around them. The frigid air drifted to the back of his mind until all he felt was a condensing panic that told him they were headed in the wrong direction.

Nick had landed the helicopter in a field four miles back and they'd been hoofing it since to avoid alerting any daemons in the area they were coming, but somehow he suddenly knew any daemons lingering here were the least of their worries.

"What's wrong, Zander?"

Theron had stopped and was now studying him with that intense expression their leader was known for. Nick and Cerek were doing the same.

"I—" His chest squeezed tight, cutting off his words. This sensation was different from the rage he was accustomed to. It was deeper, more personal, and this time, insistent. Telling him . . . telling him *something*. But he couldn't figure out what. He turned a slow circle, looked through the trees but saw none of the forest around him. "Something's not right."

"How do you know?" Nick asked with a get-real expression.

"Because I feel it," he tossed back, still looking out at the trees. "They're not here. They're—"

Pain shot up his arm and into his neck, as if someone had hooked him with a half nelson and twisted hard. And in his head he heard Callia's voice. Calling him.

That rush of insistence morphed to urgency. "Callia's hurt," he whispered. Then louder, "There's trouble at the colony."

Zander brought his hands together. When his pinky fingers touched, the markings on his forearms and hands glowed a brilliant white just before the portal opened with a pop and sizzle.

"Aw, fuck," someone muttered. "He's opening the portal. The daemons know for sure we're here now."

Theron took a step toward him. "Zander, wait—"

He didn't. Because only one thing mattered now: Callia needed him.

Isadora jolted from sleep. Her eyes flew open. She pushed up on her hands just as a roar shook the living room of the lodge.

Beside her on the couch, bleary-eyed and sleepy, Casey did the same. "What . . . what's wrong?"

"I don't know." Isadora rushed to the window and peeled back the curtains. The sight that met her eyes tore a gasp from her chest.

"What?" Casey said, hurrying over. When she reached the window and saw the daemons below, raiding the colony, her hand flew over her mouth. "Oh, God."

"We have to get out of here." Adrenaline pulsing, Isadora whipped around and scanned the room for a weapon. Where the hell was Gryphon?

Her eyes landed on the sofa she and Casey had fallen asleep on, moved to the coffee table where the orb, now nothing but a cold piece of metal, still lay, then to the other couch, where Callia should be. "Sonofabitch, she's gone."

"Where would she have gone?" Panic filled Casey's voice.

"I don't know. I—"

The door to the living room crashed open. On instinct, Isadora pushed Casey behind her. Gryphon and—holy hell—Demetrius, in all his evil charm, charged into the room. When had Demetrius gotten here? Had Gryphon called him?

"Princess," Gryphon announced in an I-mean-business tone, "we have to get you back to Argolea. Right now."

This time Isadora wasn't about to argue. She wanted out of here too. Except . . . "Callia's missing. We can't go without her."

Gryphon and Demetrius exchanged glances, and just as Gryphon opened his mouth to answer, loud footsteps pounded down the corridor toward them.

"Get back!" Demetrius yelled, whipping around and drawing his blade.

Isadora's heart lurched to her throat. She backed Casey against the wall and held on to her sister as her pulse beat like wildfire beneath her skin. A body flashed in front of the door, and two glowing green eyes appeared just as Demetrius shifted to attack. Around Demetrius's massive shoulders, Isadora caught sight of the rest of the body in the shadows.

She shoved away from Casey and dashed between the Argonauts to put herself between Demetrius and the door. "No!"

"Hades. Princess, *move*!"

"No, Demetrius. Don't! It's Orpheus."

Orpheus chuckled at her back. "And here I thought *you* didn't care, Isa."

She ignored Orpheus and looked to Gryphon, who held his own blade with a what-the-fuck-is-this? expression on his face.

"How the hell did you—?"

"Uncle Lucian's here," Orpheus said, cutting off his brother's words. "He came to me for help. It seems Loukas has been playing for the wrong team."

Oh, gods. Callia . . .

Demetrius motioned to Casey. "We're getting you both back to Argolea right now."

Casey rushed forward. "Theron—"

"Is fine." Demetrius grabbed Casey's jacket from the couch and thrust it toward her.

"But Callia—" Casey protested as he pushed her toward the door.

Outside, roars and screams echoed up to where they stood on the second floor of the lodge, cutting off her argument. "The Misos," Casey whispered.

"We'll come back for the healer and the others after we get you home," Gryphon said quickly.

Orpheus moved to let the others pass. As Demetrius pushed Isadora out the door, she belatedly remembered the orb.

"Wait." She whipped back around and tried to push by Demetrius. But he was like a solid steel wall blocking her path. "The disk!"

"I'll get it," Orpheus announced.

Orpheus? Oh, holy hell, no. She didn't trust Orpheus with the Orb of Krónos for even a microsecond. Exigency pushed her against the flow of bodies. "Demetrius, get out of my way!"

"You really are a royal pain in my ass," Demetrius sneered. "I said we're leaving now, *Princess*, and I meant it." His arms wrapped around her legs, and then all Isadora felt was air as she was tossed over his shoulder.

"Demetrius! Let me go! I command it."

His only answer was a low, menacing rumble that vibrated through his chest and into her body, warning her the daemons weren't the only evil she needed to worry about right now.

No.

Callia stared wide-eyed as Atalanta fixed her gaze on their location in the trees. The demigod's coal black eyes were as soulless as Callia remembered, but she was bigger than Callia had thought. Easily seven feet and more powerful than any being on this planet.

Atalanta tugged on the rope at her side, the one that ran to Max's hands, then pulled hard. The motion jerked Max off balance, and he stumbled but caught himself at the last second.

Fear was replaced with motherly instinct. Callia drew in a breath and let go of the pain shooting up her arm and into her neck where Loukas held her tight. Her eyes locked on Max.

"Come on, Callie," Loukas breathed over her ear. "It's time for our little meeting."

Loukas's tight grasp made moving over the snow-covered ground awkward. Soldiers from the colony had spilled out to ward off the attack, and Loukas maneuvered her past the fight and forward, up an embankment toward the knoll of a ridge she could just barely see.

Atalanta and Max were already waiting for them when they reached the crest. Callia's gaze shot straight to her son. Max's silver eyes were wide, his blond hair disheveled. Dirt marred his skin and clothing, and his hands were bound in front of him, but there were no cuts across his skin, nothing that indicated he'd been hurt. And staring at him there like that, the knife in Callia's heart twisted even deeper, because he looked just like a younger version of Zander the first day she'd run into him in the castle, nearly eleven years before.

Breathing heavy through her nose, Callia tried to catch her bearings as sweat slid down her spine. Behind her, Loukas was also huffing from the exertion, but his body remained a solid presence at her back, reminding her who was in charge.

"Hello, *Eirene*," Atalanta said in a menacing voice, drawing Callia's attention. "We've been expecting you. Haven't we, Maximus?"

Callia cut her gaze from Atalanta to Max. He stared at Callia with wide eyes. Did he know who she was? Did he have any idea he was hers and not Atalanta's?

"Enough with the pleasantries," Loukas barked at her back. "Let's do this."

"An *ándras* of action," Atalanta said. "I like that. I trust you brought the orb?"

Loukas shifted his legs wider. "When the youngling is dead, I'll give it to you. Not before."

Panic clawed up Callia's chest. She shrieked beneath the hand clamped hard over her mouth, but the sound that came out was nothing more than a grunt.

Loukas tightened his arms around her until pain shot

through her nerve endings, cutting off her voice. Callia gripped Loukas's arms, tried to pull them free, but he was too strong.

"The Orb of Krónos is quite a treasure, Loukas," Atalanta drawled. "I never bothered to ask. However did you find it?"

"How I came to have it isn't important."

"Oh, but I think it is."

Loukas tensed at Callia's back. "My cousin found it. Now the boy—"

A feral smile slid across Atalanta's perfect face. Far down the hill, the sounds of battle drifted up to them, but Atalanta didn't seem to hear. "Shall I tell you a story, Loukas?"

"I—"

"Oh, it's a good one," she said with a smile. "One I think you'll like. You see, not long ago, an *ándras* of your world came across the Orb of Krónos high in the Aegis Mountains. Being one who is always—how shall I say this . . . looking out for himself?—he decided to see what he could get for it. He posed a riddle to Persephone who, realizing what he had, managed to steal the orb right out from under his nose."

Sweat slicked Callia's back, only it wasn't just hers. It was Loukas's as well, seeping through the cloth separating them. His heart rate picked up against her skin, and his anxiety sank into her as if it were her own.

"The gods are never to be trusted," Atalanta went on. "Remember that, Loukas. Now, Persephone took the orb to her husband, Hades, who was, as I'm sure you can guess, more than thrilled with her little find. He kept it close to him for quite some time. Which is how I encountered it."

Loukas's pulse skyrocketed. Moisture gathered on his palms where he held Callia.

"It always amazes me how single-minded males can be," Atalanta said. "Even gods. If you fuck them long enough, you can get them to forget everything. Even what they've done with something as precious as the key to the world."

Loukas swallowed hard. His muscles bunched. Out of

the corner of her eye, Callia caught movement in the brush. She looked closer and saw—It couldn't be. Her father?

Simon placed a finger over his lips, signaling her to be quiet.

Atalanta's eyes hardened on Loukas. "Did you think you could trick me? You don't have the orb. You've never had it."

"But I do."

Callia's gaze flicked to the side where Orpheus had just poofed into appearance, holding the Orb of Krónos in front of him by its long chain.

Holy . . . Hades. Where the hell had he come from? Callia's eyes grew wide all over again. Orpheus could flash on earth like they could in Argolea? That didn't make sense . . .

"Let the youngling and the female go, Atalanta," Orpheus announced. "Or I promise you'll never see this trinket again."

"Callia!"

The scream from below registered for all of them at the same time. Callia's gaze shot down the hill to where Zander was tearing toward them, lashing out with his blade right and left as he struck daemon after daemon on his way to her. A pack of daemons halfway up the hill realized where he was heading and charged.

And then things happened so fast, Callia barely registered the movements. Loukas let go of her and darted toward the trees. Atalanta's arm shot out toward Loukas and a beam of energy slammed into his body, throwing him forward. He screamed as his body hit hard, bounced, then collapsed and twitched uncontrollably against the cold earth before going deathly still.

Her father charged from the brush, blade held high. Atalanta's arm swung out and around and she backhanded Simon easily down the hill as if he were nothing but a puppet. Then she shifted and threw her arm past Callia toward where Orpheus stood holding the orb.

"Do you want this?" Orpheus yelled.

Atalanta's eyes grew wide. He pulled the orb back and

swung it forward by the chain, hurling it across the distance between them. She threw a ball of fiery energy his direction, but before it reached him, Orpheus disappeared in a poof of smoke only to reappear at her back where she couldn't see him.

Atalanta screamed in frustration. The orb had disappeared right along with Orpheus. Chest heaving, Atalanta whipped in Callia's direction, and her eyes blazed as red as her robe. "You."

"No!" Max screamed.

Callia's heart rate jerked. She took a step back and braced herself. Behind Atalanta, Orpheus shot Callia a keep-her-distracted look, then silently stooped to untie Max's hands.

Oh, gods. This was it. Callia's gaze darted to Max. He could escape. All she had to do was keep Atalanta focused on her . . .

"You will pay for what the daemon spawn has done." Atalanta lifted both arms and thrust her hands forward. But nothing happened. No heat flared from her fingers, no energy whipped from her palms. Eyes wide, the demigod looked down at her hands in shocked stupor.

Then her body jerked hard and was thrust down, much like Loukas's, and she crashed against the ground with a squeal of pain.

She rolled and stared up at Max who had both hands extended out toward her, as if *he'd* just thrown her own energy back at her.

"Don't touch her," Max said.

Atalanta took one enraged look at Max, at Orpheus by his side, then over at Callia. Then she vanished, right into thin air.

"That's right," Orpheus said to the empty ground where Atalanta had just lain. "Tuck tail and run like the lower life form you are."

Max stared down at his hands as if he couldn't believe what he'd done.

"Dude," Orpheus said, glancing at Max. "You've got the

power of transference." A victorious smile burst across his face. "That . . . totally . . . *rocks!*"

"Callia!"

Growls and shouts drifted up the hill along with the sounds of metal clanging against metal and flesh and bone. Callia tore her gaze from her son to the edge of the hill where Zander, bloody and dirty, and her father, looking much the same, battled back the ten or so daemons headed straight for them.

Oh, shit. They weren't out of this yet.

"Orpheus!" Callia screamed.

"I'm on it," he yelled. He shoved something in his pocket before he drew his blade. "Been a while since I kicked some daemon ass."

He poofed into nothingness just as Callia saw her father go down.

"No!"

Orpheus reappeared behind the seven-foot monster. His blade arced out and around, severing the daemon's head, preventing the monster from stabbing his blade into Simon's chest.

"Dad!" Callia shot a look at Max.

"Go," Max said. "Go!"

Her healer instincts kicked in. She didn't think, only ran. Skidded to a stop at her father's side. Blood poured from a wound near his ribs. Dirt and gore streaked his face and clothes. He wheezed in a breath. Air expelled from the wound as blood pooled around him.

His lung was punctured. He didn't have much time. She wasn't strong enough to heal this on her own. She had to get him to her clinic, where she had materials and supplies and could treat his wound. Fast. *Now.*

She packed her hands against the wounds. Tears burned her eyes as she looked up and around. "Zander!"

Zander's blade clashed against the sword of the daemon he was fighting. Locked together, neither able to get leverage, his head whipped her way and his eyes widened.

A burst of adrenaline seemed to rocket through him. He broke free and pulled back, then shoved his parazonium deep in the daemon's chest. It howled and roared, went down to its knees, and Zander jerked his blade free, then swung out and decapitated the beast.

Callia looked down at her father. *"Patéras . . ."*

"I . . ."

She sensed someone drop to the ground next to her. Then small hands came around to join hers over the wounds. Through a blur she looked to the side to see Max on his knees.

"Let me help."

"You can't . . ."

"I can," he said in a voice that was so sweet, it sounded like bells. "If you help me."

Emotions choking her, Callia nodded then looked down at the wound and focused her healing powers.

Warmth gathered beneath her hands, beneath Max's. She felt him aiding her, together the two of them stronger than one. But her father's hand closing over both of theirs interrupted the process.

"No," he rasped.

Callia's eyes shot to her father's face. "Dad—"

"No, *agkelos*. Let me go."

Moisture blurred her vision all over again, especially when he called her angel in the old language like he had when she was a child. Before everything that had happened with Zander had changed their relationship forever. *"Patéras . . ."*

"My time is done here, Callia." His voice was so low, she barely heard him. His breathing strained. "Your mother was right. I want to . . . tell her. I'm . . . ready."

Pain knifed through her heart and into her soul.

Her father looked at Max. "I'm sorry," he rasped. "I'm sorry for everything . . . I did. Take care of her. Love her . . . the way I should have."

His eyes slid closed.

Strong arms closed around her from behind just as the tears spilled over her lashes.

"Dad!"

But he didn't hear her. He was already gone.

Those arms pulled and turned her, and then she felt Zander's muscular chest against her cheek. *"Thea."*

She balled her bloody hands against Zander's shirt. Cursed every god she could think of. He was her father, and he'd loved her, even if sometimes she hadn't understood that love. And today, he'd come here to help her. To help save her son.

Her son.

She sniffled at that thought. Pushed back from Zander and looked up at his handsome, familiar, bruised and dirty face. "Max," she whispered. "His name is Maximus."

As the rest of the Argonauts fought back the remaining daemons, they both looked at the boy still on his knees beside them.

In death there was life. She thought of the decision her father had made the day her son was born. One life for another. Though she would never agree with his choice, a small part of her understood how a parent could never sit back and watch their child die.

She wiped her eyes with her sleeve and tried to smile, even though she knew it probably did no good. She was filthy, covered in blood, and death surrounded them. But she'd dreamed of this moment for ten long years.

"Do you know who we are?" she asked softly.

Max looked from her to Zander and back again. Caution filled his wary gaze, but slowly, he nodded. "The old lady in white . . . She showed me. I . . ." He glanced between them again, and his voice dropped to a whisper. "I didn't think you were real."

A flood of emotions burst through the dam Callia had erected around her heart. "Oh, we're real. And we've been looking for you."

"You have?" Max's eyebrows lifted, and hope rushed across his face.

She nodded, and her smile grew. One—this time—she didn't have to force.

"Yeah," Zander said, his own voice choked with emotion. "We have."

CHAPTER TWENTY-THREE

Zander drew a calming breath as he stood on the porch of Callia's father's house in the hills on the outskirts of Tiyrns. Correction—Callia's house now. His nerves had always hit the big time whenever he'd come here to see her. Almost eleven years later, and that fact hadn't changed a bit. Everything else though? Yeah, everything else was a thousand times different. And right now, about as bad as he could imagine.

He lifted his hand. Knocked. Leaves danced on the light breeze and drifted to the ground out on the grass. The house was huge, built like a Tudor mansion in the human realm. Much bigger than they ever needed, and he hoped Callia wasn't attached to it, because where they were headed, this house definitely couldn't follow.

The door pulled open, and Callia stood on the other side. She didn't smile, but her eyes brightened when she saw him, and he figured, considering everything she'd been through the last forty-eight hours, that was as good a greeting as he was going to get.

"Come in out of the cold." Her hand landed on his forearm and heat gathered beneath her touch to warm the cold spaces inside him left from his conversation with the king. All that pent-up anxiety he'd amassed in the last hour seemed to slide right out of his body. Being close to her calmed him in a way nothing else ever could.

She closed the door at his back and rubbed her arms while he wiped his boots on the rug in her entryway. "Where's Max?" he asked.

"Sleeping." She led him into the formal living area, with

its high-backed chairs and uncomfortable couches. "He's been so tired. I guess that's not a surprise, but . . ." She glanced toward the stairs that led up to the second floor. "I worry."

"He's fine," he said, moving toward her and resting his hands on her upper arms to warm her himself. "You checked him out. You had another healer check him out. Physically, he's fine."

"It's mentally I'm worried about."

"Something tells me he's tougher than either of us realizes, *thea*."

A wary look passed over her eyes just before she pulled out of his grasp and moved to stand in front of the fireplace. "I take it your conversation with the king didn't go so well."

Zander clenched his jaw. The king. Her *biological* father. The one who didn't give a shit about anyone but himself. Even now, when he knew Callia was his daughter and Max was his grandson. The heir to the throne of Argolea and the one who would never be recognized. "He's frickin' senile."

"Yeah," she said on a breath, staring into the flames. "Sounds like it went very well."

She knew what the king had said. He didn't even need to tell her.

"Look." Zander moved toward her. "Screw him. If he wants to act like nothing's changed, that's fine with me. But I won't be his patsy. Pack up only the things you and Max really need. We can be out of here by nightfall, before anyone even knows we're gone."

She turned to face him, and the brightness he'd seen in her eyes when he'd walked in the door was long gone. "We're not going with you."

His eyebrows snapped together. "What?"

"Oh, wow." She brought her hands up to her cheeks, breathed deeply. "This is harder than I thought it would be." She dropped her arms, focused on him. "We're not going with you, Zander. I've thought about this a lot over the last twenty-four hours and I . . . It won't work."

"What are you talking about?" A sliver of panic wedged its way into his chest, and he tried to read her emotions but couldn't.

"You, me . . . us." She waved her hands between them. "I think there's a point at which it's either meant to be or it's not. And we passed that point. Too much has changed, and I . . . I don't want to go back. There will always be a place in my heart for you, but I have to focus on Max now. He has to be the center of my world. No one else."

"Callia, wait. If this is about what the king said—"

"No, Zander," she said softly. "This is about me. And what I want and don't want. All my life people have been telling me what to do, and I'm done with it. It's time for me to make my own decisions. And right now . . ." She drew in a steadying breath. "Right now I want to stay right here."

His chest pinched. And through the link he shared with her, he tried to find the lie he knew had to be hidden in her words. But he came up empty. Was she blocking him from her feelings, or . . . was she finally telling him the truth?

"You don't . . ." He could barely think the words, let alone say them. "Want me?"

"I think—no, I know—that going to the human realm with you would be a mistake." Her voice softened. "I want you to bind yourself to Isadora, Zander. It's the right thing for you to do."

That pain pierced his chest. And his heart, the one she'd thawed and softened and brought back to life burst into a thousand pieces right there in her father's stuffy living room.

Days ago, he'd stood on that cliff with Titus, looking down at the ravine below, and he'd wanted to die. But then at least he'd been numb. So used to feeling nothing, he'd thought death would be a welcome respite. Now he knew what true pain was. And not even death could save him from this torture.

Everything he'd confessed to her at the colony rushed through his head. And this time he didn't miss the fact she'd never once told him she loved him back or talked about a future with him past finding their son. Could he have been a bigger fool? She hadn't wanted him then. Not in the same way he'd wanted her. He'd let his wants and needs consume him and override the signals he should have picked up from the first through his link to her.

He waited for the rage to overtake him. Craved it. But it was nowhere to be found. And wasn't that just fucking ironic? The one time he needed it to keep him sane, it was long gone.

"Zander. Wait—"

He couldn't. He moved for the door and freedom. Outside he stopped on the front walk and shakily breathed in the crisp air.

He'd waited eight hundred–plus years for her and finally found his humanity. And in the end all he had to show for it was a son who didn't know him and a fiancée he didn't want. The only consolation was at least he knew he wasn't immortal anymore. Now he just had to wait for Callia to die of old age so he could finally die too.

Isadora ran her hands through her short hair and stared at her reflection in the vanity of her suite. The long-sleeved white wedding gown was heavy and itchy, and it reminded her of the gowns she used to wear. So much had happened and yet nothing was different. Here she was, the same cloistered female she'd been weeks ago, before Casey had come into her life, before she'd discovered Callia was her half-sister. In a matter of hours she'd be bound, property no longer belonging to her father, but to Zander.

Her soul screamed for freedom. She felt like crawling out of her skin. When the panic built to explosive levels, she clamped her hands on the vanity and stared at her reflection.

But she didn't see her face. The mirror faded in and out, and an image appeared. Fuzzy at first, but growing clearer. Her features came into view. She was lying down. Not on the bed in her suite, but somewhere else, surrounded by flickering light and rugged stone. Her skin was tanned, her face flushed. Someone—warmth rushed through her veins when the image panned back and sharpened—was kissing her neck, her shoulders, the tops of her breasts. A male. She couldn't see his face, but his muscular back was bare, his ass tight, his body thrusting against hers as candlelight flickered over them.

Isadora swallowed hard as she watched, transfixed by the scene in front of her. Her body writhed underneath the massive male's, and the moan of pleasure that rang in her ears told her loud and clear that she was enjoying every single thing he was doing to her.

Heat gathered in her veins, slid low until she ached. She pressed her thighs together, bit back her own moan. Her eyes grew wider as she leaned closer to the mirror, trying to see his face. Knowing now how Zander felt about Callia, she couldn't possibly be enjoying his touch this much. It was wrong. It was . . .

And then the male lifted his head. Just as the image of her in the mirror reached the peak and she threw her hair back and groaned in ecstasy.

Isadora gasped and scrambled away from the mirror. Her chair fell back on the hard floor with a clank. Terror clawed its way up her throat as her body shook. No. It couldn't be. Something . . . something was very wrong. The first vision of the future she'd had in over a month couldn't be right. Because there was no way in this realm or the next that she would ever be alone with Demetrius like that.

"Took you long enough."

Isadora whipped around and found herself staring at Persephone. The goddess of the Underworld wore a white gown tied at the waist with a gold sash and she sat on a plush chair in Isadora's sitting area. Her long legs were crossed, one elegant foot swaying lightly. A gold sandal hung from her purple-painted toes. "I was about to level this city." Persephone's green eyes hardened. "I don't like waiting, little queen. I spend my life waiting."

Oh, shit. Their agreement. Isadora had nearly forgotten. "You're here because—"

"Because you just got your powers back. And now, they belong to me. For one month. That"—Persephone nodded toward the mirror—"was hot, by the way. I can't wait to see what happens next."

"You can't—"

Persephone rose to her full height, taller than the Argonauts and with more power in her pinky than any of them had in his entire body. Too late Isadora remembered the goddess could wipe her and this whole castle out if she wanted with nothing more than her breath. "I can. And I will. One month, little queen. You've lasted this long without your powers; one more month won't kill you."

In a poof, Persephone was gone. Isadora reached for the corner post of her massive bed before she collapsed. Outside, the bells began to ring, signaling her impending binding.

It felt like tiny knives were stabbing her from every angle. Her lungs seemed suddenly too small. She didn't understand what she'd just seen, but some instinct deep inside said if she stayed here, it was going to come true. Whether she bound herself to Zander or not.

She couldn't let that happen. She couldn't stay. She *wouldn't* let Demetrius touch her like that.

She turned, frantic as she scanned her room and tried to come up with a plan. Every idea fizzled in her mind. Orpheus had taken his invisibility cloak back. She'd never get out of the castle without someone seeing her. And the orb . . . No one seemed to know what had happened to the orb after the encounter with Atalanta.

Oh, gods, oh, gods, oh, gods . . .

"My lady," Saphira said, stepping into the room, holding a steaming mug in one hand and the dreaded gold veil that would shield her from Zander until the last possible second in the other. "They're ready for you."

Isadora's chest rose and fell in short, labored breaths.

Clutching the bedpost, she lifted her eyes and tried to focus. Shock raced across Saphira's delicate features when she realized Isadora was in the midst of a major panic attack.

Shock? Get in line.

The handmaiden dropped the veil in her hands and rushed close.

"Oh, my lady." Still holding the mug in one hand, Saphira wrapped her other arm around Isadora and supported her weight. Isadora clutched onto the female's thin shoulders. "Blast the king for doing this to you. It's not right."

"I . . . can't . . . breathe."

"Of course you can't. No one could in your place." Saphira led Isadora to the ottoman in the sitting area. Determination hardened her features. "You're not doing this. I won't let you."

"You . . . you . . . cannot . . . stop it. No one . . . can." *Oh, gods . . .*

Saphira clenched her jaw and pushed the mug into Isadora's hands. "Drink this."

"I—"

"Drink it," she said in a commanding voice, one Isadora had never heard from the female. "You'll feel better once you do."

Hand shaking, Isadora brought the cup to her lips. She smelled lavender and something else in the tea. Something vaguely familiar. The steaming liquid blazed a heated trail down Isadora's throat and warmed her from the inside out. Her muscles slowly relaxed one by one.

Saphira knelt at Isadora's feet. "There. Better?"

Slowly, Isadora nodded. Took another sip. The panic attack was waning. But if she thought too much about what had to happen next . . .

Saphira's chilled hands gripped Isadora's knees through the thin fabric of her gown. "I have friends who can help you."

"H-how?"

"They can take you away from this until your father passes. Once he's gone, they can bring you back."

Isadora's brow lowered. It couldn't be that simple, could it? Something in the back of her head yelled, *No!* But she was having trouble listening. Her brain felt heavy and . . . foggy.

Saphira pushed the cup back to her lips. "Drink again."

Right. Drink. That's what she should do. It would make her feel better. But . . .

Her muscles didn't seem to work. When Saphira tilted the cup, Isadora had no choice but to take another sip. As the warm liquid slid into her belly, she felt the last bit of stress slide right out of her body.

A feral smile swept across Saphira's face. "Good. That's good, Princess."

Something in Saphira's expression set off warning bells in Isadora's mind, but they were drowned out by one thought. "C-Casey." She couldn't be away from her sister for long. It was part of their connection as the Chosen.

"Don't you worry your little head about Casey. I promise you won't have to think of her much longer." Saphira rose as if it was all decided. She pulled Isadora to her feet, caught her when she swayed. And vaguely the princess realized her handmaiden was stronger than she'd ever seemed before. Which was just . . . strange.

"I'll get you out of here, Princess. And in a matter of hours, this will all be just a memory. You trust me don't you?"

As if on cue, Isadora nodded, though she felt as if she saw herself doing it from a great distance and had no control over the action.

Saphira smiled again. "Good. And I've never let you down, have I?"

No. But that little voice in the back of Isadora's head that was quickly being smothered screamed that it only took once . . .

CHAPTER TWENTY-FOUR

Callia looked up from the book in her lap and stared out the window at the rain drizzling Tiyrns. It was useless to try to read today. First her father's funeral rite at the Stone Circle, then the rain and soon . . . Zander's binding.

She closed the book, leaned her head against the cool glass and drew deep breaths. Even her favorite window seat and a copy of *Gone with the Wind*, which Orpheus had given to her after they returned home, didn't ease the ache in her soul.

This was all for the best. For her, for Zander, for everyone. If she repeated it enough times, maybe she'd believe it.

A sound at her back brought her head around. Max stood in the doorway to the kitchen with his hands shoved into the front pockets of his jeans and a look of worry across his handsome face. She swiped at her cheeks, pushed away from the window. "I didn't hear you."

After the funeral rite, he'd come home and lain down for a nap, just like he had yesterday. She knew he was fine, but she still worried. And every time she thought about the way he'd extracted Atalanta's energy on that hill and turned it back on her . . .

Even Max didn't realize how truly special he was. Now she understood how he'd stayed alive in the Underworld all that time and how he'd held his own against Atalanta's daemons, even if he didn't. Whatever powers they'd used on him he'd been able to twist around and utilize to his benefit. The gift of transference was an incredible power. One many—not just Atalanta—would love to get their hands on. And for that and other reasons, he wasn't getting out of her sight. But, Callia knew from her own limited experience transferring illnesses, it was also draining. No wonder he looked like he could sleep for a week and never catch up.

She forced a smile she didn't feel and moved toward him. "Would you like something to eat?"

He shook his blond head. "I . . . I heard the bells."

"What bells?"

"The castle bells. Today at the Stone Circle, Casey told me what they mean."

Meddling Misos. Callia closed her eyes. Shook her head. Felt that ache all over again. "Your newfound aunt needs to learn to keep her mouth shut."

He moved down the two steps into the sunken living room, with its dark woods and formal furnishings, his little, perfect, bare feet making not a single sound on the hardwood floors her father had loved so much. "You're doing this because of me, aren't you?"

The anger she heard in his voice and the way his eyes flashed that swirling smoky gray before resettling to their normal silver color reminded her of Zander. "I don't know what you're talking about."

"I'm stronger than you think."

That ache intensified. "I don't want you to have to be strong, Max," she whispered as he stopped in front of her. "You've been strong long enough. It's time for us to do that for you."

He reached out and took her hand, and as she looked down she saw the markings on his forearms that ran down his fingers and now spread out to entwine hers. And she had a memory flash. Of that suite in the half-breed colony. Of her and Zander in that big bed. Of his fingers intertwined with hers. Of those markings over and around her as if she were a part of them herself.

"I didn't think you wanted me," he said in a soft voice, looking down at their hands. "I dreamed about it at night. But during the day, I convinced myself you didn't. That you couldn't . . . That someone like me was . . . unlovable."

His silver eyes lifted to hers, and she knew he saw the tears in hers but she didn't look away. Or answer. Because she owed him this much.

"The little old lady with the glass told me to remember my humanity. I didn't think it would matter, but . . . I was wrong. Humanity can't save a person, but it can give you hope. And without that . . . well, you might as well just become one of Atalanta's daemons."

That ache in her chest engulfed her entire being until she thought it might just consume her.

"It seems like a silly little thing," he said softer, "but sometimes hope can be enough to make all the difference."

She leaned over so they were face-to-face. "You're not supposed to be smarter than me at ten years of age."

One corner of his mouth curled up. "Good genes?"

"Good something."

"I practiced flashing earlier today." The grin on Max's face lightened the ache in her chest. And gods, his smile at full force was dazzling. "Casey told me how it works. Want to see? We could go outside right now and I could show you. I bet I could flash all the way to the castle if I tried."

Wonderful. A manipulator. Just like his father. Between the two of them, she didn't stand a chance.

"There are guards all over the castle," she said. "After everything that happened, they're being extra cautious with security for the . . . event."

The binding ceremony. Zander's binding. Her stomach pitched hard. She couldn't possibly be contemplating going to the castle. Not now. What good would it do? Nothing had changed. They still couldn't leave with him and he'd never go without her. Butterflies took flight in her stomach.

"I'm pretty sure I can get us in." The look of utter confidence on his face struck her, and in that moment he was the picture-perfect image of Zander.

She would never be free of the guardian. No matter where she went or what she did, Zander was always going to be a part of her. And though she'd tried to convince herself what she felt for him was trivial, in the end it was everything. *He* was everything. Max was right. She couldn't kill his hope because she thought it would make things easier. She'd spent her whole life resenting those who laid claim to her, and yet the one person she now knew she truly belonged to was the only one who thought she didn't care.

Her heart pounded hard in her chest. Images, memories, pictures of Zander were all she could see.

Max lifted his brows. "Ready?"

"No," she whispered as her pulse beat like wildfire. When it came to Zander she was never ready. But this time, at least, she knew she was doing the right thing.

"Yo, Z. It's time."

Zander turned from the window he'd been staring out the last twenty minutes and looked across the gigantic bedroom suite on the third floor of the castle—correction, *his* bedroom suite—toward Titus, decked out in his Argonaut dress uniform, dwarfing the doorframe and anteroom beyond.

The guardian wore the same ensemble Zander did— tight-fitting dark trousers, a white tunic cinched at the waist, the traditional leather breastplate decorated with the seal of his forefather and a cloak made of differing colors based on a guardian's lineage, which fell over his left arm and was anchored at his shoulder with a bronze leaf. Titus, being from Odysseus's line, wore a blue cloak. Zander's was amber.

Titus let out a low whistle as he looked around the room. "Sweet digs. You could hold a party in here and still have room to house the Misos while they look for a new base camp."

Zander glanced around the massive and stifling room with its soaring ceilings and gold *everything* as his stomach rolled all over again. Man, he hated this. Hated every part of it. He was so fucked it wasn't even funny. And there wasn't a goddamn thing he could do about it.

He drew in a steadying breath and wished for his old friend, rage, to push its way forward so he had an excuse to escape. But it didn't. It was nowhere to be found.

"You okay, old man?" Titus asked quietly from the door.

Realizing he was staring off into space and that this was a conversation he didn't want to have with anyone—especially someone who could read his pathetic mind—Zander gave his head a shake and forced his feet forward. "I'm fine. Let's just go do this and get it the hell over with."

"Spoken like another happy groom," Titus muttered, stepping out of the doorway to let Zander pass.

They made it to the top of the grand stairs before his skin started to itch under the greaves—the ancient shin guards that ran from his boots to his knees over his pants. To keep the panic at bay, Zander focused on the sensation of the leather rubbing the cloth into his skin as he moved, and counted the minutes until he could be back in his room—alone—staring out at nothing.

The royal temple was located in the courtyard of the castle. By now the Council would be seated, including the other Argonauts and Orpheus who—motherfucker—he still couldn't believe was being fast-tracked to replace Lucian when he retired. Sure, he owed Orpheus for saving Callia and Max on that hillside, and as Gryphon was a guardian himself, that left Orpheus as Lucian's only blood relative who was eligible for the seat. But Orpheus on the Council of Elders had *bad news* written all over it. Even Zander could see that much.

He was so caught up in his thoughts, he didn't notice the commotion one floor down near the main doors until he and Titus rounded the newel post at the top of the first floor.

"Looks like the Executive Guard's finally good for something," Titus mumbled at his side. "At least they're keeping the rubberneckers back from your nuptials."

Zander peered down to where someone was arguing with the two guards at the door. When the guard on the left tried to muscle the person back, a small voice said, "Get your hands off her." The guard went sailing backward to land on his ass on the shiny marble floor.

Zander froze. He knew that voice. He moved down three steps, his eyes searching for his son.

"Zander! Wait!" Callia broke free of the second guard and sprinted across the lobby toward him. Zander's eyes grew wide. Shouts rang out behind Callia. In his peripheral vision, Zander saw Titus speed past him toward the door, but he barely cared. All he saw was her.

"What's wrong?" he asked when she reached him. "Max. I thought I heard—"

"Max is fine." Callia's chest rose and fell with her labored breathing, and her cheeks were rosy and wet, as if she'd just run a mile in the rain. "He can't flash to save his life, though." A hysterical laugh slipped from her perfect mouth. "He can take down a demigod, but he can't flash. He gets that from my side of the family, you know. Overachievers have trouble with the simplest tasks."

His brow lowered as his eyes searched her face. He was having trouble following her, had no idea why she was here, but couldn't look away if his life depended on it. "Callia, if nothing's wrong with Max, then what are you doing here?"

"I . . ." Her eyes shifted to the side, and his followed. He caught sight of his son, just as wet and out of sorts as she was, near the main doors, helping Titus set the guard on his feet.

Callia stepped in front of him, blocking his view, until all he saw was her face. "See? He's fine. I . . . I needed to see you. To talk to you before . . ." She swallowed hard, pressed her hands to her flushed cheeks. "Oh, gods. This sounded so much saner in my head on the way over here."

"What are you—?"

"Oh, Zander. I lied." Her hands moved to his chest, and even beneath the layer of leather and cloth, his skin warmed from the contact. "When you came to see me yesterday I thought I was making things easier, but I see now I wasn't. All I was doing was taking away your hope, and no one should have to live without that. I mean, you might as well be a daemon without it. And you're not a daemon, are you?" She looked up at him with the softest eyes he'd ever seen. Like amethysts mined from the purest ores, polished to a gleaming shine.

Of course, she made no sense whatsoever, but when she looked at him like that, as if some part of her still cared, he could almost believe the things that had happened between them—all the really awful stuff—were nothing more than memories.

"Did you hear what I said, Zander?" Her hands landed gently on his face, and that warmth spread hot over his skin, drawing him back to her words. "I was wrong to take that from you. Just as I was wrong to keep my love for you to myself. It doesn't change anything, I know that, but it wasn't right and I—"

He gripped her arms. "What did you just say?"

"I said I was wrong."

"No. The other part."

Her face went all dreamy, just as it had in every fantasy he'd had of her over the years. "I said I love you. I've always loved you. Even when I thought I had a reason to hate you, I loved you. I should have told you before—so many times— but I was scared. I'm not scared anymore."

His brain and heart clicked into gear at the exact same time. And even before the first bell tolled outside in the courtyard, he was pulling her toward the main doors.

"Zander. Wait. What are you doing?"

"We'll go right now. We'll get Max and go. The portal won't be heavily guarded, not with everyone here. We—"

"No."

The finality to her voice and the way she stopped short brought him around to look at her.

"No," she said softer. "We're not going anywhere. Nothing's changed, Zander."

"But you said—"

She moved in close, and the heat from her body drifted

up and around him, warming that place he thought had gone cold. "I said I love you, and I do. But that doesn't change our reality." Her hands rested gently on his breastplate again, right over the symbol of Achilles branded into the leather. "I'm your vulnerability, aren't I?" At his silence she lifted her eyes, eyes so clear he was sure he could see himself in them. "Your weakness, your Achilles' heel. Zander, why didn't you tell me?"

"Because it doesn't matter."

"Yes, it does. Right now it's all that matters."

"That isn't your curse to bear."

She slid her arm around his back and ran her fingers over the scars there now. Her scars, which he'd taken from her when he'd opened himself fully to her. "It's not yours either."

"Thea—"

"I would go to the ends of the earth with you if I could, Zander, but I can't. We both know Atalanta is going to be gunning for Casey and Isadora and me. And Max isn't safe in the human realm either."

"I can protect you both."

Her hand curved around his cheek, and reflexively he leaned into her touch, wanting it everywhere, anywhere. "And who's going to protect you? If something happens to me, it happens to you. And then who will take care of Max? We can't abandon him there again."

"I . . ." His heart squeezed tight because he was getting exactly what he wanted—her love—and yet, he would never have her. She was right. How could he take them into the human realm and know there was a strong chance doing so could condemn their son all over again? And yet if he stayed here . . .

He closed his eyes as the pain in his chest condensed to the only thing he could feel. "I can't live without you."

Her other hand came up to frame his face. "You don't have to. You never have to. I'm always going to be right here."

Yeah, but he wouldn't be. He looked down at her. "The king won't change his mind. He—"

"You promised me you would make all of this right. Do you remember that? At the colony? Zander, this is your chance to do that." She took a deep breath. "You have to go through with the binding ceremony. You have to marry Isadora."

"No—"

"Do you think I want this?" Her eyes filled with tears. "I want you and us and the life we should have had a long time ago, but that can't happen. And more than that, I want our son to grow up in a world where what happened to me won't happen to another female."

She moved in close until it was all he could do not to grab her and hold on for dear life. "Zander, you have a chance to change things, to make a difference, to help Isadora reshape our world. It's ironic, don't you think, that Argolea was a realm set aside by the gods, a place of peace, and yet we have as many problems as they do on earth?" Her voice dropped to a whisper. "Make this right for Max. And for me. You can do that for us. You're the only one who can."

"What you're asking me to do . . ." His eyes fell closed again. "I can't love another. I've tried. Gods, I've tried. But you're it for me, *thea*. Just you."

"I will always be yours, Zander." Her voice quivered. "And not because some curse says I am. Open your eyes and look at me." He did, and when he focused on her violet eyes he saw everything he felt reflected back on her face. "I'm yours because I love you. Because the connection we share is stronger than anything the king decrees or does. No binding ceremony can break that. For me there's no one but you. But we need you here. To stay in this realm, to be there for Max, to help the Argonauts and to make our world better. If you leave we can't go with you. But if you stay . . . Oh, Zander, there's so much good that can come from it."

His heart broke into a thousand pieces. He never thought—not in a million years—that her love wouldn't be enough. But it wasn't. Fate seemed to be pushing them in different directions and he was powerless to stop it.

He rested his forehead against hers and just tried to breathe. But even that hurt. "This sucks."

Her fingers twined around to run through the hair at the nape of his neck. "It does. I agree."

Silence settled between them. And like it always did, the silky smooth glide of her fingers against his skin calmed him from the inside out.

"A true leader sets aside his personal wants for the good of the whole," she whispered. "And he makes sacrifices. Ones that, in the end, justify all that came before." When he lifted his head and frowned at her, a sad smile spread across her perfect face. "Someone once told me that."

"Sounds like a moron. I'm not a leader."

"No, but you're a guardian. The best one I know. And you're a father. That makes you a leader, whether you think so or not. Zander, do you know your irises are silver?"

What was left of his heart pinched. Tight. He rested his forehead against hers once more. "Because of you."

"Oh . . ."

"You're holding up the proceedings, Argonaut."

The king's irritated voice echoing from above brought tension to Zander's shoulders all over again. He glared up to the balcony where the fragile king stood leaning against the banister in his white regal suit, a scowl on his wrinkled face and a cane in one hand. It was clear he couldn't see them, but he could hear them, and Zander had no doubt the now-blind king could picture what was happening below.

Theron, dressed in his uniform and red cloak, stood at the king's right, Casey at his left. Neither the leader of the Argonauts nor his bride looked thrilled with the situation, and the king was positively fuming.

Callia's soft fingers against his cheek drew his face back to hers. "Ignore him."

"He's your biological father. He should care."

"He's doing what he thinks is best. Look at me." When he did, the shine of tears in her eyes told him this was as hard for her as it was for him. Probably harder. "Don't let him poison our last few seconds together."

"Thea . . ."

She brushed the hair back from his temples, and her voice hitched when she said, "I love you, Zander. Always. Remember that whenever things get to be too much. Me and Max. We're yours no matter where you go or what you do. Nothing, *no one*, can change that."

Mine. As he looked down into her eyes, he saw his life broken into two parts. The way it was before her, empty and meaningless, and the way it had been since she'd come into it, full and with purpose. She'd uncovered the humanity in him, given him balance and healed him in a way no one else ever could. And though part of him burned with the heat of a thousand suns knowing they couldn't be together, she was right. She was his. Would always be his.

He drew in a shaky breath and memorized every curve, every angle, every line and plane of her gorgeous face so he could call it up whenever he needed. For the rest of his life. No matter how long that may be.

"I love you, *thea*. Only you."

Two tears spilled over her sooty lashes to slide down her creamy skin.

"Zander," the king announced in a hard tone from above, breaking their bittersweet moment, "this binding ceremony will go on as scheduled. You cannot stop it. My daughter will be bound today. Acacia," he barked at his side.

"What?" Casey said next to him, irritation coating her words as well.

"Find something more appropriate for Callia to wear. Even though I can't see her, I know how she dresses. She can't have her binding ceremony in commoner's clothing."

Callia's eyes grew wide. And hope, just the tiniest shred,

slivered its way into Zander's chest. They both looked up at the king.

"Contrary to what you all think," the king said with a scowl, "I'm not a heartless bastard. I still believe sacrifice is necessary, but not at the expense of one daughter over another."

Lucian stepped up next to the king then, peering over the banister with a less-than-thrilled expression on his face.

"After much debate," the king went on, "Lord Lucian has finally agreed to recognize Maximus as a legitimate heir to the throne, until such time as Isadora produces her own heir. Acacia, go tell your sister she was just granted a reprieve. At least until I figure out what in Hades to do with her."

A wide grin swept across Casey's face. She shot a look at Theron, who was also smiling, before she darted off toward Isadora's rooms.

Zander whipped back to Callia. And though excitement flared in his veins, he tamped it down because there was still one matter left unaddressed.

"Oh, my gods," Callia whispered.

"Thea." He gripped her arms. "You don't have to do what he commands. I won't let him dictate your life the way he does Isadora's. It has to be your choice. If you don't want—"

She threw her arms around his neck and pressed her mouth to his. And when she eased back, her smile beamed. "I want you. I've always only ever wanted you. Zander, bind yourself to me. To us," she corrected, glancing at Max, still standing with Titus, smiling himself. "Today. Right now. We'll figure everything else out later."

His chest filled to bursting. Only this time, it was happiness, not rage, that consumed him. And he knew it always would be. "Ah, *thea*," he said softly, closing his arms around her and drawing her tight against him. "I don't need a ceremony to tell me what I already know. Our lives have been entwined from the very start. Do you think I could ever choose anyone but you?"

Her victory smile widened. "No, thank the Fates, you can't." She leaned in to kiss him. "And I won't ever let you. You're mine, Guardian. Forever."

He smiled himself as his lips met hers. "It's about damn time."

Eternal Guardians Lexicon

ándras; pl. *ándres*—Male Argolean.

agkelos—Term of endearment; angel.

Argolea—Realm established by Zeus for the blessed heroes and their descendants.

Argonauts—Eternal guardian warriors who protect Argolea. In every generation, one from the original seven bloodlines (Heracles, Achilles, Jason, Odysseus, Perseus, Theseus, and Bellerophon) is chosen to continue the guardian tradition.

Council of Elders—Twelve lords of Argolea who advise the king

daemons—Beasts who were once human, recruited from the Fields of Asphodel (purgatory) by Atalanta to join her army.

élencho—Mind-control technique Argonauts use on humans

Fields of Asphodel—Purgatory

gigia—Grandmother

gynaíka; pl. *gynaíkes*—Female Argolean

Horae—Three goddesses of balance controlling life and order

Isles of the Blessed—Heaven

ilithios—Idiot

matéras—Mother

meli—Term of endearment; beloved.

Medean witches—Covens in the mountains of Argolea that follow the teachings and traditions of Medea

Misos—Half-human/half-Argolean race that lives hidden among humans

ochi—No

oraios—Beautiful

Orb of Krónos—Four-chambered disk with the power to release the Titans from Tartarus

patéras pl. *patéres*—Father

rompa—Ancient red robe worn by members of the Argolean Council

skata—Swearword

syzygos—Wife

Tartarus—Realm of the Underworld similar to hell

thea—Term of endearment; goddess.

yios—Son

BARBARA MONAJEM

Author of *Sunrise in a Garden of Love & Evil*

THE ROAD TO BAYOU GAVOTTE

Rose Fairburn is on the run. Her vampire nature can't protect her from everything, especially not herself. Now, when she should be worried about escaping her past, she can only think about one thing. Her kind can't live without blood or sex. Love they must forego.

Jack Tallis can slake her thirst. Tall. Handsome. Trustworthy. And not a man alive can resist a vamp's allure. But . . . Jack can. And he has other secrets. The shadows hide mysteries darker than Rose can even dream, and all will be revealed in the fetish clubs of one strange Louisiana town. . . .

Tastes of LOVE & EVIL

ISBN 13: 978-0-505-52862-9

INTERACT WITH DORCHESTER ONLINE!

Want to learn more about your favorite books and authors?
Want to talk with other readers that like to read the same books as you?
Want to see up-to-the-minute Dorchester news?

VISIT DORCHESTER AT:

DorchesterPub.com
Twitter.com/DorchesterPub
Facebook.com (Search Pages)

DISCUSS DORCHESTER'S NOVELS AT:

Dorchester Forums at DorchesterPub.com
GoodReads.com
LibraryThing.com
Myspace.com/books
Shelfari.com
WeRead.com

✂ ❑ **YES!**

Sign me up for the Love Spell Book Club and send my FREE BOOKS! If I choose to stay in the club, I will pay only $8.50* each month, a savings of $6.48!

NAME: _____

ADDRESS: _____

TELEPHONE: _____

EMAIL: _____

❑ I want to pay by credit card.

❑ **VISA**   ❑ **MasterCard.**   ❑ **DISCOVER**

ACCOUNT #: _____

EXPIRATION DATE: _____

SIGNATURE: _____

Mail this page along with $2.00 shipping and handling to:
Love Spell Book Club
PO Box 6640
Wayne, PA 19087
Or fax (must include credit card information) to:
610-995-9274
You can also sign up online at **www.dorchesterpub.com**.
*Plus $2.00 for shipping. Offer open to residents of the U.S. and Canada only.
Canadian residents please call 1-800-481-9191 for pricing information.
If under 18, a parent or guardian must sign. Terms, prices and conditions subject to change. Subscription subject to acceptance. Dorchester Publishing reserves the right to reject any order or cancel any subscription.